THE ST. PAUL STORIES
OF F. SCOTT FITZGERALD

THE ST. PAUL STORIES
OF
F. SCOTT FITZGERALD

Edited by

PATRICIA HAMPL

&

DAVE PAGE

BOREALIS
BOOKS

Borealis Books is an imprint of the Minnesota Historical Society Press.

www.borealisbooks.org

Introduction ©2004 by Patricia Hampl. Other new material ©2004 by the Minnesota Historical Society. All rights reserved. No part of this book may be used or reproduced in any manner whatsoever without written permission, except in the case of brief quotations embodied in critical articles and reviews. For information, write to Borealis Books, 345 Kellogg Blvd. W., St. Paul, MN 55102-1906.

www.mnhs.org/mhspress

The Minnesota Historical Society Press is a member of the
Association of American University Presses.

Manufactured in the United States of America

10 9 8 7 6 5 4 3

∞ The paper used in this publication meets the minimum requirements of the American National Standard for Information Sciences—Permanence for Printed Library Materials, ANSI Z39.48-1984.

International Standard Book Number 0-87351-512-9

Library of Congress Cataloging-in-Publication Data

Fitzgerald, F. Scott (Francis Scott), 1896–1940.
  The St. Paul stories of F. Scott Fitzgerald / edited by Patricia Hampl and Dave Page.
    p.   cm.
  Includes bibliographical references.
  ISBN 0-87351-512-9 (pbk. : alk. paper)
  1. Saint Paul (Minn.)—Fiction.   I. Hampl, Patricia   II. Page, Dave.   III. Title.
  PS3511.I9A6 2004
  813'.52—dc22

                                2004009910

The following stories are reprinted by arrangement with the original publisher, Scribner, an imprint of Simon & Schuster Inc. "The Scandal Detectives" copyright 1928 by Curtis Publishing Co.; "A Night at the Fair" copyright 1928 by Curtis Publishing Co.; "He Thinks He's Wonderful" copyright 1928 by Curtis Publishing Co.; "The Captured Shadow" copyright 1928 by Curtis Publishing Co.; and "Forging Ahead" copyright 1929 by Curtis Publishing Co. are reprinted from *The Basil and Josephine Stories of F. Scott Fitzgerald,* ed. Jackson R. Bryer and John Kuehl (New York: Charles Scribner's Sons, 1973). "A Short Trip Home," copyright 1927 by Curtis Publishing Co.; "At Your Age" copyright 1929 by Curtis Publishing Co.; and "A Freeze-Out" copyright 1931 by Curtis Publishing Co. are reprinted from Matthew J. Bruccoli, *The Short Stories of F. Scott Fitzgerald: A New Collection* (New York: Charles Scribner's Sons, 1989).

Frontispiece: F. Scott Fitzgerald, about 1920 (Minnesota Historical Society)

THE ST. PAUL STORIES
OF F. SCOTT FITZGERALD

INTRODUCTION

PATRICIA HAMPL

I belong here, where everything is civilized and gay and rotted and polite. And I wouldn't mind a bit if in a few years Zelda + I could snuggle up together under a stone in some old graveyard here. That is really a happy thought + not melancholy at all. . . .

A strangely funereal wish from a man barely thirty-nine. But it came true for Scott Fitzgerald only five years later, and eight years after that for Zelda. Neither of them made it to fifty.

Fitzgerald wasn't planning a pleasantly domestic eternity in his hometown in Minnesota. Nor was he imagining himself in New York or on the Riviera, places forever associated with him and his fiction. In this 1935 letter he was talking about Baltimore where he was then living, contending with the disappointing reception of *Tender Is the Night*, his fourth novel and the longest and hardest in coming. He would soon write his bitter confessional "Crack Up" essays and was nursing his sense of failure in Maryland, ancestral home of his father — also considered a failure. "Baltimore is warm but pleasant," he writes. "It is so rich with memories — it is nice to look up the street + see the statue of my great uncle, + to know Poe is buried here and that many ancestors of mine have walked in the old town by the bay."

Fitzgerald could wax nostalgic at the drop of a place name. His beautiful essay on New York, "My Lost City," is another valentine to a beloved city. But his hometown sentiments could be considerably more tart: "I no longer regard St. Paul as my home," he writes coolly to Marie Hersey Hamm in 1934, "any more than the

Eastern seaboard or the Riviera." He had been too long a vaga-
bond and meant "no disloyalty," he tells his old friend (who, after
all, still lived in St. Paul), but he reminds her that "my father was
an Easterner and I went East to college and I never did quite adjust myself to those damn Minnesota winters. It was always freezing my cheeks, being a rotten skater etc — though many events
there will always fill me with a tremendous nostalgia." Yet he
doesn't wing off into a fond recitation of St. Paul memories. The
next sentence shivers with dislike: "Anyhow all recent reports
paint it as a city of gloom and certainly the ones from the remnants of the McQuillan family are anything but cheerful."

Baltimore was the town he associated with his gentle, ineffec-
tive (and alcoholic) father, Edward Fitzgerald, and Maryland was
home to dim romantic figures Fitzgerald could think of, with
pleasantly vague colonial pride, as "ancestors." In fact, his "rich
memories" of Baltimore were not memories at all, but historical
and literary associations and allusions. The great-uncle for whom
Fitzgerald said he was named was Francis Scott Key, the author of
"The Star-Spangled Banner." But he wasn't an uncle, "only a distant cousin," as Fitzgerald's daughter, Scottie Fitzgerald Smith,
wrote much later and more exactly.

Fitzgerald's appropriation of Poe as a kindred spirit is also
strangely tainted. Whether Fitzgerald thought of him this way or
not, Poe was a writer whose addictions mirrored his own alcoholism. Baltimore evoked bittersweet defeat and literary an-
tecedents, not memories of a personal past. For Fitzgerald, Baltimore was a gently decaying corner of the "rotted" South, a city in
which death and failure dwelt honorably, at home in an older, finer
world where such frayed words as *civility* and *breeding* had meaning and even some force.

St. Paul, by contrast, was the bully northern town of Fitzgerald's eccentric mother Molly McQuillan and her Irish family, the
moralizing moneymakers who were called on to bankroll the family when mild, good-looking Edward Fitzgerald proved to be a

failure, first in his wicker furniture company (an unfortunately southern business venture for Minnesota) and later as a salesman for Procter and Gamble. No tender rot and brave gaiety here — St. Paul was all ice and insult.

Though Fitzgerald wrote several unremarkable stories while Zelda was in Johns Hopkins Hospital, in which Baltimore and Maryland details surface, there are no Fitzgerald "Baltimore stories," no rhapsodic evocations of Maryland in his fiction, as St. Paul is evoked and rhapsodized and returned to again and again. Near the end of *The Great Gatsby,* when Nick Carraway delivers his grieving meditation on the American tragedy he has just narrated, he doesn't turn to New York, where the novel's ruinous action has taken place, but to the Midwest and finally to St. Paul, in what is surely one of the most lyrical love notes ever written to an American city:

> One of my most vivid memories is of coming back West from prep school and later from college at Christmas time. Those who went farther than Chicago would gather in the old dim Union Station at six o'clock of a December evening, with a few Chicago friends, already caught up into their own holiday gayeties, to bid them a hasty good-by. I remember the fur coats of the girls returning from Miss This-or-That's and the chatter of frozen breath and the hands waving overhead as we caught sight of old acquaintances, and the matchings of invitations: "Are you going to the Ordways'? the Herseys'? the Schultzes'?" and the long green tickets clasped tight in our gloved hands. And last the murky yellow cars of the Chicago, Milwaukee & St. Paul railroad looking cheerful as Christmas itself on the tracks beside the gate.
>
> When we pulled out into the winter night and the real snow, our snow, began to stretch out beside us and twinkle against the windows, and the dim lights of small Wisconsin stations moved by, a sharp wild brace came suddenly into the air. We drew in deep breaths of it as we walked back from dinner through the cold vestibules, unutterably aware of our identity

with this country for one strange hour, before we melted indistinguishably into it again.

That's my Middle West—not the wheat or the prairies or the lost Swede towns, but the thrilling returning trains of my youth, and the street lamps and sleigh bells in the frosty dark and shadows of holly wreaths thrown by lighted windows on the snow. I am part of that, a little solemn with the feel of those long winters, a little complacent from growing up in the Carraway house in a city where dwellings are still called through decades by a family's name. . . .

After Gatsby's death the East was haunted for me . . . distorted beyond my eyes' power of correction. So when the blue smoke of brittle leaves was in the air and the wind blew the wet laundry stiff on the line I decided to come back home.

In practical terms Fitzgerald also retained a trust with St. Paul. Like Nick, he too decided to come back home at a pivotal moment. When Zelda was pregnant in 1921, the Fitzgeralds first went south to her family in Montgomery, Alabama, thinking they would await their baby's birth there. But the summer heat was devastating. And Zelda's father, Judge Sayre, cheerlessly enforced Prohibition in his house on Pleasant Avenue, another insupportable condition of life there.

In August they fled north to Scott's hometown ("the worst move I ever made in my life," he later claimed). Scottie, the Fitzgeralds' only child, was born in St. Paul on October 26, 1921. The family stayed in various rented houses and hotel suites in St. Paul's Summit and Crocus Hill neighborhoods. They eventually moved to the White Bear Yacht Club to spend the following summer. Wherever they rented, these rowdy celebs were complained about, and asked to quiet down. They were evicted at least twice. Apparently, being a loud neighbor was a crime in St. Paul, though the police department allowed gangsters (relatively small fry in Fitzgerald's day, but later Dillinger, Ma Barker, and her boys, to name a few) to lie low in the city if they behaved themselves. Still, as Fitzgerald wrote his college friend Edmund Wilson in the spring of 1922, "St. Paul is dull as hell." He signed the letter, "Yours in this hell-hole of life + time."

By September 1922, a little over a year after they had arrived, they were gone. Fitzgerald had just finished "Winter Dreams," his most resonant St. Paul story and something of a first run at *The Great Gatsby*. It was the last time the Fitzgeralds lived in Minnesota.

His parents soon left as well. Edward and Mollie Fitzgerald moved from their rented Summit Avenue row house in the early 1920s and settled in a fashionable Washington, D.C., residential hotel for the rest of their lives. Scott and Zelda headed to New York and Long Island where they rejoined the riotous American bash that Nick Carraway would soon document in his remorseless midwestern voice.

* * *

The early celebrity Scott Fitzgerald first enjoyed—and later suffered from—is almost impossible to imagine for a literary writer today, no matter how successful. The fame that assaulted Fitzgerald after the publication of his first novel, *This Side of Paradise,* in March 1920, when he was just twenty-three, is usually reserved in our own times for rock star "icons." Which is exactly what Scott Fitzgerald became overnight—and Zelda too, his consort and the embodiment of his dashing flapper heroines.

Ernest Hemingway's fame eventually surpassed Fitzgerald's during his lifetime, but as a young man even Hemingway was never the phenom Fitzgerald became after his first novel hit the bookstores. Fitzgerald's fame, coming so soon after the First World War, coincided with the spike of American popular culture that was an unprecedented marker of modernity. His glamour as the representative of "the lost generation" flashed during the brief moment before the movies and pop music would provide whole new fields and demographics for celebrity, the moment when a writer could be a rock star before there were rock stars.

Fitzgerald wasn't simply absorbed into the culture as a writer, even a terrifically gifted writer. He became a model for whatever it meant to be young, wild, free, and new under the post-war sun. You didn't even have to read him to feel you "got" him. He and Zelda were splashed all over the tabloids. While Hemingway in Paris was dutifully sitting under the Picassos in the shadowy apartment on rue de Fleurus, clinging to every modernist judgment Gertrude Stein was handing down about the contemporary sentence, Fitzgerald in New York was busy not only writing but publicly *being* modern. And outrageous. He and Zelda were buzz, ultimate buzz.

It didn't last long. With the Crash and the Depression, compounded by the personal devastation of his alcoholism and Zelda's breakdowns, Fitzgerald entered the black hole of his own stardom. He became a convenient tabloid cartoon of Roaring Twenties excess and egotism just as, a decade earlier, he had been lionized as its brash and fashionable hero. From the start, his audience conflated him with his work—probably the most lethal cocktail fame can offer its darlings.

Fitzgerald's self and his work have for so long been shaken together to create a popular image that, even with the reams of meticulous and impassioned scholarly attention that have followed since his death in 1940, it seems impossible to separate those two essences that were fused in the lightning flash of his youthful success at the dawn of the American twentieth-century imperium. "The life" and "the work" of F. Scott Fitzgerald long ago became, and have remained, the legend.

More than a legend, a convenient cautionary tale for a culture risen from its Puritan roots: the high-living, indulgent midwestern egoist who meets an early and tragic end, a failure like his graceful father, his books no longer much read, desperately trying to make ends meet, keeping up appearances in a modest Hollywood apartment, waiting for movie work to come in. Fitzgerald's rise and fall have become so much a part of American cultural iconography that he is invoked by his first name, like a black sheep uncle—Scott, we say, Scott and Zelda. Nobody calls Hemingway "Ernest" in this way; his preferred nickname, "Papa," was an image-enhancing honorific he conferred on himself and urged on others.

The tabloid accounts of Fitzgerald diving into the fountain at the Plaza, the glam photogravure portraits of Scott and Zelda posing like louche matinee idols, the surreal drunkenness, the weeklong parties and manic spending, the entourage of maids and drivers and governesses, the clubs and expensive hotels, alcoholic fights and lavish morning-after apologies—all of it swirled in the goblet of fame along with the steady stream of stylish stories that he managed to write and publish in the glossies of the day, most notably *The Saturday Evening Post.*

Reading a voice as vivid and immediate, by turns hip and lyrically intimate, as Fitzgerald's, how could a reader entirely distinguish him from his characters and from that third beast that hounded him—his legend? More to the point, how was the ambitious young man who woke up one day and found himself famous supposed to make the distinction?

* * *

It was a success beyond even Fitzgerald's extravagant imaginings. He had come back home to St. Paul from New York in July 1919, a solid failure. He was twenty-two years old. By his count New York was his fifth bitter defeat—he had not finished Princeton and he had not made it to Europe as an officer in the Army before the war was over. Zelda Sayre had broken off their engagement, hedging her bets on a lover whose prospects depended on his imagination. And Maxwell Perkins at Scribner's had rejected his first try at a novel, *The Romantic Egoist.*

He had failed miserably at all he had hoped for and tried for in the East and came home without evident prospects. Back in St. Paul, Fitzgerald holed up on the third floor of his parents' rented

599 Summit Avenue row house and set about revising his rejected novel. He spent July and August of 1919 ripping it apart and recasting it before he sent it back to Perkins at the end of the summer.

On September 16, the postman rang, and F. Scott Fitzgerald held in his hand a letter from Maxwell Perkins accepting the retooled book. Its new title was *This Side of Paradise*. According to a vignette ratified by Fitzgerald in his rueful 1937 essay "Early Success," he was so elated about the news that he "ran along the streets, stopping automobiles to tell friends and acquaintances." He had his ticket out—and up (his first word as a baby was "Up"). The following week he celebrated his twenty-third birthday.

Later that fall he acquired an agent, Harold Ober of the prestigious Reynolds literary agency. This lifelong business and personal relationship had its start, oddly enough, from a St. Paul connection. Grace Flandrau, a popular novelist ten years older than Fitzgerald and married into an old Summit Avenue family, was a Reynolds agency author, and she arranged for Fitzgerald to be taken on there.

By November, hardly two months after Scribner's had accepted the novel, Ober sold Fitzgerald's first story to *The Saturday Evening Post*—for $400. It was another heady success: his one earlier commercial story sale, "Babes in the Woods"—sold in the spring of 1919 to *The Smart Set*, edited by H. L. Mencken and George Jean Nathan—had earned Fitzgerald $30. He had spent that money, he later wrote in the memoir piece "Early Success," "on a magenta fan for a girl in Alabama." But he also wrote, in another essay, that he bought himself a pair of flannels with that first sweet money. Either way, the pattern was set for style as necessity.

* * *

Barely a week after receiving Perkins's acceptance letter, and still flying high (or perhaps just incredibly relieved), Fitzgerald wrote a euphoric note to an old St. Paul friend who was back East at college. It begins:

> In a house below the average
> Of a street above the average
> In a room below the roof
> > With a lot above the ears
> > I shall write Alida Bigelow
> > Shall indite Alida Bigelow . . .

He's gleeful, of course, delighted to report "Scribner has accepted my book. Ain't I Smart?" Still, the precision of the social ranking he notes in this ditty is telling, especially sent to a St. Paul girl who would also know exactly how to vet a Summit Avenue address.

The point of mentioning it, no doubt, is that Fitzgerald now feels released from such distinctions. The claws of class don't quite clutch him anymore. Now he's a Writer. He is outfitted with a New York publisher, a New York agent, and his stories are selling for delirious sums to the best magazines. He's self-made, born again as a success, the person who now does the naming and social ranking instead of the one being named and ranked. He can afford to write a cheery bit of dismissive doggerel about his family's house and situation. He's almost out of here.

A few years later he wrote a review of Grace Flandrau's St. Paul novel, *Being Respectable,* for a St. Paul paper, and gave a sharp reading of the city's social and economic history. St. Paul, he says, though it is "bloodbrother of Indianapolis, Minneapolis, Kansas City, Milwaukee, and Co., feels itself a little superior to the others. . . . In the fifties the climate of St. Paul was reputed exceptionally healthy. Consequently there arrived an element from the East who had both money and fashionable education. These Easterners mingled with the rising German and Irish stock, whose second generation left the cobbler's last, forgot the steerage, and became passionately 'swell' on its own account. But the pace was set by the tubercular Easterners. Hence the particular social complacency of St. Paul."

There's the Nick Carraway word again—complacency. Clearly a word that carried a charge for Fitzgerald, defining his sense of St. Paul and what was behind the "innocence" of the Midwest and beyond that what fired the aging innocence of America itself. In his view, this enraging complacency was the stew of raw capitalism, cooked down over three generations into the entitlements of inherited wealth.

Fitzgerald was famously sensitive to class and wealth. This sensitivity—even touchiness—was burned into him, not by his boarding school in New Jersey or by "the East," but much earlier in Minnesota with the dry ice of provincial St. Paul's own social touchiness. Fitzgerald's mild, failed father and his rather odd mother in her gigantic funereal hats did not participate much in the social life of the St. Paul gentry, but his mother's McQuillan connection made it possible for their son to do so—and to feel his (or their) implicit inferiority. Before he went East to prep school, Fitzgerald attended St. Paul Academy (even today the premier private school of the city), he attended the right dancing school, he went to parties in the mansions of Summit Avenue. He wasn't an outsider but something even more conflicted and embittering: a (relatively) poor boy in a rich boy's world.

As late as 1938 he was still brooding. He wrote to Anne Ober, his agent's wife, from Hollywood where he was trying to hang onto a studio job (he lost it). Mrs. Ober had taken over as a kind of surrogate mother for Scottie, and Fitzgerald confided his worries about his daughter's possible "shame" at Vassar "being a poor girl in a rich girl's school." He admitted, "That was always my experience." He had always felt himself "a poor boy in a rich town; a poor boy in a rich boy's school; a poor boy in a rich man's club at Princeton. So I guess she can stand it. However, I have never been able to forgive the rich for being rich, and it has colored my entire life and works." The chip of a Summit Avenue mansion was still on his shoulder.

Summit appears as Crest Avenue in "The Popular Girl," a long, almost novella-length story Fitzgerald wrote in St. Paul in 1921. "That's our show street," the heroine of the story says as she and her companion—transparently named Scott—take a spin in her roadster. But Fitzgerald's narrative voice-over can't let the local girl have her civic pride in the grand boulevard. He describes the mansions as "a half-mile of pretentious stone houses put up in the gloomy 90's. These were adorned with monstrous driveways and porte-cocheres which had once echoed to the hoofs of good horses and with huge circular windows that corseted the second stories."

Fitzgerald even appears to give an irritated little salute to his parents' "below the average" red stone row house: "past a block of dark frame horrors, a deserted row of grim red brick—an unfortunate experiment."

At the end of their ride the girl repeats her boosterish remark. "This is our show street," she says again.

But Fitzgerald gives "Scott" the last damning word: "A museum of American architectural failures," he replies.

St. Paul, with its topography of bluffs and flats (the rich perched on a rim above, the working class on the plain below), no doubt encouraged Fitzgerald's fierce awareness of social and class distinctions. So did his parents' dependence on his mother's family money. He watched the capital city elite conduct its intense and introverted social life, rounds of parties and dances, as snowbound and fashion-conscious as any provincial capital in a Russian novel. As Nick Carraway said, Fitzgerald too was "part of that, a little solemn with the feel of those long winters."

But unlike well-born, firmly ensconced Nick, Fitzgerald was not "a little complacent from growing up in the Carraway house in a city where dwellings are still called through decades by a family's name." Fitzgerald couldn't afford to be complacent— even as a child, he was driven. "If anybody can poison Scotty or stop his mouth in some way," a classmate remarks in the St. Paul Academy school paper in 1909, "the school at large and myself will be obliged."

His family's "dwellings" weren't the ancestral piles of the Herseys, the Ordways, the Schultzes (local names Nick Carraway invokes in *The Great Gatsby* without the fig leaf of pseudonyms). The Fitzgerald family dwellings weren't architectural failures — or successes. They were rental units. For years Mollie and Edward Fitzgerald roved the secondary streets north and south of Summit as well as the "below the average" western edge of the neighborhood, moving from one apartment or row house to another almost every year, tenants, not owners, always pitching their tent within the tight compass of St. Paul respectability.

*   *   *

"I cannot comprehend," Franz Kafka's friend Willi Haas once wrote, "how anyone could understand Kafka who was not born in Prague between 1880 and 1890." An extreme remark, but places can intersect history to exert uncanny powers on a fervent imagination. It's tempting to claim a similar if lesser constellation of place and time between Fitzgerald and old St. Paul. It was not simply the city where he was born and raised (after all, he had spent impressionable childhood years in Buffalo, New York, during the ten years his father worked for Procter and Gamble). St. Paul appears again and again in his fiction as something more than just backdrop or setting, and in his memoir vignettes and letters the city surfaces with the dull ache of a chronic pain, a memory still looking for the relief of meaning.

The city serves, in his fiction, as Fitzgerald's geography of youthful romance — the locus of those dangerous life-defining "winter dreams" of his striving young men. That youthful ardor and arrogance (or arch complacency — his St. Paul characters display them all) turn the Midwest and especially the provincial capital of the cold northland into a figure of newly imperial America, clutching its proud innocence in one hand as it grabs with the other for the big bad world "out there" — New York, France, Hollywood, wherever the action is.

St. Paul bears the spiritual exhaustion of all the heavy lifting of Fitzgerald's desperate boyhood ambition, his almost frantic desire for fame. For fame, he sensed instinctively, was the only way out. For getting out (and of course up) is perhaps the deepest of all midwestern dreams. Fitzgerald's imperial dream of grandeur was bred of the dissatisfactions of an exiled royal who knows he is meant for better things.

St. Paul stamped Fitzgerald's imagination with frosty silver, marking his relationship to wealth and even his understanding of—and mistrust of—capitalism. His was the St. Paul of James J. Hill and Archbishop John Ireland, trailing the bright clouds of its late nineteenth-century boom-town success stories in which a canny young Canadian shipping clerk could turn himself into The Empire Builder, and an Irish priest could turn immigrant Catholics into a political and cultural power beyond their age-old hierarchical European limitations.

The greatest wealth Fitzgerald saw enshrined in the mansions of Summit Avenue had been made from transportation (first the river, then the railroads) and what might be called the domestic settling of the West. Some of the fantastically turreted Summit Avenue castles were built by the fortunes of dry-goods merchants. These family firms had furnished a massive swath of the Dakotas and Montana with everything from cooking oil and sewing machines to school desks and blackboards in the last decades of the nineteenth century and even into the twentieth.

St. Paul, Catholic and mercantile (unlike Protestant, wheat-and-commodities-speculating Minneapolis), was insular and self-regarding, and as Fitzgerald wrote, it prided itself on being "a three generation town" in distinction from two-generation upstarts like Minneapolis and Indianapolis. It tended its snobberies and its evergreen midwestern idealism with a self-regarding sense of purity that often surfaces in Fitzgerald's fiction like a shark fin rising in still water. Nick Carraway's dangerous "complacency" is bred precisely of his conflation of goodness and good luck, personal integrity and honor pleasantly wedded to inherited wealth and position. "Just remember," Nick's complacency-rich father tells his son as he starts out from St. Paul, "that all the people in this world haven't had the advantages that you've had."

The resonant voice of entitlement. Such unquestioning belief in one's own decency and lofty position formed a kind of nouveau midwestern *noblesse oblige* that Fitzgerald regarded with fierce outsider rage. In one of the "Crack-Up" essays from his abyss of 1936, he writes of how he had almost lost Zelda as a poor boy without prospects, and then with his first novel and the sudden wealth from short stories in big magazines (many of those early stories set in St. Paul) he had won her after all. "The man with the jingle of money in his pocket who married the girl a year later," he wrote, "would always cherish an abiding distrust, an animosity, toward the leisure class — not the conviction of a revolutionist but the smoldering hatred of a peasant."

Fitzgerald's reserved his deepest grudge for inherited wealth, "the leisure class." In using that term, he invokes another one-time Minnesotan, Thorstein Veblen, whose *Theory of the Leisure Class*, published in 1899, was a startling (and still classic) study of wealth, culture, and ethics. Veblen's book introduced the damning term "conspicuous consumption," a concept Scott and Zelda were to embody with abandon.

In supposedly classless American culture, Fitzgerald is a rare twentieth-century writer, counting up the silver, attending to the inheritances, narrowing his critical eye to the life and habits of the idle (or busy) rich. His bitter acuity about class-consciousness, bred of his St. Paul experience, has gotten him in trouble with generations of critics. While his eminence as an American writer has long been unquestioned, his attitude (or supposed attitude) toward wealth continues to nick his reputation as if behind the incandescent writing there is the dirty little itch of a wannabe.

During his lifetime and even now Fitzgerald has been attacked as an apologist for the rich, a social climber and relentless snob without either political consciousness or an awareness of economic imperatives. There is the famous Hemingway exchange in "The Snows of Kilamanjaro" in which Fitzgerald is supposed to have said, "The rich are different from you and me," thereby allowing Hemingway to write the arch reply, "Yes, they have more money."

Except it turns out this exchange never happened. Even decent Max Perkins couldn't seem to correct the inaccuracy. He was present at a lunch in New York in 1936 when Hemingway said, "I am getting to know the rich." To which the literary critic Mary Colum, the other person at the table, delivered the snapper reply. Fitzgerald wasn't at the table or in the city at the time. But then good stories have a way of propelling themselves beyond facts. And it surely was a story Hemingway didn't want told at *his* expense.

As the Depression deepened (and Fitzgerald's personal and financial troubles with it), he knew that this playboy image was the prevailing critical skinny on him — and that it was inexorably turning him into yesterday's news. This could exasperate him. But mostly it mystified him. Just a month before his death, he writes to Edmund Wilson about a shockingly disloyal essay he had come across by John Peale Bishop, another old Princeton friend. "He reproached me," Fitzgerald tells Wilson with dismay, "with being a suck around the rich. I've had this before but nobody seems able to name these rich." He wonders what could have caused this vicious attack from an old friend. "It can't be jealousy," he says with resignation, "for there isn't much to be jealous of any more."

Fitzgerald didn't see where this indelible idea of his attachment to "the rich" came from perhaps because he had long ceased to believe in — or exist in — his playboy image. Didn't people understand that *Tender Is the Night* was not a celebration of the rich? Didn't they see it was a dissection of the fragrant corpse of capitalism? Well, no.

Fitzgerald's drinking, that insignia of the Roaring Twenties, remained and even increased, but it was hardly a party anymore. Yet he couldn't see how permanent such public images become, how they refuse to leave "the work" pristine in its accomplishment. Fitzgerald thought of himself as belonging to the left politically. He welcomed "the Great Change" as he called the progressive or even socialist movement he saw rising up from the frustrations and inequities unmasked by the Depression. He wrote to Scottie in college in 1938 that he considered himself "a left-wing sympathizer and would be proud if you were. In any case, I should feel outraged if you identified yourself with Nazism or Red-Baiting in any form."

It's strange that Fitzgerald was seen — is still often perceived — as a fly caught in the amber of the flapper era, weirdly gifted as a writer but essentially brainless. But he was reified as an icon of that historical moment rather than fully absorbed as its sardonic voice and sometimes its tragic scourge. He accepted with touching (and unfortunate) modesty the judgment of his old friend Edmund Wilson and others that he wasn't an intellectual, not even much of a thinker.

He never gave himself credit for the sharp intelligence of his native lyric gift. Yet Fitzgerald's poetic method captured in swift images not only an American time but an American consciousness. That pulse, so accurately taken, continues to beat. His poetic understanding often trumps writers as strong and enduring as Dos Passos and Hemingway and his fellow Minnesotan Sinclair Lewis, who approach the massive cultural shifts of the period with wholly narrative tools and accredited "political" readings.

Fitzgerald had an intuitive grasp of the American project in his times. His politics had a prophetic rather than a theoretical cast. "We will be the Romans in the next generation," he wrote, "as the English are now." He perceived the double helix of American capitalism and American popular culture rising out of the ashes of the First World War. And he saw, with the stiff, old-fashioned provincial grief of Nick Carraway, that the old moral compass was smashed.

* * *

In March 1922 Wilson published a long, insightful essay about Fitzgerald in *The Bookman*. Scott and Zelda were living in St. Paul at the time with their new baby. Fitzgerald had already written two novels — but not the two we think of today. *The Great Gatsby* wasn't published until 1925, and *Tender Is the Night* was a long time coming nine years later in 1934. The Fitzgerald of Wilson's essay is the shooting star of the early short stories and his first two "lost generation" novels — the coming-of-age *This Side of Paradise* and its young married sequel, *The Beautiful and Damned*.

Wilson was doing Fitzgerald a big favor — writing about him in a prestigious literary journal, honoring his pop icon pal with a serious critical once-over. He sent Fitzgerald the piece before it was published. With his characteristic schoolboy probity before Wilson, his "intellectual conscience" (as he called Wilson in a "Crack-Up" essay), Fitzgerald didn't make a peep about the dismissive opening of the essay. Wilson retailed there a remark, now famous, first made by Edna St. Vincent Millay:

> It has been said by a celebrated person that to meet F. Scott Fitzgerald is to think of a stupid old woman with whom someone has left a diamond; she is extremely proud of the diamond and shows it to everyone who comes by, and everyone is surprised that such an ignorant old woman should possess so valuable a jewel; for in nothing does she appear so inept as in the remarks she makes about the diamond.

This kind of intellectual condescension followed Fitzgerald all his life. He seemed to accept it. As a young man he was a bigger success than most of the people making such remarks, and perhaps he could afford to brush off arch literary insults. As a considerably chastened older writer trying to earn a living by writing popular stories while keeping himself and his dream of another novel alive, he felt he "had been only a mediocre caretaker . . . even of my talent," and perhaps felt he deserved the humiliations dealt him. In any case, Fitzgerald could be touchingly modest, even self-denigrating about his intellectual stature. But

his assessment of the writers of his times has proved to be aston-
ishingly accurate—he had an uncanny way of picking the big tal-
ents and seeing the lightweights and phonies. His historical and
political reading of his times was also usually acute, even if it was
a matter of lyric instinct rather than scholarly reflection.

In his profile of Fitzgerald as a young success, Wilson diplo-
matically shades the reference to him as a stupid old woman (a
comment made by his then-lover Millay about his faithful friend
Fitzgerald) while still admitting its "symbolic truth." But the real
theme of the manuscript Wilson sent Fitzgerald is three points he
feels are essential to understanding the gifted young writer: "In
the first place, he comes from the Middle West—from St. Paul,
Minnesota."

Wilson immediately lifts Fitzgerald's reputation to the height
of the already established Sinclair Lewis. "Fitzgerald is as much of
the Middle West of large cities and country clubs," he writes with
wonderful East coast snobbery, "as Sinclair Lewis is of the Middle
West of the prairies and little towns. What we find in him is
much what we find in the more prosperous strata of these cities:
sensitivity and eagerness for life without a sound base of culture
and taste; a structure of millionaire residences, brilliant expensive
hotels and exhilarating social activities built not on the eighteenth
century but simply on the flat Western land. "

The second thing Wilson points out is that Fitzgerald is
Irish—which is a bit like reaffirming his St. Paul origins or at
least more fully defining them. And the third thing to know
about F. Scott Fitzgerald: he's a drinker.

"Now as to the liquor thing," Fitzgerald nervously writes back
in response to the manuscript, "it's true, but nevertheless I'm going to ask you take it out. It leaves a loophole through which I can
be attacked and discredited by every moralist who reads the article." He also reminds Wilson a bit fussily that he was "not Irish
on Father's side."

Wilson made the changes—in the published piece there are

only two, not three, things "worth knowing" about F. Scott Fitzgerald, and his drinking isn't one of them. Wilson also allows him to be "partly Irish" instead of "Irish."

By 1935, when Fitzgerald writes to Maxwell Perkins from Baltimore, with Zelda in a nearby mental hospital and his own youth behind him, his dreams for his latest novel in tatters, he makes a pathetic distinction about the role of drinking in his artistic life. "A short story," he tells Perkins, "can be written on a bottle, but for a novel you need the mental speed that enables you to keep the whole pattern in your head and ruthlessly sacrifice the sideshows."

It was the kind of double standard he had always kept in his artistic life. Novels were the real thing—art, reputation, and any chance for immortality lay there. They were literature. The short story was a job, not always an honorable one. When his fee at *The Saturday Evening Post* reached its high point (in 1929 for "At Your Age," a St. Paul story), Fitzgerald savaged himself in a letter to Hemingway, "Here's a last flicker of the old cheap pride. The *Post* now pays the old whore $4,000 a screw." Yet as early as 1921 when he and Zelda were living on Goodrich Avenue in St. Paul and he was still in his ascendancy, Fitzgerald was already beating himself up for his success with the popular short story. He had printed up stationery that read:

F. Scott Fitzgerald
Hack Writer and Plagiarist
Saint Paul, Minnesota

In 1924 he wrote Max Perkins from Rome on the Piazza de Spagna where his hero Keats had died, saying, "I now get $2,000.00 a story but I hate worse than hell to do them." He told Perkins he was thinking of doing "a book of good stories" and "some cheap ones," making promises about "no more intervals of trash" in order to "go on as a novelist." The high life, the drinking (which of course went on with or without Zelda, high life or low, first in youthful "parties," later in grim solitary binges) and a general inability to settle to any kind of domestic life—all of it cast the short story into the diabolical role of financial lifesaver and artistic killer.

But he may have known he was blaming the wrong villain. "Strange to say," he wrote to Mencken, "my whole heart was in my first trash." The short story, so embedded in commercial taste and the formulas of romantic fiction, was how he made his living. It is difficult to translate the purchasing power of $4,000 in 1931 (or $400 in 1919) into current early twenty-first century value. But the usual conversion would assume that $4,000 in 1929, for example, would be something like $25,000 or $30,000 now. And Fitzgerald, in his glory years, was publishing six or eight stories a year. In 1924, at the height of the Roaring Twenties (though not yet at the height of Fitzgerald's short story fees with the glossies), two-thirds of Americans earned less than $1,500 a year.

Some of the stories (a surprising number with St. Paul settings and characters) are enduring pieces of the American canon— "Winter Dreams," "The Ice Palace," "Absolution," "The Diamond As Big as the Ritz," "Babylon Revisited." In March 1928, stalled on his ambitious plan for a novel (eventually *Tender Is the Night*), Fitzgerald abruptly turned to a series of stories from his adolescence featuring an alter ego he named Basil Duke Lee. In the eight Basil stories Fitzgerald takes a backward look at his coming-of-age in St. Paul.

But the Basil stories did not earn the fabulous sums that *The Saturday Evening Post* was willing to pay because they had a regional flavor. Quite the opposite. They were modish tales of a big dreamer determined to turn himself into a big deal. Basil's provincial St. Paul background was eloquent shorthand for the classic American plot of the nobody who makes himself into a somebody. Not simply a very midwestern story but a very American story. All eight stories were published in *The Post* in the months preceding the Crash of 1929. As Fitzgerald put it in "The Crack-Up," the national Crash mirrored his own. And Zelda's. Her first lengthy hospitalization, in Switzerland for much of 1931, occasioned a very different kind of backward glance and introspection than the Basil stories could accommodate for all their sharp social awareness.

"It's odd," he wrote to Zelda just two months before his death, "that my old talent for the short story vanished." He tried to puzzle it out. "It was partly that times changed, " he thought, "editors changed, but part of it was tied up somehow with you and me — the happy ending." And there was no happy ending, they both now understood. He was doing whatever spec work was thrown his way in Hollywood, she was living either with her mother in Asheville or, when things got bad, returning to the hospital for a while.

The last of Fitzgerald's stories that might be called a St. Paul story was "The Freeze-Out," published in *The Saturday Evening Post* in December 1931. It earned him $4,000, still top-dollar. Though he schemed with Max Perkins at Scribner's and with Harold Ober, his savvy literary agent, about bringing out a collection of the Basil stories or perhaps reworking them more thoughtfully into a novel, this never came about in his lifetime.

* * *

Fitzgerald died believing himself a failure. His books were no longer much read (his last royalty statement was for the grimly unlucky figure of $13.13), his wife was in a mental hospital, he couldn't provide a home for his child, he was demolished by drinking and weakened by heart disease, living in Hollywood, that cruelest American dream city.

Even as a young writer pulling in fantastic sums from magazines, Fitzgerald was chronically short of cash. He used both the Reynolds agency and Scribner's as a kind of ATM, asking for (and getting) advances that he paid back when magazine payments came in. But his financial problems became truly dire during the Depression with the private hospital costs for Zelda, private schools for Scottie, and his own inability to play the game as deftly as he once had. He may have played fast and loose with his agent and editor for money, but when he was really desperate, he was loath to turn to friends or even his wealthy younger sister.

He only felt able to ask two friends (and no family) for loans. One was Gerald Murphy from his high-living French Riviera days. The other was Oscar Kalman, an old St. Paul friend who also did not let him down. The Minnesota connection was staid (Kalman was an established investment broker with homes on Summit Avenue and White Bear Lake) but loyal, and Fitzgerald knew he could go there.

While he said he didn't want his daughter to be a midwesterner, he wrote Kalman that he wanted her "to have some sense of life in the middle-west + to have some friends there." He and Zelda had vague but recurring plans that Scottie should make her debut in St. Paul. But Zelda was in Asheville and Fitzgerald said his heart was always there with her, "yet a part of me will always live in St. Paul which I think of as a tough + usually impolite city and am indebted to for the ability to take it."

Even at the end, eclipsed and ill, Fitzgerald could still rise to meet his obscurity with the courage of a crowned poet who had crossed over from the Lethe of success. "I would rather impress my image (even though an image the size of a nickel)," he wrote to Mencken, his old *Smart Set* editor, "than be known. . . . I would as soon be as anonymous as Rimbaud. . . . It is simply that having once found the intensity of art, nothing else that can happen in life can ever again seem as important as the creative process."

This remark makes its point obliquely, but it underscores Fitzgerald's enduring struggle with the opposing values of fame and art. Success was "the bitch goddess," as he said with rueful middle-aged disgust. But the "image" he strives finally to "impress" (on the world, on literature) is his sensibility, not something as flimsy as his personality. Like his great literary hero, Keats, he understood that fame was simply greatness in art. And it had to be "anonymous." The fame that adhered to the great ones was not to be confused with celebrity. The real fame, the one Keats consciously sought and Fitzgerald is looking for too with eyes almost dead and gone, is nothing less than immortality. It is the laurel wreath awarded by the gods to those rare lyric champions who dare to lose themselves and *become* the work.

With his perfect pitch for the resonant detail, Fitzgerald no doubt would have relished the fact that he started life in St. Paul, born on Laurel Avenue, and that his last address was on Laurel Avenue in Hollywood. He perhaps had not gone so far after all.

He and Zelda, like his own parents, never owned a house, never pitched a tent for long. For all his "rambling," as Fitzgerald called his manic geographic lurchings in his letter to his old St. Paul friend Marie Hersey, he ended, at least poetically, where he had begun, on a street named for the poet's tree. It was a detail he would have known how to use for one of his impetuous heroes glittering and skidding toward his improbable dream of success.

THE ST. PAUL STORIES
OF F. SCOTT FITZGERALD

BABES IN THE WOODS

In January 1917, after his breakup with his first great love, Ginevra King, Fitzgerald wrote about their initial encounter in "Babes in the Woods." It was published in the May 1917 issue of Princeton's Nassau Literary Magazine. King, a debutante from a wealthy Chicago family, roomed at boarding school with Marie Hersey, one of Fitzgerald's St. Paul friends. "The name 'Ginevra King,'" Fitzgerald scrawled in his ledger in July 1911, years before he met her. "Again the name Ginevra," he noted in January 1913. Fitzgerald finally met King at a dinner party in January 1915, when she came to St. Paul to visit Hersey. During the spring of 1919, while he was living in New York, Fitzgerald was trying to convince another young woman — Zelda Sayre — that he could support her with his writing. He sent out over a hundred inquiries, but he sold only one story in June, earning $30 from the literary magazine The Smart Set for a slightly revised version of "Babes in the Woods." This first professional appearance was completely overshadowed by Scribner's acceptance that September of This Side of Paradise, in which "Babes in the Woods" appears yet again, as two subchapters. All three versions reproduce Fitzgerald's preoccupation with Ginevra before he met her.

Published in *The Smart Set*, September 1919
Collected in *The Apprentice Fiction of F. Scott Fitzgerald* (1919)

I
· · · · ·

SHE PAUSED AT THE TOP OF THE STAIRCASE. The emotions of divers on springboards, leading ladies on opening nights, and lumpy, be-striped young men on the day of the Big Game, crowded through her. She felt as if she should have descended to a burst of drums or to a discordant blend of gems from *Thaïs* and *Carmen*. She had never been so worried about her appearance, she had never been so satisfied with it. She had been sixteen years old for six months.

"Isabelle!" called Elaine, her cousin, from the doorway of the dressing-room.

"I'm ready." She caught a slight lump of nervousness in her throat.

"I've had to send back to the house for another pair of slippers—it'll be just a minute."

Isabelle started toward the dressing-room for a last peek at a mirror, but something decided her to stand there and gaze down the stairs. They curved tantalizingly and she could just catch a glimpse of two pairs of masculine feet in the hall below.

Pump-shod in uniform black, they gave no hint of identity, but eagerly she wondered if one pair were attached to Stephen Palms. This young man, as yet unmet, had taken up a considerable part of her day—the first day of her arrival.

Going up in a machine from the station Elaine had volunteered, amid a rain of questions and comment, revelation and exaggeration—

"You remember Stephen Palms; well, he is simply mad to see you again. He's stayed over a day from college and he's coming tonight. He's heard *so* much about you———"

It had pleased her to know this. It put them on more equal terms, although she was accustomed to stage her own romances with or without a send-off.

But following her delighted tremble of anticipation came a sinking sensation which made her ask:

"How do you mean he's heard about me? What sort of things?"

Elaine smiled — she felt more or less in the capacity of a show-woman with her more exotic cousin.

"He knows you're good-looking and all that." She paused — "I guess he knows you've been kissed."

Isabelle had shuddered a bit under the fur robe. She was accustomed to be followed by this, but it never failed to arouse in her the same feeling of resentment; yet — in a strange town it was an advantage.

She was a "speed," was she? Well, let them find out! She wasn't quite old enough to be sorry or nearly old enough to be glad.

Out of the window Isabelle watched the high-piled snow glide by in the frosty morning. It was ever so much colder here than in Baltimore, she had not remembered; the glass of the side door was iced and the windows were shirred with snow in the corners.

Her mind played still with one subject: Did *he* dress like that boy there who walked so calmly down what was evidently a bustling business street, in moccasins and winter-carnival costume? How very *western!* Of course he wasn't that way; he went to college, was a freshman or something.

Really she had no distinct idea of him. A two-year-back picture had not impressed her except by the big eyes, which he had probably grown up to by now.

However, in the last two weeks, when her Christmas visit to Elaine had been decided on, he had assumed the proportions of a worthy adversary. Children, the most astute of matchmakers, plot and plan quickly, and Elaine had cleverly played a correspondence sonata to Isabelle's excitable temperament. Isabelle was, and had been for some time, capable of very strong, if very transient emotions.

They drew up at a white stone building, set back from the

snowy street. Mrs. Hollis greeted her warmly and her various younger cousins were produced from the corners where they skulked politely. Isabelle met them quite tactfully. At her best she allied all with whom she came in contact, except older girls and some women. All the impressions that she made were conscious. The half-dozen girls she renewed acquaintance with that morning were all rather impressed—and as much by her direct personality as by her reputation.

Stephen Palms was an open subject of conversation. Evidently he was a bit light of love. He was neither popular nor unpopular. Every girl there seemed to have had an affair with him at some time or other, but no one volunteered any really useful information. He was going to "fall for her". . .

Elaine had issued that statement to her young set and they were retailing it back to Elaine as fast as they set eyes on Isabelle. Isabelle resolved that, if necessary, she would force herself to like him—she owed it to Elaine—even though she were terribly disappointed. Elaine had painted him in such glowing colors—he was good-looking, had a "line," and was properly inconstant.

In fact, he summed up all the romance that her age and environment led her to desire. Were those his dancing shoes that "shimmied" tentatively around the soft rug below?

All impressions, and in fact all ideas, were terribly kaleidoscopic to Isabelle. She had that curious mixture of the social and artistic temperaments, found so often in two classes, society girls and actresses. Her education, or rather her sophistication, had been absorbed from the boys who had dangled from her favor, her tact was instinctive, and her capacity for love affairs was limited only by the number of boys she met. Flirt smiled from her large, black-brown eyes and figured in her intense physical magnetism.

So she waited at the head of the stairs at the Country Club that evening while slippers were fetched. Just as she was getting impatient, Elaine came out of the dressing-room beaming with her accustomed good nature and high spirits, and together they descended the broad stairs while the nervous searchlight of Isabelle's mind flashed on two ideas. She was glad she had high color tonight and she wondered if he danced well.

Downstairs, in the Club's great room, the girls she had met in the afternoon surrounded her for a moment, looking unbelievably changed by the soft yellow light; then she heard Elaine's voice repeating a cycle of names and she found herself bowing to a sextet of black and white and terrible stiff figures.

The name Palms figured somewhere, but she did not place him at first. A confused and very juvenile moment of awkward backings and bumpings, and all found themselves arranged talking to the persons they least desired to.

Isabelle maneuvered herself and Duncan Collard, a freshman from Harvard with whom she had once played hopscotch, to a seat on the stairs. A reference, supposedly humorous, to the past was all she needed.

What Isabelle could do socially with one idea was remarkable. First, she repeated it rapturously in an enthusiastic contralto with a trace of a Southern accent; then she held it off at a distance and smiled at it — her wonderful smile; then she delivered it in variations and played a sort of mental catch with it, all this in the nominal form of dialogue.

Duncan was fascinated and totally unconscious that this was being done, not for him, but for the eyes that glistened under the shining, carefully watered hair, a little to her left. As an actor even in the fullest flush of his own conscious magnetism gets a lasting impression of most of the people in the front row, so Isabelle sized up Stephen Palms. First, he was light, and from her feeling of disappointment, she knew that she had expected him to be dark and of pencil slenderness. For the rest, a faint flush and a straight romantic profile, the effect set off by a close-fitting dress suit and a silk ruffled shirt of the kind that women still delight in on men, but men were just beginning to get tired of.

Stephen was just quietly smiling.

"Don't *you* think so?" she said suddenly, turning to him innocent-eyed.

He nodded and smiled—an expectant, waiting smile.

Then there was a stir and Elaine led the way over to their table. Stephen struggled to her side and whispered:

"You're my dinner partner—Isabelle."

Isabelle gasped—this was rather right in line. But really she felt as if a good speech had been taken from the star and given to a minor character—she mustn't lose the leadership a bit. The dinner table glittered with laughter at the confusion of getting places and then curious eyes were turned on her, sitting near the head.

She was enjoying this immensely, and Duncan Collard was so engrossed with the added sparkle of her rising color that he forgot to pull out Elaine's chair and fell into a dim confusion. Stephen was on the other side, full of confidence and vanity, looking at her most consciously. He began directly and so did Duncan.

"I've heard a lot about you since you wore braids——"

"Wasn't it funny this afternoon——"

Both stopped.

Isabelle turned to Stephen shyly.

Her face was always enough answer for anyone, but she decided to speak.

"How—who from?"

"From everybody—for all the years since you've been away."

She blushed appropriately.

On her right, Duncan was hors-de-combat already although he hadn't quite realized it.

"I'll tell you what I remembered about you all these years," Stephen continued.

She leaned slightly toward him and looked modestly at the celery before her.

Duncan sighed—he knew Stephen and the situations that Stephen was born to handle. He turned to Elaine and asked her if she was going away to school next year.

II
. . . . .

Isabelle and Stephen were distinctly not innocent, nor were they otherwise. Moreover, amateur standing had very little value in the game they were beginning — they were each playing a part that they might play for years. They had both started with good looks and excitable temperaments, and the rest was the result of certain accessible popular novels, and dressing-room conversation culled from a slightly older set.

When Isabelle's eyes, wide and innocent, proclaimed the ingénue most, Stephen was proportionately less deceived. He waited for the mask to drop off, but at the same time he did not question her right to wear it.

She, on her part, was not impressed by his studied air of blasé sophistication. She had lived in a larger city and had slightly an advantage in range. But she accepted his pose. It was one of a dozen little conventions of this kind of affair. He was aware that he was getting this particular favor now because she had been coached. He knew that he stood for merely the best thing in sight, and that he would have to improve his opportunity before he lost his advantage.

So they proceeded, with an infinite guile that would have horrified the parents of both.

After the half dozen little dinners were over, the dance began.

Everything went smoothly — boys cut in on Isabelle every few feet and then squabbled in the corners with: "You might let me get more than an *inch!*" and "She didn't like it either — she told me so next time I cut in."

It was true — she told everyone so, and gave every hand a parting pressure that said, "You know that your dances are *making* my evening."

But time passed, two hours of it, and the less subtle beaux had better learn to focus their pseudo-passionate glances elsewhere, for eleven o'clock found Isabelle and Stephen sitting on a leather lounge in a little den off the reading room. She was conscious that they were a handsome pair and seemed to belong distinctly on this leather lounge while lesser lights fluttered and chattered downstairs. Boys who passed the door looked in enviously—girls who passed only laughed and frowned, and grew wise within themselves.

They had now reached a very definite stage. They had traded ages and accounts of their lives since they had met last. She had listened to much that she had heard before. He was a freshman at college and was on his class hockey team. He had learned that some of the boys she went with in Baltimore were "terrible speeds" and came to parties intoxicated—most of them were twenty or so, and drove alluring Stutzes. A good half of them seemed to have flunked out of various boarding schools and colleges, but some of them bore sporting names that made him look at her admiringly.

As a matter of fact, Isabelle's closer acquaintance with the colleges was chiefly through older cousins. She had bowing acquaintances with a lot of young men who thought she was "a pretty kid" and "worth keeping an eye on." But Isabelle strung the names into a fabrication of gaiety that would have dazzled a Viennese nobleman. Such is the power of young contralto voices on leather sofas.

I have said that they had reached a very definite stage—nay more, a very critical stage. Stephen had stayed over a day to see her and his train left at twelve-eighteen that night. His trunk and suitcase awaited him at the station and his watch was already beginning to hang heavy in his pocket.

"Isabelle," he said suddenly, "I want to tell you something."

They had been talking lightly about "that funny look in her eyes," and on the relative attractions of dancing and sitting out, and Isabelle knew from the change in his manner exactly what was coming—indeed, she had been wondering how soon it would come.

Stephen reached above their heads and turned out the electric light, so they were in the dark except for the glow from the red lamps that fell through the door from the reading-room. Then he began:

"I don't know — I don't know whether or not you know what you — what I'm going to say. Lordy, Isabelle — this sounds like a line, but it isn't."

"I know," said Isabelle softly.

"We may never meet again like this — I have darned hard luck sometimes."

He was leaning away from her on the other arm of the lounge, but she could see his black eyes plainly in the dark.

"You'll see me again — silly." There was just the slightest emphasis on the last word — so that it became almost a term of endearment.

He continued a bit huskily:

"I've fallen for a lot of people — girls — and I guess you have, too — boys, I mean — but honestly you — " He broke off suddenly and leaned forward, chin on his hands, a favorite and studied gesture. "Oh, what's the use? You'll go your way and I suppose I'll go mine."

Silence for a moment. Isabelle was quite stirred — she wound her handkerchief into a tight ball and by the faint light that streamed over her, dropped it deliberately on the floor. Their hands touched for an instant, but neither spoke. Silences were becoming more frequent and more delicious. Outside another stray couple had come up and were experimenting on the piano in the next room. After the usual preliminary of "chopsticks," one of them started "Babes in the Wood" and a light tenor carried the words into the den —

> *Give me your hand,*
> *I understand,*
> *We're off to Slumberland.*

Isabelle hummed it softly and trembled as she felt Stephen's hand close over hers.

"Isabelle," he whispered, "you know I'm mad about you. You *do* give a darn about me?"

"Yes."

"How much do you care—do you like anyone better?"

"No." He could scarcely hear her, although he bent so near that he felt her breath against his cheek.

"Isabelle, I'm going back to college for six long months and why shouldn't we—if I could only just have one thing to remember you by——"

"Close the door."

Her voice had just stirred so that he half wondered whether she had spoken at all.

As he swung the door softly shut, the music seemed quivering just outside.

> *Moonlight is bright,*
> *Kiss me good-night.*

What a wonderful song, she thought—everything was wonderful tonight, most of all this romantic scene in the den with their hands clinging and the inevitable looming charmingly close.

The future vista of her life seemed an unending succession of scenes like this, under moonlight and pale starlight, and in the backs of warm limousines and in low, cozy roadsters stopped under sheltering trees—only the boy might change, and this one was so nice.

"Isabelle!"

His whisper blended in the music and they seemed to float nearer together.

Her breath came faster.

"Can't I kiss you, Isabelle?"

Lips half-parted, she turned her head to him in the dark.

Suddenly the ring of voices, the sound of running footsteps surged toward them.

Like a flash Stephen reached up and turned on the light and when the door opened and three boys, the wrathy and dance-craving Duncan among them, rushed in, he was turning over the magazines on the table, while she sat without moving, serene and unembarrassed, and even greeted them with a welcoming smile. But her heart was beating wildly and she felt somehow as if she had been deprived.

It was evidently over. There was a clamor for a dance, there was a glance that passed between them, on his side despair, on hers regret, and then the evening went on, with the reassured beaux and the eternal cutting in.

At quarter to twelve Stephen shook hands with her gravely, in a small crowd assembled to wish him good-speed.

For an instant he lost his poise and she felt slightly unnecessary, when a satirical voice from a concealed wit on the edge of the company cried:

"Take her outside, Stephen."

As he took her hand he pressed it a little and she returned the pressure as she had done to twenty hands that evening — that was all.

At two-o'clock, back at Hollis', Elaine asked her if she and Stephen had had a "time" in the den. Isabelle turned to her quietly. In her eyes was the light of the idealist, the inviolate dreamer of Joan-like dreams.

"No!" she answered. "I don't do that sort of thing any more — he asked me to, but I said 'No.'"

As she crept into bed she wondered what he'd say in his special delivery tomorrow. He had such a good-looking mouth — would she ever — ?

"Fourteen angels were watching them," sang Elaine sleepily from the next room.

"Damn!" muttered Isabelle as she explored the cold sheets cautiously. "Damn!"

THE CAMEL'S BACK

During Christmas week 1919, *while waiting in St. Paul for the publication of* This Side of Paradise, *Fitzgerald heard about a well-known man in town who crashed a party disguised as a camel, enlisting a taxi-driver as the rear half. "I can't seem to find out exactly what happened," he told his friends, "but I'm going to write about it as if it was ten times funnier than anything you've said." A few days later he moved to New Orleans, where he wrote "The Camel's Back" in twenty-two consecutive hours. After the story was published, Louis Hill, the son of the railroad tycoon James J. Hill, wrote his daughter Maudie in boarding school that "under separate cover I am sending to you a story by Scott Fitzgerald, the St. Paul boy who wrote the book* [This Side of Paradise] *which has taken so well. This is the story of Eddie Saunders and the camel at our Christmas party at the house. Perry Parkhurst is Eddie Saunders and evidently the Mrs. Nolak is Mrs. Geason and the 'Tate' house is our house. The 'Club' is the University Club." Fitzgerald was familiar with the Hill family's Christmas costume parties, having escorted Marie Hersey to one of the events in* 1915. *"The Camel's Back," his third story to be published in the* Post, *brought him a raise from* $400 *to* $500. *He used the money to buy a diamond and platinum wristwatch for Zelda. He later sold an option for the story's movie rights.*

The Saturday Evening Post, April 24, 1920
Collected in *Tales of the Jazz Age* (1922)

I
. . . . .

THE GLAZED EYE OF THE TIRED READER resting for a second
on the above title will presume it to be merely metaphorical. Stories about the cup and the lip and the bad penny and the new
broom rarely have anything to do with cups or lips or pennies or
brooms. This story is the exception. It has to do with a material,
visible, and large-as-life camel's back.

Starting from the neck we shall work toward the tail. I want
you to meet Mr. Perry Parkhurst, twenty-eight, lawyer, native of
Toledo. Perry has nice teeth, a Harvard diploma, parts his hair in
the middle. You have met him before — in Cleveland, Portland,
St. Paul, Indianapolis, Kansas City, and so forth. Baker Brothers,
New York, pause on their semi-annual trip through the West to
clothe him; Montmorency & Co. dispatch a young man post-haste
every three months to see that he has the correct number of little
punctures on his shoes. He has a domestic roadster now, will have
a French roadster if he lives long enough, and doubtless a Chinese
tank if it comes into fashion. He looks like the advertisement of
the young man rubbing his sunset-colored chest with liniment
and goes East every other year to his class reunion.

I want you to meet his Love. Her name is Betty Medill, and she
would take well in the movies. Her father gives her three hundred
a month to dress on, and she has tawny eyes and hair and feather
fans of five colors. I shall also introduce her father, Cyrus Medill.
Though he is to all appearances flesh and blood, he is, strange to
say, commonly known in Toledo as the Aluminum Man. But
when he sits in his club window with two or three Iron Men, and
the White Pine Man, and the Brass Man, they look very much as
you and I do, only more so, if you know what I mean.

Now during the Christmas holidays of 1919 there took place
in Toledo, counting only the people with the italicized *the,* forty-
one dinner parties, sixteen dances, six luncheons, male and female,

16

twelve teas, four stag dinners, two weddings, and thirteen bridge parties. It was the cumulative effect of all this that moved Perry Parkhurst on the twenty-ninth day of December to a decision.

This Medill girl would marry him and she wouldn't marry him. She was having such a good time that she hated to take such a definite step. Meanwhile, their secret engagement had got so long that it seemed as if any day it might break off of its own weight. A little man named Warburton, who knew it all, persuaded Perry to superman her, to get a marriage license and go up to the Medill house and tell her she'd have to marry him at once or call it off forever. So he presented himself, his heart, his license, and his ultimatum, and within five minutes they were in the midst of a violent quarrel, a burst of sporadic open fighting such as occurs near the end of all long wars and engagements. It brought about one of those ghastly lapses in which two people who are in love pull up sharp, look at each other coolly, and think it's all been a mistake. Afterward they usually kiss wholesomely and assure the other person it was all their fault. Say it all was my fault! Say it was! I want to hear you say it!

But while reconciliation was trembling in the air, while each was, in a measure, stalling it off, so that they might the more voluptuously and sentimentally enjoy it when it came, they were permanently interrupted by a twenty-minute phone call for Betty from a garrulous aunt. At the end of eighteen minutes Perry Parkhurst, urged on by pride and suspicion and injured dignity, put on his long fur coat, picked up his light brown soft hat, and stalked out the door.

"It's all over," he muttered brokenly as he tried to jam his car into first. "It's all over—if I have to choke you for an hour, damn you!" This last to the car, which had been standing some time and was quite cold.

He drove downtown—that is, he got into a snow rut that led him downtown. He sat slouched down very low in his seat, much too dispirited to care where he went.

In front of the Clarendon Hotel he was hailed from the side-walk by a bad man named Baily, who had big teeth and lived at the hotel and had never been in love.

"Perry," said the bad man softly when the roadster drew up be-side him at the curb, "I've got six quarts of the doggonedest still champagne you ever tasted. A third of it's yours, Perry, if you'll come up-stairs and help Martin Macy and me drink it."

"Baily," said Perry tensely, "I'll drink your champagne. I'll drink every drop of it. I don't care if it kills me."

"Shut up, you nut!" said the bad man gently. "They don't put wood alcohol in champagne. This is the stuff that proves the world is more than six thousand years old. It's so ancient that the cork is petrified. You have to pull it with a stone drill."

"Take me up-stairs," said Perry moodily. "If that cork sees my heart it'll fall out from pure mortification."

The room up-stairs was full of those innocent hotel pictures of little girls eating apples and sitting in swings and talking to dogs. The other decorations were neckties and a pink man reading a pink paper devoted to ladies in pink tights.

"When you have to go into the highways and byways——" said the pink man, looking reproachfully at Baily and Perry.

"Hello, Martin Macy," said Perry shortly, "where's this stone-age champagne?"

"What's the rush? This isn't an operation, understand. This is a party."

Perry sat down dully and looked disapprovingly at all the neckties.

Baily leisurely opened the door of a wardrobe and brought out six handsome bottles.

"Take off that darn fur coat!" said Martin Macy to Perry. "Or maybe you'd like to have us open all the windows."

"Give me champagne," said Perry.

"Going to the Townsends' circus ball to-night?"

"Am not!"

"'Vited?"

"Uh-huh."

"Why not go?"

"Oh, I'm sick of parties," exclaimed Perry. "I'm sick of 'em. I've been to so many that I'm sick of 'em."

"Maybe you're going to the Howard Tates' party?"

"No, I tell you; I'm sick of 'em."

"Well," said Macy consolingly, "the Tates' is just for college kids anyways."

"I tell you———"

"I thought you'd be going to one of 'em anyways. I see by the papers you haven't missed a one this Christmas."

"Hm," grunted Perry morosely.

He would never go to any more parties. Classical phrases played in his mind—that side of his life was closed, closed. Now when a man says "closed, closed" like that, you can be pretty sure that some woman has double-closed him, so to speak. Perry was also thinking that other classical thought, about how cowardly suicide is. A noble thought that one—warm and inspiring. Think of all the fine men we should lose if suicide were not so cowardly!

An hour later was six o'clock, and Perry had lost all resemblance to the young man in the liniment advertisement. He looked like a rough draft for a riotous cartoon. They were singing—an impromptu song of Baily's improvisation:

> *One Lump Perry, the parlor snake,*
> *Famous through the city for the way he drinks his tea;*
> *Plays with it, toys with it,*
> *Makes no noise with it,*
> *Balanced on a napkin on his well-trained knee———*

"Trouble is," said Perry, who had just banged his hair with Baily's comb and was tying an orange tie round it to get the effect of Julius Cæsar, "that you fellas can't sing worth a damn. Soon's I leave th' air and start singin' tenor you start singin' tenor too."

"'M a natural tenor," said Macy gravely. "Voice lacks cultivation, tha's all. Gotta natural voice, m'aunt used say. Naturally good singer."

"Singers, singers, all good singers," remarked Baily, who was at the telephone. "No, not the cabaret; I want night egg. I mean some dog-gone clerk 'at's got food — food! I want——"

"Julius Cæsar," announced Perry, turning round from the mirror. "Man of iron will and stern 'termination."

"Shut up!" yelled Baily. "Say, iss Mr. Baily. Sen' up enormous supper. Use y'own judgment. Right away."

He connected the receiver and the hook with some difficulty, and then with his lips closed and an expression of solemn intensity in his eyes went to the lower drawer of his dresser and pulled it open.

"Lookit!" he commanded. In his hands he held a truncated garment of pink gingham.

"Pants," he exclaimed gravely. "Lookit!"

This was a pink blouse, a red tie, and a Buster Brown collar.

"Lookit!" he repeated. "Costume for the Townsends' circus ball. I'm li'l' boy carries water for the elephants."

Perry was impressed in spite of himself.

"I'm going to be Julius Cæsar," he announced after a moment of concentration.

"Thought you weren't going!" said Macy.

"Me? Sure, I'm goin'. Never miss a party. Good for the nerves — like celery."

"Cæsar!" scoffed Baily. "Can't be Cæsar! He is not about a circus. Cæsar's Shakespeare. Go as a clown."

Perry shook his head.

"Nope; Cæsar."

"Cæsar?"

"Sure. Chariot."

Light dawned on Baily.

"That's right. Good idea."

Perry looked round the room searchingly.

"You lend me a bathrobe and this tie," he said finally.

Baily considered.

"No good."

"Sure, tha's all I need. Cæsar was a savage. They can't kick if I come as Cæsar, if he was a savage."

"No," said Baily, shaking his head slowly. "Get a costume over at a costumer's. Over at Nolak's."

"Closed up."

"Find out."

After a puzzling five minutes at the phone a small, weary voice managed to convince Perry that it was Mr. Nolak speaking, and that they would remain open until eight because of the Townsends' ball. Thus assured, Perry ate a great amount of filet mignon and drank his third of the last bottle of champagne. At eight-fifteen the man in the tall hat who stands in front of the Clarendon found him trying to start his roadster.

"Froze up," said Perry wisely. "The cold froze it. The cold air."

"Froze, eh?"

"Yes. Cold air froze it."

"Can't start it?"

"Nope. Let it stand here till summer. One those hot ole August days'll thaw it out awright."

"Goin' let it stand?"

"Sure. Let 'er stand. Take a hot thief to steal it. Gemme taxi."

The man in the tall hat summoned a taxi.

"Where to, mister?"

"Go to Nolak's—costume fella."

II
. . . . .

Mrs. Nolak was short and ineffectual looking, and on the cessation of the world war had belonged for a while to one of the new nationalities. Owing to unsettled European conditions she had never since been quite sure what she was. The shop in which she and her husband performed their daily stint was dim and ghostly, and peopled with suits of armor and Chinese mandarins, and enormous papier-mâché birds suspended from the ceiling. In a vague background many rows of masks glared eyelessly at the visitor, and there were glass cases full of crowns and scepters, and jewels and enormous stomachers, and paints, and crêpe hair, and wigs of all colors.

When Perry ambled into the shop Mrs. Nolak was folding up the last troubles of a strenuous day, so she thought, in a drawer full of pink silk stockings.

"Something for you?" she queried pessimistically.

"Want costume of Julius Hur, the charioteer."

Mrs. Nolak was sorry, but every stitch of charioteer had been rented long ago. Was it for the Townsends' circus ball?

It was.

"Sorry," she said, "but I don't think there's anything left that's really circus."

This was an obstacle.

"Hm," said Perry. An idea struck him suddenly. "If you've got a piece of canvas I could go's a tent."

"Sorry, but we haven't anything like that. A hardware store is where you'd have to go to. We have some very nice Confederate soldiers."

"No. No soldiers."

"And I have a very handsome king."

He shook his head.

"Several of the gentlemen," she continued hopefully, "are wearing stovepipe hats and swallow-tail coats and going as ringmasters — but we're all out of tall hats. I can let you have some crêpe hair for a mustache."

"Want somep'n 'stinctive."

"Something — let's see. Well, we have a lion's head, and a goose, and a camel — "

"Camel?" The idea seized Perry's imagination, gripped it fiercely.

"Yes, but it needs two people."

"Camel. That's the idea. Lemme see it."

The camel was produced from his resting place on a top shelf. At first glance he appeared to consist entirely of a very gaunt, cadaverous head and a sizable hump, but on being spread out he was found to possess a dark brown, unwholesome-looking body made of thick, cottony cloth.

"You see it takes two people," explained Mrs. Nolak, holding out the camel in frank admiration. "If you have a friend he could be part of it. You see there's sorta pants for two people. One pair is for the fella in front, and the other pair for the fella in back. The fella in front does the lookin' out through these here eyes, an' the fella in back he's just gotta stoop over an' folla the front fella round."

"Put it on," commanded Perry.

Obediently Mrs. Nolak put her tabby-cat face inside the camel's head and turned it from side to side ferociously.

Perry was fascinated.

"What noise does a camel make?"

"What?" asked Mrs. Nolak as her face emerged, somewhat smudgy. "Oh, what noise? Why, he sorta brays."

"Lemme see it in a mirror."

Before a wide mirror Perry tried on the head and turned from side to side appraisingly. In the dim light the effect was distinctly pleasing. The camel's face was a study in pessimism, decorated with numerous abrasions, and it must be admitted that his coat was in that state of general negligence peculiar to camels — in fact, he needed to be cleaned and pressed — but distinctive he certainly was. He was majestic. He would have attracted attention in any gathering, if only by his melancholy cast of feature and the look of hunger lurking round his shadowy eyes.

"You see you have to have two people," said Mrs. Nolak again.

Perry tentatively gathered up the body and legs and wrapped them about him, tying the hind legs as a girdle round his waist. The effect on the whole was bad. It was even irreverent — like one of those mediæval pictures of a monk changed into a beast by the ministrations of Satan. At the very best the ensemble resembled a humpbacked cow sitting on her haunches among blankets.

"Don't look like anything at all," objected Perry gloomily.

"No," said Mrs. Nolak; "you see you got to have two people."

A solution flashed upon Perry.

"You got a date to-night?"

"Oh, I couldn't possibly——"

"Oh, come on," said Perry encouragingly. "Sure you can! Here! Be good sport, and climb into these hind legs."

With difficulty he located them, and extended their yawning depths ingratiatingly. But Mrs. Nolak seemed loath. She backed perversely away.

"Oh, no——"

"C'mon! You can be the front if you want to. Or we'll flip a coin."

"Oh, no——"

"Make it worth your while."

Mrs. Nolak set her lips firmly together.

"Now you just stop!" she said with no coyness implied. "None of the gentlemen ever acted up this way before. My husband——"

"You got a husband?" demanded Perry. "Where is he?"

"He's home."

"Wha's telephone number?"

After considerable parley he obtained the telephone number pertaining to the Nolak penates and got into communication with that small, weary voice he had heard once before that day. But Mr. Nolak, though taken off his guard and somewhat confused by Perry's brilliant flow of logic, stuck staunchly to his point. He refused firmly, but with dignity, to help out Mr. Parkhurst in the capacity of back part of a camel.

Having rung off, or rather having been rung off on, Perry sat down on a three-legged stool to think it over. He named over to himself those friends on whom he might call, and then his mind paused as Betty Medill's name hazily and sorrowfully occurred to him. He had a sentimental thought. He would ask her. Their love affair was over, but she could not refuse this last request. Surely it was not much to ask—to help him keep up his end of social obligation for one short night. And if she insisted, she could be the front part of the camel and he would go as the back. His magnanimity pleased him. His mind even turned to rosy-colored dreams of a tender reconciliation inside the camel—there hidden away from all the world. . . .

"Now you'd better decide right off."

The bourgeois voice of Mrs. Nolak broke in upon his mellow fancies and roused him to action. He went to the phone and called up the Medill house. Miss Betty was out; had gone out to dinner.

Then, when all seemed lost, the camel's back wandered curiously into the store. He was a dilapidated individual with a cold in his head and a general trend about him of downwardness. His cap was pulled down low on his head, and his chin was pulled down low on his chest, his coat hung down to his shoes, he looked run-down, down at the heels, and—Salvation Army to the contrary—down and out. He said that he was the taxicab-driver that the gentleman had hired at the Clarendon Hotel. He had been instructed to wait outside, but he had waited some time, and a suspicion had grown upon him that the gentleman had gone out the back way with purpose to defraud him—gentlemen sometimes did—so he had come in. He sank down onto the three-legged stool.

"Wanta go to a party?" demanded Perry sternly.

"I gotta work," answered the taxi-driver lugubriously. "I gotta keep my job."

"It's a very good party."

"'S a very good job."

"Come on!" urged Perry. "Be a good fella. See — it's pretty!" He held the camel up and the taxi-driver looked at it cynically.

"Huh!"

Perry searched feverishly among the folds of the cloth.

"See!" he cried enthusiastically, holding up a selection of folds. "This is your part. You don't even have to talk. All you have to do is to walk — and sit down occasionally. You do all the sitting down. Think of it. I'm on my feet all the time and *you* can sit down some of the time. The only time *I* can sit down is when we're lying down, and you can sit down when — oh, any time. See?"

"What's 'at thing?" demanded the individual dubiously. "A shroud?"

"Not at all," said Perry indignantly. "It's a camel."

"Huh?"

Then Perry mentioned a sum of money, and the conversation left the land of grunts and assumed a practical tinge. Perry and the taxi-driver tried on the camel in front of the mirror.

"You can't see it," explained Perry, peering anxiously out through the eyeholes, "but honestly, ole man, you look sim'ly great! Honestly!"

A grunt from the hump acknowledged this somewhat dubious compliment.

"Honestly, you look great!" repeated Perry enthusiastically. "Move round a little."

The hind legs moved forward, giving the effect of a huge cat-camel hunching his back preparatory to a spring.

"No; move sideways."

The camel's hips went neatly out of joint; a hula dancer would have writhed in envy.

"Good, isn't it?" demanded Perry, turning to Mrs. Nolak for approval.

"It looks lovely," agreed Mrs. Nolak.

"We'll take it," said Perry.

The bundle was stowed under Perry's arm and they left the shop.

"Go to the party!" he commanded as he took his seat in the back.

"What party?"

"Fanzy-dress party."

"Where'bouts is it?"

This presented a new problem. Perry tried to remember, but the names of all those who had given parties during the holidays danced confusedly before his eyes. He could ask Mrs. Nolak, but on looking out the window he saw that the shop was dark. Mrs. Nolak had already faded out, a little black smudge far down the snowy street.

"Drive uptown," directed Perry with fine confidence. "If you see a party, stop. Otherwise I'll tell you when we get there."

He fell into a hazy daydream and his thoughts wandered again to Betty—he imagined vaguely that they had had a disagreement because she refused to go to the party as the back part of the camel. He was just slipping off into a chilly doze when he was wakened by the taxi-driver opening the door and shaking him by the arm.

"Here we are, maybe."

Perry looked out sleepily. A striped awning led from the curb up to a spreading gray stone house, from which issued the low drummy whine of expensive jazz. He recognized the Howard Tate house.

"Sure," he said emphatically; "'at's it! Tate's party to-night. Sure, everybody's goin'."

"Say," said the individual anxiously after another look at the awning, "you sure these people ain't gonna romp on me for cumin' here?"

Perry drew himself up with dignity.

"'F anybody says anything to you, just tell 'em you're part of my costume."

The visualization of himself as a thing rather than a person seemed to reassure the individual.

"All right," he said reluctantly.

Perry stepped out under the shelter of the awning and began unrolling the camel.

"Let's go," he commanded.

Several minutes later a melancholy, hungry-looking camel, emitting clouds of smoke from his mouth and from the tip of his noble hump, might have been seen crossing the threshhold of the Howard Tate residence, passing a startled footman without so much as a snort, and heading directly for the main stairs that led up to the ballroom. The beast walked with a peculiar gait which varied between an uncertain lockstep and a stampede — but can best be described by the word "halting." The camel had a halting gait — and as he walked he alternately elongated and contracted like a gigantic concertina.

III
. . . . .

The Howard Tates are, as every one who lives in Toledo knows, the most formidable people in town. Mrs. Howard Tate was a Chicago Todd before she became a Toledo Tate, and the family generally affect that conscious simplicity which has begun to be the earmark of American aristocracy. The Tates have reached the stage where they talk about pigs and farms and look at you icy-eyed if you are not amused. They have begun to prefer retainers rather than friends as dinner guests, spend a lot of money in a quiet way, and, having lost all sense of competition, are in process of growing quite dull.

The dance this evening was for little Millicent Tate, and though all ages were represented, the dancers were mostly from school and college — the younger married crowd was at the Townsends' circus ball up at the Tallyho Club. Mrs. Tate was standing just inside the ballroom, following Millicent round with her eyes, and beaming whenever she caught her eye. Beside her were two middle-aged sycophants, who were saying what a perfectly exquisite child Millicent was. It was at this moment that Mrs. Tate was grasped firmly by the skirt and her youngest daughter, Emily, aged eleven, hurled herself with an "Oof!" into her mother's arms.

"Why, Emily, what's the trouble?"

"Mamma," said Emily, wild-eyed but voluble, "there's something out on the stairs."

"What?"

"There's a thing out on the stairs, mamma. I think it's a big dog, mamma, but it doesn't look like a dog."

"What do you mean, Emily?"

The sycophants waved their heads sympathetically.

"Mamma, it looks like a — like a camel."

Mrs. Tate laughed.

"You saw a mean old shadow, dear, that's all."

"No, I didn't. No, it was some kind of thing, mamma — big. I was going down-stairs to see if there were any more people, and this dog or something, he was coming up-stairs. Kinda funny, mamma, like he was lame. And then he saw me and gave a sort of growl, and then he slipped at the top of the landing, and I ran."

Mrs. Tate's laugh faded.

"The child must have seen something," she said.

The sycophants agreed that the child must have seen something — and suddenly all three women took an instinctive step away from the door as the sounds of muffled steps were audible just outside.

And then three startled gasps rang out as a dark brown form rounded the corner, and they saw what was apparently a huge beast looking down at them hungrily.

"Oof!" cried Mrs. Tate.

"O-o-oh!" cried the ladies in a chorus.

The camel suddenly humped his back, and the gasps turned to shrieks.

"Oh — look!"

"What is it?"

The dancing stopped, but the dancers hurrying over got quite a different impression of the invader; in fact, the young people immediately suspected that it was a stunt, a hired entertainer come to amuse the party. The boys in long trousers looked at it rather disdainfully, and sauntered over with their hands in their pockets, feeling that their intelligence was being insulted. But the girls uttered little shouts of glee.

"It's a camel!"

"Well, if he isn't the funniest!"

The camel stood there uncertainly, swaying slightly from side to side, and seeming to take in the room in a careful, appraising glance; then as if he had come to an abrupt decision he turned and ambled swiftly out the door.

Mr. Howard Tate had just come out of the library on the lower floor, and was standing chatting with a young man in the hall. Suddenly they heard the noise of shouting up-stairs, and almost immediately a succession of bumping sounds, followed by the precipitous appearance at the foot of the stairway of a large brown beast that seemed to be going somewhere in a great hurry.

"Now what the devil!" said Mr. Tate, starting.

The beast picked itself up not without dignity and, affecting an air of extreme nonchalance, as if he had just remembered an important engagement, started at a mixed gait toward the front door. In fact, his front legs began casually to run.

"See here now," said Mr. Tate sternly. "Here! Grab it, Butterfield! Grab it!"

The young man enveloped the rear of the camel in a pair of compelling arms, and, realizing that further locomotion was impossible, the front end submitted to capture and stood resignedly in a state of some agitation. By this time a flood of young people was pouring down-stairs, and Mr. Tate, suspecting everything from an ingenious burglar to an escaped lunatic, gave crisp directions to the young man:

"Hold him! Lead him in here; we'll soon see."

The camel consented to be led into the library, and Mr. Tate, after locking the door, took a revolver from a table drawer and instructed the young man to take the thing's head off. Then he gasped and returned the revolver to its hiding-place.

"Well, Perry Parkhurst!" he exclaimed in amazement.

"Got the wrong party, Mr. Tate," said Perry sheepishly. "Hope I didn't scare you."

"Well — you gave us a thrill, Perry." Realization dawned on him. "You're bound for the Townsends' circus ball."

"That's the general idea."

"Let me introduce Mr. Butterfield, Mr. Parkhurst." Then turning to Perry: "Butterfield is staying with us for a few days."

"I got a little mixed up," mumbled Perry. "I'm very sorry."

"Perfectly all right; most natural mistake in the world. I've got a clown rig and I'm going down there myself after a while." He turned to Butterfield. "Better change your mind and come down with us."

The young man demurred. He was going to bed.

"Have a drink, Perry?" suggested Mr. Tate.

"Thanks, I will."

"And, say," continued Tate quickly, "I'd forgotten all about your — friend here." He indicated the rear part of the camel. "I didn't mean to seem discourteous. Is it any one I know? Bring him out."

"It's not a friend," explained Perry hurriedly. "I just rented him."

"Does he drink?"

"Do you?" demanded Perry, twisting himself tortuously round.

There was a faint sound of assent.

"Sure he does!" said Mr. Tate heartily. "A really efficient camel ought to be able to drink enough so it'd last him three days."

"Tell you," said Perry anxiously, "he isn't exactly dressed up enough to come out. If you give me the bottle I can hand it back to him and he can take his inside."

From under the cloth was audible the enthusiastic smacking sound inspired by this suggestion. When a butler had appeared with bottles, glasses, and siphon, one of the bottles was handed back; thereafter the silent partner could be heard imbibing long potations at frequent intervals.

Thus passed a benign hour. At ten o'clock Mr. Tate decided that they'd better be starting. He donned his clown's costume; Perry replaced the camel's head, and side by side they traversed on foot the single block between the Tate house and the Tallyho Club.

The circus ball was in full swing. A great tent fly had been put up inside the ballroom and round the walls had been built rows of booths representing the various attractions of a circus side show, but these were now vacated and over the floor swarmed a shouting, laughing medley of youth and color—clowns, bearded ladies, acrobats, bareback riders, ringmasters, tattooed men, and charioteers. The Townsends had determined to assure their party of success, so a great quantity of liquor had been surreptitiously brought over from their house and was now flowing freely. A green ribbon ran along the wall completely round the ballroom, with pointing arrows alongside and signs which instructed the uninitiated to "Follow the green line!" The green line led down to the bar, where waited pure punch and wicked punch and plain dark-green bottles.

On the wall above the bar was another arrow, red and very wavy, and under it the slogan: "Now follow this!"

But even amid the luxury of costume and high spirits represented there, the entrance of the camel created something of a stir, and Perry was immediately surrounded by a curious, laughing crowd attempting to penetrate the identity of this beast that stood by the wide doorway eying the dancers with his hungry, melancholy gaze.

And then Perry saw Betty standing in front of a booth, talking to a comic policeman. She was dressed in the costume of an Egyptian snake-charmer: her tawny hair was braided and drawn through brass rings, the effect crowned with a glittering Oriental tiara. Her fair face was stained to a warm olive glow and on her arms and the half moon of her back writhed painted serpents with single eyes of venomous green. Her feet were in sandals and her skirt was slit to the knees, so that when she walked one caught a glimpse of other slim serpents painted just above her bare ankles. Wound about her neck was a glittering cobra. Altogether a charming costume — one that caused the more nervous among the older women to shrink away from her when she passed, and the more troublesome ones to make great talk about "shouldn't be allowed" and "perfectly disgraceful."

But Perry, peering through the uncertain eyes of the camel, saw only her face, radiant, animated, and glowing with excitement, and her arms and shoulders, whose mobile, expressive gestures made her always the outstanding figure in any group. He was fascinated and his fascination exercised a sobering effect on him. With a growing clarity the events of the day came back — rage rose within him, and with a half-formed intention of taking her away from the crowd he started toward her — or rather he elongated slightly, for he had neglected to issue the preparatory command necessary to locomotion.

But at this point fickle Kismet, who for a day had played with him bitterly and sardonically, decided to reward him in full for the amusement he had afforded her. Kismet turned the tawny eyes of the snake-charmer to the camel. Kismet led her to lean toward the man beside her and say, "Who's that? That camel?"

"Darned if I know."

But a little man named Warburton, who knew it all, found it necessary to hazard an opinion:

"It came in with Mr. Tate. I think part of it's probably Warren Butterfield, the architect from New York, who's visiting the Tates."

Something stirred in Betty Medill — that age-old interest of the provincial girl in the visiting man.

"Oh," she said casually after a slight pause.

At the end of the next dance Betty and her partner finished up within a few feet of the camel. With the informal audacity that was the key-note of the evening she reached out and gently rubbed the camel's nose.

"Hello, old camel."

The camel stirred uneasily.

"You 'fraid of me?" said Betty, lifting her eyebrows in reproof. "Don't be. You see I'm a snake-charmer, but I'm pretty good at camels too."

The camel bowed very low and some one made the obvious remark about beauty and the beast.

Mrs. Townsend approached the group.

"Well, Mr. Butterfield," she said helpfully, "I wouldn't have recognized you."

Perry bowed again and smiled gleefully behind his mask.

"And who is this with you?" she inquired.

"Oh," said Perry, his voice muffled by the thick cloth and quite unrecognizable, "he isn't a fellow, Mrs. Townsend. He's just part of my costume."

Mrs. Townsend laughed and moved away. Perry turned again to Betty.

"So," he thought, "this is how much she cares! On the very day of our final rupture she starts a flirtation with another man—an absolute stranger."

On an impulse he gave her a soft nudge with his shoulder and waved his head suggestively toward the hall, making it clear that he desired her to leave her partner and accompany him.

"By-by, Rus," she called to her partner. "This old camel's got me. Where we going, Prince of Beasts?"

The noble animal made no rejoinder, but stalked gravely along in the direction of a secluded nook on the side stairs.

There she seated herself, and the camel, after some seconds of confusion which included gruff orders and sounds of a heated dispute going on in his interior, placed himself beside her—his hind legs stretching out uncomfortably across two steps.

"Well, old egg," said Betty cheerfully, "how do you like our happy party?"

The old egg indicated that he liked it by rolling his head ecstatically and executing a gleeful kick with his hoofs.

"This is the first time that I ever had a tête-à-tête with a man's valet 'round"—she pointed to the hind legs—"or whatever that is."

"Oh," mumbled Perry, "he's deaf and blind."

"I should think you'd feel rather handicapped—you can't very well toddle, even if you want to."

The camel hung his head lugubriously.

"I wish you'd say something," continued Betty sweetly. "Say you like me, camel. Say you think I'm beautiful. Say you'd like to belong to a pretty snake-charmer."

The camel would.

"Will you dance with me, camel?"

The camel would try.

Betty devoted half an hour to the camel. She devoted at least half an hour to all visiting men. It was usually sufficient. When she approached a new man the current débutantes were accustomed to scatter right and left like a close column deploying before a machine-gun. And so to Perry Parkhurst was awarded the unique privilege of seeing his love as others saw her. He was flirted with violently!

IV
· · · · ·

This paradise of frail foundation was broken into by the sounds of a general ingress to the ballroom; the cotillion was beginning. Betty and the camel joined the crowd, her brown hand resting lightly on his shoulder, defiantly symbolizing her complete adoption of him.

When they entered the couples were already seating themselves at tables round the walls, and Mrs. Townsend, resplendent as a super bareback rider with rather too rotund calves, was standing in the centre with the ringmaster in charge of arrangements. At a signal to the band every one rose and began to dance.

"Isn't it just slick!" sighed Betty. "Do you think you can possibly dance?"

Perry nodded enthusiastically. He felt suddenly exuberant. After all, he was here incognito talking to his love — he could wink patronizingly at the world.

So Perry danced the cotillion. I say danced, but that is stretching the word far beyond the wildest dreams of the jazziest terpsichorean. He suffered his partner to put her hands on his helpless shoulders and pull him here and there over the floor while he hung his huge head docilely over her shoulder and made futile dummy motions with his feet. His hind legs danced in a manner all their own, chiefly by hopping first on one foot and then on the other. Never being sure whether dancing was going on or not, the hind legs played safe by going through a series of steps whenever the music started playing. So the spectacle was frequently presented of the front part of the camel standing at ease and the rear keeping up a constant energetic motion calculated to rouse a sympathetic perspiration in any soft-hearted observer.

He was frequently favored. He danced first with a tall lady covered with straw who announced jovially that she was a bale of hay and coyly begged him not to eat her.

"I'd like to; you're so sweet," said the camel gallantly.

Each time the ringmaster shouted his call of "Men up!" he lumbered ferociously for Betty with the cardboard wienerwurst or the photograph of the bearded lady or whatever the favor chanced to be. Sometimes he reached her first, but usually his rushes were unsuccessful and resulted in intense interior arguments.

"For Heaven's sake," Perry would snarl, fiercely between his clenched teeth, "get a little pep! I could have gotten her that time if you'd picked your feet up."

"Well, gimme a little warnin'!"

"I did, darn you."

"I can't see a dog-gone thing in here."

"All you have to do is follow me. It's just like dragging a load of sand round to walk with you."

"Maybe you wanta try back here."

"You shut up! If these people found you in this room they'd give you the worst beating you ever had. They'd take your taxi license away from you!"

Perry surprised himself by the ease with which he made this monstrous threat, but it seemed to have a soporific influence on his companion, for he gave out an "aw gwan" and subsided into abashed silence.

The ringmaster mounted to the top of the piano and waved his hand for silence.

"Prizes!" he cried. "Gather round!"

"Yea! Prizes!"

Self-consciously the circle swayed forward. The rather pretty girl who had mustered the nerve to come as a bearded lady trembled with excitement, thinking to be rewarded for an evening's hideousness. The man who had spent the afternoon having tattoo marks painted on him skulked on the edge of the crowd, blushing furiously when any one told him he was sure to get it.

"Lady and gent performers of this circus," announced the ringmaster jovially, "I am sure we will all agree that a good time has been had by all. We will now bestow honor where honor is due by bestowing the prizes. Mrs. Townsend has asked me to bestow the prizes. Now, fellow performers, the first prize is for that lady who has displayed this evening the most striking, becoming" — at this point the bearded lady sighed resignedly — "and original costume." Here the bale of hay pricked up her ears, "Now I am sure that the decision which has been agreed upon will be unanimous with all here present. The first prize goes to Miss Betty Medill, the charming Egyptian snake-charmer."

There was a burst of applause, chiefly masculine, and Miss Betty Medill, blushing beautifully through her olive paint, was passed up to receive her award. With a tender glance the ringmaster handed down to her a huge bouquet of orchids.

"And now," he continued, looking round him, "the other prize is for that man who has the most amusing and original costume. This prize goes without dispute to a guest in our midst, a gentleman who is visiting here but whose stay we all hope will be long and merry — in short, to the noble camel who has entertained us all by his hungry look and his brilliant dancing throughout the evening."

He ceased and there was a violent clapping and yeaing, for it was a popular choice. The prize, a large box of cigars, was put aside for the camel, as he was anatomically unable to accept it in person.

"And now," continued the ringmaster, "we will wind up the cotillion with the marriage of Mirth to Folly!

"Form for the grand wedding march, the beautiful snake-charmer and the noble camel in front!"

Betty skipped forward cheerily and wound an olive arm round the camel's neck. Behind them formed the procession of little boys, little girls, country jakes, fat ladies, thin men, sword-swallowers, wild men of Borneo, and armless wonders, many of them well in their cups, all of them excited and happy and dazzled by the flow of light and color round them, and by the familiar faces, strangely unfamiliar under bizarre wigs and barbaric paint. The voluptuous chords of the wedding march done in blasphemous syncopation issued in a delirious blend from the trombones and saxophones — and the march began.

"Aren't you glad, camel?" demanded Betty sweetly as they stepped off. "Aren't you glad we're going to be married and you're going to belong to the nice snake-charmer ever afterward?"

The camel's front legs pranced, expressing excessive joy.

"Minister! Minister! Where's the minister?" cried voices out of the revel. "Who's going to be the clergyman?"

The head of Jumbo, obese Negro, waiter at the Tallyho Club for many years, appeared rashly through a half-opened pantry door.

"Oh, Jumbo!"

"Get old Jumbo. He's the fella!"

"Come on, Jumbo. How 'bout marrying us a couple?"

"Yea!"

Jumbo was seized by four comedians, stripped of his apron, and escorted to a raised daïs at the head of the ball. There his collar was removed and replaced back side forward with ecclesiastical effect. The parade separated into two lines, leaving an aisle for the bride and groom.

"Lawdy, man," roared Jumbo, "Ah got ole Bible 'n' ev'ythin', sho nuff."

He produced a battered Bible from an interior pocket.

"Yea! Jumbo's got a Bible!"

"Razor, too, I'll bet!"

Together the snake-charmer and the camel ascended the cheering aisle and stopped in front of Jumbo.

"Where's yo license, camel?"

A man near by prodded Perry.

"Give him a piece of paper. Anything'll do."

Perry fumbled confusedly in his pocket, found a folded paper, and pushed it out through the camel's mouth. Holding it upside down, Jumbo pretended to scan it earnestly.

"Dis yeah's a special camel's license," he said. "Get you ring ready, camel."

Inside the camel Perry turned round and addressed his worse half.

"Gimme a ring, for Heaven's sake!"

"I ain't got none," protested a weary voice.

"You have. I saw it."

"I ain't goin' to take it offen my hand."

"If you don't I'll kill you."

There was a gasp and Perry felt a huge affair of rhinestone and brass inserted into his hand.

Again he was nudged from the outside.

"Speak up!"

"I do!" cried Perry quickly.

He heard Betty's responses given in a debonair tone, and even in this burlesque the sound thrilled him.

Then he had pushed the rhinestone through a tear in the camel's coat and was slipping it on her finger, muttering ancient and historic words after Jumbo. He didn't want any one to know about this ever. His one idea was to slip away without having to disclose his identity, for Mr. Tate had so far kept his secret well. A dignified young man, Perry—and this might injure his infant law practice.

"Embrace the bride!"

"Unmask, camel, and kiss her!"

Instinctively his heart beat high as Betty turned to him laughingly and began to stroke the cardboard muzzle. He felt his self-control giving way, he longed to surround her with his arms and declare his identity and kiss those lips that smiled only a foot away—when suddenly the laughter and applause round them died off and a curious hush fell over the hall. Perry and Betty looked up in surprise. Jumbo had given vent to a huge "Hello!" in such a startled voice that all eyes were bent on him.

"Hello!" he said again. He had turned round the camel's marriage license, which he had been holding upside down, produced spectacles, and was studying it agonizingly.

"Why," he exclaimed, and in the pervading silence his words were heard plainly by every one in the room, "this yeah's a sho-nuff marriage permit."

"What?"

"Huh?"

"Say it again, Jumbo!"

"Sure you can read?"

Jumbo waved them to silence and Perry's blood burned to fire in his veins as he realized the break he had made.

"Yassuh!" repeated Jumbo. "This yeah's a sho-nuff license, and the pa'ties concerned one of 'em is dis yeah young lady, Miz Betty Medill, and th' other's Mistah Perry Pa'khurst."

There was a general gasp, and a low rumble broke out as all eyes fell on the camel. Betty shrank away from him quickly, her tawny eyes giving out sparks of fury.

"Is you Mistah Pa'khurst, you camel?"

Perry made no answer. The crowd pressed up closer and stared at him. He stood frozen rigid with embarrassment, his cardboard face still hungry and sardonic as he regarded the ominous Jumbo.

"Y'all bettah speak up!" said Jumbo slowly, "this yeah's a mighty serious mattah. Outside mah duties at this club ah happens to be a sho-nuff minister in the Firs' Cullud Baptis' Church. It done look to me as though y'all is gone an' got married."

V
· · · · ·

The scene that followed will go down forever in the annals of the Tallyho Club. Stout matrons fainted, one-hundred-per-cent Americans swore, wild-eyed débutantes babbled in lightning groups instantly formed and instantly dissolved, and a great buzz of chatter, virulent yet oddly subdued, hummed through the chaotic ballroom. Feverish youths swore they would kill Perry or Jumbo or themselves or some one, and the Baptis' preacheh was besieged by a tempestuous covey of clamorous amateur lawyers, asking questions, making threats, demanding precedents, ordering the bonds annulled, and especially trying to ferret out any hint of prearrangement in what had occurred.

In the corner Mrs. Townsend was crying softly on the shoulder of Mr. Howard Tate, who was trying vainly to comfort her; they were exchanging "all my fault's" volubly and voluminously. Outside on a snow-covered walk Mr. Cyrus Medill, the Aluminum Man, was being paced slowly up and down between two brawny charioteers, giving vent now to a string of unrepeatables, now to wild pleadings that they'd just let him get at Jumbo. He was facetiously attired for the evening as a wild man of Borneo, and the most exacting stage-manager would have acknowledged any improvement in casting the part to be quite impossible.

Meanwhile the two principals held the real centre of the stage. Betty Medill — or was it Betty Parkhurst? — storming furiously, was surrounded by the plainer girls — the prettier ones were too busy talking about her to pay much attention to her — and over on the other side of the hall stood the camel, still intact except for his headpiece, which dangled pathetically on his chest. Perry was earnestly engaged in making protestations of his innocence to a ring of angry, puzzled men. Every few minutes, just as he had apparently proved his case, some one would mention the marriage certificate, and the inquisition would begin again.

A girl named Marion Cloud, considered the second best belle of Toledo, changed the gist of the situation by a remark she made to Betty.

"Well," she said maliciously, "it'll all blow over, dear. The courts will annul it without question."

Betty's angry tears dried miraculously in her eyes, her lips shut tight together, and she looked stonily at Marion. Then she rose and, scattering her sympathizers right and left, walked directly across the room to Perry, who stared at her in terror. Again silence crept down upon the room.

"Will you have the decency to grant me five minutes' conversation — or wasn't that included in your plans?"

He nodded, his mouth unable to form words.

Indicating coldly that he was to follow her she walked out into the hall with her chin uptilted and headed for the privacy of one of the little card-rooms.

Perry started after her, but was brought to a jerky halt by the failure of his hind legs to function.

"You stay here!" he commanded savagely.

"I can't," whined a voice from the hump, "unless you get out first and let me get out."

Perry hesitated, but unable any longer to tolerate the eyes of the curious crowd he muttered a command and the camel moved carefully from the room on its four legs.

Betty was waiting for him.

"Well," she began furiously, "you see what you've done! You and that crazy license! I told you you shouldn't have gotten it!"

"My dear girl, I——"

"Don't say 'dear girl' to me! Save that for your real wife if you ever get one after this disgraceful performance. And don't try to pretend it wasn't all arranged. You know you gave that colored waiter money! You know you did! Do you mean to say you didn't try to marry me?"

"No—of course——"

"Yes, you'd better admit it! You tried it, and now what are you going to do? Do you know my father's nearly crazy? It'll serve you right if he tries to kill you. He'll take his gun and put some cold steel in you. Even if this wed—this *thing* can be annulled it'll hang over me all the rest of my life!"

Perry could not resist quoting softly: "'Oh, camel, wouldn't you like to belong to the pretty snake-charmer for all your——'"

"Shut up!" cried Betty.

There was a pause.

"Betty," said Perry finally, "there's only one thing to do that will really get us out clear. That's for you to marry me."

"Marry you!"

"Yes. Really it's the only——"

"You shut up! I wouldn't marry you if—if——"

"I know. If I were the last man on earth. But if you care anything about your reputation——"

"Reputation!" she cried. "You're a nice one to think about my reputation *now.* Why didn't you think about my reputation before you hired that horrible Jumbo to—to———"

Perry tossed up his hands hopelessly.

"Very well. I'll do anything you want. Lord knows I renounce all claims!"

"But," said a new voice, "I don't."

Perry and Betty started, and she put her hand to her heart.

"For Heaven's sake, what was that?"

"It's me," said the camel's back.

In a minute Perry had whipped off the camel's skin, and a lax, limp object, his clothes hanging on him damply, his hand clenched tightly on an almost empty bottle, stood defiantly before them.

"Oh," cried Betty, "you brought that object in here to frighten me! You told me he was deaf—that awful person!"

The camel's back sat down on a chair with a sigh of satisfaction.

"Don't talk 'at way about me, lady. I ain't no person. I'm your husband."

"Husband!"

The cry was wrung simultaneously from Betty and Perry.

"Why, sure. I'm as much your husband as that gink is. The smoke didn't marry you to the camel's front. He married you to the whole camel. Why, that's my ring you got on your finger!"

With a little yelp she snatched the ring from her finger and flung it passionately at the floor.

"What's all this?" demanded Perry dazedly.

"Jes' that you better fix me an' fix me right. If you don't I'm a-gonna have the same claim you got to bein' married to her!"

"That's bigamy," said Perry, turning gravely to Betty.

Then came the supreme moment of Perry's evening, the ultimate chance on which he risked his fortunes. He rose and looked first at Betty, where she sat weakly, aghast at this new complication, and then at the individual who swayed from side to side on his chair, uncertainly, menacingly.

"Very well," said Perry slowly to the individual, "you can have her. Betty, I'm going to prove to you that as far as I'm concerned our marriage was entirely accidental. I'm going to renounce utterly my rights to have you as my wife, and give you to—to the man whose ring you wear—your lawful husband."

There was a pause and four horror-stricken eyes were turned on him.

"Good-by, Betty," he said brokenly. "Don't forget me in your new-found happiness. I'm going to leave for the Far West on the morning train. Think of me kindly, Betty."

With a last glance at them he turned and his head rested on his chest as his hand touched the door-knob.

"Good-by," he repeated. He turned the door-knob.

But at this sound the snakes and silk and tawny hair precipitated themselves violently toward him.

"Oh, Perry, don't leave me! Perry, Perry, take me with you!"

Her tears flowed damply on his neck. Calmly he folded his arms about her.

"I don't care," she cried. "I love you and if you can wake up a minister at this hour and have it done over again I'll go West with you."

Over her shoulder the front part of the camel looked at the back part of the camel—and they exchanged a particularly subtle, esoteric sort of wink that only true camels can understand.

BERNICE BOBS HER HAIR

Fitzgerald wrote "Barbara Bobs Her Hair" while he was living in New York in the spring of 1919. It was rejected by every magazine to which it was sent, including The Saturday Evening Post. *"Barbara" languished until Fitzgerald's newly acquired agent, Harold Ober at the Paul Reynolds Agency, managed to sell another rejected Fitzgerald piece called "Variety" to the* Post *editor, George Horace Lorimer, who renamed it "Head and Shoulders." Encouraged by the agency's success, Fitzgerald revised "Barbara" in January 1920 by giving it a new ending and changing the title. The roots of the story are in a note Fitzgerald wrote his younger sister, Annabel, in 1915, soon after he met Ginevra King. "Here are some leading questions for a girl to use . . . a) You dance so much better than you did last year. b) How about giving me that sporty necktie when you're thru with it? c) You've got the longest eyelashes! (This will embarrass him, but he likes it.) d) I hear you've got a 'line'! Avoid a) When do you go back to school? . . . Never try to give a boy the affect that you're popular — Ginevra always starts by saying she's a poor unpopular woman without any beaux." Above this list, Fitzgerald wrote, "Written by me at 19 or so. Basis of Bernice." The $500 he received for the piece — equal to nearly $4,500 in 2004 — prompted Fitzgerald to announce to Maxwell Perkins, his editor at Scribner's, that while he did not enjoy writing short stories, he would "just do it for money." The following year he would tell Ober, "by God and Lorimer, I'm going to make a fortune yet."*

The Saturday Evening Post, May 1, 1920
Collected in *Flappers and Philosophers* (1920)

I
· · · · ·

AFTER DARK ON SATURDAY NIGHT one could stand on the first tee of the golf-course and see the country-club windows as a yellow expanse over a very black and wavy ocean. The waves of this ocean, so to speak, were the heads of many curious caddies, a few of the more ingenious chauffeurs, the golf professional's deaf sister—and there were usually several stray, diffident waves who might have rolled inside had they so desired. This was the gallery.

The balcony was inside. It consisted of the circle of wicker chairs that lined the wall of the combination clubroom and ballroom. At these Saturday-night dances it was largely feminine; a great babel of middle-aged ladies with sharp eyes and icy hearts behind lorgnettes and large bosoms. The main function of the balcony was critical. It occasionally showed grudging admiration, but never approval, for it is well known among ladies over thirty-five that when the younger set dance in the summer-time it is with the very worst intentions in the world, and if they are not bombarded with stony eyes stray couples will dance weird barbaric interludes in the corners, and the more popular, more dangerous, girls will sometimes be kissed in the parked limousines of unsuspecting dowagers.

But, after all, this critical circle is not close enough to the stage to see the actors' faces and catch the subtler byplay. It can only frown and lean, ask questions and make satisfactory deductions from its set of postulates, such as the one which states that every young man with a large income leads the life of a hunted partridge. It never really appreciates the drama of the shifting, semi-cruel world of adolescence. No; boxes, orchestra-circle, principals, and chorus are represented by the medley of faces and voices that sway to the plaintive African rhythm of Dyer's dance orchestra.

From sixteen-year-old Otis Ormonde, who has two more years at Hill School, to G. Reece Stoddard, over whose bureau at home hangs a Harvard law diploma; from little Madeleine Hogue, whose hair still feels strange and uncomfortable on top of her head, to Bessie MacRae, who has been the life of the party a little too long — more than ten years — the medley is not only the centre of the stage but contains the only people capable of getting an unobstructed view of it.

With a flourish and a bang the music stops. The couples exchange artificial, effortless smiles, facetiously repeat "*la*-de-*da-da* dum-*dum*," and then the clatter of young feminine voices soars over the burst of clapping.

A few disappointed stags caught in midfloor as they had been about to cut in subsided listlessly back to the walls, because this was not like the riotous Christmas dances — these summer hops were considered just pleasantly warm and exciting, where even the younger marrieds rose and performed ancient waltzes and terrifying fox trots to the tolerant amusement of their younger brothers and sisters.

Warren McIntyre, who casually attended Yale, being one of the unfortunate stags, felt in his dinner-coat pocket for a cigarette and strolled out onto the wide, semidark veranda, where couples were scattered at tables, filling the lantern-hung night with vague words and hazy laughter. He nodded here and there at the less absorbed and as he passed each couple some half-forgotten fragment of a story played in his mind, for it was not a large city and every one was Who's Who to every one else's past. There, for example, were Jim Strain and Ethel Demorest, who had been privately engaged for three years. Every one knew that as soon as Jim managed to hold a job for more than two months she would marry him. Yet how bored they both looked, and how wearily Ethel regarded Jim sometimes, as if she wondered why she had trained the vines of her affection on such a wind-shaken poplar.

Warren was nineteen and rather pitying with those of his friends who hadn't gone East to college. But, like most boys, he bragged tremendously about the girls of his city when he was away from it. There was Genevieve Ormonde, who regularly made the rounds of dances, house-parties, and football games at Princeton, Yale, Williams, and Cornell; there was black-eyed Roberta Dillon, who was quite as famous to her own generation as Hiram Johnson or Ty Cobb; and, of course, there was Marjorie Harvey, who besides having a fairylike face and a dazzling, bewildering tongue was already justly celebrated for having turned five cartwheels in succession during the last pump-and-slipper dance at New Haven.

Warren, who had grown up across the street from Marjorie, had long been "crazy about her." Sometimes she seemed to reciprocate his feeling with a faint gratitude, but she had tried him by her infallible test and informed him gravely that she did not love him. Her test was that when she was away from him she forgot him and had affairs with other boys. Warren found this discouraging, especially as Marjorie had been making little trips all summer, and for the first two or three days after each arrival home he saw great heaps of mail on the Harveys' hall table addressed to her in various masculine handwritings. To make matters worse, all during the month of August she had been visited by her cousin Bernice from Eau Claire, and it seemed impossible to see her alone. It was always necessary to hunt round and find some one to take care of Bernice. As August waned this was becoming more and more difficult.

Much as Warren worshipped Marjorie, he had to admit that Cousin Bernice was sorta dopeless. She was pretty, with dark hair and high color, but she was no fun on a party. Every Saturday night he danced a long arduous duty dance with her to please Marjorie, but he had never been anything but bored in her company.

"Warren"—a soft voice at his elbow broke in upon his thoughts, and he turned to see Marjorie, flushed and radiant as usual. She laid a hand on his shoulder and a glow settled almost imperceptibly over him.

"Warren," she whispered, "do something for me—dance with

Bernice. She's been stuck with little Otis Ormonde for almost an hour."

Warren's glow faded.

"Why—sure," he answered half-heartedly.

"You don't mind, do you? I'll see that you don't get stuck."

"'Sall right."

Marjorie smiled—that smile that was thanks enough.

"You're an angel, and I'm obliged loads."

With a sigh the angel glanced round the veranda, but Bernice and Otis were not in sight. He wandered back inside, and there in front of the women's dressing-room he found Otis in the centre of a group of young men who were convulsed with laughter. Otis was brandishing a piece of timber he had picked up, and discoursing volubly.

"She's gone in to fix her hair," he announced wildly. "I'm waiting to dance another hour with her."

Their laughter was renewed.

"Why don't some of you cut in?" cried Otis resentfully. "She likes more variety."

"Why, Otis," suggested a friend, "you've just barely got used to her."

"Why the two-by-four, Otis?" inquired Warren, smiling.

"The two-by-four? Oh, this? This is a club. When she comes out I'll hit her on the head and knock her in again."

Warren collapsed on a settee and howled with glee.

"Never mind, Otis," he articulated finally. "I'm relieving you this time."

Otis simulated a sudden fainting attack and handed the stick to Warren.

"If you need it, old man," he said hoarsely.

No matter how beautiful or brilliant a girl may be, the reputation of not being frequently cut in on makes her position at a dance unfortunate. Perhaps boys prefer her company to that of the butterflies with whom they dance a dozen times an evening, but youth in this jazz-nourished generation is temperamentally restless, and the idea of fox-trotting more than one full fox trot with the same girl is distasteful, not to say odious. When it comes to several dances and the intermissions between she can be quite sure that a young man, once relieved, will never tread on her wayward toes again.

Warren danced the next full dance with Bernice, and finally, thankful for the intermission, he led her to a table on the veranda. There was a moment's silence while she did unimpressive things with her fan.

"It's hotter here than in Eau Claire," she said.

Warren stifled a sigh and nodded. It might be for all he knew or cared. He wondered idly whether she was a poor conversationalist because she got no attention or got no attention because she was a poor conversationalist.

"You going to be here much longer?" he asked, and then turned rather red. She might suspect his reasons for asking.

"Another week," she answered, and stared at him as if to lunge at his next remark when it left his lips.

Warren fidgeted. Then with a sudden charitable impulse he decided to try part of his line on her. He turned and looked at her eyes.

"You've got an awfully kissable mouth," he began quietly.

This was a remark that he sometimes made to girls at college proms when they were talking in just such half dark as this. Bernice distinctly jumped. She turned an ungraceful red and became clumsy with her fan. No one had ever made such a remark to her before.

"Fresh!"—the word had slipped out before she realized it, and she bit her lip. Too late she decided to be amused, and offered him a flustered smile.

Warren was annoyed. Though not accustomed to have that remark taken seriously, still it usually provoked a laugh or a paragraph of sentimental banter. And he hated to be called fresh, except in a joking way. His charitable impulse died and he switched the topic.

"Jim Strain and Ethel Demorest sitting out as usual," he commented.

This was more in Bernice's line, but a faint regret mingled with her relief as the subject changed. Men did not talk to her about kissable mouths, but she knew that they talked in some such way to other girls.

"Oh, yes," she said, and laughed. "I hear they've been mooning round for years without a red penny. Isn't it silly?"

Warren's disgust increased. Jim Strain was a close friend of his brother's, and anyway he considered it bad form to sneer at people for not having money. But Bernice had had no intention of sneering. She was merely nervous.

II
. . . . .

When Marjorie and Bernice reached home at half after midnight they said good night at the top of the stairs. Though cousins, they were not intimates. As a matter of fact Marjorie had no female intimates — she considered girls stupid. Bernice on the contrary all through this parent-arranged visit had rather longed to exchange those confidences flavored with giggles and tears that she considered an indispensable factor in all feminine intercourse. But in this respect she found Marjorie rather cold; felt somehow the same difficulty in talking to her that she had in talking to men. Marjorie never giggled, was never frightened, seldom embarrassed, and in fact had very few of the qualities which Bernice considered appropriately and blessedly feminine.

As Bernice busied herself with tooth-brush and paste this night she wondered for the hundredth time why she never had any attention when she was away from home. That her family were the wealthiest in Eau Claire; that her mother entertained tremendously, gave little dinners for her daughter before all dances, and bought her a car of her own to drive round in, never occurred to her as factors in her home-town social success. Like most girls she had been brought up on the warm milk prepared by Annie Fellows Johnston and on novels in which the female was beloved because of certain mysterious womanly qualities, always mentioned but never displayed.

Bernice felt a vague pain that she was not at present engaged in being popular. She did not know that had it not been for Marjorie's campaigning she would have danced the entire evening with one man; but she knew that even in Eau Claire other girls with less position and less pulchritude were given a much bigger rush. She attributed this to something subtly unscrupulous in those girls. It had never worried her, and if it had her mother would have assured her that the other girls cheapened themselves and that men really respected girls like Bernice.

She turned out the light in her bathroom, and on an impulse decided to go in and chat for a moment with her aunt Josephine, whose light was still on. Her soft slippers bore her noiselessly down the carpeted hall, but hearing voices inside she stopped near the partly opened door. Then she caught her own name, and without any definite intention of eavesdropping lingered — and the thread of the conversation going on inside pierced her consciousness sharply as if it had been drawn through with a needle.

"She's absolutely hopeless!" It was Marjorie's voice. "Oh, I know what you're going to say! So many people have told you how pretty and sweet she is, and how she can cook! What of it? She has a bum time. Men don't like her."

"What's a little cheap popularity?"

Mrs. Harvey sounded annoyed.

"It's everything when you're eighteen," said Marjorie emphatically. "I've done my best. I've been polite and I've made men dance with her, but they just won't stand being bored. When I think of that gorgeous coloring wasted on such a ninny, and think what Martha Carey could do with it — oh!"

"There's no courtesy these days."

Mrs. Harvey's voice implied that modern situations were too much for her. When she was a girl all young ladies who belonged to nice families had glorious times.

"Well," said Marjorie, "no girl can permanently bolster up a lame-duck visitor, because these days it's every girl for herself. I've even tried to drop her hints about clothes and things, and she's been furious—given me the funniest looks. She's sensitive enough to know she's not getting away with much, but I'll bet she consoles herself by thinking that she's very virtuous and that I'm too gay and fickle and will come to a bad end. All unpopular girls think that way. Sour grapes! Sarah Hopkins refers to Genevieve and Roberta and me as gardenia girls! I'll bet she'd give ten years of her life and her European education to be a gardenia girl and have three or four men in love with her and be cut in on every few feet at dances."

"It seems to me," interrupted Mrs. Harvey rather wearily, "that you ought to be able to do something for Bernice. I know she's not very vivacious."

Marjorie groaned.

"Vivacious! Good grief! I've never heard her say anything to a boy except that it's hot or the floor's crowded or that she's going to school in New York next year. Sometimes she asks them what kind of car they have and tells them the kind she has. Thrilling!"

There was a short silence, and then Mrs. Harvey took up her refrain:

"All I know is that other girls not half so sweet and attractive get partners. Martha Carey, for instance, is stout and loud, and her mother is distinctly common. Roberta Dillon is so thin this year that she looks as though Arizona were the place for her. She's dancing herself to death."

"But, mother," objected Marjorie impatiently, "Martha is cheerful and awfully witty and an awfully slick girl, and Roberta's a marvellous dancer. She's been popular for ages!"

Mrs. Harvey yawned.

"I think it's that crazy Indian blood in Bernice," continued Marjorie. "Maybe she's a reversion to type. Indian women all just sat round and never said anything."

"Go to bed, you silly child," laughed Mrs. Harvey. "I wouldn't have told you that if I'd thought you were going to remember it. And I think most of your ideas are perfectly idiotic," she finished sleepily.

There was another silence, while Marjorie considered whether or not convincing her mother was worth the trouble. People over forty can seldom be permanently convinced of anything. At eighteen our convictions are hills from which we look; at forty-five they are caves in which we hide.

Having decided this, Marjorie said good night. When she came out into the hall it was quite empty.

III
. . . . .

While Marjorie was breakfasting late next day Bernice came into the room with a rather formal good morning, sat down opposite, stared intently over and slightly moistened her lips.

"What's on your mind?" inquired Marjorie, rather puzzled.

Bernice paused before she threw her hand-grenade.

"I heard what you said about me to your mother last night."

Marjorie was startled, but she showed only a faintly heightened color and her voice was quite even when she spoke.

"Where were you?"

"In the hall. I didn't mean to listen—at first."

After an involuntary look of contempt Marjorie dropped her eyes and became very interested in balancing a stray corn-flake on her finger.

"I guess I'd better go back to Eau Claire—if I'm such a nuisance." Bernice's lower lip was trembling violently and she continued on a wavering note: "I've tried to be nice, and—and I've been first neglected and then insulted. No one ever visited me and got such treatment."

Marjorie was silent.

"But I'm in the way, I see. I'm a drag on you. Your friends don't like me." She paused, and then remembered another one of her grievances. "Of course I was furious last week when you tried to hint to me that that dress was unbecoming. Don't you think I know how to dress myself?"

"No," murmured Marjorie less than half-aloud.

"What?"

"I didn't hint anything," said Marjorie succinctly. "I said, as I remember, that it was better to wear a becoming dress three times straight than to alternate it with two frights."

"Do you think that was a very nice thing to say?"

"I wasn't trying to be nice." Then after a pause: "When do you want to go?"

Bernice drew in her breath sharply.

"Oh!" It was a little half-cry.

Marjorie looked up in surprise.

"Didn't you say you were going?"

"Yes, but——"

"Oh, you were only bluffing!"

They stared at each other across the breakfast-table for a moment. Misty waves were passing before Bernice's eyes, while Marjorie's face wore that rather hard expression that she used when slightly intoxicated undergraduates were making love to her.

"So you were bluffing," she repeated as if it were what she might have expected.

Bernice admitted it by bursting into tears. Marjorie's eyes showed boredom.

"You're my cousin," sobbed Bernice. "I'm v-v-visiting you. I was to stay a month, and if I go home my mother will know and she'll wah-wonder——"

Marjorie waited until the shower of broken words collapsed into little sniffles.

"I'll give you my month's allowance," she said coldly, "and you can spend this last week anywhere you want. There's a very nice hotel——"

Bernice's sobs rose to a flute note, and rising of a sudden she fled from the room.

An hour later, while Marjorie was in the library absorbed in composing one of those non-committal, marvellously elusive letters that only a young girl can write, Bernice reappeared, very red-eyed and consciously calm. She cast no glance at Marjorie but took a book at random from the shelf and sat down as if to read. Marjorie seemed absorbed in her letter and continued writing. When the clock showed noon Bernice closed her book with a snap.

"I suppose I'd better get my railroad ticket."

This was not the beginning of the speech she had rehearsed upstairs, but as Marjorie was not getting her cues—wasn't urging her to be reasonable; it's all a mistake—it was the best opening she could muster.

"Just wait till I finish this letter," said Marjorie without looking round. "I want to get it off in the next mail."

After another minute, during which her pen scratched busily, she turned round and relaxed with an air of "at your service." Again Bernice had to speak.

"Do you want me to go home?"

"Well," said Marjorie, considering, "I suppose if you're not having a good time you'd better go. No use being miserable."

"Don't you think common kindness——"

"Oh, please don't quote *Little Women!*" cried Marjorie impatiently. "That's out of style."

"You think so?"

"Heavens, yes! What modern girl could live like those inane females?"

"They were the models for our mothers."

Marjorie laughed.

"Yes, they were — not! Besides, our mothers were all very well in their way, but they know very little about their daughters' problems."

Bernice drew herself up.

"Please don't talk about my mother."

Marjorie laughed.

"I don't think I mentioned her."

Bernice felt that she was being led away from her subject.

"Do you think you've treated me very well?"

"I've done my best. You're rather hard material to work with."

The lids of Bernice's eyes reddened.

"I think you're hard and selfish, and you haven't a feminine quality in you."

"Oh, my Lord!" cried Marjorie in desperation. "You little nut! Girls like you are responsible for all the tiresome colorless marriages; all those ghastly inefficiencies that pass as feminine qualities. What a blow it must be when a man with imagination marries the beautiful bundle of clothes that he's been building ideals round, and finds that she's just a weak, whining, cowardly mass of affectations!"

Bernice's mouth had slipped half open.

"The womanly woman!" continued Marjorie. "Her whole early life is occupied in whining criticisms of girls like me who really do have a good time."

Bernice's jaw descended farther as Marjorie's voice rose.

"There's some excuse for an ugly girl whining. If I'd been irretrievably ugly I'd never have forgiven my parents for bringing me into the world. But you're starting life without any handicap——" Marjorie's little fist clinched. "If you expect me to weep with you you'll be disappointed. Go or stay, just as you like." And picking up her letters she left the room.

Bernice claimed a headache and failed to appear at luncheon. They had a matinée date for the afternoon, but the headache persisting, Marjorie made explanation to a not very downcast boy. But when she returned late in the afternoon she found Bernice with a strangely set face waiting for her in her bedroom.

"I've decided," began Bernice without preliminaries, "that maybe you're right about things — possibly not. But if you'll tell me why your friends aren't — aren't interested in me I'll see if I can do what you want me to."

Marjorie was at the mirror shaking down her hair.

"Do you mean it?"

"Yes."

"Without reservations? Will you do exactly what I say?"

"Well, I———"

"Well nothing! Will you do exactly as I say?"

"If they're sensible things."

"They're not! You're no case for sensible things."

"Are you going to make — to recommend———"

"Yes, everything. If I tell you to take boxing-lessons you'll have to do it. Write home and tell your mother you're going to stay another two weeks."

"If you'll tell me———"

"All right — I'll just give you a few examples now. First, you have no ease of manner. Why? Because you're never sure about your personal appearance. When a girl feels that she's perfectly groomed and dressed she can forget that part of her. That's charm. The more parts of yourself you can afford to forget the more charm you have."

"Don't I look all right?"

"No; for instance, you never take care of your eyebrows. They're black and lustrous, but by leaving them straggly they're a blemish. They'd be beautiful if you'd take care of them in one-tenth the time you take doing nothing. You're going to brush them so that they'll grow straight."

Bernice raised the brows in question.

"Do you mean to say that men notice eyebrows?"

"Yes—subconsciously. And when you go home you ought to have your teeth straightened a little. It's almost imperceptible, still——"

"But I thought," interrupted Bernice in bewilderment, "that you despised little dainty feminine things like that."

"I hate dainty minds," answered Marjorie. "But a girl has to be dainty in person. If she looks like a million dollars she can talk about Russia, ping-pong, or the League of Nations and get away with it."

"What else?"

"Oh, I'm just beginning! There's your dancing."

"Don't I dance all right?"

"No, you don't—you lean on a man; yes, you do—ever so slightly. I noticed it when we were dancing together yesterday. And you dance standing up straight instead of bending over a little. Probably some old lady on the side-line once told you that you looked so dignified that way. But except with a very small girl it's much harder on the man, and he's the one that counts."

"Go on." Bernice's brain was reeling.

"Well, you've got to learn to be nice to men who are sad birds. You look as if you'd been insulted whenever you're thrown with any except the most popular boys. Why, Bernice, I'm cut in on every few feet—and who does most of it? Why, those very sad birds. No girl can afford to neglect them. They're the big part of any crowd. Young boys too shy to talk are the very best conversational practice. Clumsy boys are the best dancing practice. If you can follow them and yet look graceful you can follow a baby tank across a barb-wire sky-scraper."

Bernice sighed profoundly, but Marjorie was not through.

"If you go to a dance and really amuse, say, three sad birds that dance with you; if you talk so well to them that they forget they're stuck with you, you've done something. They'll come back next time, and gradually so many sad birds will dance with you that the attractive boys will see there's no danger of being stuck — then they'll dance with you."

"Yes," agreed Bernice faintly. "I think I begin to see."

"And finally," concluded Marjorie, "poise and charm will just come. You'll wake up some morning knowing you've attained it, and men will know it too."

Bernice rose.

"It's been awfully kind of you — but nobody's ever talked to me like this before, and I feel sort of startled."

Marjorie made no answer but gazed pensively at her own image in the mirror.

"You're a peach to help me," continued Bernice.

Still Marjorie did not answer, and Bernice thought she had seemed too grateful.

"I know you don't like sentiment," she said timidly.

Marjorie turned to her quickly.

"Oh, I wasn't thinking about that. I was considering whether we hadn't better bob your hair."

Bernice collapsed backward upon the bed.

IV
. . . . .

On the following Wednesday evening there was a dinner-dance at the country club. When the guests strolled in Bernice found her place-card with a slight feeling of irritation. Though at her right sat G. Reece Stoddard, a most desirable and distinguished young bachelor, the all-important left held only Charley Paulson. Charley lacked height, beauty, and social shrewdness, and in her new enlightenment Bernice decided that his only qualification to be her partner was that he had never been stuck with her. But this feeling of irritation left with the last of the soup-plates, and Marjorie's specific instruction came to her. Swallowing her pride she turned to Charley Paulson and plunged.

"Do you think I ought to bob my hair, Mr. Charley Paulson?" Charley looked up in surprise.

"Why?"

"Because I'm considering it. It's such a sure and easy way of attracting attention."

Charley smiled pleasantly. He could not know this had been rehearsed. He replied that he didn't know much about bobbed hair. But Bernice was there to tell him.

"I want to be a society vampire, you see," she announced coolly, and went on to inform him that bobbed hair was the necessary prelude. She added that she wanted to ask his advice, because she had heard he was so critical about girls.

Charley, who knew as much about the psychology of women as he did of the mental states of Buddhist contemplatives, felt vaguely flattered.

"So I've decided," she continued, her voice rising slightly, "that early next week I'm going down to the Sevier Hotel barber-shop, sit in the first chair, and get my hair bobbed." She faltered, noticing that the people near her had paused in their conversation and were listening; but after a confused second Marjorie's coaching told, and she finished her paragraph to the vicinity at large. "Of course I'm charging admission, but if you'll all come down and encourage me I'll issue passes for the inside seats."

There was a ripple of appreciative laughter, and under cover of it G. Reece Stoddard leaned over quickly and said close to her ear: "I'll take a box right now."

She met his eyes and smiled as if he had said something surpassingly brilliant.

"Do you believe in bobbed hair?" asked G. Reece in the same undertone.

"I think it's unmoral," affirmed Bernice gravely. "But, of course, you've either got to amuse people or feed 'em or shock 'em." Marjorie had culled this from Oscar Wilde. It was greeted with a ripple of laughter from the men and a series of quick, intent looks from the girls. And then as though she had said nothing of wit or moment Bernice turned again to Charley and spoke confidentially in his ear.

"I want to ask you your opinion of several people. I imagine you're a wonderful judge of character."

Charley thrilled faintly—paid her a subtle compliment by overturning her water.

Two hours later, while Warren McIntyre was standing passively in the stag line abstractedly watching the dancers and wondering whither and with whom Marjorie had disappeared, an unrelated perception began to creep slowly upon him—a perception that Bernice, cousin to Marjorie, had been cut in on several times in the past five minutes. He closed his eyes, opened them and looked again. Several minutes back she had been dancing with a visiting boy, a matter easily accounted for; a visiting boy would know no better. But now she was dancing with some one else, and there was Charley Paulson headed for her with enthusiastic determination in his eye. Funny—Charley seldom danced with more than three girls an evening.

Warren was distinctly surprised when—the exchange having been effected—the man relieved proved to be none other than G. Reece Stoddard himself. And G. Reece seemed not at all jubilant at being relieved. Next time Bernice danced near, Warren regarded her intently. Yes, she was pretty, distinctly pretty; and tonight her face seemed really vivacious. She had that look that no woman, however histrionically proficient, can successfully counterfeit—she looked as if she were having a good time. He liked the way she had her hair arranged, wondered if it was brilliantine that made it glisten so. And that dress was becoming—a dark red that set off her shadowy eyes and high coloring. He remembered that he had thought her pretty when she first came to town, before he had realized that she was dull. Too bad she was dull—dull girls unbearable—certainly pretty though.

His thoughts zigzagged back to Marjorie. This disappearance

would be like other disappearances. When she reappeared he would demand where she had been — would be told emphatically that it was none of his business. What a pity she was so sure of him! She basked in the knowledge that no other girl in town interested him; she defied him to fall in love with Genevieve or Roberta.

Warren sighed. The way to Marjorie's affections was a labyrinth indeed. He looked up. Bernice was again dancing with the visiting boy. Half unconsciously he took a step out from the stag line in her direction, and hesitated. Then he said to himself that it was charity. He walked toward her — collided suddenly with G. Reece Stoddard.

"Pardon me," said Warren.

But G. Reece had not stopped to apologize. He had again cut in on Bernice.

That night at one o'clock Marjorie, with one hand on the electric-light switch in the hall, turned to take a last look at Bernice's sparkling eyes.

"So it worked?"

"Oh, Marjorie, yes!" cried Bernice.

"I saw you were having a gay time."

"I did! The only trouble was that about midnight I ran short of talk. I had to repeat myself — with different men of course. I hope they won't compare notes."

"Men don't," said Marjorie, yawning, "and it wouldn't matter if they did — they'd think you were even trickier."

She snapped out the light, and as they started up the stairs Bernice grasped the banister thankfully. For the first time in her life she had been danced tired.

"You see," said Marjorie at the top of the stairs, "one man sees another man cut in and he thinks there must be something there. Well, we'll fix up some new stuff to-morrow. Good night."

"Good night."

As Bernice took down her hair she passed the evening before her in review. She had followed instructions exactly. Even when Charley Paulson cut in for the eighth time she had simulated delight and had apparently been both interested and flattered. She had not talked about the weather or Eau Claire or automobiles or her school, but had confined her conversation to me, you, and us.

But a few minutes before she fell asleep a rebellious thought was churning drowsily in her brain—after all, it was she who had done it. Marjorie, to be sure, had given her her conversation, but then Marjorie got much of her conversation out of things she read. Bernice had bought the red dress, though she had never valued it highly before Marjorie dug it out of her trunk—and her own voice had said the words, her own lips had smiled, her own feet had danced. Marjorie nice girl—vain, though—nice evening—nice boys—like   Warren—Warren—Warren—what's-his-name—Warren——

She fell asleep.

V
. . . . .

To Bernice the next week was a revelation. With the feeling that people really enjoyed looking at her and listening to her came the foundation of self-confidence. Of course there were numerous mistakes at first. She did not know, for instance, that Draycott Deyo was studying for the ministry; she was unaware that he had cut in on her because he thought she was a quiet, reserved girl. Had she known these things she would not have treated him to the line which began "Hello, Shell Shock!" and continued with the bathtub story—"It takes a frightful lot of energy to fix my hair in the summer—there's so much of it—so I always fix it first and powder my face and put on my hat; then I get into the bathtub, and dress afterward. Don't you think that's the best plan?"

Though Draycott Deyo was in the throes of difficulties concerning baptism by immersion and might possibly have seen a connection, it must be admitted that he did not. He considered feminine bathing an immoral subject, and gave her some of his ideas on the depravity of modern society.

But to offset that unfortunate occurrence Bernice had several signal successes to her credit. Little Otis Ormonde pleaded off from a trip East and elected instead to follow her with a puppylike devotion, to the amusement of his crowd and to the irritation of G. Reece Stoddard, several of whose afternoon calls Otis completely ruined by the disgusting tenderness of the glances he bent on Bernice. He even told her the story of the two-by-four and the dressing-room to show her how frightfully mistaken he and every one else had been in their first judgment of her. Bernice laughed off that incident with a slight sinking sensation.

Of all Bernice's conversation perhaps the best known and most universally approved was the line about the bobbing of her hair.

"Oh, Bernice, when you goin' to get the hair bobbed?"

"Day after to-morrow maybe," she would reply, laughing. "Will you come and see me? Because I'm counting on you, you know."

"Will we? You know! But you better hurry up."

Bernice, whose tonsorial intentions were strictly dishonorable, would laugh again.

"Pretty soon now. You'd be surprised."

But perhaps the most significant symbol of her success was the gray car of the hypercritical Warren McIntyre, parked daily in front of the Harvey house. At first the parlor-maid was distinctly startled when he asked for Bernice instead of Marjorie; after a week of it she told the cook that Miss Bernice had gotta holda Miss Marjorie's best fella.

And Miss Bernice had. Perhaps it began with Warren's desire to rouse jealousy in Marjorie; perhaps it was the familiar though unrecognized strain of Marjorie in Bernice's conversation; perhaps it was both of these and something of sincere attraction besides. But somehow the collective mind of the younger set knew within a week that Marjorie's most reliable beau had made an amazing face-about and was giving an indisputable rush to Marjorie's guest. The question of the moment was how Marjorie would take it. Warren called Bernice on the 'phone twice a day, sent her notes, and they were frequently seen together in his roadster, obviously engrossed in one of those tense, significant conversations as to whether or not he was sincere.

Marjorie on being twitted only laughed. She said she was mighty glad that Warren had at last found some one who appreciated him. So the younger set laughed, too, and guessed that Marjorie didn't care and let it go at that.

One afternoon when there were only three days left of her visit Bernice was waiting in the hall for Warren, with whom she was going to a bridge party. She was in rather a blissful mood, and when Marjorie — also bound for the party — appeared beside her and began casually to adjust her hat in the mirror, Bernice was utterly unprepared for anything in the nature of a clash. Marjorie did her work very coldly and succinctly in three sentences.

"You may as well get Warren out of your head," she said coldly.

"What?" Bernice was utterly astounded.

"You may as well stop making a fool of yourself over Warren McIntyre. He doesn't care a snap of his fingers about you."

For a tense moment they regarded each other — Marjorie scornful, aloof; Bernice astounded, half-angry, half-afraid. Then two cars drove up in front of the house and there was a riotous honking. Both of them gasped faintly, turned, and side by side hurried out.

All through the bridge party Bernice strove in vain to master a rising uneasiness. She had offended Marjorie, the sphinx of sphinxes. With the most wholesome and innocent intentions in the world she had stolen Marjorie's property. She felt suddenly and horribly guilty. After the bridge game, when they sat in an informal circle and the conversation became general, the storm gradually broke. Little Otis Ormonde inadvertently precipitated it.

"When you going back to kindergarten, Otis?" some one had asked.

"Me? Day Bernice gets her hair bobbed."

"Then your education's over," said Marjorie quickly. "That's only a bluff of hers. I should think you'd have realized."

"That a fact?" demanded Otis, giving Bernice a reproachful glance.

Bernice's ears burned as she tried to think up an effectual come-back. In the face of this direct attack her imagination was paralyzed.

"There's a lot of bluffs in the world," continued Marjorie quite pleasantly. "I should think you'd be young enough to know that, Otis."

"Well," said Otis, "maybe so. But gee! With a line like Bernice's——"

"Really?" yawned Marjorie. "What's her latest bon mot?"

No one seemed to know. In fact, Bernice, having trifled with her muse's beau, had said nothing memorable of late.

"Was that really all a line?" asked Roberta curiously.

Bernice hesitated. She felt that wit in some form was demanded of her, but under her cousin's suddenly frigid eyes she was completely incapacitated.

"I don't know," she stalled.

"Splush!" said Marjorie. "Admit it!"

Bernice saw that Warren's eyes had left a ukulele he had been tinkering with and were fixed on her questioningly.

"Oh, I don't know!" she repeated steadily. Her cheeks were glowing.

"Splush!" remarked Marjorie again.

"Come through, Bernice," urged Otis. "Tell her where to get off." Bernice looked round again — she seemed unable to get away from Warren's eyes.

"I like bobbed hair," she said hurriedly, as if he had asked her a question, "and I intend to bob mine."

"When?" demanded Marjorie.

"Any time."

"No time like the present," suggested Roberta.

Otis jumped to his feet.

"Good stuff!" he cried. "We'll have a summer bobbing party. Sevier Hotel barber-shop, I think you said."

In an instant all were on their feet. Bernice's heart throbbed violently.

"What?" she gasped.

Out of the group came Marjorie's voice, very clear and contemptuous.

"Don't worry — she'll back out!"

"Come on, Bernice!" cried Otis, starting toward the door.

Four eyes — Warren's and Marjorie's — stared at her, challenged her, defied her. For another second she wavered wildly.

"All right," she said swiftly, "I don't care if I do."

An eternity of minutes later, riding down-town through the late afternoon beside Warren, the others following in Roberta's car close behind, Bernice had all the sensations of Marie Antoinette bound for the guillotine in a tumbrel. Vaguely she wondered why she did not cry out that it was all a mistake. It was all she could do to keep from clutching her hair with both hands to protect it from the suddenly hostile world. Yet she did neither. Even the thought of her mother was no deterrent now. This was the test supreme of her sportsmanship; her right to walk unchallenged in the starry heaven of popular girls.

Warren was moodily silent, and when they came to the hotel he drew up at the curb and nodded to Bernice to precede him out. Roberta's car emptied a laughing crowd into the shop, which presented two bold plate-glass windows to the street.

Bernice stood on the curb and looked at the sign, Sevier Barber-Shop. It was a guillotine indeed, and the hangman was the first barber, who, attired in a white coat and smoking a cigarette, leaned nonchalantly against the first chair. He must have heard of her; he must have been waiting all week, smoking eternal cigarettes beside that portentous, too-often-mentioned first chair. Would they blind-fold her? No, but they would tie a white cloth round her neck lest any of her blood—nonsense—hair—should get on her clothes.

"All right, Bernice," said Warren quickly.

With her chin in the air she crossed the sidewalk, pushed open the swinging screen-door, and giving not a glance to the uproar-ious, riotous row that occupied the waiting bench, went up to the first barber.

"I want you to bob my hair."

The first barber's mouth slid somewhat open. His cigarette dropped to the floor.

"Huh?"

"My hair—bob it!"

Refusing further preliminaries, Bernice took her seat on high. A man in the chair next to her turned on his side and gave her a glance, half lather, half amazement. One barber started and spoiled little Willy Schuneman's monthly haircut. Mr. O'Reilly in the last chair grunted and swore musically in ancient Gaelic as a razor bit into his cheek. Two bootblacks became wide-eyed and rushed for her feet. No, Bernice didn't care for a shine.

Outside a passer-by stopped and stared; a couple joined him; half a dozen small boys' noses sprang into life, flattened against the glass; and snatches of conversation borne on the summer breeze drifted in through the screen-door.

"Lookada long hair on a kid!"

"Where'd yuh get 'at stuff? 'At's a bearded lady he just fin-ished shavin'."

But Bernice saw nothing, heard nothing. Her only living sense told her that this man in the white coat had removed one tortoise-shell comb and then another; that his fingers were fumbling clum-sily with unfamiliar hairpins; that this hair, this wonderful hair of hers, was going—she would never again feel its long voluptuous pull as it hung in a dark-brown glory down her back. For a second she was near breaking down, and then the picture before her swam mechanically into her vision — Marjorie's mouth curling in a faint ironic smile as if to say:

"Give up and get down! You tried to buck me and I called your bluff. You see you haven't got a prayer."

And some last energy rose up in Bernice, for she clinched her hands under the white cloth, and there was a curious narrowing of her eyes that Marjorie remarked on to some one long afterward.

Twenty minutes later the barber swung her round to face the mirror, and she flinched at the full extent of the damage that had been wrought. Her hair was not curly, and now it lay in lank lifeless blocks on both sides of her suddenly pale face. It was ugly as sin — she had known it would be ugly as sin. Her face's chief charm had been a Madonna-like simplicity. Now that was gone and she was — well, frightfully mediocre — not stagy; only ridiculous, like a Greenwich Villager who had left her spectacles at home.

As she climbed down from the chair she tried to smile — failed miserably. She saw two of the girls exchange glances; noticed Marjorie's mouth curved in attenuated mockery — and that Warren's eyes were suddenly very cold.

"You see" — her words fell into an awkward pause — "I've done it."

"Yes, you've — done it," admitted Warren.

"Do you like it?"

There was a half-hearted "Sure" from two or three voices, another awkward pause, and then Marjorie turned swiftly and with serpentlike intensity to Warren.

"Would you mind running me down to the cleaners?" she asked. "I've simply got to get a dress there before supper. Roberta's driving right home and she can take the others."

Warren stared abstractedly at some infinite speck out the window. Then for an instant his eyes rested coldly on Bernice before they turned to Marjorie.

"Be glad to," he said slowly.

VI
. . . . .

Bernice did not fully realize the outrageous trap that had been set for her until she met her aunt's amazed glance just before dinner.

"Why, Bernice!"

"I've bobbed it, Aunt Josephine."

"Why, child!"

"Do you like it?"

"Why, Ber-nice!"

"I suppose I've shocked you."

"No, but what'll Mrs. Deyo think tomorrow night? Bernice, you should have waited until after the Deyos' dance—you should have waited if you wanted to do that."

"It was sudden, Aunt Josephine. Anyway, why does it matter to Mrs. Deyo particularly?"

"Why, child," cried Mrs. Harvey, "in her paper on 'The Foibles of the Younger Generation' that she read at the last meeting of the Thursday Club she devoted fifteen minutes to bobbed hair. It's her pet abomination. And the dance is for you and Marjorie!"

"I'm sorry."

"Oh, Bernice, what'll your mother say? She'll think I let you do it."

"I'm sorry."

Dinner was an agony. She had made a hasty attempt with a curling-iron, and burned her finger and much hair. She could see that her aunt was both worried and grieved, and her uncle kept saying, "Well, I'll be darned!" over and over in a hurt and faintly hostile tone. And Marjorie sat very quietly, intrenched behind a faint smile, a faintly mocking smile.

Somehow she got through the evening. Three boys called; Marjorie disappeared with one of them, and Bernice made a listless unsuccessful attempt to entertain the two others—sighed thankfully as she climbed the stairs to her room at half past ten. What a day!

When she had undressed for the night the door opened and Marjorie came in.

"Bernice," she said, "I'm awfully sorry about the Deyo dance. I'll give you my word of honor I'd forgotten all about it."

"'Sall right," said Bernice shortly. Standing before the mirror she passed her comb slowly through her short hair.

"I'll take you down-town to-morrow," continued Marjorie, "and the hairdresser'll fix it so you'll look slick. I didn't imagine you'd go through with it. I'm really mighty sorry."

"Oh, 'sall right!"

"Still it's your last night, so I suppose it won't matter much."

Then Bernice winced as Marjorie tossed her own hair over her shoulders and began to twist it slowly into two long blond braids until in her cream-colored negligée she looked like a delicate painting of some Saxon princess. Fascinated, Bernice watched the braids grow. Heavy and luxurious they were, moving under the supple fingers like restive snakes—and to Bernice remained this relic and the curling-iron and a to-morrow full of eyes. She could see G. Reece Stoddard, who liked her, assuming his Harvard manner and telling his dinner partner that Bernice shouldn't have been allowed to go to the movies so much; she could see Draycott Deyo exchanging glances with his mother and then being conscientiously charitable to her. But then perhaps by to-morrow Mrs. Deyo would have heard the news; would send round an icy little note requesting that she fail to appear—and behind her back they would all laugh and know that Marjorie had made a fool of her; that her chance at beauty had been sacrificed to the jealous whim of a selfish girl. She sat down suddenly before the mirror, biting the inside of her cheek.

"I like it," she said with an effort. "I think it'll be becoming."

Marjorie smiled.

"It looks all right. For heaven's sake, don't let it worry you!"

"I won't."

"Good night, Bernice."

But as the door closed something snapped within Bernice. She sprang dynamically to her feet, clinching her hands, then swiftly and noiselessly crossed over to her bed and from underneath it dragged out her suitcase. Into it she tossed toilet articles and a change of clothing. Then she turned to her trunk and quickly dumped in two drawerfuls of lingerie and summer dresses. She moved quietly, but with deadly efficiency, and in three-quarters of an hour her trunk was locked and strapped and she was fully dressed in a becoming new travelling suit that Marjorie had helped her pick out.

Sitting down at her desk she wrote a short note to Mrs. Harvey, in which she briefly outlined her reasons for going. She sealed it, addressed it, and laid it on her pillow. She glanced at her watch. The train left at one, and she knew that if she walked down to the Marborough Hotel two blocks away she could easily get a taxicab.

Suddenly she drew in her breath sharply and an expression flashed into her eyes that a practised character reader might have connected vaguely with the set look she had worn in the barber's chair — somehow a development of it. It was quite a new look for Bernice — and it carried consequences.

She went stealthily to the bureau, picked up an article that lay there, and turning out all the lights stood quietly until her eyes became accustomed to the darkness. Softly she pushed open the door to Marjorie's room. She heard the quiet, even breathing of an untroubled conscience asleep.

She was by the bedside now, very deliberate and calm. She acted swiftly. Bending over she found one of the braids of Marjorie's hair, followed it up with her hand to the point nearest the head, and then holding it a little slack so that the sleeper would feel no pull, she reached down with the shears and severed it. With the pigtail in her hand she held her breath. Marjorie had muttered something in her sleep. Bernice deftly amputated the other braid, paused for an instant, and then flitted swiftly and silently back to her own room.

Down-stairs she opened the big front door, closed it carefully behind her, and feeling oddly happy and exuberant stepped off the porch into the moonlight, swinging her heavy grip like a shopping-bag. After a minute's brisk walk she discovered that her left hand still held the two blond braids. She laughed unexpectedly—had to shut her mouth hard to keep from emitting an absolute peal. She was passing Warren's house now, and on the impulse she set down her baggage, and swinging the braids like pieces of rope flung them at the wooden porch, where they landed with a slight thud. She laughed again, no longer restraining herself.

"Huh!" she giggled wildly. "Scalp the selfish thing!"

Then picking up her suitcase she set off at a half-run down the moonlit street.

THE ICE PALACE

"The idea of 'The Ice Palace' grew out of a conversation with a girl out in St. Paul, Minnesota, my home," Fitzgerald wrote in a 1920 letter. As he and the girl were riding home from a movie, she said, "Here comes winter." Fitzgerald wondered aloud whether Swedes were melancholy because of the cold. Two weeks later he was walking in a Montgomery cemetery with Zelda. "She told me," he said, "I could never understand how she felt about the Confederate graves, and I told her I understood so well that I could put it on paper." He returned to St. Paul and wrote "The Ice Palace" before the end of the year. He bragged to his typist that it would earn him a substantial sum from the Post, *because the magazine was "going strongly for local color." He was right. The* Post *paid him $400 but delayed publication, much to his consternation. Fitzgerald hoped the story would establish him as a serious writer before the release of* This Side of Paradise. *Although the description of the ice palace is central to the story, it is unlikely that he ever saw one in St. Paul. He said that he questioned older people about ice palaces of the previous century and looked up old newspaper engravings at the library. The first ice palace St. Paul built during Fitzgerald's lifetime went up in 1917, while he was away at Princeton. The next one was constructed in 1930, eight years after he left St. Paul for good.*

The Saturday Evening Post, May 22, 1920
Collected in Flappers and Philosophers (1920)

I

. . . . .

THE SUNLIGHT DRIPPED OVER THE HOUSE like golden paint over an art jar, and the freckling shadows here and there only intensified the rigor of the bath of light. The Butterworth and Larkin houses flanking were intrenched behind great stodgy trees; only the Happer house took the full sun, and all day long faced the dusty road-street with a tolerant kindly patience. This was the city of Tarleton in southernmost Georgia, September afternoon.

Up in her bedroom window Sally Carrol Happer rested her nineteen-year-old chin on a fifty-two-year-old sill and watched Clark Darrow's ancient Ford turn the corner. The car was hot—being partly metallic it retained all the heat it absorbed or evolved—and Clark Darrow sitting bolt upright at the wheel wore a pained, strained expression as though he considered himself a spare part, and rather likely to break. He laboriously crossed two dust ruts, the wheels squeaking indignantly at the encounter, and then with a terrifying expression he gave the steering-gear a final wrench and deposited self and car approximately in front of the Happer steps. There was a plaintive heaving sound, a death-rattle, followed by a short silence; and then the air was rent by a startling whistle.

Sally Carrol gazed down sleepily. She started to yawn, but finding this quite impossible unless she raised her chin from the window-sill, changed her mind and continued silently to regard the car, whose owner sat brilliantly if perfunctorily at attention as he waited for an answer to his signal. After a moment the whistle once more split the dusty air.

"Good mawnin'."

With difficulty Clark twisted his tall body round and bent a distorted glance on the window.

"'Tain't mawnin', Sally Carrol."

"Isn't it, sure enough?"

"What you doin'?"

"Eatin' 'n apple."

"Come on go swimmin'—want to?"

"Reckon so."

"How 'bout hurryin' up?"

"Sure enough."

Sally Carrol sighed voluminously and raised herself with profound inertia from the floor, where she had been occupied in alternately destroying parts of a green apple and painting paper tops for her younger sister. She approached a mirror, regarded her expression with a pleased and pleasant languor, dabbed two spots of rouge on her lips and a grain of powder on her nose, and covered her bobbed corn-colored hair with a rose-littered sun bonnet. Then she kicked over the painting water, said, "Oh, damn!"—but let it lay—and left the room.

"How you, Clark?" she inquired a minute later as she slipped nimbly over the side of the car.

"Mighty fine, Sally Carrol."

"Where we go swimmin'?"

"Out to Walley's pool. Told Marylyn we'd call by an' get her an' Joe Ewing."

Clark was dark and lean, and when on foot was rather inclined to stoop. His eyes were ominous and his expression somewhat petulant except when startlingly illuminated by one of his frequent smiles. Clark had "a income"—just enough to keep himself in ease and his car in gasolene—and he had spent the two years since he graduated from Georgia Tech in dozing round the lazy streets of his home town, discussing how he could best invest his capital for an immediate fortune.

Hanging round he found not at all difficult; a crowd of little girls had grown up beautifully, the amazing Sally Carrol foremost among them; and they enjoyed being swum with and danced with and made love to in the flower-filled summery evenings—and they all liked Clark immensely. When feminine company palled there were half a dozen other youths who were always just about to do something, and meanwhile were quite willing to join him in a few holes of golf, or a game of billiards, or the consumption of a quart of "hard yella licker." Every once in a while one of these contemporaries made a farewell round of calls before going up to New York or Philadelphia or Pittsburgh to go into business, but mostly they just stayed round in this languid parade of dreamy skies and firefly evenings and noisy niggery street fairs — and especially of gracious, soft-voiced girls, who were brought up on memories instead of money.

The Ford having been excited into a sort of restless resentful life Clark and Sally Carrol rolled and rattled down Valley Avenue into Jefferson Street, where the dust road became a pavement; along opiate Millicent Place, where there were half a dozen prosperous, substantial mansions; and on into the down-town section. Driving was perilous here, for it was shopping time; the population idled casually across the streets and a drove of low-moaning oxen were being urged along in front of a placid street car; even the shops seemed only yawning their doors and blinking their windows in the sunshine before retiring into a state of utter and finite coma.

"Sally Carrol," said Clark suddenly, "it a fact that you're engaged?"

She looked at him quickly.

"Where'd you hear that?"

"Sure enough, you engaged?"

"'At's a nice question!"

"Girl told me you were engaged to a Yankee you met up in Asheville last summer."

Sally Carrol sighed.

"Never saw such an old town for rumors."

"Don't marry a Yankee, Sally Carrol. We need you round here."

Sally Carrol was silent a moment.

"Clark," she demanded suddenly, "who on earth shall I marry?"

"I offer my services."

"Honey, you couldn't support a wife," she answered cheerfully. "Anyway, I know you too well to fall in love with you."

"'At doesn't mean you ought to marry a Yankee," he persisted.

"S'pose I love him?"

He shook his head.

"You couldn't. He'd be a lot different from us, every way."

He broke off as he halted the car in front of a rambling, dilapidated house. Marylyn Wade and Joe Ewing appeared in the doorway.

"'Lo, Sally Carrol."

"Hi!"

"How you-all?"

"Sally Carrol," demanded Marylyn as they started off again, "you engaged?"

"Lawdy, where'd all this start? Can't I look at a man 'thout everybody in town engagin' me to him?"

Clark stared straight in front of him at a bolt on the clattering wind-shield.

"Sally Carrol," he said with a curious intensity, "don't you like us?"

"What?"

"Us down here?"

"Why, Clark, you know I do. I adore all you boys."

"Then why you gettin' engaged to a Yankee?"

"Clark, I don't know. I'm not sure what I'll do, but—well, I want to go places and see people. I want my mind to grow. I want to live where things happen on a big scale."

"What you mean?"

"Oh, Clark, I love you, and I love Joe here, and Ben Arrot, and you-all, but you'll—you'll——"

"We'll all be failures?"

"Yes. I don't mean only money failures, but just sort of—of ineffectual and sad, and—oh, how can I tell you?"

"You mean because we stay here in Tarleton?"

"Yes, Clark; and because you like it and never want to change things or think or go ahead."

He nodded and she reached over and pressed his hand.

"Clark," she said softly, "I wouldn't change you for the world. You're sweet the way you are. The things that'll make you fail I'll love always—the living in the past, the lazy days and nights you have, and all your carelessness and generosity."

"But you're goin' away?"

"Yes—because I couldn't ever marry you. You've a place in my heart no one else ever could have, but tied down here I'd get restless. I'd feel I was—wastin' myself. There's two sides to me, you see. There's the sleepy old side you love; an' there's a sort of energy—the feelin' that makes me do wild things. That's the part of me that may be useful somewhere, that'll last when I'm not beautiful any more."

She broke off with characteristic suddenness and sighed, "Oh, sweet cooky!" as her mood changed.

Half closing her eyes and tipping back her head till it rested on the seat-back she let the savory breeze fan her eyes and ripple the fluffy curls of her bobbed hair. They were in the country now, hurrying between tangled growths of bright-green coppice and grass and tall trees that sent sprays of foliage to hang a cool welcome over the road. Here and there they passed a battered Negro cabin, its oldest white-haired inhabitant smoking a corncob pipe beside the door, and half a dozen scantily clothed pickaninnies parading tattered dolls on the wild-grown grass in front. Farther out were lazy cotton-fields, where even the workers seemed intangible shadows lent by the sun to the earth, not for toil, but to while away some age-old tradition in the golden September fields. And round the drowsy picturesqueness, over the trees and shacks and muddy rivers, flowed the heat, never hostile, only comforting, like a great warm nourishing bosom for the infant earth.

"Sally Carrol, we're here!"

"Poor chile's soun' asleep."

"Honey, you dead at last outa sheer laziness?"

"Water, Sally Carrol! Cool water waitin' for you!"

Her eyes opened sleepily.

"Hi!" she murmured, smiling.

II
· · · · ·

In November Harry Bellamy, tall, broad, and brisk, came down
from his Northern city to spend four days. His intention was to
settle a matter that had been hanging fire since he and Sally Carrol had met in Asheville, North Carolina, in midsummer. The set-
tlement took only a quiet afternoon and an evening in front of a
glowing open fire, for Harry Bellamy had everything she wanted;
and, besides, she loved him — loved him with that side of her she
kept especially for loving. Sally Carrol had several rather clearly
defined sides.

On his last afternoon they walked, and she found their steps
tending half-unconsciously toward one of her favorite haunts, the
cemetery. When it came in sight, gray-white and golden-green
under the cheerful late sun, she paused, irresolute, by the iron
gate.

"Are you mournful by nature, Harry?" she asked with a faint
smile.

"Mournful? Not I."

"Then let's go in here. It depresses some folks, but I like it."

They passed through the gateway and followed a path that led
through a wavy valley of graves — dusty-gray and mouldy for the
fifties; quaintly carved with flowers and jars for the seventies; or-
nate and hideous for the nineties, with fat marble cherubs lying in
sodden sleep on stone pillows, and great impossible growths of
nameless granite flowers. Occasionally they saw a kneeling figure
with tributary flowers, but over most of the graves lay silence and
withered leaves with only the fragrance that their own shadowy
memories could waken in living minds.

They reached the top of a hill where they were fronted by a tall, round headstone, freckled with dark spots of damp and half grown over with vines.

"Margery Lee," she read; "1844–1873. Wasn't she nice? She died when she was twenty-nine. Dear Margery Lee," she added softly. "Can't you see her, Harry?"

"Yes, Sally Carrol."

He felt a little hand insert itself into his.

"She was dark, I think; and she always wore her hair with a ribbon in it, and gorgeous hoop-skirts of alice blue and old rose."

"Yes."

"Oh, she was sweet, Harry! And she was the sort of girl born to stand on a wide, pillared porch and welcome folks in. I think perhaps a lot of men went away to war meanin' to come back to her; but maybe none of 'em ever did."

He stooped down close to the stone, hunting for any record of marriage.

"There's nothing here to show."

"Of course not. How could there be anything there better than just 'Margery Lee,' and that eloquent date?"

She drew close to him and an unexpected lump came into his throat as her yellow hair brushed his cheek.

"You see how she was, don't you, Harry?"

"I see," he agreed gently. "I see through your precious eyes. You're beautiful now, so I know she must have been."

Silent and close they stood, and he could feel her shoulders trembling a little. An ambling breeze swept up the hill and stirred the brim of her floppidy hat.

"Let's go down there!"

She was pointing to a flat stretch on the other side of the hill where along the green turf were a thousand grayish-white crosses stretching in endless, ordered rows like the stacked arms of a battalion.

"Those are the Confederate dead," said Sally Carrol simply.

They walked along and read the inscriptions, always only a name and a date, sometimes quite indecipherable.

"The last row is the saddest—see, 'way over there. Every cross has just a date on it, and the word 'Unknown.'"

She looked at him and her eyes brimmed with tears.

"I can't tell you how real it is to me, darling—if you don't know."

"How you feel about it is beautiful to me."

"No, no, it's not me, it's them—that old time that I've tried to have live in me. These were just men, unimportant evidently or they wouldn't have been 'unknown'; but they died for the most beautiful thing in the world—the dead South. You see," she continued, her voice still husky, her eyes glistening with tears, "people have these dreams they fasten onto things, and I've always grown up with that dream. It was so easy because it was all dead and there weren't any disillusions comin' to me. I've tried in a way to live up to those past standards of noblesse oblige—there's just the last remnants of it, you know, like the roses of an old garden dying all round us—streaks of strange courtliness and chivalry in some of these boys an' stories I used to hear from a Confederate soldier who lived next door, and a few old darkies. Oh, Harry, there was something, there was something! I couldn't ever make you understand, but it was there."

"I understand," he assured her again quietly.

Sally Carrol smiled and dried her eyes on the tip of a handkerchief protruding from his breast pocket.

"You don't feel depressed, do you, lover? Even when I cry I'm happy here, and I get a sort of strength from it."

Hand in hand they turned and walked slowly away. Finding soft grass she drew him down to a seat beside her with their backs against the remnants of a low broken wall.

"Wish those three old women would clear out," he complained. "I want to kiss you, Sally Carrol."

"Me, too."

They waited impatiently for the three bent figures to move off, and then she kissed him until the sky seemed to fade out and all her smiles and tears to vanish in an ecstasy of eternal seconds.

Afterward they walked slowly back together, while on the corners twilight played at somnolent black-and-white checkers with the end of day.

"You'll be up about mid-January," he said, "and you've got to stay a month at least. It'll be slick. There's a winter carnival on, and if you've never really seen snow it'll be like fairy-land to you. There'll be skating and skiing and tobogganing and sleigh-riding, and all sorts of torchlight parades on snowshoes. They haven't had one for years, so they're going to make it a knock-out."

"Will I be cold, Harry?" she asked suddenly.

"You certainly won't. You may freeze your nose, but you won't be shivery cold. It's hard and dry, you know."

"I guess I'm a summer child. I don't like any cold I've ever seen."

She broke off and they were both silent for a minute.

"Sally Carrol," he said very slowly, "what do you say to—March?"

"I say I love you."

"March?"

"March, Harry."

III
· · · · ·

All night in the Pullman it was very cold. She rang for the porter to ask for another blanket, and when he couldn't give her one she tried vainly, by squeezing down into the bottom of her berth and doubling back the bedclothes, to snatch a few hours' sleep. She wanted to look her best in the morning.

She rose at six and sliding uncomfortably into her clothes stumbled up to the diner for a cup of coffee. The snow had filtered into the vestibules and covered the floor with a slippery coating.

It was intriguing, this cold, it crept in everywhere. Her breath was quite visible and she blew into the air with a naïve enjoyment. Seated in the diner she stared out the window at white hills and valleys and scattered pines whose every branch was a green platter for a cold feast of snow. Sometimes a solitary farmhouse would fly by, ugly and bleak and lone on the white waste; and with each one she had an instant of chill compassion for the souls shut in there waiting for spring.

As she left the diner and swayed back into the Pullman she experienced a surging rush of energy and wondered if she was feeling the bracing air of which Harry had spoken. This was the North, the North—her land now!

> *Then blow, ye winds, heigho!*
> *A-roving I will go,*

she chanted exultantly to herself.

"What's 'at?" inquired the porter politely.

"I said: 'Brush me off.'"

The long wires of the telegraph-poles doubled; two tracks ran up beside the train—three—four; came a succession of white-roofed houses, a glimpse of a trolley-car with frosted windows, streets—more streets—the city.

She stood for a dazed moment in the frosty station before she saw three fur-bundled figures descending upon her.

"There she is!"

"Oh, Sally Carrol!"

Sally Carrol dropped her bag.

"Hi!"

A faintly familiar icy-cold face kissed her, and then she was in a group of faces all apparently emitting great clouds of heavy smoke; she was shaking hands. There were Gordon, a short, eager man of thirty who looked like an amateur knocked-about model for Harry, and his wife, Myra, a listless lady with flaxen hair under a fur automobile cap. Almost immediately Sally Carrol thought of her as vaguely Scandinavian. A cheerful chauffeur adopted her bag, and amid ricochets of half-phrases, exclamations, and perfunctory listless "my dears" from Myra, they swept each other from the station.

Then they were in a sedan bound through a crooked succession of snowy streets where dozens of little boys were hitching sleds behind grocery wagons and automobiles.

"Oh," cried Sally Carrol, "I want to do that! Can we, Harry?"

"That's for kids. But we might——"

"It looks like such a circus!" she said regretfully.

Home was a rambling frame house set on a white lap of snow, and there she met a big, gray-haired man of whom she approved, and a lady who was like an egg, and who kissed her—these were Harry's parents. There was a breathless indescribable hour crammed full of half-sentences, hot water, bacon and eggs and confusion; and after that she was alone with Harry in the library, asking him if she dared smoke.

It was a large room with a Madonna over the fire-place and rows upon rows of books in covers of light gold and dark gold and shiny red. All the chairs had little lace squares where one's head should rest, the couch was just comfortable, the books looked as if they had been read—some—and Sally Carrol had an instantaneous vision of the battered old library at home, with her father's huge medical books, and the oil-paintings of her three great-uncles, and the old couch that had been mended up for forty-five years and was still luxurious to dream in. This room struck her as being neither attractive nor particularly otherwise. It was simply a room with a lot of fairly expensive things in it that all looked about fifteen years old.

"What do you think of it up here?" demanded Harry eagerly. "Does it surprise you? Is it what you expected, I mean?"

"You are, Harry," she said quietly, and reached out her arms to him.

But after a brief kiss he seemed anxious to extort enthusiasm from her.

"The town, I mean. Do you like it? Can you feel the pep in the air?"

"Oh, Harry," she laughed, "you'll have to give me time. You can't just fling questions at me."

She puffed at her cigarette with a sigh of contentment.

"One thing I want to ask you," he began rather apologetically; "you Southerners put quite an emphasis on family, and all that — not that it isn't quite all right, but you'll find it a little different here. I mean — you'll notice a lot of things that'll seem to you sort of vulgar display at first, Sally Carrol; but just remember that this is a three-generation town. Everybody has a father, and about half of us have grandfathers. Back of that we don't go."

"Of course," she murmured.

"Our grandfathers, you see, founded the place, and a lot of them had to take some pretty queer jobs while they were doing the founding. For instance, there's one woman who at present is about the social model for the town; well, her father was the first public ash man — things like that."

"Why," said Sally Carrol, puzzled, "did you s'pose I was goin' to make remarks about people?"

"Not at all," interrupted Harry; "and I'm not apologizing for any one either. It's just that — well, a Southern girl came up here last summer and said some unfortunate things, and — oh, I just thought I'd tell you."

Sally Carrol felt suddenly indignant — as though she had been unjustly spanked — but Harry evidently considered the subject closed, for he went on with a great surge of enthusiasm.

"It's carnival time, you know. First in ten years. And there's an ice palace they're building now that's the first they've had since eighty-five. Built out of blocks of the clearest ice they could find — on a tremendous scale."

She rose and walking to the window pushed aside the heavy Turkish portières and looked out.

"Oh!" she cried suddenly. "There's two little boys makin' a snow man! Harry, do you reckon I can go out an' help 'em?"

"You dream! Come here and kiss me."

She left the window rather reluctantly.

"I don't guess this is a very kissable climate, is it? I mean, it makes you so you don't want to sit round, doesn't it?"

"We're not going to. I've got a vacation for the first week you're here, and there's a dinner-dance to-night."

"Oh, Harry," she confessed, subsiding in a heap, half in his lap, half in the pillows, "I sure do feel confused. I haven't got an idea whether I'll like it or not, an' I don't know what people expect, or anythin'. You'll have to tell me, honey."

"I'll tell you," he said softly, "if you'll just tell me you're glad to be here."

"Glad—just awful glad!" she whispered, insinuating herself into his arms in her own peculiar way. "Where you are is home for me, Harry."

And as she said this she had the feeling for almost the first time in her life that she was acting a part.

That night, amid the gleaming candles of a dinner-party, where the men seemed to do most of the talking while the girls sat in a haughty and expensive aloofness, even Harry's presence on her left failed to make her feel at home.

"They're a good-looking crowd, don't you think?" he demanded. "Just look round. There's Spud Hubbard, tackle at Princeton last year, and Junie Morton—he and the red-haired fellow next to him were both Yale hockey captains; Junie was in my class. Why, the best athletes in the world come from these States round here. This is a man's country, I tell you. Look at John J. Fishburn!"

"Who's he?" asked Sally Carol innocently.

"Don't you know?"

"I've heard the name."

"Greatest wheat man in the Northwest, and one of the greatest financiers in the country."

She turned suddenly to a voice on her right.

"I guess they forgot to introduce us. My name's Roger Patton."

"My name is Sally Carrol Happer," she said graciously.

"Yes, I know. Harry told me you were coming."

"You a relative?"

"No, I'm a professor."

"Oh," she laughed.

"At the university. You're from the South, aren't you?"

"Yes; Tarleton, Georgia."

She liked him immediately—a reddish-brown mustache under watery blue eyes that had something in them that these other eyes lacked, some quality of appreciation. They exchanged stray sentences through dinner, and she made up her mind to see him again.

After coffee she was introduced to numerous good-looking young men who danced with conscious precision and seemed to take it for granted that she wanted to talk about nothing except Harry.

"Heavens," she thought, "they talk as if my being engaged made me older than they are—as if I'd tell their mothers on them!"

In the South an engaged girl, even a young married woman, expected the same amount of half-affectionate badinage and flattery that would be accorded a débutante, but here all that seemed banned. One young man, after getting well started on the subject of Sally Carrol's eyes, and how they had allured him ever since she entered the room, went into a violent confusion when he found she was visiting the Bellamys—was Harry's fiancée. He seemed to feel as though he had made some risqué and inexcusable blunder, became immediately formal, and left her at the first opportunity.

She was rather glad when Roger Patton cut in on her and suggested that they sit out a while.

"Well," he inquired, blinking cheerily, "how's Carmen from the South?"

"Mighty fine. How's—how's Dangerous Dan McGrew? Sorry, but he's the only Northerner I know much about."

He seemed to enjoy that.

"Of course," he confessed, "as a professor of literature I'm not supposed to have read Dangerous Dan McGrew."

"Are you a native?"

"No, I'm a Philadelphian. Imported from Harvard to teach French. But I've been here ten years."

"Nine years, three hundred and sixty-four days longer than me."

"Like it here?"

"Uh-huh. Sure do!"

"Really?"

"Well, why not? Don't I look as if I were havin' a good time?"

"I saw you look out the window a minute ago—and shiver."

"Just my imagination," laughed Sally Carrol. "I'm used to havin' everythin' quiet outside, an' sometimes I look out an' see a flurry of snow, an' it's just as if somethin' dead was movin'."

He nodded appreciatively.

"Ever been North before?"

"Spent two Julys in Asheville, North Carolina."

"Nice-looking crowd, aren't they?" suggested Patton, indicating the swirling floor.

Sally Carrol started. This had been Harry's remark.

"Sure are! They're—canine."

"What?"

She flushed.

"I'm sorry; that sounded worse than I meant it. You see I always think of people as feline or canine, irrespective of sex."

"Which are you?"

"I'm feline. So are you. So are most Southern men an' most of these girls here."

"What's Harry?"

"Harry's canine distinctly. All the men I've met to-night seem to be canine."

"What does 'canine' imply? A certain conscious masculinity as opposed to subtlety?"

"Reckon so. I never analyzed it — only I just look at people an' say 'canine' or 'feline' right off. It's right absurd, I guess."

"Not at all. I'm interested. I used to have a theory about these people. I think they're freezing up."

"What?"

"I think they're growing like Swedes — Ibsenesque, you know. Very gradually getting gloomy and melancholy. It's these long winters. Ever read any Ibsen?"

She shook her head.

"Well, you find in his characters a certain brooding rigidity. They're righteous, narrow, and cheerless, without infinite possibilities for great sorrow or joy."

"Without smiles or tears?"

"Exactly. That's my theory. You see there are thousands of Swedes up here. They come, I imagine, because the climate is very much like their own, and there's been a gradual mingling. There're probably not half a dozen here to-night, but — we've had four Swedish governors. Am I boring you?'

"I'm mighty interested."

"Your future sister-in-law is half Swedish. Personally I like her, but my theory is that Swedes react rather badly on us as a whole. Scandinavians, you know, have the largest suicide rate in the world."

"Why do you live here if it's so depressing?"

"Oh, it doesn't get me. I'm pretty well cloistered, and I suppose books mean more than people to me anyway."

"But writers all speak about the South being tragic. You know — Spanish señoritas, black hair and daggers an' haunting music."

He shook his head.

"No, the Northern races are the tragic races—they don't indulge in the cheering luxury of tears."

Sally Carrol thought of her graveyard. She supposed that that was vaguely what she had meant when she said it didn't depress her.

"The Italians are about the gayest people in the world—but it's a dull subject," he broke off. "Anyway, I want to tell you you're marrying a pretty fine man."

Sally Carrol was moved by an impulse of confidence.

"I know. I'm the sort of person who wants to be taken care of after a certain point, and I feel sure I will be."

"Shall we dance? You know," he continued as they rose, "it's encouraging to find a girl who knows what she's marrying for. Nine-tenths of them think of it as a sort of walking into a moving-picture sunset."

She laughed, and liked him immensely.

Two hours later on the way home she nestled near Harry in the back seat.

"Oh, Harry," she whispered, "it's so co-old!"

"But it's warm in here, darling girl."

"But outside it's cold; and oh, that howling wind!"

She buried her face deep in his fur coat and trembled involuntarily as his cold lips kissed the tip of her ear.

IV
. . . . .

The first week of her visit passed in a whirl. She had her promised toboggan-ride at the back of an automobile through a chill January twilight. Swathed in furs she put in a morning tobogganing on the country-club hill; even tried skiing, to sail through the air for a glorious moment and then land in a tangled laughing bundle on a soft snowdrift. She liked all the winter sports, except an afternoon spent snow-shoeing over a glaring plain under pale yellow sunshine, but she soon realized that these things were for children—that she was being humored and that the enjoyment round her was only a reflection of her own.

At first the Bellamy family puzzled her. The men were reliable and she liked them; to Mr. Bellamy especially, with his iron-gray hair and energetic dignity, she took an immediate fancy, once she found that he was born in Kentucky; this made of him a link between the old life and the new. But toward the women she felt a definite hostility. Myra, her future sister-in-law, seemed the essence of spiritless conventionality. Her conversation was so utterly devoid of personality that Sally Carrol, who came from a country where a certain amount of charm and assurance could be taken for granted in the women, was inclined to despise her.

"If those women aren't beautiful," she thought, "they're nothing. They just fade out when you look at them. They're glorified domestics. Men are the centre of every mixed group."

Lastly there was Mrs. Bellamy, whom Sally Carrol detested. The first day's impression of an egg had been confirmed—an egg with a cracked, veiny voice and such an ungracious dumpiness of carriage that Sally Carrol felt that if she once fell she would surely scramble. In addition, Mrs. Bellamy seemed to typify the town in being innately hostile to strangers. She called Sally Carrol "Sally," and could not be persuaded that the double name was anything more than a tedious ridiculous nickname. To Sally Carrol this shortening of her name was like presenting her to the public half clothed. She loved "Sally Carrol"; she loathed "Sally." She knew also that Harry's mother disapproved of her bobbed hair; and she had never dared smoke down-stairs after that first day when Mrs. Bellamy had come into the library sniffing violently.

Of all the men she met she preferred Roger Patton, who was a frequent visitor at the house. He never again alluded to the Ibsen-esque tendency of the populace, but when he came in one day and found her curled upon the sofa bent over *Peer Gynt* he laughed and told her to forget what he'd said—that it was all rot.

And then one afternoon in her second week she and Harry hovered on the edge of a dangerously steep quarrel. She considered that he precipitated it entirely, though the Serbia in the case was an unknown man who had not had his trousers pressed.

They had been walking homeward between mounds of high-piled snow and under a sun which Sally Carrol scarcely recognized. They passed a little girl done up in gray wool until she resembled a small Teddy bear, and Sally Carrol could not resist a gasp of maternal appreciation.

"Look! Harry!"

"What?"

"That little girl—did you see her face?"

"Yes, why?"

"It was red as a little strawberry. Oh, she was cute!"

"Why, your own face is almost as red as that already! Everybody's healthy here. We're out in the cold as soon as we're old enough to walk. Wonderful climate!"

She looked at him and had to agree. He was mighty healthy-looking; so was his brother. And she had noticed the new red in her own cheeks that very morning.

Suddenly their glances were caught and held, and they stared for a moment at the street-corner ahead of them. A man was standing there, his knees bent, his eyes gazing upward with a tense expression as though he were about to make a leap toward the chilly sky. And then they both exploded into a shout of laughter, for coming closer they discovered it had been a ludicrous momentary illusion produced by the extreme bagginess of the man's trousers.

"Reckon that's one on us," she laughed.

"He must be a Southerner, judging by those trousers," suggested Harry mischievously.

"Why, Harry!"

Her surprised look must have irritated him.

"Those damn Southerners!"

Sally Carrol's eyes flashed.

"Don't call 'em that!"

"I'm sorry, dear," said Harry, malignantly apologetic, "but you know what I think of them. They're sort of—sort of degenerates—not at all like the old Southerners. They've lived so long down there with all the colored people that they've gotten lazy and shiftless."

"Hush your mouth, Harry!" she cried angrily. "They're not! They may be lazy—anybody would be in that climate—but they're my best friends, an' I don't want to hear 'em criticised in any such sweepin' way. Some of 'em are the finest men in the world."

"Oh, I know. They're all right when they come North to college, but of all the hangdog, ill-dressed, slovenly lot I ever saw, a bunch of small-town Southerners are the worst!"

Sally Carrol was clinching her gloved hands and biting her lip furiously.

"Why," continued Harry, "there was one in my class at New Haven, and we all thought that at last we'd found the true type of Southern aristocrat, but it turned out that he wasn't an aristocrat at all—just the son of a Northern carpetbagger, who owned about all the cotton round Mobile."

"A Southerner wouldn't talk the way you're talking now," she said evenly.

"They haven't the energy!"

"Or the somethin' else."

"I'm sorry, Sally Carrol, but I've heard you say yourself that you'd never marry——"

"That's quite different. I told you I wouldn't want to tie my life to any of the boys that are round Tarleton now, but I never made any sweepin' generalities."

They walked along in silence.

"I probably spread it on a bit thick, Sally Carrol. I'm sorry."

She nodded but made no answer. Five minutes later as they stood in the hallway she suddenly threw her arms round him.

"Oh, Harry," she cried, her eyes brimming with tears, "let's get married next week. I'm afraid of having fusses like that. I'm afraid, Harry. It wouldn't be that way if we were married."

But Harry, being in the wrong, was still irritated.

"That'd be idiotic. We decided on March."

The tears in Sally Carrol's eyes faded; her expression hardened slightly.

"Very well—I suppose I shouldn't have said that."

Harry melted.

"Dear little nut!" he cried. "Come and kiss me and let's forget."

That very night at the end of a vaudeville performance the orchestra played "Dixie" and Sally Carrol felt something stronger and more enduring than her tears and smiles of the day brim up inside her. She leaned forward gripping the arms of her chair until her face grew crimson.

"Sort of get you, dear?" whispered Harry.

But she did not hear him. To the spirited throb of the violins and the inspiring beat of the kettledrums her own old ghosts were marching by and on into the darkness, and as fifes whistled and sighed in the low encore they seemed so nearly out of sight that she could have waved good-by.

> *Away, away,*
> *Away down South in Dixie!*
> *Away, away,*
> *Away down South in Dixie!*

V
. . . . .

It was a particularly cold night. A sudden thaw had nearly cleared the streets the day before, but now they were traversed again with a powdery wraith of loose snow that travelled in wavy lines before the feet of the wind, and filled the lower air with a fine-particled mist. There was no sky—only a dark, ominous tent that draped in the tops of the streets and was in reality a vast approaching army of snowflakes — while over it all, chilling away the comfort from the brown-and-green glow of lighted windows and muffling the steady trot of the horse pulling their sleigh, interminably washed the north wind. It was a dismal town after all, she thought — dismal.

Sometimes at night it had seemed to her as though no one lived here — they had all gone long ago — leaving lighted houses to be covered in time by tombing heaps of sleet. Oh, if there should be snow on her grave! To be beneath great piles of it all winter long, where even her headstone would be a light shadow against light shadows. Her grave — a grave that should be flower-strewn and washed with sun and rain.

She thought again of those isolated country houses that her train had passed, and of the life there the long winter through — the ceaseless glare through the windows, the crust forming on the soft drifts of snow, finally the slow, cheerless melting, and the harsh spring of which Roger Patton had told her. Her spring — to lose it forever — with its lilacs and the lazy sweetness it stirred in her heart. She was laying away that spring — afterward she would lay away that sweetness.

With a gradual insistence the storm broke. Sally Carrol felt a film of flakes melt quickly on her eyelashes, and Harry reached over a furry arm and drew down her complicated flannel cap. Then the small flakes came in skirmish-line, and the horse bent his neck patiently as a transparency of white appeared momentarily on his coat.

"Oh, he's cold, Harry," she said quickly.

"Who? The horse? Oh, no, he isn't. He likes it!"

After another ten minutes they turned a corner and came in sight of their destination. On a tall hill outlined in vivid glaring green against the wintry sky stood the ice palace. It was three stories in the air, with battlements and embrasures and narrow icicled windows, and the innumerable electric lights inside made a gorgeous transparency of the great central hall. Sally Carrol clutched Harry's hand under the fur robe.

"It's beautiful!" he cried excitedly. "My golly, it's beautiful, isn't it! They haven't had one here since eighty-five!"

Somehow the notion of there not having been one since eighty-five oppressed her. Ice was a ghost, and this mansion of it was surely peopled by those shades of the eighties, with pale faces and blurred snow-filled hair.

"Come on, dear," said Harry.

She followed him out of the sleigh and waited while he hitched the horse. A party of four — Gordon, Myra, Roger Patton, and another girl — drew up beside them with a mighty jingle of bells. There were quite a crowd already, bundled in fur or sheepskin, shouting and calling to each other as they moved through the snow, which was now so thick that people could scarcely be distinguished a few yards away.

"It's a hundred and seventy feet tall," Harry was saying to a muffled figure beside him as they trudged toward the entrance; "covers six thousand square yards."

She caught snatches of conversation: "One main hall" — "walls twenty to forty inches thick" — "and the ice cave has almost a mile of——"

— "this Canuck who built it——"

They found their way inside, and dazed by the magic of the great crystal walls Sally Carrol found herself repeating over and over two lines from "Kubla Khan":

> *It was a miracle of rare device,*
> *A sunny pleasure-dome with caves of ice!*

In the great glittering cavern with the dark shut out she took a seat on a wooden bench, and the evening's oppression lifted. Harry was right — it was beautiful; and her gaze travelled the smooth surface of the walls, the blocks for which had been selected for their purity and clearness to obtain this opalescent, translucent effect.

"Look! Here we go—oh, boy!" cried Harry.

A band in a far corner struck up "Hail, Hail, the Gang's All Here!" which echoed over to them in wild muddled acoustics, and then the lights suddenly went out; silence seemed to flow down the icy sides and sweep over them. Sally Carrol could still see her white breath in the darkness, and a dim row of pale faces over on the other side.

The music eased to a sighing complaint, and from outside drifted in the full-throated resonant chant of the marching clubs. It grew louder like some pæn of a viking tribe traversing an ancient wild; it swelled—they were coming nearer; then a row of torches appeared, and another and another, and keeping time with their moccasined feet a long column of gray-mackinawed figures swept in, snowshoes slung at their shoulders, torches soaring and flickering as their voices rose along the great walls.

The gray column ended and another followed, the light streaming luridly this time over red toboggan caps and flaming crimson mackinaws, and as they entered they took up the refrain; then came a long platoon of blue and white, of green, of white, of brown and yellow.

"Those white ones are the Wacouta Club," whispered Harry eagerly. "Those are the men you've met round at dances."

The volume of the voices grew; the great cavern was a phantasmagoria of torches waving in great banks of fire, of colors and the rhythm of soft-leather steps. The leading column turned and halted, platoon deployed in front of platoon until the whole procession made a solid flag of flame, and then from thousands of voices burst a mighty shout that filled the air like a crash of thunder, and sent the torches wavering. It was magnificent, it was tremendous! To Sally Carrol it was the North offering sacrifice on some mighty altar to the gray pagan God of Snow. As the shout died the band struck up again and there came more singing, and then long reverberating cheers by each club. She sat very quiet listening while the staccato cries rent the stillness; and then she started, for there was a volley of explosion, and great clouds of smoke went up here and there through the cavern — the flashlight photographers at work — and the council was over. With the band at their head the clubs formed in column once more, took up their chant, and began to march out.

"Come on!" shouted Harry. "We want to see the labyrinths down-stairs before they turn the lights off!"

They all rose and started toward the chute — Harry and Sally Carrol in the lead, her little mitten buried in his big fur gantlet. At the bottom of the chute was a long empty room of ice, with the ceiling so low that they had to stoop — and their hands were parted. Before she realized what he intended Harry had darted down one of the half-dozen glittering passages that opened into the room and was only a vague receding blot against the green shimmer.

"Harry!" she called.

"Come on!" he cried back.

She looked round the empty chamber; the rest of the party had evidently decided to go home, were already outside somewhere in the blundering snow. She hesitated and then darted in after Harry.

"Harry!" she shouted.

She had reached a turning-point thirty feet down; she heard a faint muffled answer far to the left, and with a touch of panic fled toward it. She passed another turning, two more yawning alleys.

"Harry!"

No answer. She started to run straight forward, and then turned like lightning and sped back the way she had come, enveloped in a sudden icy terror.

She reached a turn—was it here?—took the left and came to what should have been the outlet into the long, low room, but it was only another glittering passage with darkness at the end. She called again, but the walls gave back a flat, lifeless echo with no reverberations. Retracing her steps she turned another corner, this time following a wide passage. It was like the green lane between the parted waters of the Red Sea, like a damp vault connecting empty tombs.

She slipped a little now as she walked, for ice had formed on the bottom of her overshoes; she had to run her gloves along the half-slippery, half-sticky walls to keep her balance.

"Harry!"

Still no answer. The sound she made bounced mockingly down to the end of the passage.

Then on an instant the lights went out, and she was in complete darkness. She gave a small, frightened cry, and sank down into a cold little heap on the ice. She felt her left knee do something as she fell, but she scarcely noticed it as some deep terror far greater than any fear of being lost settled upon her. She was alone with this presence that came out of the North, the dreary loneliness that rose from ice-bound whalers in the Arctic seas, from smokeless, trackless wastes where were strewn the whitened bones of adventure. It was an icy breath of death; it was rolling down low across the land to clutch at her.

With a furious, despairing energy she rose again and started blindly down the darkness. She must get out. She might be lost in here for days, freeze to death and lie embedded in the ice like corpses she had read of, kept perfectly preserved until the melting of a glacier. Harry probably thought she had left with the others—he had gone by now; no one would know until late next day. She reached pitifully for the wall. Forty inches thick, they had said—forty inches thick!

"Oh!"

On both sides of her along the walls she felt things creeping, damp souls that haunted this palace, this town, this North.

"Oh, send somebody—send somebody!" she cried aloud.

Clark Darrow—he would understand; or Joe Ewing; she couldn't be left here to wander forever—to be frozen, heart, body, and soul. This her—this Sally Carrol! Why, she was a happy thing. She was a happy little girl. She liked warmth and summer and Dixie. These things were foreign—foreign.

"You're not crying," something said aloud. "You'll never cry any more. Your tears would just freeze; all tears freeze up here!"

She sprawled full length on the ice.

"Oh, God!" she faltered.

A long single file of minutes went by, and with a great weariness she felt her eyes closing. Then some one seemed to sit down near her and take her face in warm, soft hands. She looked up gratefully.

"Why, it's Margery Lee," she crooned softly to herself. "I knew you'd come." It really was Margery Lee, and she was just as Sally Carrol had known she would be, with a young, white brow, and wide, welcoming eyes, and a hoop-skirt of some soft material that was quite comforting to rest on.

"Margery Lee."

It was getting darker now and darker—all those tombstones ought to be repainted, sure enough, only that would spoil 'em, of course. Still, you ought to be able to see 'em.

Then after a succession of moments that went fast and then slow, but seemed to be ultimately resolving themselves into a multitude of blurred rays converging toward a pale-yellow sun, she heard a great cracking noise break her new-found stillness.

It was the sun, it was a light; a torch, and a torch beyond that, and another one, and voices; a face took flesh below the torch, heavy arms raised her, and she felt something on her cheek—it felt wet. Some one had seized her and was rubbing her face with snow. How ridiculous—with snow!

"Sally Carrol! Sally Carrol!"

It was Dangerous Dan McGrew; and two other faces she didn't know.

"Child, child! We've been looking for you two hours! Harry's half-crazy!"

Things came rushing back into place—the singing, the

torches, the great shout of the marching clubs. She squirmed in Patton's arms and gave a long low cry.

"Oh, I want to get out of here! I'm going back home. Take me home"—her voice rose to a scream that sent a chill to Harry's heart as he came racing down the next passage—"to-morrow!" she cried with delirious, unrestrained passion—"To-morrow! To-morrow! To-morrow!"

VI
. . . . .

The wealth of golden sunlight poured a quite enervating yet oddly comforting heat over the house where day long it faced the dusty stretch of road. Two birds were making a great to-do in a cool spot found among the branches of a tree next door, and down the street a colored woman was announcing herself melodiously as a purveyor of strawberries. It was April afternoon.

Sally Carrol Happer, resting her chin on her arm, and her arm on an old window-seat, gazed sleepily down over the spangled dust whence the heat waves were rising for the first time this spring. She was watching a very ancient Ford turn a perilous corner and rattle and groan to a jolting stop at the end of the walls. She made no sound, and in a minute a strident familiar whistle rent the air. Sally Carrol smiled and blinked.

"Good mawnin'."

A head appeared tortuously from under the car-top below.

"'Tain't mawnin', Sally Carrol."

"Sure enough!" she said in affected surprise. "I guess maybe not."

"What you doin'?"

"Eatin' green peach. 'Spect to die any minute."

Clark twisted himself a last impossible notch to get a view of her face.

"Water's warm as a kettla steam, Sally Carrol. Wanta go swimmin'?"

"Hate to move," sighed Sally Carrol lazily, "but I reckon so."

WINTER DREAMS

In September 1922, shortly before he left St. Paul to return to New York, Fitzgerald wrote "Winter Dreams." It is the last story he wrote in his hometown. By then, he was a celebrity writer whose name attracted readers to the popular magazines of the day. Editor Carl Hovey of The Metropolitan *wanted that kind of cachet to reverse the declining fortunes of his magazine. He offered Fitzgerald $900 for each of his next six stories, a considerable raise over the $500 he was earning from the* Post. *The setting is White Bear Lake, then a fashionable resort community just north of St. Paul. Fitzgerald had known the area since boyhood and had just spent the summer living at the White Bear Yacht Club (Sherry Island Golf Club in the story). He described "Winter Dreams" as a "sort of 1st draft of the Gatsby idea." It includes his most romantic evocation of Summit Avenue, St. Paul's famous boulevard.*

The Metropolitan Magazine, December 1922
Collected in *All the Sad Young Men* (1926)

I

. . . . .

SOME OF THE CADDIES WERE POOR AS SIN and lived in one-room houses with a neurasthenic cow in the front yard, but Dexter Green's father owned the second best grocery-store in Black Bear—the best one was "The Hub," patronized by the wealthy people from Sherry Island—and Dexter caddied only for pocket-money.

In the fall when the days became crisp and gray, and the long Minnesota winter shut down like the white lid of a box, Dexter's skis moved over the snow that hid the fairways of the golf course. At these times the country gave him a feeling of profound melancholy—it offended him that the links should lie in enforced fallowness, haunted by ragged sparrows for the long season. It was dreary, too, that on the tees where the gay colors fluttered in summer there were now only the desolate sand-boxes knee-deep in crusted ice. When he crossed the hills the wind blew cold as misery, and if the sun was out he tramped with his eyes squinted up against the hard dimensionless glare.

In April the winter ceased abruptly. The snow ran down into Black Bear Lake scarcely tarrying for the early golfers to brave the season with red and black balls. Without elation, without an interval of moist glory, the cold was gone.

Dexter knew that there was something dismal about this Northern spring, just as he knew there was something gorgeous about the fall. Fall made him clinch his hands and tremble and repeat idiotic sentences to himself, and make brisk abrupt gestures of command to imaginary audiences and armies. October filled him with hope which November raised to a sort of ecstatic triumph, and in this mood the fleeting brilliant impressions of the summer at Sherry Island were ready grist to his mill. He became a golf champion and defeated Mr. T. A. Hedrick in a marvellous match played a hundred times over the fairways of his imagination, a match each detail of which he changed about untiringly—sometimes he won with almost laughable ease, sometimes he came up magnificently from behind. Again, stepping from a Pierce-Arrow automobile, like Mr. Mortimer Jones, he strolled frigidly into the lounge of the Sherry Island Golf Club—or perhaps, surrounded by an admiring crowd, he gave an exhibition of fancy diving from the spring-board of the club raft. . . . Among those who watched him in open-mouthed wonder was Mr. Mortimer Jones.

And one day it came to pass that Mr. Jones—himself and not his ghost—came up to Dexter with tears in his eyes and said that Dexter was the———best caddy in the club, and wouldn't he decide not to quit if Mr. Jones made it worth his while, because every other———caddy in the club lost one ball a hole for him—regularly———

"No, sir," said Dexter decisively, "I don't want to caddy any more." Then, after a pause: "I'm too old."

"You're not more than fourteen. Why the devil did you decide just this morning that you wanted to quit? You promised that next week you'd go over to the State tournament with me."

"I decided I was too old."

Dexter handed in his "A Class" badge, collected what money was due him from the caddy master, and walked home to Black Bear Village.

"The best———caddy I ever saw," shouted Mr. Mortimer Jones over a drink that afternoon. "Never lost a ball! Willing! Intelligent! Quiet! Honest! Grateful!"

The little girl who had done this was eleven—beautifully ugly as little girls are apt to be who are destined after a few years to be inexpressibly lovely and bring no end of misery to a great number of men. The spark, however, was perceptible. There was a general ungodliness in the way her lips twisted down at the corners when she smiled, and in the—Heaven help us!—in the almost passionate quality of her eyes. Vitality is born early in such women. It was utterly in evidence now, shining through her thin frame in a sort of glow.

She had come eagerly out on to the course at nine o'clock with a white linen nurse and five small new golf-clubs in a white canvas bag which the nurse was carrying. When Dexter first saw her she was standing by the caddy house, rather ill at ease and trying to conceal the fact by engaging her nurse in an obviously unnatural conversation graced by startling and irrelevant grimaces from herself.

"Well, it's certainly a nice day, Hilda," Dexter heard her say. She drew down the corners of her mouth, smiled, and glanced furtively around, her eyes in transit falling for an instant on Dexter.

Then to the nurse:

"Well, I guess there aren't very many people out here this morning, are there?"

The smile again — radiant, blatantly artificial — convincing.

"I don't know what we're supposed to do now," said the nurse, looking nowhere in particular.

"Oh, that's all right. I'll fix it up."

Dexter stood perfectly still, his mouth slightly ajar. He knew that if he moved forward a step his stare would be in her line of vision — if he moved backward he would lose his full view of her face. For a moment he had not realized how young she was. Now he remembered having seen her several times the year before — in bloomers.

Suddenly, involuntarily, he laughed, a short abrupt laugh — then, startled by himself, he turned and began to walk quickly away.

"Boy!"

Dexter stopped.

"Boy——"

Beyond question he was addressed. Not only that, but he was treated to that absurd smile, that preposterous smile — the memory of which at least a dozen men were to carry into middle age.

"Boy, do you know where the golf teacher is?"

"He's giving a lesson."

"Well, do you know where the caddy-master is?"

"He isn't here yet this morning."

"Oh." For a moment this baffled her. She stood alternately on her right and left foot.

"We'd like to get a caddy," said the nurse. "Mrs. Mortimer Jones sent us out to play golf, and we don't know how without we get a caddy."

Here she was stopped by an ominous glance from Miss Jones, followed immediately by the smile.

"There aren't any caddies here except me," said Dexter to the nurse, "and I got to stay here in charge until the caddy-master gets here."

"Oh."

Miss Jones and her retinue now withdrew, and at a proper distance from Dexter became involved in a heated conversation, which was concluded by Miss Jones taking one of the clubs and hitting it on the ground with violence. For further emphasis she raised it again and was about to bring it down smartly upon the nurse's bosom, when the nurse seized the club and twisted it from her hands.

"You damn little mean old *thing!*" cried Miss Jones wildly.

Another argument ensued. Realizing that the elements of the comedy were implied in the scene, Dexter several times began to laugh, but each time restrained the laugh before it reached audibility. He could not resist the monstrous conviction that the little girl was justified in beating the nurse.

The situation was resolved by the fortuitous appearance of the caddy-master, who was appealed to immediately by the nurse.

"Miss Jones is to have a little caddy, and this one says he can't go."

"Mr. McKenna said I was to wait here till you came," said Dexter quickly.

"Well, he's here now." Miss Jones smiled cheerfully at the caddy-master. Then she dropped her bag and set off at a haughty mince toward the first tee.

"Well?" The caddy-master turned to Dexter. "What you standing there like a dummy for? Go pick up the young lady's clubs."

"I don't think I'll go out to-day," said Dexter.

"You don't——"

"I think I'll quit."

The enormity of his decision frightened him. He was a favorite caddy, and the thirty dollars a month he earned through the summer were not to be made elsewhere around the lake. But he had received a strong emotional shock, and his perturbation required a violent and immediate outlet.

It is not so simple as that, either. As so frequently would be the case in the future, Dexter was unconsciously dictated to by his winter dreams.

II
. . . . .

Now, of course, the quality and the seasonability of these winter dreams varied, but the stuff of them remained. They persuaded Dexter several years later to pass up a business course at the State university—his father, prospering now, would have paid his way—for the precarious advantage of attending an older and more famous university in the East, where he was bothered by his scanty funds. But do not get the impression, because his winter dreams happened to be concerned at first with musings on the rich, that there was anything merely snobbish in the boy. He wanted not association with glittering things and glittering people—he wanted the glittering things themselves. Often he reached out for the best without knowing why he wanted it—and sometimes he ran up against the mysterious denials and prohibitions in which life indulges. It is with one of those denials and not with his career as a whole that this story deals.

He made money. It was rather amazing. After college he went to the city from which Black Bear Lake draws its wealthy patrons. When he was only twenty-three and had been there not quite two years, there were already people who liked to say: "Now *there's* a boy—" All about him rich men's sons were peddling bonds precariously, or investing patrimonies precariously, or plodding through the two dozen volumes of the "George Washington Commercial Course," but Dexter borrowed a thousand dollars on his college degree and his confident mouth, and bought a partnership in a laundry.

It was a small laundry when he went into it but Dexter made a specialty of learning how the English washed fine woollen golf-stockings without shrinking them, and within a year he was catering to the trade that wore knickerbockers. Men were insisting that their Shetland hose and sweaters go to his laundry just as they had insisted on a caddy who could find golfballs. A little later he was doing their wives' lingerie as well—and running five branches in different parts of the city. Before he was twenty-seven he owned the largest string of laundries in his section of the country. It was then that he sold out and went to New York. But the part of his story that concerns us goes back to the days when he was making his first big success.

When he was twenty-three Mr. Hart—one of the gray-haired men who like to say "Now there's a boy"—gave him a guest card to the Sherry Island Golf Club for a week-end. So he signed his name one day on the register, and that afternoon played golf in a foursome with Mr. Hart and Mr. Sandwood and Mr. T. A. Hedrick. He did not consider it necessary to remark that he had once carried Mr. Hart's bag over this same links, and that he knew every trap and gully with his eyes shut—but he found himself glancing at the four caddies who trailed them, trying to catch a gleam or gesture that would remind him of himself, that would lessen the gap which lay between his present and his past.

It was a curious day, slashed abruptly with fleeting, familiar impressions. One minute he had the sense of being a trespasser — in the next he was impressed by the tremendous superiority he felt toward Mr. T. A. Hedrick, who was a bore and not even a good golfer any more.

Then, because of a ball Mr. Hart lost near the fifteenth green, an enormous thing happened. While they were searching the stiff grasses of the rough there was a clear call of "Fore!" from behind a hill in their rear. And as they all turned abruptly from their search a bright new ball sliced abruptly over the hill and caught Mr. T. A. Hedrick in the abdomen.

"By Gad!" cried Mr. T. A. Hedrick, "they ought to put some of these crazy women off the course. It's getting to be outrageous."

A head and a voice came up together over the hill:

"Do you mind if we go through?"

"You hit me in the stomach!" declared Mr. Hedrick wildly.

"Did I?" The girl approached the group of men. "I'm sorry. I yelled 'Fore!'"

Her glance fell casually on each of the men — then scanned the fairway for her ball.

"Did I bounce into the rough?"

It was impossible to determine whether this question was ingenuous or malicious. In a moment, however, she left no doubt, for as her partner came up over the hill she called cheerfully:

"Here I am! I'd have gone on the green except that I hit something."

As she took her stance for a short mashie shot, Dexter looked at her closely. She wore a blue gingham dress, rimmed at throat and shoulders with a white edging that accentuated her tan. The quality of exaggeration, of thinness, which had made her passionate eyes and down-turning mouth absurd at eleven, was gone now. She was arrestingly beautiful. The color in her cheeks was centered like the color in a picture — it was not a "high" color, but a sort of fluctuating and feverish warmth, so shaded that it seemed at any moment it would recede and disappear. This color and the mobility of her mouth gave a continual impression of flux, of intense life, of passionate vitality — balanced only partially by the sad luxury of her eyes.

She swung her mashie impatiently and without interest, pitching the ball into a sand-pit on the other side of the green. With a quick, insincere smile and a careless "Thank you!" she went on after it.

"That Judy Jones!" remarked Mr. Hedrick on the next tee, as they waited — some moments — for her to play on ahead. "All she needs is to be turned up and spanked for six months and then to be married off to an old-fashioned cavalry captain."

"My God, she's good-looking!" said Mr. Sandwood, who was just over thirty.

"Good-looking!" cried Mr. Hedrick contemptuously, "she always looks as if she wanted to be kissed! Turning those big cow-eyes on every calf in town!"

It was doubtful if Mr. Hedrick intended a reference to the maternal instinct.

"She'd play pretty good golf if she'd try," said Mr. Sandwood.

"She has no form," said Mr. Hedrick solemnly.

"She has a nice figure," said Mr. Sandwood.

"Better thank the Lord she doesn't drive a swifter ball," said Mr. Hart, winking at Dexter.

Later in the afternoon the sun went down with a riotous swirl of gold and varying blues and scarlets, and left the dry, rustling night of Western summer. Dexter watched from the veranda of the Golf Club, watched the even overlap of the waters in the little wind, silver molasses under the harvest-moon. Then the moon held a finger to her lips and the lake became a clear pool, pale and quiet. Dexter put on his bathing-suit and swam out to the farthest raft, where he stretched dripping on the wet canvas of the springboard.

There was a fish jumping and a star shining and the lights around the lake were gleaming. Over on a dark peninsula a piano was playing the songs of last summer and of summers before that—songs from *Chin-Chin* and *The Count of Luxemburg* and *The Chocolate Soldier*—and because the sound of a piano over a stretch of water had always seemed beautiful to Dexter he lay perfectly quiet and listened.

The tune the piano was playing at that moment had been gay and new five years before when Dexter was a sophomore at college. They had played it at a prom once when he could not afford the luxury of proms, and he had stood outside the gymnasium and listened. The sound of the tune precipitated in him a sort of ecstasy and it was with that ecstasy he viewed what happened to him now. It was a mood of intense appreciation, a sense that, for once, he was magnificently attune to life and that everything about him was radiating a brightness and a glamour he might never know again.

A low, pale oblong detached itself suddenly from the darkness of the Island, spitting forth the reverberate sound of a racing motor-boat. Two white streamers of cleft water rolled themselves out behind it and almost immediately the boat was beside him, drowning out the hot tinkle of the piano in the drone of its spray. Dexter raising himself on his arms was aware of a figure standing at the wheel, of two dark eyes regarding him over the lengthening space of water—then the boat had gone by and was sweeping in an immense and purposeless circle of spray round and round in the middle of the lake. With equal eccentricity one of the circles flattened out and headed back toward the raft.

"Who's that?" she called, shutting off her motor. She was so near now that Dexter could see her bathing-suit, which consisted apparently of pink rompers.

The nose of the boat bumped the raft, and as the latter tilted rakishly he was precipitated toward her. With different degrees of interest they recognized each other.

"Aren't you one of those men we played through this afternoon?" she demanded.

He was.

"Well, do you know how to drive a motor-boat? Because if you do I wish you'd drive this one so I can ride on the surf-board behind. My name is Judy Jones" — she favored him with an absurd smirk — rather, what tried to be a smirk, for, twist her mouth as she might, it was not grotesque, it was merely beautiful — "and I live in a house over there on the Island, and in that house there is a man waiting for me. When he drove up at the door I drove out of the dock because he says I'm his ideal."

There was a fish jumping and a star shining and the lights around the lake were gleaming. Dexter sat beside Judy Jones and she explained how her boat was driven. Then she was in the water, swimming to the floating surf-board with a sinuous crawl. Watching her was without effort to the eye, watching a branch waving or a sea-gull flying. Her arms, burned to butternut, moved sinuously among the dull platinum ripples, elbow appearing first, casting the forearm back with a cadence of falling water, then reaching out and down, stabbing a path ahead.

They moved out into the lake; turning, Dexter saw that she was kneeling on the low rear of the now uptilted surf-board.

"Go faster," she called, "fast as it'll go."

Obediently he jammed the lever forward and the white spray mounted at the bow. When he looked around again the girl was standing up on the rushing board, her arms spread wide, her eyes lifted toward the moon.

"It's awful cold," she shouted. "What's your name?"

He told her.

"Well, why don't you come to dinner to-morrow night?"

His heart turned over like the fly-wheel of the boat, and, for the second time, her casual whim gave a new direction to his life.

III

· · · · ·

Next evening while he waited for her to come down-stairs, Dexter peopled the soft deep summer room and the sun-porch that opened from it with the men who had already loved Judy Jones.

He knew the sort of men they were—the men who when he first went to college had entered from the great prep schools with graceful clothes and the deep tan of healthy summers. He had seen that, in one sense, he was better than these men. He was newer and stronger. Yet in acknowledging to himself that he wished his children to be like them he was admitting that he was but the rough, strong stuff from which they eternally sprang.

When the time had come for him to wear good clothes, he had known who were the best tailors in America, and the best tailors in America had made him the suit he wore this evening. He had acquired that particular reserve peculiar to his university, that set it off from other universities. He recognized the value to him of such a mannerism and he had adopted it; he knew that to be careless in dress and manner required more confidence than to be careful. But carelessness was for his children. His mother's name had been Krimslich. She was a Bohemian of the peasant class and she had talked broken English to the end of her days. Her son must keep to the set patterns.

At a little after seven Judy Jones came down-stairs. She wore a blue silk afternoon dress, and he was disappointed at first that she had not put on something more elaborate. This feeling was accentuated when, after a brief greeting, she went to the door of a butler's pantry and pushing it open called: "You can serve dinner, Martha." He had rather expected that a butler would announce dinner, that there would be a cocktail. Then he put these thoughts behind him as they sat down side by side on a lounge and looked at each other.

"Father and mother won't be here," she said thoughtfully.

He remembered the last time he had seen her father, and he was glad the parents were not to be here to-night—they might wonder who he was. He had been born in Keeble, a Minnesota village fifty miles farther north, and he always gave Keeble as his home instead of Black Bear Village. Country towns were well enough to come from if they weren't inconveniently in sight and used as footstools by fashionable lakes.

They talked of his university, which she had visited frequently during the past two years, and of the near-by city which supplied Sherry Island with its patrons, and whither Dexter would return next day to his prospering laundries.

During dinner she slipped into a moody depression which gave Dexter a feeling of uneasiness. Whatever petulance she uttered in her throaty voice worried him. Whatever she smiled at — at him, at a chicken liver, at nothing — it disturbed him that her smile could have no root in mirth, or even in amusement. When the scarlet corners of her lips curved down, it was less a smile than an invitation to a kiss.

Then, after dinner, she led him out on the dark sun-porch and deliberately changed the atmosphere.

"Do you mind if I weep a little?" she said.

"I'm afraid I'm boring you," he responded quickly.

"You're not. I like you. But I've just had a terrible afternoon. There was a man I cared about, and this afternoon he told me out of a clear sky that he was poor as a church-mouse. He'd never even hinted it before. Does this sound horribly mundane?"

"Perhaps he was afraid to tell you."

"Suppose he was," she answered. "He didn't start right. You see, if I'd thought of him as poor — well, I've been mad about loads of poor men, and fully intended to marry them all. But in this case, I hadn't thought of him that way, and my interest in him wasn't strong enough to survive the shock. As if a girl calmly informed her fiancé that she was a widow. He might not object to widows, but——

"Let's start right," she interrupted herself suddenly. "Who are you, anyhow?"

For a moment Dexter hesitated. Then:

"I'm nobody," he announced. "My career is largely a matter of futures."

"Are you poor?"

"No," he said frankly, "I'm probably making more money than

any man my age in the Northwest. I know that's an obnoxious re-mark, but you advised me to start right."

There was a pause. Then she smiled and the corners of her mouth drooped and an almost imperceptible sway brought her closer to him, looking up into his eyes. A lump rose in Dexter's throat, and he waited breathless for the experiment, facing the un-predictable compound that would form mysteriously from the el-ements of their lips. Then he saw — she communicated her excite-ment to him, lavishly, deeply, with kisses that were not a promise but a fulfillment. They aroused in him not hunger demanding re-newal but surfeit that would demand more surfeit . . . kisses that were like charity, creating want by holding back nothing at all.

It did not take him many hours to decide that he had wanted Judy Jones ever since he was a proud, desirous little boy.

IV
. . . . .

It began like that — and continued, with varying shades of inten-sity, on such a note right up to the dénouement. Dexter surren-dered a part of himself to the most direct and unprincipled per-sonality with which he had ever come in contact. Whatever Judy wanted, she went after with the full pressure of her charm. There was no divergence of method, no jockeying for position or pre-meditation of effects — there was a very little mental side to any of her affairs. She simply made men conscious to the highest degree of her physical loveliness. Dexter had no desire to change her. Her deficiencies were knit up with a passionate energy that tran-scended and justified them.

When, as Judy's head lay against his shoulder that first night, she whispered, "I don't know what's the matter with me. Last night I thought I was in love with a man and to-night I think I'm in love with you — " — it seemed to him a beautiful and romantic thing to say. It was the exquisite excitability that for the moment he controlled and owned. But a week later he was compelled to view this same quality in a different light. She took him in her roadster to a picnic supper, and after supper she disappeared, like-wise in her roadster, with another man. Dexter became enor-mously upset and was scarcely able to be decently civil to the other people present. When she assured him that she had not kissed the other man, he knew she was lying — yet he was glad that she had taken the trouble to lie to him.

He was, as he found before the summer ended, one of a varying dozen who circulated about her. Each of them had at one time been favored above all others — about half of them still basked in the solace of occasional sentimental revivals. Whenever one showed signs of dropping out through long neglect, she granted him a brief honeyed hour, which encouraged him to tag along for a year or so longer. Judy made these forays upon the helpless and defeated without malice, indeed half unconscious that there was anything mischievous in what she did.

When a new man came to town every one dropped out — dates were automatically cancelled.

The helpless part of trying to do anything about it was that she did it all herself. She was not a girl who could be "won" in the kinetic sense — she was proof against cleverness, she was proof against charm; if any of these assailed her too strongly she would immediately resolve the affair to a physical basis, and under the magic of her physical splendor the strong as well as the brilliant played her game and not their own. She was entertained only by the gratification of her desires and by the direct exercise of her own charm. Perhaps from so much youthful love, so many youthful lovers, she had come, in self-defense, to nourish herself wholly from within.

Succeeding Dexter's first exhilaration came restlessness and dis-satisfaction. The helpless ecstasy of losing himself in her was opi-ate rather than tonic. It was fortunate for his work during the win-ter that those moments of ecstasy came infrequently. Early in their acquaintance it had seemed for a while that there was a deep and spontaneous mutual attraction — that first August, for example — three days of long evenings on her dusky veranda, of strange wan kisses through the late afternoon, in shadowy alcoves or behind the protecting trellises of the garden arbors, of mornings when she was fresh as a dream and almost shy at meeting him in the clarity of the rising day. There was all the ecstasy of an engagement about it, sharpened by his realization that there was no engagement. It was during those three days that, for the first time, he had asked her to marry him. She said "maybe some day," she said "kiss me," she said "I'd like to marry you," she said "I love you" — she said — nothing.

The three days were interrupted by the arrival of a New York man who visited at her house for half September. To Dexter's agony, rumor engaged them. The man was the son of the president of a great trust company. But at the end of a month it was reported that Judy was yawning. At a dance one night she sat all evening in a motor-boat with a local beau, while the New Yorker searched the club for her frantically. She told the local beau that she was bored with her visitor, and two days later he left. She was seen with him at the station, and it was reported that he looked very mournful indeed.

On this note the summer ended. Dexter was twenty-four, and he found himself increasingly in a position to do as he wished. He joined two clubs in the city and lived at one of them. Though he was by no means an integral part of the stag-lines at these clubs, he managed to be on hand at dances where Judy Jones was likely to appear. He could have gone out socially as much as he liked — he was an eligible young man, now, and popular with down-town fathers. His confessed devotion to Judy Jones had rather solidified his position. But he had no social aspirations and rather despised the dancing men who were always on tap for the Thursday or Saturday parties and who filled in at dinners with the younger married set. Already he was playing with the idea of going East to New York. He wanted to take Judy Jones with him. No disillusion as to the world in which she had grown up could cure his illusion as to her desirability.

Remember that — for only in the light of it can what he did for her be understood.

Eighteen months after he first met Judy Jones he became engaged to another girl. Her name was Irene Scheerer, and her father was one of the men who had always believed in Dexter. Irene was light-haired and sweet and honorable, and a little stout, and she had two suitors whom she pleasantly relinquished when Dexter formally asked her to marry him.

Summer, fall, winter, spring, another summer, another fall — so much he had given of his active life to the incorrigible lips of Judy Jones. She had treated him with interest, with encouragement, with malice, with indifference, with contempt. She had inflicted on him the innumerable little slights and indignities possible in such a case — as if in revenge for having ever cared for him at all. She had beckoned him and yawned at him and beckoned him again and he had responded often with bitterness and narrowed eyes. She had brought him ecstatic happiness and intolerable agony of spirit. She had caused him untold inconvenience and not a little trouble. She had insulted him, and she had ridden over him, and she had played his interest in her against his interest in his work — for fun. She had done everything to him except to criticise him — this she had not done — it seemed to him only because it might have sullied the utter indifference she manifested and sincerely felt toward him.

When autumn had come and gone again it occurred to him that he could not have Judy Jones. He had to beat this into his mind but he convinced himself at last. He lay awake at night for a while and argued it over. He told himself the trouble and the pain she had caused him, he enumerated her glaring deficiencies as a wife. Then he said to himself that he loved her, and after a while he fell asleep. For a week, lest he imagined her husky voice over the telephone or her eyes opposite him at lunch, he worked hard and late, and at night he went to his office and plotted out his years.

At the end of a week he went to a dance and cut in on her once. For almost the first time since they had met he did not ask her to sit out with him or tell her that she was lovely. It hurt him that she did not miss these things — that was all. He was not jealous when he saw that there was a new man to-night. He had been hardened against jealousy long before.

He stayed late at the dance. He sat for an hour with Irene Scheerer and talked about books and about music. He knew very little about either. But he was beginning to be master of his own time now, and he had a rather priggish notion that he — the young and already fabulously successful Dexter Green — should know more about such things.

That was in October, when he was twenty-five. In January, Dexter and Irene became engaged. It was to be announced in June, and they were to be married three months later.

The Minnesota winter prolonged itself interminably, and it was almost May when the winds came soft and the snow ran down into Black Bear Lake at last. For the first time in over a year Dexter was enjoying a certain tranquility of spirit. Judy Jones had been in Florida, and afterward in Hot Springs, and somewhere she had been engaged, and somewhere she had broken it off. At first, when Dexter had definitely given her up, it had made him sad that people still linked them together and asked for news of her, but when he began to be placed at dinner next to Irene Scheerer people didn't ask him about her any more — they told him about her. He ceased to be an authority on her.

May at last. Dexter walked the streets at night when the darkness was damp as rain, wondering that so soon, with so little done, so much of ecstasy had gone from him. May one year back had been marked by Judy's poignant, unforgivable, yet forgiven turbulence — it had been one of those rare times when he fancied she had grown to care for him. That old penny's worth of happiness he had spent for this bushel of content. He knew that Irene would be no more than a curtain spread behind him, a hand moving among gleaming tea-cups, a voice calling to chil-. dren . . . fire and loveliness were gone, the magic of nights and the wonder of the varying hours and seasons . . . slender lips, down-turning, dropping to his lips and bearing him up into a heaven of eyes. . . . The thing was deep in him. He was too strong and alive for it to die lightly.

In the middle of May when the weather balanced for a few days on the thin bridge that led to deep summer he turned in one night at Irene's house. Their engagement was to be announced in a week now — no one would be surprised at it. And to-night they would sit together on the lounge at the University Club and look on for an hour at the dancers. It gave him a sense of solidity to go with her — she was so sturdily popular, so intensely "great."

He mounted the steps of the brownstone house and stepped inside.

"Irene," he called.

Mrs. Scheerer came out of the living-room to meet him.

"Dexter," she said, "Irene's gone up-stairs with a splitting headache. She wanted to go with you but I made her go to bed."

"Nothing serious, I——"

"Oh, no. She's going to play golf with you in the morning. You can spare her for just one night, can't you, Dexter?"

Her smile was kind. She and Dexter liked each other. In the living-room he talked for a moment before he said good-night.

Returning to the University Club, where he had rooms, he stood in the doorway for a moment and watched the dancers. He leaned against the door-post, nodded at a man or two — yawned.

"Hello, darling."

The familiar voice at his elbow startled him. Judy Jones had left a man and crossed the room to him — Judy Jones, a slender enamelled doll in cloth of gold: gold in a band at her head, gold in two slipper points at her dress's hem. The fragile glow of her face seemed to blossom as she smiled at him. A breeze of warmth and light blew through the room. His hands in the pockets of his dinner-jacket tightened spasmodically. He was filled with a sudden excitement.

"When did you get back?" he asked casually.

"Come here and I'll tell you about it."

She turned and he followed her. She had been away — he could have wept at the wonder of her return. She had passed through enchanted streets, doing things that were like provocative music. All mysterious happenings, all fresh and quickening hopes, had gone away with her, come back with her now.

She turned in the doorway.

"Have you a car here? If you haven't, I have."

"I have a coupé."

In then, with a rustle of golden cloth. He slammed the door. Into so many cars she had stepped — like this — like that — her back against the leather, so — her elbow resting on the door — waiting. She would have been soiled long since had there been anything to soil her — except herself — but this was her own self outpouring.

With an effort he forced himself to start the car and back into the street. This was nothing, he must remember. She had done this before, and he had put her behind him, as he would have crossed a bad account from his books.

He drove slowly down-town and, affecting abstraction, traversed the deserted streets of the business section, peopled here and there where a movie was giving out its crowd or where consumptive or pugilistic youth lounged in front of pool halls. The clink of glasses and the slap of hands on the bars issued from saloons, cloisters of glazed glass and dirty yellow light.

She was watching him closely and the silence was embarrassing, yet in this crisis he could find no casual word with which to profane the hour. At a convenient turning he began to zigzag back toward the University Club.

"Have you missed me?" she asked suddenly.

"Everybody missed you."

He wondered if she knew of Irene Scheerer. She had been back only a day—her absence had been almost contemporaneous with his engagement.

"What a remark!" Judy laughed sadly—without sadness. She looked at him searchingly. He became absorbed in the dashboard.

"You're handsomer than you used to be," she said thoughtfully. "Dexter, you have the most rememberable eyes."

He could have laughed at this, but he did not laugh. It was the sort of thing that was said to sophomores. Yet it stabbed at him.

"I'm awfully tired of everything, darling." She called every one darling, endowing the endearment with careless, individual comraderie. "I wish you'd marry me."

The directness of this confused him. He should have told her now that he was going to marry another girl, but he could not tell her. He could as easily have sworn that he had never loved her.

"I think we'd get along," she continued, on the same note, "unless probably you've forgotten me and fallen in love with another girl."

Her confidence was obviously enormous. She had said, in effect, that she found such a thing impossible to believe, that if it were true he had merely committed a childish indiscretion—and probably to show off. She would forgive him, because it was not a matter of any moment but rather something to be brushed aside lightly.

"Of course you could never love anybody but me," she continued. "I like the way you love me. Oh, Dexter, have you forgotten last year?"

"No, I haven't forgotten."

"Neither have I!"

Was she sincerely moved—or was she carried along by the wave of her own acting?

"I wish we could be like that again," she said, and he forced himself to answer:

127

"I don't think we can."

"I suppose not. . . . I hear you're giving Irene Scheerer a violent rush."

There was not the faintest emphasis on the name, yet Dexter was suddenly ashamed.

"Oh, take me home," cried Judy suddenly; "I don't want to go back to that idiotic dance — with those children."

Then, as he turned up the street that led to the residence district, Judy began to cry quietly to herself. He had never seen her cry before.

The dark street lightened, the dwellings of the rich loomed up around them, he stopped his coupé in front of the great white bulk of the Mortimer Joneses house, somnolent, gorgeous, drenched with the splendor of the damp moonlight. Its solidity startled him. The strong walls, the steel of the girders, the breadth and beam and pomp of it were there only to bring out the contrast with the young beauty beside him. It was sturdy to accentuate her slightness — as if to show what a breeze could be generated by a butterfly's wing.

He sat perfectly quiet, his nerves in wild clamor, afraid that if he moved he would find her irresistibly in his arms. Two tears had rolled down her wet face and trembled on her upper lip.

"I'm more beautiful than anybody else," she said brokenly, "why can't I be happy?" Her moist eyes tore at his stability — her mouth turned slowly downward with an exquisite sadness: "I'd like to marry you if you'll have me, Dexter. I suppose you think I'm not worth having, but I'll be so beautiful for you, Dexter."

A million phrases of anger, pride, passion, hatred, tenderness fought on his lips. Then a perfect wave of emotion washed over him, carrying off with it a sediment of wisdom, of convention, of doubt, of honor. This was his girl who was speaking, his own, his beautiful, his pride.

"Won't you come in?" He heard her draw in her breath sharply. Waiting.

"All right," his voice was trembling, "I'll come in."

V
· · · · ·

It was strange that neither when it was over nor a long time afterward did he regret that night. Looking at it from the perspective of ten years, the fact that Judy's flare for him endured just one month seemed of little importance. Nor did it matter that by his yielding he subjected himself to a deeper agony in the end and gave serious hurt to Irene Scheerer and to Irene's parents, who had befriended him. There was nothing sufficiently pictorial about Irene's grief to stamp itself on his mind.

Dexter was at bottom hard-minded. The attitude of the city on his action was of no importance to him, not because he was going to leave the city, but because any outside attitude on the situation seemed superficial. He was completely indifferent to popular opinion. Nor, when he had seen that it was no use, that he did not possess in himself the power to move fundamentally or to hold Judy Jones, did he bear any malice toward her. He loved her, and he would love her until the day he was too old for loving — but he could not have her. So he tasted the deep pain that is reserved only for the strong, just as he had tasted for a little while the deep happiness.

Even the ultimate falsity of the grounds upon which Judy terminated the engagement, that she did not want to "take him away" from Irene — Judy, who had wanted nothing else — did not revolt him. He was beyond any revulsion or any amusement.

He went East in February with the intention of selling out his laundries and settling in New York — but the war came to America in March and changed his plans. He returned to the West, handed over the management of the business to his partner, and went into the first officers' training-camp in late April. He was one of those young thousands who greeted the war with a certain amount of relief, welcoming the liberation from webs of tangled emotion.

VI
· · · · ·

This story is not his biography, remember, although things creep into it which have nothing to do with those dreams he had when he was young. We are almost done with them and with him now. There is only one more incident to be related here, and it happens seven years farther on.

It took place in New York, where he had done well—so well that there were no barriers too high for him. He was thirty-two years old, and, except for one flying trip immediately after the war, he had not been West in seven years. A man named Devlin from Detroit came into his office to see him in a business way, and then and there this incident occurred, and closed out, so to speak, this particular side of his life.

"So you're from the Middle West," said the man Devlin with careless curiosity. "That's funny—I thought men like you were probably born and raised on Wall Street. You know—wife of one of my best friends in Detroit came from your city. I was an usher at the wedding."

Dexter waited with no apprehension of what was coming.

"Judy Simms," said Devlin with no particular interest; "Judy Jones she was once."

"Yes, I knew her." A dull impatience spread over him. He had heard, of course, that she was married—perhaps deliberately he had heard no more.

"Awfully nice girl," brooded Devlin meaninglessly, "I'm sort of sorry for her."

"Why?" Something in Dexter was alert, receptive, at once.

"Oh, Lud Simms has gone to pieces in a way. I don't mean he ill-uses her, but he drinks and runs around——"

"Doesn't she run around?"

"No. Stays at home with her kids."

"Oh."

"She's a little too old for him," said Devlin.

"Too old!" cried Dexter. "Why, man, she's only twenty-seven."

He was possessed with a wild notion of rushing out into the streets and taking a train to Detroit. He rose to his feet spasmodically.

"I guess you're busy," Devlin apologized quickly. "I didn't realize——"

"No, I'm not busy," said Dexter, steadying his voice. "I'm not busy at all. Not busy at all. Did you say she was—twenty-seven? No, I said she was twenty-seven."

"Yes, you did," agreed Devlin dryly.

"Go on, then. Go on."

"What do you mean?"

"About Judy Jones."

Devlin looked at him helplessly.

"Well, that's—I told you all there is to it. He treats her like the devil. Oh, they're not going to get divorced or anything. When he's particularly outrageous she forgives him. In fact, I'm inclined to think she loves him. She was a pretty girl when she first came to Detroit."

A pretty girl! The phrase struck Dexter as ludicrous.

"Isn't she—a pretty girl, any more?"

"Oh, she's all right."

"Look here," said Dexter, sitting down suddenly, "I don't understand. You say she was a 'pretty girl' and now you say she's 'all right.' I don't understand what you mean—Judy Jones wasn't a pretty girl, at all. She was a great beauty. Why, I knew her, I knew her. She was——"

Devlin laughed pleasantly.

"I'm not trying to start a row," he said. "I think Judy's a nice girl and I like her. I can't understand how a man like Lud Simms could fall madly in love with her, but he did." Then he added: "Most of the women like her."

Dexter looked closely at Devlin, thinking wildly that there must be a reason for this, some insensitivity in the man or some private malice.

"Lots of women fade just like that," Devlin snapped his fingers. "You must have seen it happen. Perhaps I've forgotten how pretty she was at her wedding. I've seen her so much since then, you see. She has nice eyes."

A sort of dulness settled down upon Dexter. For the first time in his life he felt like getting very drunk. He knew that he was laughing loudly at something Devlin had said, but he did not know what it was or why it was funny. When, in a few minutes, Devlin went he lay down on his lounge and looked out the window at the New York sky-line into which the sun was sinking in dull lovely shades of pink and gold.

He had thought that having nothing else to lose he was invulnerable at last—but he knew that he had just lost something more, as surely as if he had married Judy Jones and seen her fade away before his eyes.

The dream was gone. Something had been taken from him. In a sort of panic he pushed the palms of his hands into his eyes and tried to bring up a picture of the waters lapping on Sherry Island and the moonlit veranda, and gingham on the golf-links and the dry sun and the gold color of her neck's soft down. And her mouth damp to his kisses and her eyes plaintive with melancholy and her freshness like new fine linen in the morning. Why, these things were no longer in the world! They had existed and they existed no longer.

For the first time in years the tears were streaming down his face. But they were for himself now. He did not care about mouth and eyes and moving hands. He wanted to care, and he could not care. For he had gone away and he could never go back any more. The gates were closed, the sun was gone down, and there was no beauty but the gray beauty of steel that withstands all time. Even the grief he could have borne was left behind in the country of illusion, of youth, of the richness of life, where his winter dreams had flourished.

"Long ago," he said, "long ago, there was something in me, but now that thing is gone. Now that thing is gone, that thing is gone. I cannot cry. I cannot care. That thing will come back no more."

A SHORT TRIP HOME

Fitzgerald wrote "A Short Trip Home" in October 1927 while living in Delaware. He was trying to earn money to work on his fourth novel, which would become Tender Is the Night, *after the disappointing sales of* The Great Gatsby. *It was the only one of Fitzgerald's supernatural stories to be published in the* Post. *Although Lorimer, the* Post *editor, rarely purchased genre fiction of this kind, the story earned Fitzgerald $3,500 (equal to over $36,000 in 2004) and was the featured selection in the issue it appeared. The story includes a description of the neighborhood around Seven Corners, still one of St. Paul's best-known intersections. Fitzgerald credited Booth Tarkington, another Princeton man, as a literary model for his fiction. But while Tarkington shied away from adolescent sexuality, Fitzgerald took up the challenge in this story.*

The Saturday Evening Post, December 17, 1927
Collected in *Taps at Reveille* (1935)

I
. . . . .

I WAS NEAR HER, for I had lingered behind in order to get the short walk with her from the living room to the front door. That was a lot, for she had flowered suddenly and I, being a man and only a year older, hadn't flowered at all, had scarcely dared to come near her in the week we'd been home. Nor was I going to say anything in that walk of ten feet, or touch her; but I had a vague hope she'd do something, give a gay little performance of some sort, personal only in so far as we were alone together.

She had bewitchment suddenly in the twinkle of short hairs on her neck, in the sure, clear confidence that at about eighteen begins to deepen and sing in attractive American girls. The lamp light shopped in the yellow strands of her hair.

Already she was sliding into another world — the world of Joe Jelke and Jim Catcher waiting for us now in the car. In another year she would pass beyond me forever.

As I waited, feeling the others outside in the snowy night, feeling the excitement of Christmas week and the excitement of Ellen here, blooming away, filling the room with "sex appeal" — a wretched phrase to express a quality that isn't like that at all — a maid came in from the dining room, spoke to Ellen quietly and handed her a note. Ellen read it and her eyes faded down, as when the current grows weak on rural circuits, and smouldered off into space. Then she gave me an odd look — in which I probably didn't show — and without a word, followed the maid into the dining room and beyond. I sat turning over the pages of a magazine for a quarter of an hour.

Joe Jelke came in, red-faced from the cold, his white silk muffler gleaming at the neck of his fur coat. He was a senior at New Haven, I was a sophomore. He was prominent, a member of Scroll and Keys, and, in my eyes, very distinguished and handsome.

"Isn't Ellen coming?"

"I don't know," I answered discreetly. "She was all ready."

"Ellen!" he called. "Ellen!"

He had left the front door open behind him and a great cloud of frosty air rolled in from outside. He went halfway up the stairs — he was a familiar in the house — and called again, till Mrs. Baker came to the banister and said that Ellen was below. Then the maid, a little excited, appeared in the dining-room door.

"Mr. Jelke," she called in a low voice.

Joe's face fell as he turned toward her, sensing bad news.

"Miss Ellen says for you to go on to the party. She'll come later."

"What's the matter?"

"She can't come now. She'll come later."

He hesitated, confused. It was the last big dance of vacation, and he was mad about Ellen. He had tried to give her a ring for Christmas, and failing that, got her to accept a gold mesh bag that must have cost two hundred dollars. He wasn't the only one — there were three or four in the same wild condition, and all in the ten days she'd been home — but his chance came first, for he was rich and gracious and at that moment the "desirable" boy of St. Paul. To me it seemed impossible that she could prefer another, but the rumor was she'd described Joe as much too perfect. I suppose he lacked mystery for her, and when a man is up against that with a young girl who isn't thinking of the practical side of marriage yet — well———.

"She's in the kitchen," Joe said angrily.

"No, she's not." The maid was defiant and a little scared.

"She is."

"She went out the back way, Mr. Jelke."

"I'm going to see."

I followed him. The Swedish servants washing dishes looked up sideways at our approach and an interested crashing of pans marked our passage through. The storm door, unbolted, was flapping in the wind and as we walked out into the snowy yard we saw the tail light of a car turn the corner at the end of the back alley.

"I'm going after her," Joe said slowly. "I don't understand this at all."

I was too awed by the calamity to argue. We hurried to his car and drove in a fruitless, despairing zigzag all over the residence section, peering into every machine on the streets. It was half an hour before the futility of the affair began to dawn upon him—St. Paul is a city of almost three hundred thousand people—and Jim Cathcart reminded him that we had another girl to stop for. Like a wounded animal he sank into a melancholy mass of fur in the corner, from which position he jerked upright every few minutes and waved himself backward and forward a little in protest and despair.

Jim's girl was ready and impatient, but after what had happened her impatience didn't seem important. She looked lovely though. That's one thing about Christmas vacation—the excitement of growth and change and adventure in foreign parts transforming the people you've known all your life. Joe Jelke was polite to her in a daze—he indulged in one burst of short, loud, harsh laughter by way of conversation—and we drove to the hotel.

The chauffeur approached it on the wrong side—the side on which the line of cars was not putting forth guests—and because of that we came suddenly upon Ellen Baker just getting out of a small coupé. Even before we came to a stop, Joe Jelke had jumped excitedly from the car.

Ellen turned toward us, a faintly distracted look—perhaps of surprise, but certainly not of alarm—in her face; in fact, she didn't seem very aware of us. Joe approached her with a stern, dignified, injured and, I thought, just exactly correct reproof in his expression. I followed.

Seated in the coupé—he had not dismounted to help Ellen out—was a hard thin-faced man of about thirty-five with an air of being scarred, and a slight sinister smile. His eyes were a sort of taunt to the whole human family—they were the eyes of an animal, sleepy and quiescent in the presence of another species. They were helpless yet brutal, unhopeful yet confident. It was as if they felt themselves powerless to originate activity, but infinitely capable of profiting by a single gesture of weakness in another.

Vaguely I placed him as one of the sort of men whom I had been conscious of from my earliest youth as "hanging around" — leaning with one elbow on the counters of tobacco stores, watching, through heaven knows what small chink of the mind, the people who hurried in and out. Intimate to garages, where he had vague business conducted in undertones, to barber shops, and to the lobbies of theatres — in such places, anyhow, I placed the type, if type it was, that he reminded me of. Sometimes his face bobbed up in one of Tad's more savage cartoons, and I had always from earliest boyhood thrown a nervous glance toward the dim borderland where he stood, and seen him watching me and despising me. Once, in a dream, he had taken a few steps toward me, jerking his head back and muttering: "Say, kid" in what was intended to be a reassuring voice, and I had broken for the door in terror. This was that sort of man.

Joe and Ellen faced each other silently; she seemed, as I have said, to be in a daze. It was cold, but she didn't notice that her coat had blown open; Joe reached out and pulled it together, and automatically she clutched it with her hand.

Suddenly the man in the coupé, who had been watching them silently, laughed. It was a bare laugh, done with the breath — just a noisy jerk of the head — but it was an insult if I had ever heard one; definite and not to be passed over. I wasn't surprised when Joe, who was quick tempered, turned to him angrily and said:

"What's your trouble?"

The man waited a moment, his eyes shifting and yet staring, and always seeing. Then he laughed again in the same way. Ellen stirred uneasily.

"Who is this — this——" Joe's voice trembled with annoyance.

"Look out now," said the man slowly.

Joe turned to me.

"Eddie, take Ellen and Catherine in, will you?" he said quickly. . . . "Ellen, go with Eddie."

"Look out now," the man repeated.

Ellen made a little sound with her tongue and teeth, but she didn't resist when I took her arm and moved her toward the side door of the hotel. It struck me as odd that she should be so helpless, even to the point of acquiescing by her silence in this imminent trouble.

"Let it go, Joe!" I called back over my shoulder. "Come inside!"

Ellen, pulling against my arm, hurried us on. As we were caught up into the swinging doors I had the impression that the man was getting out of his coupé.

Ten minutes later, as I waited for the girls outside the women's dressing-room, Joe Jelke and Jim Cathcart stepped out of the elevator. Joe was very white, his eyes were heavy and glazed, there was a trickle of dark blood on his forehead and on his white muffler. Jim had both their hats in his hand.

"He hit Joe with brass knuckles," Jim said in a low voice. "Joe was out cold for a minute or so. I wish you'd send a bell boy for some witch-hazel and court-plaster."

It was late and the hall was deserted; brassy fragments of the dance below reached us as if heavy curtains were being blown aside and dropping back into place. When Ellen came out I took her directly downstairs. We avoided the receiving line and went into a dim room set with scraggly hotel palms where couples sometimes sat out during the dance; there I told her what had happened.

"It was Joe's own fault," she said, surprisingly. "I told him not to interfere."

This wasn't true. She had said nothing, only uttered one curious little click of impatience.

"You ran out the back door and disappeared for almost an hour," I protested. "Then you turned up with a hard-looking customer who laughed in Joe's face."

"A hard-looking customer," she repeated, as if tasting the sound of the words.

"Well, wasn't he? Where on earth did you get hold of him, Ellen?"

"On the train," she answered. Immediately she seemed to regret this admission. "You'd better stay out of things that aren't your business, Eddie. You see what happened to Joe."

Literally I gasped. To watch her, seated beside me, immaculately glowing, her body giving off wave after wave of freshness and delicacy—and to hear her talk like that.

"But that man's a thug!" I cried. "No girl could be safe with him. He used brass knuckles on Joe—brass knuckles!"

"Is that pretty bad?"

She asked this as she might have asked such a question a few years ago. She looked at me at last and really wanted an answer; for a moment it was as if she were trying to recapture an attitude that had almost departed; then she hardened again. I say "hardened," for I began to notice that when she was concerned with this man her eyelids fell a little, shutting other things—everything else—out of view.

That was a moment I might have said something, I suppose, but in spite of everything, I couldn't light into her. I was too much under the spell of her beauty and its success. I even began to find excuses for her—perhaps that man wasn't what he appeared to be; or perhaps—more romantically—she was involved with him against her will to shield some one else. At this point people began to drift into the room and come up to speak to us. We couldn't talk any more, so we went in and bowed to the chaperones. Then I gave her up to the bright restless sea of the dance, where she moved in an eddy of her own among the pleasant islands of colored favors set out on tables and the south winds from the brasses moaning across the hall. After a while I saw Joe Jelke sitting in a corner with a strip of court-plaster on his forehead watching Ellen as if she herself had struck him down, but I didn't go up to him. I felt queer myself—like I feel when I wake up after sleeping through an afternoon, strange and portentous, as if something had gone on in the interval that changed the values of everything and that I didn't see.

The night slipped on through successive phases of cardboard horns, amateur tableaux, and flashlights for the morning papers. Then was the grand march and supper, and about two o'clock some of the committee, dressed up as revenue agents, pinched the party, and a facetious newspaper was distributed, burlesquing the events of the evening. And all the time out of the corner of my eye I watched the shining orchid on Ellen's shoulder as it moved like Stuart's plume about the room. I watched it with a definite foreboding until the last sleepy groups had crowded into the elevators, and then, bundled to the eyes in great shapeless fur coats, drifted out into the clear dry Minnesota night.

II
. . . . .

There is a sloping mid-section of our city which lies between the residence quarter on the hill and the business district on the level of the river. It is a vague part of town, broken by its climb into triangles and odd shapes—there are names like Seven Corners—and I don't believe a dozen people could draw an accurate map of it, though every one traversed it by trolley, auto, or shoe leather twice a day. And though it was a busy section, it would be hard for me to name the business that comprised its activity. There were always long lines of trolley cars waiting to start somewhere; there was a big movie theatre and many small ones with posters of Hoot Gibson and Wonder Dogs and Wonder Horses outside; there were small stores with "Old King Brady" and "The Liberty Boys of '76" in the windows, and marbles, cigarettes, and candy inside; and—one definite place at least—a fancy costumer whom we all visited at least once a year. Some time during boyhood I became aware that one side of a certain obscure street there were bawdy houses, and all through the district were pawnshops, cheap jewellers, small athletic clubs and gymnasiums, and somewhat too blatantly run-down saloons.

The morning after the Cotillion Club party, I woke up late and lazy, with the happy feeling that for a day or two more there was no chapel, no classes — nothing to do but wait for another party tonight. It was crisp and bright — one of those days when you forget how cold it is until your cheek freezes — and the events of the evening before seemed dim and far away. After luncheon I started downtown on foot through a light, pleasant snow of small flakes that would probably fall all afternoon, and I was about half through that halfway section of town — so far as I know, there's no inclusive name for it — when suddenly whatever idle thought was in my head blew away like a hat and I began thinking hard of Ellen Baker. I began worrying about her as I'd never worried about anything outside myself before. I began to loiter, with an instinct to go up on the hill again and find her and talk to her; then I remembered that she was at tea, and I went on again, but still thinking of her, and harder than ever. Right then the affair opened up again.

It was snowing, I said, and it was four o'clock on a December afternoon, when there is a promise of darkness in the air and the street lamps are just going on. I passed a combination pool parlor and restaurant, with a stove loaded with hot-dogs in the window, and a few loungers hanging around the door. The lights were on inside — not bright lights but just a few pale yellow high up on the ceiling — and the glow they threw out into the frosty dusk wasn't bright enough to tempt you to stare inside. As I went past, thinking hard of Ellen all this time, I took in the quartet of loafers out of the corner of my eye. I hadn't gone half a dozen steps down the street when one of them called to me, not by name but in a way clearly intended for my ear. I thought it was a tribute to my raccoon coat and paid no attention, but a moment later whoever it was called to me again in a peremptory voice. I was annoyed and turned around. There, standing in the group not ten feet away and looking at me with the half-sneer on his face with which he'd looked at Joe Jelke, was the scarred, thin-faced man of the night before.

He had on a black fancy-cut coat, buttoned up to his neck as if he were cold. His hands were deep in his pockets and he wore a derby and high button shoes. I was startled, and for a moment I hesitated, but I was most of all angry, and knowing that I was quicker with my hands than Joe Jelke, I took a tentative step back toward him. The other men weren't looking at me — I don't think they saw me at all — but I knew that this one recognized me; there was nothing casual about his look, no mistake.

"Here I am. What are you going to do about it?" his eyes seemed to say.

I took another step toward him and he laughed soundlessly, but with active contempt, and drew back into the group. I followed. I was going to speak to him — I wasn't sure what I was going to say — but when I came up he had either changed his mind and backed off, or else he wanted me to follow him inside, for he had slipped off and the three men watched my intent approach without curiosity. They were the same kind — sporty, but, unlike him, smooth rather than truculent; I didn't find any personal malice in their collective glance.

"Did he go inside?" I asked.

They looked at one another in that cagy way; a wink passed between them, and after a perceptible pause, one said:

"Who go inside?"

"I don't know his name."

There was another wink. Annoyed and determined, I walked past them and into the pool room. There were a few people at a lunch counter along one side and a few more playing billiards, but he was not among them.

Again I hesitated. If his idea was to lead me into any blind part of the establishment — there were some half-open doors farther back—I wanted more support. I went up to the man at the desk.

"What became of the fellow who just walked in here?"

Was he on his guard immediately, or was that my imagination?

"What fellow?"

"Thin face—derby hat."

"How long ago?"

"Oh—a minute."

He shook his head again. "Didn't see him," he said.

I waited. The three men from outside had come in and were lined up beside me at the counter. I felt that all of them were looking at me in a peculiar way. Feeling helpless and increasingly uneasy, I turned suddenly and went out. A little way down the street I turned again and took a good look at the place, so I'd know it and could find it again. On the next corner I broke impulsively into a run, found a taxicab in front of the hotel, and drove back up the hill.

Ellen wasn't home. Mrs. Baker came downstairs and talked to me. She seemed entirely cheerful and proud of Ellen's beauty, and ignorant of anything being amiss or of anything unusual having taken place the night before. She was glad that vacation was almost over—it was a strain and Ellen wasn't very strong. Then she said something that relieved my mind enormously. She was glad that I had come in, for of course Ellen would want to see me, and the time was so short. She was going back at half-past eight tonight.

"Tonight!" I exclaimed. "I thought it was the day after tomorrow."

"She's going to visit the Brokaws in Chicago," Mrs. Baker said. "They want her for some party. We just decided it today. She's leaving with the Ingersoll girls tonight."

I was so glad I could barely restrain myself from shaking her hand. Ellen was safe. It had been nothing all along but a moment of the most casual adventure. I felt like an idiot, but I realized how much I cared about Ellen and how little I could endure anything terrible happening to her.

"She'll be in soon?"

"Any minute now. She just phoned from the University Club."

I said I'd be over later—I lived almost next door and I wanted to be alone. Outside I remembered I didn't have a key, so I started up the Bakers' driveway to take the old cut we used in childhood through the intervening yard. It was still snowing, but the flakes were bigger now against the darkness, and trying to locate the buried walk I noticed that the Bakers' back door was ajar.

I scarcely know why I turned and walked into that kitchen. There was a time when I would have known the Bakers' servants by name. That wasn't true now, but they knew me, and I was aware of a sudden suspension as I came in—not only a suspension of talk but of some mood or expectation that had filled them. They began to go to work too quickly; they made unnecessary movements and clamor—those three. The parlor maid looked at me in a frightened way and I suddenly guessed she was waiting to deliver another message. I beckoned her into the pantry.

"I know all about this," I said. "It's a very serious business. Shall I go to Mrs. Baker now, or will you shut and lock that back door?"

"Don't tell Mrs. Baker, Mr. Stinson!"

"Then I don't want Miss Ellen disturbed. If she is—and if she is I'll know of it——" I delivered some outrageous threat about going to all the employment agencies and seeing she never got another job in the city. She was thoroughly intimidated when I went out; it wasn't a minute before the back door was locked and bolted behind me.

Simultaneously I heard a big car drive up in front, chains crunching on the soft snow; it was bringing Ellen home, and I went in to say good-by.

Joe Jelke and two other boys were along, and none of the three could manage to take their eyes off her, even to say hello to me.

She had one of those exquisite rose skins frequent in our part of the country, and beautiful until the little veins begin to break at about forty; now, flushed with the cold, it was a riot of lovely delicate pinks like many carnations. She and Joe had reached some sort of reconciliation, or at least he was too far gone in love to remember last night; but I saw that though she laughed a lot she wasn't really paying any attention to him or any of them. She wanted them to go, so that there'd be a message from the kitchen, but I knew that the message wasn't coming — that she was safe. There was talk of the Pump and Slipper dance at New Haven and of the Princeton Prom, and then, in various moods, we four left and separated quickly outside. I walked home with a certain depression of spirit and lay for an hour in a hot bath thinking that vacation was all over for me now that she was gone; feeling, even more deeply than I had yesterday, that she was out of my life.

And something eluded me, some one more thing to do, something that I had lost amid the events of the afternoon, promising myself to go back and pick it up, only to find that it had escaped me. I associated it vaguely with Mrs. Baker, and now I seemed to recall that it had poked up its head somewhere in the stream of conversation with her. In my relief about Ellen I had forgotten to ask her a question regarding something she had said.

The Brokaws — that was it — where Ellen was to visit. I knew Bill Brokaw well; he was in my class at Yale. Then I remembered and sat bolt upright in the tub — the Brokaws weren't in Chicago this Christmas; they were at Palm Beach!

Dripping I sprang out of the tub, threw an insufficient union suit around my shoulders, and sprang for the phone in my room. I got the connection quick, but Miss Ellen had already started for the train.

Luckily our car was in, and while I squirmed, still damp, into my clothes, the chauffeur brought it around to the door. The night was cold and dry, and we made good time to the station through the hard, crusty snow. I felt queer and insecure starting out this way, but somehow more confident as the station loomed up bright and new against the dark, cold air. For fifty years my family had owned the land on which it was built and that made my temerity seem all right somehow. There was always a possibility that I was rushing in where angels feared to tread, but that sense of having a solid foothold in the past made me willing to make a fool of myself. This business was all wrong — terribly wrong. Any idea I had entertained that it was harmless dropped away now; between Ellen and some vague overwhelming catastrophe there stood me, or else the police and a scandal. I'm no moralist — there was another element here, dark and frightening, and I didn't want Ellen to go through it alone.

There are three competing trains from St. Paul to Chicago that all leave within a few minutes of half-past eight. Hers was the Burlington, and as I ran across the station I saw the grating being pulled over and the light above it go out. I knew, though, that she had a drawing-room with the Ingersoll girls, because her mother had mentioned buying the ticket, so she was, literally speaking, tucked in until tomorrow.

The C., M. & St. P. gate was down at the other end and I raced for it and made it. I had forgotten one thing, though, and that was enough to keep me awake and worried half the night. This train got into Chicago ten minutes after the other. Ellen had that much time to disappear into one of the largest cities in the world.

I gave the porter a wire to my family to send from Milwaukee, and at eight o'clock next morning I pushed violently by a whole line of passengers, clamoring over their bags parked in the vestibule, and shot out of the door with a sort of scramble over the porter's back. For a moment the confusion of a great station, the voluminous sounds and echoes and cross-currents of bells and smoke struck me helpless. Then I dashed for the exit and toward the only chance I knew of finding her.

I had guessed right. She was standing at the telegraph counter, sending off heaven knows what black lie to her mother, and her expression when she saw me had a sort of terror mixed up with its surprise. There was cunning in it too. She was thinking quickly — she would have liked to walk away from me as if I weren't there, and go about her own business, but she couldn't. I was too matter-of-fact a thing in her life. So we stood silently watching each other and each thinking hard.

"The Brokaws are in Florida," I said after a minute.

"It was nice of you to take such a long trip to tell me that."

"Since you've found it out, don't you think you'd better go on to school?"

"Please let me alone, Eddie," she said.

"I'll go as far as New York with you. I've decided to go back early myself."

"You'd better let me alone." Her lovely eyes narrowed and her face took on a look of dumb-animal-like resistance. She made a visible effort, the cunning flickered back into it, then both were gone, and in their stead was a cheerful reassuring smile that all but convinced me.

"Eddie, you silly child, don't you think I'm old enough to take care of myself?" I didn't answer. "I'm going to meet a man, you understand. I just want to see him today. I've got my ticket East on the five o'clock train. If you don't believe it, here it is in my bag."

"I believe you."

"The man isn't anybody that you know and — frankly, I think you're being awfully fresh and impossible."

"I know who the man is."

Again she lost control of her face. That terrible expression came back into it and she spoke with almost a snarl:

"You'd better let me alone."

I took the blank out of her hand and wrote out an explanatory telegram to her mother. Then I turned to Ellen and said a little roughly:

"We'll take the five o'clock train East together. Meanwhile you're going to spend the day with me."

The mere sound of my own voice saying this so emphatically encouraged me, and I think it impressed her too; at any rate, she submitted — at least temporarily — and came along without protest while I bought my ticket.

When I start to piece together the fragments of that day a sort of confusion begins, as if my memory didn't want to yield up any of it, or my consciousness let any of it pass through. There was a bright, fierce morning during which we rode about in a taxicab and went to a department store where Ellen said she wanted to buy something and then tried to slip away from me by a back way. I had the feeling, for an hour, that someone was following us along Lake Shore Drive in a taxicab, and I would try to catch them by turning quickly or looking suddenly into the chauffeur's mirror; but I could find no one, and when I turned back I could see that Ellen's face was contorted with mirthless, unnatural laughter.

All morning there was a raw, bleak wind off the lake, but when we went to the Blackstone for lunch a light snow came down past the windows and we talked almost naturally about our friends, and about casual things. Suddenly her tone changed; she grew serious and looked me in the eye, straight and sincere.

"Eddie, you're the oldest friend I have," she said, "and you oughtn't to find it too hard to trust me. If I promise you faithfully on my word of honor to catch that five o'clock train, will you let me alone a few hours this afternoon?"

"Why?"

"Well" — she hesitated and hung her head a little — "I guess everybody has a right to say — good-by."

"You want to say good-by to that——"

"Yes, yes," she said hastily; "just a few hours, Eddie, and I promise faithfully that I'll be on that train."

"Well, I suppose no great harm could be done in two hours. If you really want to say good-by——"

I looked up suddenly, and surprised a look of such tense cunning in her face that I winced before it. Her lip was curled up and her eyes were slits again; there wasn't the faintest touch of fairness and sincerity in her whole face.

We argued. The argument was vague on her part and somewhat hard and reticent on mine. I wasn't going to be cajoled again into any weakness or be infected with any—and there was a contagion of evil in the air. She kept trying to imply, without any convincing evidence to bring forward, that everything was all right. Yet she was too full of the thing itself—whatever it was—to build up a real story, and she wanted to catch at any credulous and acquiescent train of thought that might start in my head, and work that for all it was worth. After every reassuring suggestion she threw out, she stared at me eagerly, as if she hoped I'd launch into a comfortable moral lecture with the customary sweet at the end—which in this case would be her liberty. But I was wearing her away a little. Two or three times it needed just a touch of pressure to bring her to the point of tears—which, of course, was what I wanted—but I couldn't seem to manage it. Almost I had her—almost possessed her interior attention—then she would slip away.

I bullied her remorselessly into a taxi about four o'clock and started for the station. The wind was raw again, with a sting of snow in it, and the people in the streets, waiting for busses and street cars too small to take them all in, looked cold and disturbed and unhappy. I tried to think how lucky we were to be comfortably off and taken care of, but all the warm, respectable world I had been part of yesterday had dropped away from me. There was something we carried with us now that was the enemy and the opposite of all that; it was in the cabs beside us, the streets we passed through. With a touch of panic, I wondered if I wasn't slipping almost imperceptibly into Ellen's attitude of mind. The column of passengers waiting to go aboard the train were as remote from me as people from another world, but it was I that was drifting away and leaving them behind.

My lower was in the same car with her compartment. It was an old-fashioned car, its lights somewhat dim, its carpets and uphol-stery full of the dust of another generation. There were half a dozen other travellers, but they made no special impression on me, except that they shared the unreality that I was beginning to feel everywhere around me. We went into Ellen's compartment, shut the door, and sat down.

Suddenly I put my arms around her and drew her over to me, just as tenderly as I knew how — as if she were a little girl — as she was. She resisted a little, but after a moment she submitted and lay tense and rigid in my arms.

"Ellen," I said helplessly, "you asked me to trust you. You have much more reason to trust me. Wouldn't it help to get rid of all this, if you told me a little?"

"I can't," she said, very low — "I mean, there's nothing to tell."

"You met this man on the train coming home and you fell in love with him, isn't that true?"

"I don't know."

"Tell me, Ellen. You fell in love with him?"

"I don't know. Please let me alone."

"Call it anything you want," I went on, "he has some sort of hold over you. He's trying to use you; he's trying to get something from you. He's not in love with you."

"What does that matter?" she said in a weak voice.

"It does matter. Instead of trying to fight this — this thing — you're trying to fight me. And I love you, Ellen. Do you hear? I'm telling you all of a sudden, but it isn't new with me. I love you."

She looked at me with a sneer on her gentle face; it was an ex-pression I had seen on men who were tight and didn't want to be taken home. But it was human. I was reaching her, faintly and from far away, but more than before.

"Ellen, I want you to answer me one question. Is he going to be on this train?"

She hesitated; then, an instant too late, she shook her head.

"Be careful, Ellen. Now I'm going to ask you one thing more, and I wish you'd try very hard to answer. Coming West, when did this man get on the train?"

"I don't know," she said with an effort.

Just at that moment I became aware, with the unquestionable knowledge reserved for facts, that he was just outside the door. She knew it, too; the blood left her face and that expression of low-animal perspicacity came creeping back. I lowered my face into my hands and tried to think.

We must have sat there, with scarcely a word, for well over an hour. I was conscious that the lights of Chicago, then of Englewood and of endless suburbs, were moving by, and then there were no more lights and we were out on the dark flatness of Illinois. The train seemed to draw in upon itself; it took on an air of being alone. The porter knocked at the door and asked if he could make up the berth, but I said no and he went away.

After a while I convinced myself that the struggle inevitably coming wasn't beyond what remained of my sanity, my faith in the essential all-rightness of things and people. That this person's purpose was what we call "criminal," I took for granted, but there was no need of ascribing to him an intelligence that belonged to a higher plane of human, or inhuman, endeavor. It was still as a man that I considered him, and tried to get at his essence, his self-interest — what took the place in him of a comprehensible heart — but I suppose I more than half knew what I would find when I opened the door.

When I stood up Ellen didn't seem to see me at all. She was hunched into the corner staring straight ahead with a sort of film over her eyes, as if she were in a state of suspended animation of body and mind. I lifted her and put two pillows under her head and threw my fur coat over her knees. Then I knelt beside her and kissed her two hands, opened the door, and went out into the hall.

I closed the door behind me and stood with my back against it for a minute. The car was dark save for the corridor lights at each end. There was no sound except the groaning of the couplers, the even click-a-click of the rails, and someone's loud sleeping breath farther down the car. I became aware after a moment that the figure of a man was standing by the water cooler just outside the men's smoking room, his derby hat on his head, his coat collar turned up around his neck as if he were cold, his hands in his coat pockets. When I saw him, he turned and went into the smoking room, and I followed. He was sitting in the far corner of the long leather bench; I took the single armchair beside the door.

As I went in I nodded to him and he acknowledged my presence with one of those terrible soundless laughs of his. But this time it was prolonged, it seemed to go on forever, and mostly to cut it short, I asked: "Where are you from?" in a voice I tried to make casual.

He stopped laughing and looked at me narrowly, wondering what my game was. When he decided to answer, his voice was muffled as though he were speaking through a silk scarf, and it seemed to come from a long way off.

"I'm from St. Paul, Jack."

"Been making a trip home?"

He nodded. Then he took a long breath and spoke in a hard, menacing voice:

"You better get off at Fort Wayne, Jack."

He was dead. He was dead as hell — he had been dead all along, but what force had flowed through him, like blood in his veins, out to St. Paul and back, was leaving him now. A new outline — the outline of him dead — was coming through the palpable figure that had knocked down Joe Jelke.

He spoke again, with a sort of jerking effort:

"You get off at Fort Wayne, Jack, or I'm going to wipe you out." He moved his hand in his coat pocket and showed me the outline of a revolver.

I shook my head. "You can't touch me," I answered. "You see, I know." His terrible eyes shifted over me quickly, trying to determine whether or not I did know. Then he gave a snarl and made as though he were going to jump to his feet.

"You climb off here or else I'm going to get you, Jack!" he cried hoarsely. The train was slowing up for Fort Wayne and his voice rang loud in the comparative quiet, but he didn't move from his chair—he was too weak, I think—and we sat staring at each other while workmen passed up and down outside the window banging the brake and wheels, and the engine gave out loud mournful pants up ahead. No one got into our car. After a while the porter closed the vestibule door and passed back along the corridor, and we slid out of the murky yellow station light and into the long darkness.

What I remember next must have extended over a space of five or six hours, though it comes back to me as something without any existence in time—something that might have taken five minutes or a year. There began a slow, calculated assault on me, wordless and terrible. I felt what I can only call a strangeness stealing over me—akin to the strangeness I had felt all afternoon, but deeper and more intensified. It was like nothing so much as the sensation of drifting away, and I gripped the arms of the chair convulsively, as if to hang onto a piece in the living world. Sometimes I felt myself going out with a rush. There would be almost a warm relief about it, a sense of not caring; then, with a violent wrench of the will, I'd pull myself back into the room.

Suddenly I realized that from a while back I had stopped hating him, stopped feeling violently alien to him, and with the realization, I went cold and sweat broke out all over my head. He was getting around my abhorrence, as he had got around Ellen coming West on the train; and it was just that strength he drew from preying on people that had brought him up to the point of concrete violence in St. Paul, and that, fading and flickering out, still kept him fighting now.

He must have seen that faltering in my heart, for he spoke at once, in a low, even, almost gentle voice: "You better go now."

"Oh, I'm not going," I forced myself to say.

"Suit yourself, Jack."

He was my friend, he implied. He knew how it was with me and he wanted to help. He pitied me. I'd better go away before it was too late. The rhythm of his attack was soothing as a song: I'd better go away—*and let him get at Ellen.* With a little cry I sat bolt upright.

"What do you want of this girl?" I said, my voice shaking. "To make a sort of walking hell of her."

His glance held a quality of dumb surprise, as if I were punishing an animal for a fault of which he was not conscious. For an instant I faltered; then I went on blindly:

"You've lost her; she's put her trust in me."

His countenance went suddenly black with evil, and he cried: "You're a liar!" in a voice that was like cold hands.

"She trusts me," I said. "You can't touch her. She's safe!"

He controlled himself. His face grew bland, and I felt that curious weakness and indifference begin again inside me. What was the use of all this? What was the use?

"You haven't got much time left," I forced myself to say, and then, in a flash of intuition, I jumped at the truth. "You died, or you were killed, not far from here!"—Then I saw what I had not seen before—that his forehead was drilled with a small round hole like a larger picture nail leaves when it's pulled from a plaster wall. "And now you're sinking. You've only got a few hours. The trip home is over!"

His face contorted, lost all semblance of humanity, living or dead. Simultaneously the room was full of cold air and with a noise that was something between a paroxysm of coughing and a burst of horrible laughter, he was on his feet, reeking of shame and blasphemy.

"Come and look!" he cried. "I'll show you——"

He took a step toward me, then another, and it was exactly as if a door stood open behind him, a door yawning out to an inconceivable abyss of darkness and corruption. There was a scream of mortal agony, from him or from somewhere behind, and abruptly the strength went out of him in a long husky sigh and he wilted to the floor. . . .

How long I sat there, dazed with terror and exhaustion, I don't know. The next thing I remember is the sleepy porter shining shoes across the room from me, and outside the window the steel fires of Pittsburgh breaking the flat perspective also—something too faint for a man, too heavy for a shadow, of the night. There was something extended on the bench. Even as I perceived it it faded off and away.

Some minutes later I opened the door of Ellen's compartment. She was asleep where I had left her. Her lovely cheeks were white and wan, but she lay naturally—her hands relaxed and her breathing regular and clear. What had possessed her had gone out of her, leaving her exhausted but her own dear self again.

I made her a little more comfortable, tucked a blanket around her, extinguished the light and went out.

III
· · · · ·

When I came home for Easter vacation, almost my first act was to go down to the billiard parlor near Seven Corners. The man at the cash register quite naturally didn't remember my hurried visit of three months before.

"I'm trying to locate a certain party who, I think, came here a lot some time ago."

I described the man rather accurately, and when I had finished, the cashier called to a little jockeylike fellow who was sitting near with an air of having something very important to do that he couldn't quite remember.

"Hey, Shorty, talk to this guy, will you? I think he's looking for Joe Varland."

The little man gave me a tribal look of suspicion. I went and sat near him.

"Joe Varland's dead, fella," he said grudgingly. "He died last winter."

I described him again — his overcoat, his laugh, the habitual expression of his eyes.

"That's Joe Varland you're looking for all right, but he's dead."

"I want to find out something about him."

"What you want to find out?"

"What did he do, for instance?"

"How should I know?"

"Look here! I'm not a policeman. I just want some kind of information about his habits. He's dead now and it can't hurt him. And it won't go beyond me."

"Well" — he hesitated, looking me over — "he was a great one for traveling. He got in a row in the station in Pittsburgh and a dick got him."

I nodded. Broken pieces of the puzzle began to assemble in my head.

"Why was he a lot on trains?"

"How should I know, fella?"

"If you can use ten dollars, I'd like to know anything you may have heard on the subject."

"Well," said Shorty reluctantly, "all I know is they used to say he worked the trains."

"Worked the trains?"

"He had some racket of his own he'd never loosen up about. He used to work the girls travelling alone on the trains. Nobody ever knew much about it — he was a pretty smooth guy — but sometimes he'd turn up here with a lot of dough and he let 'em know it was the janes he got it off of."

I thanked him and gave him the ten dollars and went out, very thoughtful, without mentioning that part of Joe Varland had made a last trip home.

Ellen wasn't West for Easter, and even if she had been I wouldn't have gone to her with the information, either — at least

I've seen her almost every day this summer and we've managed to talk about everything else. Sometimes, though, she gets silent about nothing and wants to be very close to me, and I know what's in her mind.

Of course she's coming out this fall, and I have two more years at New Haven; still, things don't look so impossible as they did a few months ago. She belongs to me in a way—even if I lose her she belongs to me. Who knows? Anyhow, I'll always be there.

THE SCANDAL DETECTIVES

Stalled in his novel and needing ready cash he could only earn with more short stories, Fitzgerald turned to the rich source of his adolescent years in St. Paul. He began his Basil Duke Lee stories in Delaware before he and Zelda left for Paris in April 1928. "I have finally put your home in a story," Fitzgerald wrote his boyhood friend and Princeton classmate, Norris Jackson, upon its publication. Jackson had married Betty Ames, and they moved into her childhood home at 501 Grand Hill. She and her brother Ted had played with the neighborhood children, including Fitzgerald, in their spacious yard with "deep shadows there all day long and ever something vague in bloom." The stories reflect real events: in 1911, Fitzgerald and some of his friends formed a club called "The Gooserah," whose members attacked Reuben Warner (Hubert Blair) for stealing the affections of Margaret Armstrong (Imogene Bissel). In September 1929, shortly after the series had run its course, Fitzgerald responded to a fan letter: "The Basil Lee stories were a mistake — it was too much good material being shoved into lousy form." However, the $3,500 that Fitzgerald earned for each of eight Basil stories provided roughly half his income in 1928–29.

The Saturday Evening Post, April 28, 1928
Collected in Taps at Reveille (1935)

I

. . . . .

IT WAS A HOT AFTERNOON IN MAY and Mrs. Buckner thought that a pitcher of fruit lemonade might prevent the boys from filling up on ice cream at the drug store. She belonged to that generation, since retired, upon whom the great revolution in American family life was to be visited; but at that time she believed that her children's relation to her was as much as hers had been to her parents, for this was more than twenty years ago.

Some generations are close to those that succeed them; between others the gap is infinite and unbridgeable. Mrs. Buckner—a woman of character, a member of Society in a large Middle-Western city—carrying a pitcher of fruit lemonade through her own spacious back yard, was progressing across a hundred years. Her own thoughts would have been comprehensible to her great-grandmother; what was happening in a room above the stable would have been entirely unintelligible to them both. In what had once served as the coachman's sleeping apartment, her son and a friend were not behaving in a normal manner, but were, so to speak, experimenting in a void. They were making the first tentative combinations of the ideas and materials they found ready at their hand—ideas destined to become, in future years, first articulate, then startling, and finally commonplace. At the moment when she called up to them they were sitting with disarming quiet upon the still unhatched eggs of the mid-twentieth century.

Riply Buckner descended the ladder and took the lemonade. Basil Duke Lee looked abstractedly down at the transaction and said, "Thank you very much, Mrs. Buckner."

"Are you sure it isn't too hot up there?"

"No, Mrs. Buckner. It's fine."

It was stifling; but they were scarcely conscious of the heat, and they drank two tall glasses each of the lemonade without knowing that they were thirsty. Concealed beneath a sawed-out trapdoor from which they presently took it was a composition book bound in imitation red leather which currently absorbed much of their attention. On its first page was inscribed, if you penetrated the secret of the lemon-juice ink: "THE BOOK OF SCANDAL, written by Riply Buckner, Jr., and Basil D. Lee, Scandal Detectives."

In this book they had set down such deviations from rectitude on the part of their fellow citizens as had reached their ears. Some of these false steps were those of grizzled men, stories that had become traditions in the city and were embalmed in the composition book by virtue of indiscreet exhumations at family dinner tables. Others were the more exciting sins, confirmed or merely rumored, of boys and girls their own age. Some of the entries would have been read by adults with bewilderment, others might have inspired wrath, and there were three or four contemporary reports that would have prostrated the parents of the involved children with horror and despair.

One of the mildest items, a matter they had hesitated about setting down, though it had shocked them only last year, was: "Elwood Leaming has been to the Burlesque Show three or four times at the Star."

Another, and perhaps their favorite, because of its uniqueness, set forth that "H. P. Cramner committed some theft in the East he could be imprisoned for and had to come here" — H. P. Cramner being now one of the oldest and "most substantial" citizens of the city.

The single defect in the book was that it could only be enjoyed with the aid of the imagination, for the invisible ink must keep its secrets until that day when, the pages being held close to the fire, the items would appear. Close inspection was necessary to determine which pages had been used — already a rather grave charge against a certain couple had been superimposed upon the dismal facts that Mrs. R. B. Cary had consumption and that her son, Walter Cary, had been expelled from Pawling School. The purpose of the work as a whole was not blackmail. It was treasured against the time when its protagonists should "do something" to Basil and Riply. Its possession gave them a sense of power. Basil, for instance, had never seen Mr. H. P. Cramner make a single threatening gesture in Basil's direction but let him even hint that he was going to do something to Basil, and there preserved against him was the record of his past.

It is only fair to say that at this point the book passes entirely out of this story. Years later a janitor discovered it beneath the trapdoor, and finding it apparently blank, gave it to his little girl; so the misdeeds of Elwood Leaming and H. P. Cramner were definitely entombed at last beneath a fair copy of Lincoln's Gettysburg Address.

The book was Basil's idea. He was more the imaginative and in most ways the stronger of the two. He was a shining-eyed, brown-haired boy of fourteen, rather small as yet, and bright and lazy at school. His favorite character in fiction was Arsène Lupin, the gentleman burglar, a romantic phenomenon lately imported from Europe and much admired in the first bored decades of the century.

Riply Buckner, also in short pants, contributed to the partnership a breathless practicality. His mind waited upon Basil's imagination like a hair trigger and no scheme was too fantastic for his immediate "Let's do it!" Since the school's third baseball team, on which they had been pitcher and catcher, decomposed after an unfortunate April season, they had spent their afternoons struggling to evolve a way of life which should measure up to the mysterious energies fermenting inside them. In the cache beneath the trapdoor were some "slouch" hats and bandanna handkerchiefs, some loaded dice, half of a pair of handcuffs, a rope ladder of a tenuous crochet persuasion for rear-window escapes into the alley, and a make-up box containing two old theatrical wigs and crêpe hair of various colors—all to be used when they decided what illegal enterprises to undertake.

Their lemonades finished, they lit Home Runs and held a desultory conversation which touched on crime, professional baseball, sex, and the local stock company. This broke off at the sound of footsteps and familiar voices in the adjoining alley.

From the window, they investigated. The voices belonged to Margaret Torrence, Imogene Bissel, and Connie Davies, who were cutting through the alley from Imogene's back yard to Connie's at the end of the block. The young ladies were thirteen, twelve, and thirteen years old respectively, and they considered themselves alone, for in time to their march they were rendering a mildly daring parody in a sort of whispering giggle and coming out strongly on the finale: "Oh, my *dar*-ling *Clemen*-tine."

Basil and Riply leaned together from the window, then remembering their undershirts sank down behind the sill.

"We heard you!" they cried together.

The girls stopped and laughed. Margaret Torrence chewed exaggeratedly to indicate gum, and gum with a purpose. Basil immediately understood.

"Whereabouts?" he demanded.

"Over at Imogene's house."

They had been at Mrs. Bissel's cigarettes. The implied recklessness of their mood interested and excited the two boys and they prolonged the conversation. Connie Davies had been Riply's girl during dancing-school term; Margaret Torrence had played a part in Basil's recent past; Imogene Bissel was just back from a year in Europe. During the last month neither Basil nor Riply had thought about girls, and, thus refreshed, they became conscious that the centre of the world had shifted suddenly from the secret room to the little group outside.

"Come on up," they suggested.

"Come on out. Come on down to the Whartons' yard."

"All right."

Barely remembering to put away the Scandal Book and the box of disguises, the two boys hurried out, mounted their bicycles, and rode up the alley.

The Whartons' own children had long grown up, but their yard was still one of those predestined places where young people gather in the afternoon. It had many advantages. It was large, open to other yards on both sides, and it could be entered upon skates or bicycles from the street. It contained an old seesaw, a swing, and a pair of flying rings; but it had been a rendezvous before these were put up, for it had a child's quality—the thing that makes young people huddle inextricably on uncomfortable steps and desert the houses of their friends to herd on the obscure premises of "people nobody knows." The Whartons' yard had long been a happy compromise; there were deep shadows there all day long and ever something vague in bloom, and patient dogs around, and brown spots worn bare by countless circling wheels and dragging feet. In sordid poverty, below the bluff two hundred feet away, lived the "micks"—they had merely inherited the name, for they were now largely of Scandinavian descent—and when other amusements palled, a few cries were enough to bring a gang of them swarming up the hill, to be faced if numbers promised well, to be fled from into convenient houses if things went the other way.

It was five o'clock and there was a small crowd gathered there for that soft and romantic time before supper—a time surpassed only by the interim of summer dusk thereafter. Basil and Riply rode their bicycles around abstractedly, in and out of trees, resting now and then with a hand on someone's shoulder, shading their eyes from the glow of the late sun that, like youth itself, is too strong to face directly, but must be kept down to an undertone until it dies away.

Basil rode over to Imogene Bissel and balanced idly on his wheel before her. Something in his face then must have attracted her, for she looked up at him, looked at him really, and slowly smiled. She was to be a beauty and belle of many proms in a few years. Now her large brown eyes and large beautifully shaped mouth and the high flush over her thin cheek bones made her face gnome-like and offended those who wanted a child to look like a child. For a moment Basil was granted an insight into the future, and the spell of her vitality crept over him suddenly. For the first time in his life he realized a girl completely as something opposite and complementary to him, and he was subject to a warm chill of mingled pleasure and pain. It was a definite experience and he was immediately conscious of it. The summer afternoon became lost in her suddenly — the soft air, the shadowy hedge and banks of flowers, the orange sunlight, the laughter and voices, the tinkle of a piano over the way — the odor left all these things and went into Imogene's face as she sat there looking up at him with a smile.

For a moment it was too much for him. He let it go, incapable of exploiting it until he had digested it alone. He rode around fast in a circle on his bicycle, passing near Imogene without looking at her. When he came back after a while and asked if he could walk home with her, she had forgotten the moment, if it had ever existed for her, and was almost surprised. With Basil wheeling his bicycle beside her, they started down the street.

"Can you come out tonight?" he asked eagerly. "There'll probably be a bunch in the Whartons' yard."

"I'll ask mother."

"I'll telephone you. I don't want to go unless you'll be there."

"Why?" She smiled at him again, encouraging him.

"Because I don't want to."

"But why don't you want to?"

"Listen," he said quickly, "What boys do you like better than me?"

"Nobody. I like you and Hubert Blair best."

Basil felt no jealousy at the coupling of this name with his.

There was nothing to do about Hubert Blair but accept him philosophically, as other boys did when dissecting the hearts of other girls.

"I like you better than anybody," he said deliriously.

The weight of the pink dappled sky above him was not endurable. He was plunging along through air of ineffable loveliness while warm freshets sprang up in his blood and he turned them, and with them his whole life, like a stream toward this girl.

They reached the carriage door at the side of her house.

"Can't you come in, Basil?"

"No." He saw immediately that that was a mistake, but it was said now. The intangible present had eluded him. Still he lingered. "Do you want my school ring?"

"Yes, if you want to give it to me."

"I'll give it to you tonight." His voice shook slightly as he added, "That is, I'll trade."

"What for?"

"Something."

"What?" Her color spread; she knew.

"You know. Will you trade?"

Imogene looked around uneasily. In the honey-sweet silence that had gathered around the porch, Basil held his breath.

"You're awful," she whispered. "Maybe. . . . Good-by."

II
. . . . .

It was the best hour of the day now and Basil was terribly happy. This summer he and his mother and sister were going to the lakes and next fall he was starting away to school. Then he would go to Yale and be a great athlete, and after that — if his two dreams had fitted onto each other chronologically instead of existing independently side by side — he was due to become a gentleman burglar. Everything was fine. He had so many alluring things to think about that it was hard to fall asleep at night.

That he was now crazy about Imogene Bissel was not a distraction, but another good thing. It had as yet no poignancy, only a brilliant and dynamic excitement that was bearing him along toward the Whartons' yard through the May twilight.

He wore his favorite clothes — white duck knickerbockers, pepper-and-salt Norfolk jacket, a Belmont collar, and a gray knitted tie. With his black hair wet and shining, he made a handsome little figure as he turned in upon the familiar but now reënchanted lawn and joined the voices in the gathering darkness. Three or four girls who lived in neighboring houses were present, and almost twice as many boys; and a slightly older group adorning the side veranda made a warm, remote nucleus against the lamps of the house and contributed occasional mysterious ripples of laughter to the already overburdened night.

Moving from shadowy group to group, Basil ascertained that Imogene was not yet here. Finding Margaret Torrence, he spoke to her aside, lightly.

"Have you still got that old ring of mine?"

Margaret had been his girl all year at dancing school, signified by the fact that he had taken her to the cotillion which closed the season. The affair had languished toward the end; none the less, his question was undiplomatic.

"I've got it somewhere," Margaret replied carelessly. "Why? Do you want it back?"

"Sort of."

"All right. I never did want it. It was you that made me take it, Basil. I'll give it back to you tomorrow."

"You couldn't give it to me tonight, could you?" His heart leaped as he saw a small figure come in at the rear gate. "I sort of want to get it tonight."

"Oh, all right, Basil."

She ran across the street to her house and Basil followed. Mr. and Mrs. Torrence were on the porch, and while Margaret went upstairs for the ring he overcame his excitement and impatience and answered those questions as to the health of his parents which are so meaningless to the young. Then a sudden stiffening came over him, his voice faded off, and his glazed eyes fixed upon a scene that was materializing over the way.

From the shadows far up the street, a swift, almost flying figure emerged and floated into the patch of lamplight in front of the Whartons' house. The figure wove here and there in a series of geometric patterns, now off with a flash of sparks at the impact of skates and pavement, now gliding miraculously backward, describing a fantastic curve, with one foot lifted gracefully in the air, until the young people moved forward in groups out of the darkness and crowded to the pavement to watch. Basil gave a quiet little groan as he realized that of all possible nights, Hubert Blair had chosen this one to arrive.

"You say you're going to the lakes this summer, Basil. Have you taken a cottage?"

Basil became aware after a moment that Mr. Torrence was making this remark for the third time.

"Oh, yes, sir," he answered — "I mean, no. We're staying at the club."

"Won't that be lovely?" said Mrs. Torrence.

Across the street, he saw Imogene standing under the lamppost and in front of her Hubert Blair, his jaunty cap on the side of his head, maneuvering in a small circle. Basil winced as he heard his chuckling laugh. He did not perceive Margaret until she was beside him, pressing his ring into his hand like a bad penny. He muttered a strained hollow good-by to her parents, and, weak with apprehension, followed her back across the street.

Hanging back in a shadow, he fixed his eyes not on Imogene but on Hubert Blair. There was undoubtedly something rare about Hubert. In the eyes of children less than fifteen, the shape of the nose is the distinguishing mark of beauty. Parents may call attention to lovely eyes, shining hair, or gorgeous coloring, but the nose and its juxtaposition on the face is what the adolescent sees. Upon the lithe, stylish, athletic torso of Hubert Blair was set a conventional chubby face, and upon this face was chiseled the piquant, retroussé nose of a Harrison Fisher girl.

He was confident; he had personality, uninhibited by doubts or moods. He did not go to dancing school — his parents had moved to the city only a year ago — but already he was a legend. Though most of the boys disliked him, they did homage to his virtuosic athletic ability, and for the girls his every movement, his pleasantries, his very indifference, had a simply immeasurable fascination. Upon several previous occasions Basil had discovered this; now the discouraging comedy began to unfold once more.

Hubert took off his skates, rolled one down his arm, and caught it by the strap before it reached the pavement; he snatched the ribbon from Imogene's hair and made off with it, dodging from under her arms as she pursued him, laughing and fascinated, around the yard. He cocked one foot behind the other and pretended to lean an elbow against a tree, missed the tree on purpose, and gracefully saved himself from falling. The boys watched him noncommittally at first. Then they, too, broke out into activity, doing stunts and tricks as fast as they could think of them until those on the porch craned their necks at the sudden surge of activity in the garden. But Hubert coolly turned his back on his own success. He took Imogene's hat and began setting it in various quaint ways upon his head. Imogene and the other girls were filled with delight.

Unable any longer to endure the nauseous spectacle, Basil went up to the group and said, "Why, hello, Hube," in as negligent a tone as he could command.

Hubert answered: "Why, hello, old — old Basil the Boozle," and set the hat a different way on his head, until Basil himself couldn't resist an unwilling chortle of laughter.

"Basil the Boozle! Hello, Basil the Boozle!" The cry circled the garden. Reproachfully he distinguished Riply's voice among the others.

"Hube the Boob!" Basil countered quickly; but his ill humor detracted from the effect, though several boys repeated it appreciatively.

Gloom settled upon Basil, and through the heavy dusk the figure of Imogene began to take on a new, unattainable charm. He was a romantic boy and already he had endowed her heavily from his fancy. Now he hated her for her indifference, but he must perversely linger near in the vain hope of recovering the penny of ecstasy so wantonly expended this afternoon.

He tried to talk to Margaret with decoy animation, but Margaret was not responsive. Already a voice had gone up in the darkness calling in a child. Panic seized upon him; the blessed hour of summer evening was almost over. At a spreading of the group to let pedestrians through, he maneuvered Imogene unwillingly aside.

"I've got it," he whispered. "Here it is. Can I take you home?"

She looked at him distractedly. Her hand closed automatically on the ring.

"What? Oh, I promised Hubert he could take me home." At the sight of his face she pulled herself from her trance and forced a note of indignation. "I saw you going off with Margaret Torrence just as soon as I came into the yard."

"I didn't. I just went to get the ring."

"Yes, you did! I saw you!"

Her eyes moved back to Hubert Blair. He had replaced his roller skates and was making little rhythmic jumps and twirls on his toes, like a witch doctor throwing a slow hypnosis over an African tribe. Basil's voice, explaining and arguing, went on, but Imogene moved away. Helplessly he followed. There were other voices calling in the darkness now and unwilling responses on all sides.

"All right, mother!"

"I'll be there in a second, mother."

"Mother, can't I please stay out five minutes more?"

"I've got to go," Imogene cried. "It's almost nine."

Waving her hand and smiling absently at Basil, she started off down the street. Hubert pranced and stunted at her side, circled around her and made entrancing little figures ahead.

Only after a minute did Basil realize that another young lady was addressing him.

"What?" he demanded absently.

"Hubert Blair is the nicest boy in town and you're the most conceited," repeated Margaret Torrence with deep conviction.

He stared at her in pained surprise. Margaret wrinkled her nose at him and yielded up her person to the now-insistent demands coming from across the street. As Basil gazed stupidly after her and then watched the forms of Imogene and Hubert disappear around the corner, there was a low mutter of thunder along the sultry sky and a moment later a solitary drop plunged through the lamplit leaves overhead and splattered on the sidewalk at his feet. The day was to close in rain.

III
· · · · ·

It came quickly and he was drenched and running before he reached his house eight blocks away. But the change of weather had swept over his heart and he leaped up every few steps, swallowing the rain and crying "Yo-o-o!" aloud, as if he himself were a part of the fresh, violent disturbance of the night. Imogene was gone, washed out like the day's dust on the sidewalk. Her beauty would come back into his mind in brighter weather, but here in the storm he was alone with himself. A sense of extraordinary power welled up in him, until to leave the ground permanently with one of his wild leaps would not have surprised him. He was a lone wolf, secret and untamed; a night prowler, demoniac and free. Only when he reached his own house did his emotion begin to turn, speculatively and almost without passion, against Hubert Blair.

He changed his clothes, and putting on pajamas and dressing-gown descended to the kitchen, where he happened upon a new chocolate cake. He ate a fourth of it and most of a bottle of milk. His elation somewhat diminished, he called up Riply Buckner on the phone.

"I've got a scheme," he said.

"What about?"

"How to do something to H. B. with the S. D."

Riply understood immediately what he meant. Hubert had been so indiscreet as to fascinate other girls besides Miss Bissel that evening.

"We'll have to take in Bill Kampf," Basil said.

"All right."

"See you at recess tomorrow. . . . Good night!"

IV
. . . . .

Four days later, when Mr. and Mrs. George P. Blair were finishing dinner, Hubert was called to the telephone. Mrs. Blair took advantage of his absence to speak to her husband of what had been on her mind all day.

"George, those boys, or whatever they are, came again last night."

He frowned.

"Did you see them?"

"Hilda did. She almost caught one of them. You see, I told her about the note they left last Tuesday, the one that said, 'First warning, S. D.,' so she was ready for them. They rang the back-door bell this time and she answered it straight from the dishes. If her hands hadn't been soapy she could have caught one, because she grabbed him when he handed her a note, but her hands were soapy so he slipped away."

"What did he look like?"

"She said he might have been a very little man, but she thought he was a boy in a false face. He dodged like a boy, she said, and she thought he had short pants on. The note was like the other. It said 'Second warning, S. D.'"

"If you've got it, I'd like to see it after dinner."

Hubert came back from the phone. "It was Imogene Bissel," he said. "She wants me to come over to her house. A bunch are going over there tonight."

"Hubert," asked his father, "do you know any boy with the initials S. D.?"

"No, sir."

"Have you thought?"

"Yeah, I thought. I knew a boy named Sam Davis, but I haven't seen him for a year."

"Who was he?"

"Oh, a sort of tough. He was at Number 44 School when I went there."

"Did he have it in for you?"

"I don't think so."

"Who do you think could be doing this? Has anybody got it in for you that you know about?"

"I don't know, papa; I don't think so."

"I don't like the looks of this thing," said Mr. Blair thoughtfully. "Of course it may be only some boys, but it may be——"

He was silent. Later, he studied the note. It was in red ink and there was a skull and crossbones in the corner, but being printed, it told him nothing at all.

Meanwhile Hubert kissed his mother, set his cap jauntily on the side of his head, and passing through the kitchen stepped out on the back stoop, intending to take the usual short cut along the alley. It was a bright moonlit night and he paused for a moment on the stoop to tie his shoe. If he had but known that the telephone call just received had been a decoy, that it had not come from Imogene Bissel's house, had not indeed been a girl's voice at all, and that shadowy and grotesque forms were skulking in the alley just outside the gate, he would not have sprung so gracefully and lithely down the steps with his hands in his pockets or whistled the first bar of the Grizzly Bear into the apparently friendly night.

His whistle aroused varying emotions in the alley. Basil had given his daring and successful falsetto imitation over the telephone a little too soon, and though the Scandal Detectives had hurried, their preparations were not quite in order. They had become separated. Basil, got up like a Southern planter of the old persuasion, was just outside the Blairs' gate; Bill Kampf, with a long Balkan mustache attached by a wire to the lower cartilage of his nose, was approaching in the shadow of the fence; but Riply Buckner, in a full rabbinical beard, was impeded by a length of rope he was trying to coil, and was still a hundred feet away. The rope was an essential part of their plan; for, after much cogitation, they had decided what they were going to do to Hubert Blair. They were going to tie him up, gag him, and put him in his own garbage can.

The idea at first horrified them—it would run his suit, it was awfully dirty and he might smother. In fact the garbage can, symbol of all that was repulsive, won the day only because it made every other idea seem tame. They disposed of the objections—his suit could be cleaned, it was where he ought to be anyhow, and if they left the lid off he couldn't smother. To be sure of this they had paid a visit of inspection to the Buckners' garbage can and stared into it, fascinated, envisaging Hubert among the rinds and eggshells. Then two of them, at last, resolutely put that part out of their minds and concentrated upon the luring of him into the alley and the overwhelming of him there.

Hubert's cheerful whistle caught them off guard and each of the three stood stock-still, unable to communicate with the others. It flashed through Basil's mind that if he grabbed Hubert without Riply at hand to apply the gag as had been arranged, Hubert's cries might alarm the gigantic cook in the kitchen who had almost taken him the night before. The thought threw him into a state of indecision. At that precise moment Hubert opened the gate and came out into the alley.

The two stood five feet apart, staring at each other, and all at once Basil made a startling discovery. He discovered he liked Hubert Blair—liked him as well as any boy he knew. He had absolutely no wish to lay hands on Hubert Blair and stuff him into a garbage can, jaunty cap and all. He would have fought to prevent that contingency. As his mind, unstrung by his situation, gave pasture to this inconvenient thought, he turned and dashed out of the alley and up the street.

For a moment the apparition had startled Hubert, but when it turned and made off he was heartened and gave chase. Outdistanced, he decided after fifty yards to let well enough alone; and returning to the alley, started rather precipitously down toward the other end—and came face to face with another small and hairy stranger.

Bill Kampf, being more simply organized than Basil, had no scruples of any kind. It had been decided to put Hubert into a garbage can, and though he had nothing at all against Hubert, the idea had made a pattern on his brain which he intended to follow. He was a natural man—that is to say, a hunter—and once a creature took on the aspect of a quarry, he would pursue it without qualms until it stopped struggling.

But he had been witness to Basil's inexplicable flight, and supposing that Hubert's father had appeared and was now directly behind him, he, too, faced about and made off down the alley. Presently he met Riply Buckner, who, without waiting to inquire the cause of his flight, enthusiastically joined him. Again Hubert was surprised into pursuing a little way. Then, deciding once and for all to let well enough alone, he returned on a dead run to his house.

Meanwhile Basil had discovered that he was not pursued, and keeping in the shadows, made his way back to the alley. He was not frightened — he had simply been incapable of action. The alley was empty; neither Bill nor Riply was in sight. He saw Mr. Blair come to the back gate, open it, look up and down, and go back into the house. He came closer. There was a great chatter in the kitchen — Hubert's voice, loud and boastful, and Mrs. Blair's frightened, and the two Swedish domestics contributing bursts of hilarious laughter. Then through an open window he heard Mr. Blair's voice at the telephone:

"I want to speak to the chief of police. . . . Chief, this is George P. Blair. . . . Chief, there's a gang of toughs around here who———"

Basil was off like a flash, tearing at his Confederate whiskers as he ran.

V
. . . . .

Imogene Bissel, having just turned thirteen, was not accustomed to having callers at night. She was spending a bored and solitary evening inspecting the month's bills which were scattered over her mother's desk, when she heard Hubert Blair and his father admitted into the front hall.

"I just thought I'd bring him over myself," Mr. Blair was saying to her mother. "There seems to be a gang of toughs hanging around our alley tonight."

Mrs. Bissel had not called upon Mrs. Blair and she was considerably taken aback by this unexpected visit. She even entertained the uncharitable thought that this was a crude overture, undertaken by Mr. Blair on behalf of his wife.

"Really!" she exclaimed. "Imogene will be delighted to see Hubert, I'm sure. . . . Imogene!"

"These toughs were evidently lying in wait for Hubert," continued Mr. Blair. "But he's a pretty spunky boy and he managed to drive them away. However, I didn't want him to come down here alone."

"Of course not," she agreed. But she was unable to imagine

why Hubert should have come at all. He was a nice enough boy, but surely Imogene had seen enough of him the last three afternoons. In fact, Mrs. Bissel was annoyed, and there was a minimum of warmth in her voice when she asked Mr. Blair to come in.

They were still in the hall, and Mr. Blair was just beginning to perceive that all was not as it should be, when there was another ring at the bell. Upon the door being opened, Basil Lee, red-faced and breathless, stood on the threshold.

"How do you do, Mrs. Bissel? Hello, Imogene!" he cried in an unnecessarily hearty voice. "Where's the party?"

The salutation might have sounded to a dispassionate observer somewhat harsh and unnatural, but it fell upon the ears of an already disconcerted group.

"There isn't any party," said Imogene wonderingly.

"What?" Basil's mouth dropped open in exaggerated horror, his voice trembled slightly. "You mean to say you didn't call me up and tell me to come over here to a party?"

"Why, of course not, Basil!"

Imogene was excited by Hubert's unexpected arrival and it occurred to her that Basil had invented this excuse to spoil it. Alone of those present she was close to the truth; but she underestimated the urgency of Basil's motive, which was not jealousy but mortal fear.

"You called *me* up, didn't you, Imogene?" demanded Hubert confidently.

"Why, no, Hubert! I didn't call up anybody."

Amid a chorus of bewildered protestations, there was another ring at the doorbell and the pregnant night yielded up Riply Buckner, Jr., and William S. Kampf. Like Basil, they were somewhat rumpled and breathless, and they no less rudely and peremptorily demanded the whereabouts of the party, insisting with curious vehemence that Imogene had just now invited them over the phone.

Hubert laughed, the others began to laugh, and the tensity relaxed. Imogene, because she believed Hubert, now began to believe them all. Unable to restrain himself any longer in the presence of this unhoped-for audience, Hubert burst out with his amazing adventure.

"I guess there's a gang laying for us all!" he exclaimed. "There were some guys laying for me in our alley when I went out. There was a big fellow with gray whiskers, but when he saw me he ran away. Then I went along the alley and there was a bunch more, sort of foreigners or something, and I started after'm, and they ran. I tried to catchem, but I guess they were good and scared, because they ran too fast for *me.*"

So interested were Hubert and his father in the story that they failed to perceive that three of his listeners were growing purple in the face or to mark the uproarious laughter that greeted Mr. Bissel's polite proposal that they have a party, after all.

"Tell about the warnings, Hubert," prompted Mr. Blair. "You see, Hubert had received these warnings. Did you boys get any warnings?"

"I did," said Basil suddenly. "I got a sort of warning on a piece of paper about a week ago."

For a moment, as Mr. Blair's worried eye fell upon Basil, a strong sense not precisely of suspicion but rather of obscure misgiving passed over him. Possibly that odd aspect of Basil's eyebrows, where wisps of crêpe hair still lingered, connected itself in his subconscious mind with what was bizarre in the events of the evening. He shook his head, somewhat puzzled. Then his thoughts glided back restfully to Hubert's courage and presence of mind.

Hubert, meanwhile, having exhausted his facts, was making tentative leaps into the realms of imagination.

"I said, 'So you're the guy that's been sending these warnings,' and he swung his left at me, and I dodged and swung my right back at him. I guess I must have landed, because he gave a yell and ran. Gosh, he could run! You'd ought to of seen him, Bill—he could run as fast as you."

"Was he big?" asked Basil, blowing his nose noisily.

"Sure! About as big as father."

"Were the other ones big too?"

"Sure! They were pretty big. I didn't wait to see, I just yelled, 'You get out of here, you bunch of toughs, or I'll show you!' They started a sort of fight, but I swung my right at one of them and they didn't wait for any more."

"Hubert says he thinks they were Italians," interrupted Mr. Blair. "Didn't you, Hubert?"

"They were sort of funny-looking," Hubert said. "One fellow looked like an Italian."

Mrs. Bissel led the way to the dining room, where she had caused a cake and grape juice supper to be spread. Imogene took a chair by Hubert's side.

"Now tell me all about it, Hubert," she said, attentively folding her hands.

Hubert ran over the adventure once more. A knife now made its appearance in the belt of one conspirator; Hubert's parleys with them lengthened and grew in volume and virulence. He had told them just what they might expect if they fooled with him. They had started to draw knives, but had thought better of it and taken to flight.

In the middle of this recital there was a curious snorting sound from across the table, but when Imogene looked over, Basil was spreading jelly on a piece of coffee cake and his eyes were brightly innocent. A minute later, however, the sound was repeated, and this time she intercepted a specifically malicious expression upon his face.

"I wonder what you'd have done, Basil," she said cuttingly. "I'll bet you'd be running yet!"

Basil put the piece of coffee cake in his mouth and immediately choked on it—an accident which Bill Kampf and Riply Buckner found hilariously amusing. Their amusement at various casual incidents at table seemed to increase as Hubert's story continued.

The alley now swarmed with malefactors, and as Hubert struggled on against overwhelming odds, Imogene found herself growing restless — without in the least realizing that the tale was boring her. On the contrary, each time Hubert recollected new incidents and began again, she looked spitefully over at Basil, and her dislike for him grew.

When they moved into the library, Imogene went to the piano, where she sat alone while the boys gathered around Hubert on the couch. To her chagrin, they seemed quite content to listen indefinitely. Odd little noises squeaked out of them from time to time, but whenever the narrative slackened they would beg for more.

"Go on, Hubert. Which one did you say could run as fast as Bill Kampf?"

She was glad when, after half an hour, they all got up to go.

"It's a strange affair from beginning to end," Mr. Blair was saying. "I don't like it. I'm going to have a detective look into the matter tomorrow. What did they want of Hubert? What were they going to do to him?"

No one offered a suggestion. Even Hubert was silent, contemplating his possible fate with certain respectful awe. During breaks in his narration the talk had turned to such collateral matters as murder and ghosts, and all the boys had talked themselves into a state of considerable panic. In fact each had come to believe, in varying degrees, that a band of kidnappers infested the vicinity.

"I don't like it," repeated Mr. Blair. "In fact I'm going to see all of you boys to your own homes."

Basil greeted this offer with relief. The evening had been a mad success, but furies once aroused sometimes get out of hand. He did not feel like walking the streets alone tonight.

In the hall, Imogene, taking advantage of her mother's somewhat fatigued farewell to Mr. Blair, beckoned Hubert back into the library. Instantly attuned to adversity, Basil listened. There was a whisper and a short scuffle, followed by an indiscreet but unmistakable sound. With the corners of his mouth falling, Basil went out the door. He had stacked the cards dexterously, but Life had played a trump from its sleeve at the last.

A moment later they all started off, clinging together in a group, turning corners with cautious glances behind and ahead. What Basil and Riply and Bill expected to see as they peered warily into the sinister mouths of alleys and around great dark trees and behind concealing fences they did not know — in all probability the same hairy and grotesque desperadoes who had lain in wait for Hubert Blair that night.

VI
. . . . .

A week later Basil and Riply heard that Hubert and his mother had gone to the seashore for the summer. Basil was sorry. He had wanted to learn from Hubert some of the graceful mannerisms that his contemporaries found so dazzling and that might come in so handy next fall when he went away to school. In tribute to Hubert's passing, he practiced leaning against a tree and missing it and rolling a skate down his arm, and he wore his cap in Hubert's manner, set jauntily on the side of his head.

This was only for a while. He perceived eventually that though boys and girls would always listen to him while he talked, their mouths literally moving in response to his, they would never look at him as they had looked at Hubert. So he abandoned the loud chuckle that so annoyed his mother and set his cap straight upon his head once more.

But the change in him went deeper than that. He was no longer sure that he wanted to be a gentleman burglar, though he still read of their exploits with breathless admiration. Outside of Hubert's gate, he had for a moment felt morally alone; and he realized that whatever combinations he might make of the materials of life would have to be safely within the law. And after another week he found that he no longer grieved over losing Imogene. Meeting her, he saw only the familiar little girl he had always

known. The ecstatic moment of that afternoon had been a premature birth, an emotion left over from an already fleeting spring.

He did not know that he had frightened Mrs. Blair out of town
and that because of him a special policeman walked a placid beat
for many a night. All he knew was that the vague and restless
yearnings of three long spring months were somehow satisfied.
They reached combustion in that last week — flared up, exploded,
and burned out. His face was turned without regret toward the
boundless possibilities of summer.

A NIGHT AT THE FAIR

In Paris in May 1928, Fitzgerald continued to write the autobiographical Basil stories. "A Night at the Fair," the second to be published, touches briefly on the American Civil War, which he and his father both cared for passionately. In a foreword he contributed to Colonial and Historic Homes of Maryland *the year before he died, Fitzgerald reminisced about his childhood in Minnesota, where he posed questions about the Civil War to his father. In 1911, the year Fitzgerald left St. Paul for Newman Academy in New Jersey, the* St. Paul Pioneer Press *commemorated the fiftieth anniversary of the Civil War by running excerpts from* Battles and Leaders of the Civil War. *One of the contributors was Basil W. Duke, the brother-in-law of Confederate General John Hunt Morgan. Fitzgerald would again run across Duke's name in the Sayre household in Montgomery. Duke had written a biography of his brother-in-law, Confederate General John Hunt Morgan, who was a cousin of Zelda's grandmother; this book was in the Sayre library. "A Night at the Fair" takes place at the Minnesota State Fair, where "a grand exhibition of fireworks culminating in a representation of the Battle of Gettysburg took place in the Grand Concourse every night."*

The Saturday Evening Post, July 21, 1928
Collected in *The Basil and Josephine Stories* (1973)

I
. . . . .

THE TWO CITIES WERE SEPARATED only by a thin well-bridged river; their tails curling over the banks met and mingled, and at the juncture, under the jealous eye of each, lay, every fall, the State Fair. Because of this advantageous position, and because of the agricultural eminence of the state, the fair was one of the most magnificent in America. There were immense exhibits of grain, livestock, and farming machinery; there were horse races and automobile races and, lately, aeroplanes that really left the ground; there was a tumultuous Midway with Coney Island thrillers to whirl you through space, and a whining, tinkling hoochie-coochie show. As a compromise between the serious and the trivial, a grand exhibition of fireworks, culminating in a representation of the Battle of Gettysburg, took place in the Grand Concourse every night.

At the late afternoon of a hot September day two boys of fifteen, somewhat replete with food and pop, and fatigued by eight hours of constant motion, issued from the Penny Arcade. The one with dark, handsome, eager eyes was, according to the comic inscription in his last year's *Ancient History,* "Basil Duke Lee, Holly Avenue, St. Paul, Minnesota, United States, North America, Western Hemisphere, the World, the Universe." Though slightly shorter than his companion, he appeared taller, for he projected, so to speak, from short trousers, while Riply Buckner, Jr., had graduated into long ones the week before. This event, so simple and natural, was having a disrupting influence on the intimate friendship between them that had endured for several years.

During that time Basil, the imaginative member of the firm, had been the dominating partner, and the displacement effected by two feet of blue serge filled him with puzzled dismay — in fact, Riply Buckner had become noticeably indifferent to the pleasure of Basil's company in public. His own assumption of long trousers had seemed to promise a liberation from the restraints and inferiorities of boyhood, and the companionship of one who was, in token of his short pants, still a boy was an unwelcome reminder of how recent was his own metamorphosis. He scarcely admitted this to himself, but a certain shortness of temper with Basil, a certain tendency to belittle him with superior laughter, had been in evidence all afternoon. Basil felt the new difference keenly. In August a family conference had decided that even though he was going East to school, he was too small for long trousers. He had countered by growing an inch and a half in a fortnight, which added to his reputation for unreliability, but led him to hope that his mother might be persuaded, after all.

Coming out of the stuffy tent into the glow of sunset, the two boys hesitated, glancing up and down the crowded highway with expressions compounded of a certain ennui and a certain inarticulate yearning. They were unwilling to go home before it became necessary, yet they knew they had temporarily glutted their appetite for sights; they wanted a change in the tone, the motif, of the day. Near them was the parking space, as yet a modest yard; and as they lingered indecisively, their eyes were caught and held by a small car, red in color and slung at that proximity to the ground which indicated both speed of motion and speed of life. It was a Blatz Wildcat, and for the next five years it represented the ambition of several million American boys. Occupying it, in the posture of aloof exhaustion exacted by the sloping seat, was a blond, gay, baby-faced girl.

The two boys stared. She bent upon them a single cool glance and then returned to her avocation of reclining in a Blatz Wildcat and looking haughtily at the sky. The two boys exchanged a glance, but made no move to go. They watched the girl — when they felt that their stares were noticeable they dropped their eyes and gazed at the car.

After several minutes a young man with a very pink face and pink hair, wearing a yellow suit and hat and drawing on yellow gloves, appeared and got into the car. There was a series of frightful explosions; then, with a measured tup-tup-tup from the open cut-out, insolent, percussive, and thrilling as a drum, the car and the girl and the young man whom they had recognized as Speed Paxton slid smoothly away.

Basil and Riply turned and strolled back thoughtfully toward the Midway. They knew that Speed Paxton was dimly terrible—the wild and pampered son of a local brewer—but they envied him—to ride off into the sunset in such a chariot, into the very hush and mystery of night, beside him the mystery of that baby-faced girl. It was probably this envy that made them begin to shout when they perceived a tall youth of their own age issuing from a shooting gallery.

"Oh, El! Hey, El! Wait a minute!"

Elwood Leaming turned around and waited. He was the dissipated one among the nice boys of the town—he had drunk beer, he had learned from chauffeurs, he was already thin from too many cigarettes. As they greeted him eagerly, the hard, wise expression of a man of the world met them in his half-closed eyes.

"Hello, Rip. Put it there, Rip. Hello, Basil, old boy. Put it there."

"What you doing, El?" Riply asked.

"Nothing. What are you doing?"

"Nothing."

Elwood Leaming narrowed his eyes still further, seemed to give thought, and then made a decisive clicking sound with his teeth.

"Well, what do you say we pick something up?" he suggested. "I saw some pretty good stuff around here this afternoon."

Riply and Basil drew tense, secret breaths. A year before they had been shocked because Elwood went to the burlesque show at the Star—now here he was holding the door open to his own speedy life.

The responsibility of his new maturity impelled Riply to appear most eager. "All right with me," he said heartily.

He looked at Basil.

"All right with me," mumbled Basil.

Riply laughed, more from nervousness than from derision. "Maybe you better grow up first, Basil." He looked at Elwood, seeking approval. "You better stick around till you get to be a man."

"Oh, dry up!" retorted Basil. "How long have you had yours? Just a week!"

But he realized that there was a gap separating him from these two, and it was with a sense of tagging them that he walked along beside.

Glancing from right to left with the expression of a keen and experienced frontiersman, Elwood Leaming led the way. Several pairs of strolling girls met his mature glance and smiled encouragingly, but he found them unsatisfactory—too fat, too plain, or too hard. All at once their eyes fell upon two who sauntered along a little ahead of them, and they increased their pace, Elwood with confidence, Riply with its nervous counterfeit, and Basil suddenly in the grip of wild excitement.

They were abreast of them. Basil's heart was in his throat. He looked away as he heard Elwood's voice.

"Hello, girls! How are you this evening?"

Would they call for the police? Would his mother and Riply's suddenly turn the corner?

"Hello, yourself, kiddo!"

"Where you going, girls?"

"Nowhere."

"Well, let's all go together."

Then all of them were standing in a group and Basil was relieved to find that they were only girls his own age, after all. They were pretty, with clear skins and red lips and maturely piled-up hair. One he immediately liked better than the other—her voice was quieter and she was shy. Basil was glad when Elwood walked on with the bolder one, leaving him and Riply to follow with the other, behind.

The first lights of the evening were springing into pale existence; the afternoon crowd had thinned a little, and the lanes, empty of people, were heavy with the rich various smells of pop corn and peanuts, molasses and dust, and cooking Wienerwurst and a not-unpleasant overtone of animals and hay. The Ferris wheel, pricked out now in lights, revolved leisurely through the dusk; a few empty cars of the roller coaster rattled overhead. The heat had blown off and there was the crisp stimulating excitement of Northern autumn in the air.

They walked. Basil felt that there was some way of talking to this girl, but he could manage nothing in the key of Elwood Leaming's intense and confidential manner to the girl ahead — as if he had inadvertently discovered a kinship of taste and of hearts. So to save the progression from absolute silence — for Riply's contribution amounted only to an occasional burst of silly laughter — Basil pretended an interest in the sights they passed and kept up a sort of comment thereon.

"There's the six-legged calf. Have you seen it?"

"No, I haven't."

"There's where the man rides the motorcycle around. Did you go there?"

"No, I didn't."

"Look! They're beginning to fill the balloon. I wonder what time they start the fireworks."

"Have you been to the fireworks?"

"No, I'm going tomorrow night. Have you?"

"Yes, I been every night. My brother works there. He's one of them that helps set them off."

"Oh!"

He wondered if her brother cared that she had been picked up by strangers. He wondered even more if she felt as silly as he. It must be getting late, and he had promised to be home by half-past seven on pain of not being allowed out tomorrow night. He walked up beside Elwood.

"Hey, El," he asked, "where we going?"

Elwood turned to him and winked. "We're going around the Old Mill."

"Oh!"

Basil dropped back again — became aware that in his temporary absence Riply and the girl had linked arms. A twinge of jealousy went through him and he inspected the girl again and with more appreciation, finding her prettier than he had thought. Her eyes, dark and intimate, seemed to have wakened at the growing brilliance of the illumination overhead; there was the promise of excitement in them now, like the promise of the cooling night.

He considered taking her other arm, but it was too late; she and Riply were laughing together at something — rather, at nothing. She had asked him what he laughed at all the time and he had laughed again for an answer. Then they both laughed hilariously and sporadically together.

Basil looked disgustedly at Riply. "I never heard such a silly laugh in my life," he said indignantly.

"Didn't you?" chuckled Riply Buckner. "Didn't you, little boy?"

He bent double with laughter and the girl joined in. The words "little boy" had fallen on Basil like a jet of cold water. In his excitement he had forgotten something, as a cripple might forget his limp only to discover it when he began to run.

"You think you're so big!" he exclaimed. "Where'd you get the pants? Where'd you get the pants?" He tried to work this up with gusto and was about to add: "They're your father's pants," when he remembered that Riply's father, like his own, was dead.

The couple ahead reached the entrance to the Old Mill and waited for them. It was an off hour, and half a dozen scows bumped in the wooden offing, swayed by the mild tide of the artificial river. Elwood and his girl got into the front seat and he promptly put his arm around her. Basil helped the other girl into the rear seat, but, dispirited, he offered no resistance when Riply wedged in and sat down between.

They floated off, immediately entering upon a long echoing darkness. Somewhere far ahead a group in another boat were singing, their voices now remote and romantic, now nearer and yet more mysterious, as the canal doubled back and the boats passed close to each other with an invisible veil between.

The three boys yelled and called, Basil attempting by his vociferousness and variety to outdo Riply in the girl's eyes, but after a few moments there was no sound except his own voice and the continual bump-bump of the boat against the wooden sides, and he knew without looking that Riply had put his arm about the girl's shoulder.

They slid into a red glow — a stage set of hell, with grinning demons and lurid paper fires — he made out that Elwood and his girl sat cheek to cheek — then again into the darkness, with the gently lapping water and the passing of the singing boat now near, now far away. For a while Basil pretended that he was interested in this other boat, calling to them, commenting on their proximity. Then he discovered that the scow could be rocked and took to this poor amusement until Elwood Leaming turned around indignantly and cried:

"Hey! What are you trying to do?"

They came out finally to the entrance and the two couples broke apart. Basil jumped miserably ashore.

"Give us some more tickets," Riply cried. "We want to go around again."

"Not me," said Basil with elaborate indifference. "I have to go home."

Riply began to laugh in derision and triumph. The girl laughed too.

"Well, so long, little boy," Riply cried hilariously.

"Oh, shut up! So long, Elwood."

"So long, Basil."

The boat was already starting off; arms settled again about the girls' shoulders.

"So long, little boy!"

"So long, you big cow!" Basil cried. "Where'd you get the pants? Where'd you get the pants?"

But the boat had already disappeared into the dark mouth of the tunnel, leaving the echo of Riply's taunting laughter behind.

II
. . . . .

It is an ancient tradition that all boys are obsessed with the idea of being grown. This is because they occasionally give voice to their impatience with the restraints of youth, while those great stretches of time when they are more than content to be boys find expression in action and not in words. Sometimes Basil wanted to be just a little bit older, but no more. The question of long pants had not seemed vital to him — he wanted them, but as a costume they had no such romantic significance as, for example, a football suit or an officer's uniform, or even the silk hat and opera cape in which gentlemen burglars were wont to prowl the streets of New York by night.

But when he awoke next morning they were the most important necessity in his life. Without them he was cut off from his contemporaries, laughed at by a boy whom he had hitherto led. The actual fact that last night some chickens had preferred Riply to himself was of no importance in itself, but he was fiercely competitive, and he resented being required to fight with one hand tied behind his back. He felt that parallel situations would occur at school, and that was unbearable. He approached his mother at breakfast in a state of wild excitement.

"Why, Basil," she protested in surprise, "I thought when we talked it over you didn't especially care."

"I've got to have them," he declared. "I'd rather be dead than go away to school without them."

"Well, there's no need of being silly."

"It's true—I'd rather be dead. If I can't have long trousers I don't see any use in my going away to school."

His emotion was such that the vision of his demise began actually to disturb his mother.

"Now stop that silly talk and come and eat your breakfast. You can go down and buy some at Barton Leigh's this morning."

Mollified, but still torn by the urgency of his desire, Basil strode up and down the room.

"A boy is simply helpless without them," he declared vehemently. The phrase pleased him and he amplified it. "A boy is simply and utterly helpless without them. I'd rather be dead than go away to school—"

"Basil, stop talking like that. Somebody has been teasing you about it."

"Nobody's been teasing me," he denied indignantly—"nobody at all."

After breakfast, the maid called him to the phone.

"This is Riply," said a tentative voice. Basil acknowledged the fact coldly. "You're not sore about last night, are you?" Riply asked.

"Me? No. Who said I was sore?"

"Nobody. Well, listen, you know about us going to the fireworks together tonight."

"Yes," Basil's voice was still cold.

"Well, one of those girls—the one Elwood had—has got a sister that's even nicer than she is, and she can come out tonight and you could have her. And we thought we could meet about eight, because the fireworks don't start till nine."

"What do?"

"Well, we could go on the Old Mill again. We went around three times more last night."

There was a moment's silence. Basil looked to see if his mother's door was closed.

"Did you kiss yours?" he demanded into the transmitter.

"Sure I did!" Over the wire came the ghost of a silly laugh. "Listen, El thinks he can get his auto. We could call for you at seven."

"All right," agreed Basil gruffly, and he added, "I'm going down and get some long pants this morning."

"Are you?" Again Basil detected ghostly laughter. "Well, you be ready at seven tonight."

Basil's uncle met him at Barton Leigh's clothing store at ten, and Basil felt a touch of guilt at having put his family to all this trouble and expense. On his uncle's advice, he decided finally on two suits—a heavy chocolate brown for every day and a dark blue for formal wear. There were certain alterations to be made but it was agreed that one of the suits was to be delivered without fail that afternoon.

His momentary contriteness at having been so expensive made him save car fare by walking home from downtown. Passing along Crest Avenue, he paused speculatively to vault the high hydrant in front of the Van Schellinger house, wondering if one did such things in long trousers and if he would ever do it again. He was impelled to leap it two or three times as a sort of ceremonial farewell, and was so engaged when the Van Schellinger limousine turned into the drive and stopped at the front door.

"Oh, Basil," a voice called.

A fresh delicate face, half buried under a mass of almost white curls, was turned toward him from the granite portico of the city's second largest mansion.

"Hello, Gladys."

"Come here a minute, Basil."

He obeyed. Gladys Van Schellinger was a year younger than Basil—a tranquil, carefully nurtured girl who, so local tradition had it, was being brought up to marry in the East. She had a governess and always played with a certain few girls at her house or theirs, and was not allowed the casual freedom of children in a Midwestern city. She was never present at such rendezvous as the Whartons' yard, where the others played games in the afternoons.

"Basil, I wanted to ask you something — are you going to the State Fair tonight?"

"Why, yes, I am."

"Well, wouldn't you like to come and sit in our box and watch the fireworks?"

Momentarily he considered the matter. He wanted to accept, but he was mysteriously impelled to refuse — to forgo a pleasure in order to pursue a quest that in cold logic did not interest him at all.

"I can't. I'm awfully sorry."

A shadow of discontent crossed Gladys' face. "Oh? Well, come and see me sometime soon, Basil. In a few weeks I'm going East to school."

He walked on up the street in a state of dissatisfaction. Gladys Van Schellinger had never been his girl, nor indeed anyone's girl, but the fact that they were starting away to school at the same time gave him a feeling of kinship for her — as if they had been selected for the glamorous adventure of the East, chosen together for a high destiny that transcended the fact that she was rich and he was only comfortable. He was sorry that he could not sit with her in her box tonight.

By three o'clock, Basil, reading the *Crimson Sweater* up in his room, began giving attentive ear to every ring at the bell. He would go to the head of the stairs, lean over and call, "Hilda, was that a package for me?" And at four, dissatisfied with her indifference, her lack of feeling for important things, her slowness in going to and returning from the door, he moved downstairs and began attending to it himself. But nothing came. He phoned Barton Leigh's and was told by a busy clerk: "You'll get that suit. I'll guarantee that you'll get that suit." But he did not believe in the clerk's honor and he moved out on the porch and watched for Barton Leigh's delivery wagon.

His mother came home at five. "There were probably more alterations than they thought," she suggested helpfully. "You'll probably get it tomorrow morning."

"Tomorrow morning!" he exclaimed incredulously. "I've got to have that suit tonight."

"Well, I wouldn't be too disappointed if I were you, Basil. The stores all close at half-past five."

Basil took one agitated look up and down Holly Avenue. Then he got his cap and started on a run for the street car at the corner. A moment later a cautious afterthought caused him to retrace his steps with equal rapidity.

"If they get here, keep them for me," he instructed his mother—a man who thought of everything.

"All right," she promised dryly, "I will."

It was later than he thought. He had to wait for a trolley, and when he reached Barton Leigh's he saw with horror that the doors were locked and the blinds drawn. He intercepted a last clerk coming out and explained vehemently that he had to have his suit tonight. The clerk knew nothing about the matter. . . . Was Basil Mr. Schwartze?

No, Basil was not Mr. Schwartze. After a vague argument wherein he tried to convince the clerk that whoever promised him the suit should be fired, Basil went dispiritedly home.

He would not go to the fair without his suit—he would not go at all. He would sit at home and luckier boys would go adventuring along its Great White Way. Mysterious girls, young and reckless, would glide with them through the enchanted darkness of the Old Mill, but because of the stupidity, selfishness, and dishonesty of a clerk in a clothing store he would not be there. In a day or so the fair would be over—forever—those girls, of all living girls the most intangible, the most desirable, that sister, said to be nicest of all—would be lost out of his life. They would ride off in Blatz Wildcats into the moonlight without Basil having kissed them. No, all his life—though he would lose the clerk his position: "You see now what your act did to me" — he would look back with infinite regret upon that irretrievable hour. Like most of us, he was unable to perceive that he would have any desires in the future equivalent to those that possessed him now.

He reached home; the package had not arrived. He moped dismally about the house, consenting at half-past six to sit silently at dinner with his mother, his elbows on the table.

"Haven't you any appetite, Basil?"

"No, thanks," he said absently, under the impression he had been offered something.

"You're not going away to school for two more weeks. Why should it matter — "

"Oh, that isn't the reason I can't eat. I had a sort of headache all afternoon."

Toward the end of the meal his eye focused abstractedly on some slices of angel cake; with the air of a somnambulist, he ate three.

At seven he heard the sounds that should have ushered in a night of romantic excitement.

The Leaming car stopped outside, and a moment later Riply Buckner rang the bell. Basil rose gloomily.

"I'll go," he said to Hilda. And then to his mother, with vague impersonal reproach, "Excuse me a minute. I just want to tell them I can't go to the fair tonight."

"But of course you can go, Basil. Don't be silly. Just because _____ "

He scarcely heard her. Opening the door, he faced Riply on the steps. Beyond was the Leaming limousine, an old high car, quivering in silhouette against the harvest moon.

Clop-clop-clop! Up the street came the Barton Leigh delivery wagon. Clop-clop! A man jumped out, dumped an iron anchor to the pavement, hurried along the street, turned away, turned back again, came toward them with a long square box in his hand.

"You'll have to wait a minute," Basil was calling wildly. "It can't make any difference. I'll dress in the library. Look here, if you're a friend of mine, you'll wait a minute." He stepped out on the porch. "Hey, El, I've just got my — got to change my clothes. You can wait a minute, can't you?"

The spark of a cigarette flushed in the darkness as El spoke to the chauffeur; the quivering car came to rest with a sigh and the skies filled suddenly with stars.

III
· · · · ·

Once again the fair — but differing from the fair of the afternoon as a girl in the daytime differs from her radiant presentation of herself at night. The substance of the cardboard booths and plaster palaces was gone, the forms remained. Outlined in lights, these forms suggested things more mysterious and entrancing than themselves, and the people strolling along the network of little Broadways shared this quality, as their pale faces singly and in clusters broke the half darkness.

The boys hurried to their rendezvous, finding the girls in the deep shadow of the Temple of Wheat. Their forms had scarcely merged into a group when Basil became aware that something was wrong. In growing apprehension, he glanced from face to face and, as the introductions were made, he realized the appalling truth — the younger sister was, in point of fact, a fright, squat and dingy, with a bad complexion brooding behind a mask of cheap pink powder and a shapeless mouth that tried ceaselessly to torture itself into the mold of charm.

In a daze he heard Riply's girl say, "I don't know whether I ought to go with you. I had a sort of date with another fellow I met this afternoon."

Fidgeting, she looked up and down the street, while Riply, in astonishment and dismay, tried to take her arm.

"Come on," he urged. "Didn't I have a date with you first?"

"But I didn't know whether you'd come or not," she said perversely.

Elwood and the two sisters added their entreaties.

"Maybe I could go on the Ferris wheel," she said grudgingly, "but not the Old Mill. This fellow would be sore."

Riply's confidence reeled with the blow; his mouth fell ajar, his hand desperately pawed her arm. Basil stood glancing now with agonized politeness at his own girl, now at the others, with an expression of infinite reproach. Elwood alone was successful and content.

"Let's go on the Ferris wheel," he said impatiently. "We can't stand here all night."

At the ticket booth recalcitrant Olive hesitated once more, frowning and glancing about as if she still hoped Riply's rival would appear.

But when the swooping cars came to rest she let herself be persuaded in, and the three couples, with their troubles, were hoisted slowly into the air.

As the car rose, following the imagined curve of the sky, it occurred to Basil how much he would have enjoyed it in other company, or even alone, the fair twinkling beneath him with new variety, the velvet quality of the darkness that is on the edge of light and is barely permeated by its last attenuations. But he was unable to hurt anyone whom he thought of as an inferior. After a minute he turned to the girl beside him.

"Do you live in St. Paul or Minneapolis?" he inquired formally.

"St. Paul. I go to Number 7 School." Suddenly she moved closer. "I bet you're not so slow," she encouraged him.

He put his arm around her shoulder and found it warm. Again they reached the top of the wheel and the sky stretched out overhead, again they lapsed down through gusts of music from remote calliopes. Keeping his eyes turned carefully away, Basil pressed her to him, and as they rose again into darkness, leaned and kissed her cheek.

The significance of the contact stirred him, but out of the corner of his eye he saw her face—he was thankful when a gong struck below and the machine settled slowly to rest.

The three couples were scarcely reunited outside when Olive uttered a yelp of excitement.

"There he is!" she cried. "That Bill Jones I met this afternoon —that I had the date with."

A youth of their own age was approaching, stepping like a circus pony and twirling, with the deftness of a drum major, a small rattan cane. Under the cautious alias, the three boys recognized a friend and contemporary—none other than the fascinating Hubert Blair.

He came nearer. He greeted them all with a friendly chuckle. He took off his cap, spun it, dropped it, caught it, set it jauntily on the side of his head.

"You're a nice one," he said to Olive. "I waited here fifteen minutes this evening."

He pretended to belabor her with the cane; she giggled with delight. Hubert Blair possessed the exact tone that all girls of fourteen, and a somewhat cruder type of grown women, find irresistible. He was a gymnastic virtuoso and his figure was in constant graceful motion; he had a jaunty piquant nose, a disarming laugh, and a shrewd talent for flattery. When he took a piece of toffee from his pocket, placed it on his forehead, shook it off, and caught it in his mouth, it was obvious to any disinterested observer that Riply was destined to see no more of Olive that night.

So fascinated were the group that they failed to see Basil's eyes brighten with a ray of hope, his feet take four quick steps backward with all the guile of a gentleman burglar, his torso writhe through the parting of a tent wall into the deserted premises of the Harvester and Tractor Show. Once safe, Basil's tensity relaxed, and as he considered Riply's unconsciousness of the responsibilities presently to devolve upon him, he bent double with hilarious laughter in the darkness.

IV
· · · · ·

Ten minutes later, in a remote part of the fairgrounds, a youth made his way briskly and cautiously toward the fireworks exhibit, swinging as he walked a recently purchased rattan cane. Several girls eyed him with interest, but he passed them haughtily; he was weary of people for a brief moment—a moment which he had almost mislaid in the bustle of life—he was enjoying his long pants.

He bought a bleacher seat and followed the crowd around the race track, seeking his section. A few Union troops were moving cannon about in preparation for the Battle of Gettysburg, and, stopping to watch them, he was hailed by Gladys Van Schellinger from the box behind.

"Oh, Basil, don't you want to come and sit with us?"

He turned about and was absorbed. Basil exchanged courtesies with Mr. and Mrs. Van Schellinger and he was affably introduced to several other people as "Alice Riley's boy," and a chair was placed for him beside Gladys in front.

"Oh Basil," she whispered, glowing at him, "isn't this fun?"

Distinctly, it was. He felt a vast wave of virtue surge through him. How anyone could have preferred the society of those common girls was at this moment incomprehensible.

"Basil, won't it be fun to go East? Maybe we'll be on the same train."

"I can hardly wait," he agreed gravely. "I've got on long pants. I had to have them to go away to school."

One of the ladies in the box leaned toward him. "I know your mother very well," she said. "And I know another friend of yours. I'm Riply Buckner's aunt."

"Oh, yes!"

"Riply's such a nice boy," beamed Mrs. Van Schellinger.

And then, as if the mention of his name had evoked him, Riply Buckner came suddenly into sight. Along the now empty and brightly illuminated race track came a short but monstrous procession, a sort of Lilliputian burlesque of the wild gay life. At its head marched Hubert Blair and Olive, Hubert prancing and twirling his cane like a drum major to the accompaniment of her appreciative screams of laughter. Next followed Elwood Leaming and his young lady, leaning so close together that they walked with difficulty, apparently wrapped in each other's arms. And bringing up the rear without glory were Riply Buckner and Basil's late companion, rivaling Olive in exhibitionistic sound.

Fascinated, Basil stared at Riply, the expression of whose face was curiously mixed. At moments he would join in the general tone of the parade with silly guffaw, at others a pained expression would flit across his face, as if he doubted that, after all, the evening was a success.

The procession was attracting considerable notice — so much that not even Riply was aware of the particular attention focused upon him from this box, though he passed by it four feet away. He was out of hearing when a curious rustling sigh passed over its inhabitants and a series of discreet whispers began.

"What funny girls," Gladys said. "Was that first boy Hubert Blair?"

"Yes." Basil was listening to a fragment of conversation behind:

"His mother will certainly hear of this in the morning."

As long as Riply had been in sight, Basil had been in an agony of shame for him, but now a new wave of virtue, even stronger than the first, swept over him. His memory of the incident would have reached actual happiness, save for the fact that Riply's mother might not let him go away to school. And a few minutes later, even that seemed endurable. Yet Basil was not a mean boy. The natural cruelty of his species toward the doomed was not yet disguised by hypocrisy — that was all.

In a burst of glory, to the alternate strains of "Dixie" and "The Star-Spangled Banner," the Battle of Gettysburg ended. Outside by the waiting cars, Basil, on a sudden impulse, went up to Riply's aunt.

"I think it would be sort of a—a mistake to tell Riply's mother. He didn't do any harm. He—"

Annoyed by the event of the evening, she turned on him cool, patronizing eyes.

"I shall do as I think best," she said briefly.

He frowned. Then he turned and got into the Van Schellinger limousine.

Sitting beside Gladys in the little seats, he loved her suddenly. His hand swung gently against hers from time to time and he felt the warm bond that they were both going away to school tightening around them and pulling them together.

"Can't you come and see me tomorrow?" she urged him. "Mother's going to be away and she says I can have anybody I like."

"All right."

As the car slowed up for Basil's house, she leaned toward him swiftly. "Basil——"

He waited. Her breath was warm on his cheek. He wanted her to hurry, or, when the engine stopped, her parents, dozing in back, might hear what she said. She seemed beautiful to him then; that vague unexciting quality about her was more than compensated for by her exquisite delicacy, the fine luxury of her life.

"Basil—Basil, when you come tomorrow, will you bring that Hubert Blair?"

The chauffeur opened the door and Mr. and Mrs. Van Schellinger woke up with a start. When the car had driven off, Basil stood looking after it thoughtfully until it turned the corner of the street.

HE THINKS HE'S WONDERFUL

After setting his third published Basil story ("The Freshest Boy") at Newman Academy, Fitzgerald turned again to a St. Paul setting for "He Thinks He's Wonderful," which he wrote in Paris in August 1928. In the summer of 1908, after Edward Fitzgerald lost his job with Procter & Gamble in Buffalo, the family returned to St. Paul. They had been gone ten years, and when they returned Scott was almost twelve. Despite having an eccentric mother and a father who depended on her family's money, Fitzgerald could count on his grandmother Louisa McQuillan to give him the social status he needed to associate with the Summit Avenue gentry. He soon made friends with Arthur Foley and Jack Mitchell, whose families both lived on Summit; next to the Mitchells lived the Finches, who that summer hosted their niece Violet Stockton from Atlanta. All three boys were intrigued by her southern ways and competed for her attention. Fitzgerald later used Violet as a source for his elaborately named Ermine Gilberte Labouisse Bibble of New Orleans in "He Thinks He's Wonderful." A favorite former landmark makes an appearance in this story: Basil catches a trolley home from Wildwood, an amusement park built in 1899 on the southeastern shore of White Bear Lake by the Twin City Rapid Transit Company to give St. Paul residents a reason to ride the company's electric streetcars out to the lake.

The Saturday Evening Post, September 29, 1928
Collected in Taps at Reveille (1935)

I
. . . . .

AFTER THE COLLEGE-BOARD EXAMINATIONS in June, Basil
Duke Lee and five other boys from St. Regis School boarded the
train for the West. Two got out at Pittsburgh, one slanted south
toward St. Louis, and two stayed in Chicago; from then on Basil
was alone. It was the first time in his life that he had ever felt the
need of tranquility, but now he took long breaths of it; for, though
things had gone better toward the end, he had had an unhappy
year at school.

He wore one of those extremely flat derbies in vogue during
the twelfth year of the century, and a blue business suit become a
little too short for his constantly lengthening body. Within he was
by turns a disembodied spirit, almost unconscious of his person
and moving in a mist of impressions and emotions, and a fiercely
competitive individual trying desperately to control the rush of
events that were the steps in his own evolution from child to man.
He believed that everything was a matter of effort — the current
principle of American education — and his fantastic ambition was
continually leading him to expect too much. He wanted to be a
great athlete, popular, brilliant, and always happy. During this
year at school, where he had been punished for his "freshness," for
fifteen years of thorough spoiling at home, he had grown uselessly
introspective, and this interfered with that observation of others
which is the beginning of wisdom. It was apparent that before he
obtained much success in dealing with the world he would know
that he'd been in a fight.

He spent the afternoon in Chicago, walking the streets and
avoiding members of the underworld. He bought a detective story
called *In the Dead of the Night,* and at five o'clock recovered his
suitcase from the station check room and boarded the Chicago,
Milwaukee and St. Paul. Immediately he encountered a contemporary, also bound home from school.

Margaret Torrence was fourteen; a serious girl, considered beautiful by a sort of tradition, for she had been beautiful as a little girl. A year and a half before, after a breathless struggle, Basil had succeeded in kissing her on the forehead. They met now with extraordinary joy; for a moment each of them to the other represented home, the blue skies of the past, the summer afternoons ahead.

He sat with Margaret and her mother in the dining car that night. Margaret saw that he was no longer the ultraconfident boy of a year before; his brightness was subdued, and the air of consideration in his face — a mark of his recent discovery that others had wills as strong as his, and more power — appeared to Margaret as a charming sadness. The spell of peace after a struggle was still upon him. Margaret had always liked him — she was of the grave, conscientious type who sometimes loved him and whose love he could never return — and now she could scarcely wait to tell people how attractive he had grown.

After dinner they went back to the observation car and sat on the deserted rear platform while the train pulled them visibly westward between the dark wide farms. They talked of people they knew, of where they had gone for Easter vacation, of the plays they had seen in New York.

"Basil, we're going to get an automobile," she said, "and I'm going to learn to drive."

"That's fine." He wondered if his grandfather would let him drive the electric sometimes this summer.

The light from inside the car fell on her young face, and he spoke impetuously, borne on by the rush of happiness that he was going home: "You know something? You know you're the prettiest girl in the city?"

At the moment when the remark blurred with the thrilling night in Margaret's heart, Mrs. Torrence appeared to fetch her to bed.

Basil sat alone on the platform for a while, scarcely realizing that she was gone, at peace with himself for another hour and content that everything should remain patternless and shapeless until tomorrow.

II
. . . . .

Fifteen is of all ages the most difficult to locate — to put one's fingers on and say, "That's the way I was." The melancholy Jacques does not select it for mention, and all one can know is that somewhere between thirteen, boyhood's majority, and seventeen, when one is a sort of counterfeit young man, there is a time when youth fluctuates hourly between one world and another — pushed ceaselessly forward into unprecedented experiences and vainly trying to struggle back to the days when nothing had to be paid for. Fortunately none of our contemporaries remember much more than we do of how we behaved in those days; nevertheless the curtain is about to be drawn aside for an inspection of Basil's madness that summer.

To begin with, Margaret Torrence, in one of those moods of idealism which overcome the most matter-of-fact girls, gave it as her rapt opinion that Basil was wonderful. Having practised believing things all year at school, and having nothing much to believe at that moment, her friends accepted the fact. Basil suddenly became a legend. There were outbreaks of giggling when girls encountered him on the street, but he suspected nothing at all.

One night, when he had been home a week, he and Riply Buckner went on to an after-dinner gathering on Imogene Bissel's veranda. As they came up the walk Margaret and two other girls suddenly clung together, whispered convulsively and pursued one another around the yard, uttering strange cries — an inexplicable business that ended only when Gladys Van Schellinger, tenderly and impressively accompanied by her mother's maid, arrived in a limousine.

All of them were a little strange to one another. Those who had been East at school felt a certain superiority, which, however, was more than counterbalanced by the fact that romantic pairings and quarrels and jealousies and adventures, of which they were lamentably ignorant, had gone on while they had been away.

After the ice cream at nine they sat together on the warm stone steps in a quiet confusion that was halfway between childish teasing and adolescent coquetry. Last year the boys would have ridden their bicycles around the yard; now they had all begun to wait for something to happen.

They knew it was going to happen, the plainest girls, the shyest boys; they had begun to associate with others the romantic world of summer night that pressed deeply and sweetly on their senses. Their voices drifted in a sort of broken harmony in to Mrs. Bissel, who sat reading beside an open window.

"No, look out. You'll break it. Bay-zil!"

"Rip-lee!"

"Sure I did!"

Laughter.

> *—on Moonlight Bay*
> *We could hear their voices call—*

"Did you see———"

"Connie, don't—don't! You tickle. Look out!"

Laughter.

"Going to the lake tomorrow?"

"Going Friday."

"Elwood's home."

"Is Elwood home?"

> *—you have broken my heart—*

"Look out now!"

"Look out!"

Basil sat beside Riply on the balustrade, listening to Joe Gorman singing. It was one of the griefs of his life that he could not sing "so people could stand it," and he conceived a sudden admiration for Joe Gorman, reading into his personality the thrilling clearness of those sounds that moved so confidently through the dark air.

They evoked for Basil a more dazzling night than this, and other more remote and enchanted girls. He was sorry when the voice died away, and there was a rearranging of seats and a businesslike quiet — the ancient game of Truth had begun.

"What's your favorite color, Bill?"

"Green," supplies a friend.

"Sh-h-h! Let him alone."

Bill says, "Blue."

"What's your favorite girl's name?"

"Mary," says Bill.

"Mary Haupt! Bill's got a crush on Mary Haupt!"

She was a cross-eyed girl, a familiar personification of repulsiveness.

"Who would you rather kiss than anybody?"

Across the pause a snicker stabbed the darkness.

"My mother."

"No, but what girl?"

"Nobody."

"That's not fair. Forfeit! Come on, Margaret."

"Tell the truth, Margaret."

She told the truth and a moment later Basil looked down in surprise from his perch; he had just learned that he was her favorite boy.

"Oh, yes-s!" he exclaimed sceptically. "Oh, yes-s! How about Hubert Blair?"

He renewed a casual struggle with Riply Buckner and presently they both fell off the balustrade. The game became an inquisition into Gladys Van Schellinger's carefully chaperoned heart.

"What's your favorite sport?"

"Croquet."

The admission was greeted by a mild titter.

"Favorite boy."

"Thurston Kohler."

A murmur of disappointment.

"Who's he?"

"A boy in the East."

This was manifestly an evasion.

"Who's your favorite boy here?"

Gladys hesitated. "Basil," she said at length.

The faces turned up to the balustrade this time were less teasing, less jocular. Basil depreciated the matter with "Oh, yes-s! Sure! Oh, yes-s!" But he had a pleasant feeling of recognition, a familiar delight.

Imogene Bissel, a dark little beauty and the most popular girl in their crowd, took Gladys' place. The interlocutors were tired of gastronomic preferences — the first question went straight to the point.

"Imogene, have you ever kissed a boy?"

"No." A cry of wild unbelief. "I have not!" she declared indignantly.

"Well, have you ever been kissed?"

Pink but tranquil, she nodded, adding, "I couldn't help it."

"Who by?"

"I won't tell."

"Oh-h-h! How about Hubert Blair?"

"What's your favorite book, Imogene?"

"*Beverly of Graustark.*"

"Favorite girl?"

"Passion Johnson."

"Who's she?"

"Oh, just a girl at school."

Mrs. Bissel had fortunately left the window.

"Who's your favorite boy?"

Imogene answered steadily, "Basil Lee."

This time an impressed silence fell. Basil was not surprised — we are never surprised at our own popularity — but he knew that these were not those ineffable girls, made up out of books and faces momentarily encountered, whose voices he had heard for a moment in Joe Gorman's song. And when, presently, the first telephone rang inside, calling a daughter home, and the girls, chattering like birds, piled all together into Gladys Van Schellinger's limousine, he lingered back in the shadow so as not to seem to be showing off. Then, perhaps because he nourished a vague idea that if he got to know Joe Gorman very well he would get to sing like him, he approached him and asked him to go to Lambert's for a soda.

Joe Gorman was a tall boy with white eyebrows and a stolid face who had only recently become one of their "crowd." He did not like Basil, who, he considered, had been "stuck up" with him last year, but he was acquisitive of useful knowledge and he was momentarily overwhelmed by Basil's success with girls.

It was cheerful in Lambert's, with great moths batting against the screen door and languid couples in white dresses and light suits spread about the little tables. Over their sodas, Joe proposed that Basil come home with him to spend the night; Basil's permission was obtained over the telephone.

Passing from the gleaming store into the darkness, Basil was submerged in an unreality in which he seemed to see himself from the outside, and the pleasant events of the evening began to take on fresh importance.

Disarmed by Joe's hospitality, he began to discuss the matter.

"That was a funny thing that happened tonight," he said, with a disparaging little laugh.

"What was?"

"Why, all those girls saying I was their favorite boy." The remark jarred on Joe. "It's a funny thing," went on Basil. "I was sort of unpopular at school for a while, because I was fresh, I guess. But the thing must be that some boys are popular with boys and some are popular with girls."

He had put himself in Joe's hands, but he was unconscious of it; even Joe was only aware of a certain desire to change the subject.

"When I get my car," suggested Joe, up in his room, "we could take Imogene and Margaret and go for rides."

"All right."

"You could have Imogene and I'd take Margaret, or anybody I wanted. Of course I know they don't like me as well as they do you."

"Sure they do. It's just because you haven't been in our crowd very long yet."

Joe was sensitive on that point and the remark did not please him. But Basil continued: "You ought to be more polite to the older people if you want to be popular. You didn't say how do you do to Mrs. Bissel tonight."

"I'm hungry," said Joe quickly. "Let's go down to the pantry and get something to eat."

Clad only in their pajamas, they went downstairs. Principally to dissuade Basil from pursuing the subject, Joe began to sing in a low voice:

> *Oh, you beautiful doll,*
> *You great — big——*

But the evening, coming after the month of enforced humility at school, had been too much for Basil. He got a little awful. In the kitchen, under the impression that his advice had been asked, he broke out again:

"For instance, you oughtn't to wear those white ties. Nobody does that that goes East to school." Joe, a little red, turned around from the ice box and Basil felt a slight misgiving. But he pursued with: "For instance, you ought to get your family to send you East to school. It'd be a great thing for you. Especially if you want to go East to college you ought to first go East to school. They take it out of you."

Feeling that he had nothing special to be taken out of him, Joe found the implication distasteful. Nor did Basil appear to him at that moment to have been perfected by the process.

"Do you want cold chicken or cold ham?" They drew up chairs to the kitchen table. "Have some milk?"

"Thanks."

Intoxicated by the three full meals he had had since supper, Basil warmed to his subject. He built up Joe's life for him little by little, transformed him radiantly from what was little more than a Midwestern bumpkin to an Easterner bursting with *savoir-faire* and irresistible to girls. Going into the pantry to put away the milk, Joe paused by the open window for a breath of quiet air; Basil followed. "The thing is if a boy doesn't get it taken out of him at school, he gets it taken out of him at college," he was saying.

Moved by some desperate instinct, Joe opened the door and stepped out onto the back porch. Basil followed. The house abutted on the edge of the bluff occupied by the residential section, and the two boys stood silent for a moment, gazing at the scattered lights of the lower city. Before the mystery of the unknown human life coursing through the streets below, Basil felt the purport of his words grow thin and pale.

He wondered suddenly what he had said and why it had seemed important to him, and when Joe began to sing again softly, the quiet mood of the early evening, the side of him that was best, wisest, and most enduring, stole over him once more. The flattery, the vanity, the fatuousness of the last hour moved off, and when he spoke it was almost in a whisper:

"Let's walk around the block."

The sidewalk was warm to their bare feet. It was only midnight, but the square was deserted save for their whitish figures, inconspicuous against the starry darkness. They snorted with glee at their daring. Once a shadow, with loud human shoes, crossed the street far ahead, but the sound served only to increase their own unsubstantiality. Slipping quickly through the clearings made by gas lamps among the trees, they rounded the block, hurrying when they neared the Gorman house as though they had been really lost in a midsummer night's dream.

Up in Joe's room, they lay awake in the darkness.

"I talked too much," Basil thought. "I probably sounded pretty bossy and maybe I made him sort of mad. But probably when we walked around the block he forgot everything I said."

Alas, Joe had forgotten nothing — except the advice by which Basil had intended him to profit.

"I never saw anybody as stuck up," he said to himself wrathfully. "He thinks he's wonderful. He thinks he's so darn popular with girls."

III
. . . . .

An element of vast importance had made its appearance with the summer; suddenly the great thing in Basil's crowd was to own an automobile. Fun no longer seemed available save at great distances, at suburban lakes or remote country clubs. Walking downtown ceased to be a legitimate pastime. On the contrary, a single block from one youth's house to another's must be navigated in a car. Dependent groups formed around owners and they began to wield what was, to Basil at least, a disconcerting power.

On the morning of a dance at the lake he called up Riply Buckner.

"Hey, Rip, how you going out to Connie's tonight?"

"With Elwood Leaming."

"Has he got a lot of room?"

Riply seemed somewhat embarrassed. "Why, I don't think he has. You see, he's taking Margaret Torrence and I'm taking Imogene Bissel."

"Oh!"

Basil frowned. He should have arranged all this a week ago. After a moment he called up Joe Gorman.

"Going to the Davies' tonight, Joe?"

"Why, yes."

"Have you got room in your car—I mean, could I go with you?"

"Why, yes, I suppose so."

There was a perceptible lack of warmth in his voice.

"Sure you got plenty of room?"

"Sure. We'll call for you quarter to eight."

Basil began preparations at five. For the second time in his life he shaved, completing the operation by cutting a short straight line under his nose. It bled profusely, but on the advice of Hilda, the maid, he finally stanched the flow with little pieces of toilet paper. Quite a number of pieces were necessary; so, in order to facilitate breathing, he trimmed it down with a scissors, and with this somewhat awkward mustache of paper and gore clinging to his upper lip, wandered impatiently around the house.

At six he began working on it again, soaking off the tissue paper and dabbing at the persistently freshening crimson line. It dried at length, but when he rashly hailed his mother it opened once more and the tissue paper was called back into play.

At quarter to eight, dressed in blue coat and white flannels, he drew one last bar of powder across the blemish, dusted it carefully with his handkerchief, and hurried out to Joe Gorman's car. Joe was driving in person, and in front with him were Lewis Crum and Hubert Blair. Basil got in the big rear seat alone and they drove without stopping out of the city on the Black Bear Road, keeping their backs to him and talking in low voices together. He thought at first that they were going to pick up other boys; now he was shocked, and for a moment he considered getting out of the car, but this would imply that he was hurt. His spirit, and with it his face, hardened a little and he sat without speaking or being spoken to for the rest of the ride.

After half an hour the Davies' house, a huge rambling bungalow occupying a small peninsula in the lake, floated into sight. Lanterns outlined its shape and wavered in gleaming lines on the gold-and-rose colored water, and as they came near, the low notes of bass horns and drums were blown toward them from the lawn.

Inside Basil looked about for Imogene. There was a crowd around her seeking dances, but she saw Basil; his heart bounded at her quick intimate smile.

"You can have the fourth, Basil, and the eleventh and the second extra. . . . How did you hurt your lip?"

"Cut it shaving," he said hurriedly. "How about supper?"

"Well, I have to have supper with Riply because he brought me."

"No, you don't," Basil assured her.

"Yes, she does," insisted Riply, standing close at hand. "Why don't you get your own girl for supper?"

—but Basil had no girl, though he was as yet unaware of the fact.

After the fourth dance, Basil led Imogene down to the end of the pier, where they found seats in a motorboat.

"Now what?" she said.

He did not know. If he had really cared for her he would have known. When her hand rested on his knee for a moment he did not notice it. Instead, he talked. He told her how he had pitched on the second baseball team at school and had once beaten the first in a five-inning game. He told her that the thing was that some boys were popular with boys and some boys were popular with girls—he, for instance, was popular with girls. In short, he unloaded himself.

At length, feeling that he had perhaps dwelt disproportionately on himself, he told her suddenly that she was his favorite girl.

Imogene sat there, sighing a little in the moonlight. In another boat, lost in the darkness beyond the pier, sat a party of four. Joe Gorman was singing:

> *My little love—*
> *—in honey man,*
> *He sure has won my——*

"I thought you might want to know," said Basil to Imogene. "I thought maybe you thought I liked somebody else. The truth game didn't get around to me the other night."

"What?" asked Imogene vaguely. She had forgotten the other night, all nights except this, and she was thinking of the magic in Joe Gorman's voice. She had the next dance with him; he was going to teach her the words of a new song. Basil was sort of peculiar, telling her all this stuff. He was good-looking and attractive and all that, but—she wanted the dance to be over. She wasn't having any fun.

The music began inside—"Everybody's Doing It," played with many little nervous jerks on the violins.

"Oh, listen!" she cried, sitting up and snapping her fingers. "Do you know how to rag?"

"Listen, Imogene"—He half realized that something had slipped away—"let's sit out this dance—you can tell Joe you forgot."

She rose quickly. "Oh, no, I can't!"

Unwillingly Basil followed her inside. It had not gone well— he had talked too much again. He waited moodily for the eleventh dance so that he could behave differently. He believed now that he was in love with Imogene. His self-deception created a tightness in his throat, a counterfeit of longing and desire.

Before the eleventh dance he was aware that some party was being organized from which he was purposely excluded. There were whisperings and arguings among some of the boys, and unnatural silences when he came near. He heard Joe Gorman say to Riply Buckner, "We'll just be gone three days. If Gladys can't go, why don't you ask Connie? The chaperons'll—" he changed his sentence as he saw Basil—"and we'll all go to Smith's for ice-cream soda."

Later, Basil took Riply Buckner aside but failed to elicit any information: Riply had not forgotten Basil's attempt to rob him of Imogene tonight.

"It wasn't about anything," he insisted. "We're going to Smith's, honest. . . . How'd you cut your lip?"

"Cut it shaving."

When his dance with Imogene came she was even vaguer than before exchanging mysterious communications with various girls as they moved around the room, locked in the convulsive grip of the Grizzly Bear. He led her out to the boat again, but it was occupied, and they walked up and down the pier while he tried to talk to her and she hummed:

My little lov-in honey man———

"Imogene, listen. What I wanted to ask you when we were on the boat before was about the night we played Truth. Did you really mean what you said?"

"Oh, what do you want to talk about that silly game for?"

It had reached her ears, not once but several times, that Basil thought he was wonderful — news that was flying about with as much volatility as the rumor of his graces two weeks before. Imogene liked to agree with everyone — and she had agreed with several impassioned boys that Basil was terrible. And it was difficult not to dislike him for her own disloyalty.

But Basil thought that only ill luck ended the intermission before he could accomplish his purpose; though what he had wanted he had not known.

Finally, during the intermission, Margaret Torrence, whom he had neglected, told him the truth.

"Are you going on the touring party up to the St. Croix River?" she asked. She knew he was not.

"What party?"

"Joe Gorman got it up. I'm going with Elwood Leaming."

"No, I'm not going," he said gruffly. "I couldn't go."

"Oh!"

"I don't like Joe Gorman."

"I guess he doesn't like you much either."

"Why? What did he say?"

"Oh, nothing."

"But what? Tell me what he said."

After a minute she told him, as if reluctantly: "Well, he and Hubert Blair said you thought—you thought you were wonderful." Her heart misgave her.

But she remembered he had asked her for only one dance. "Joe said you told him that all the girls thought you were wonderful."

"I never said anything like that," said Basil indignantly, "never!"

He understood—Joe Gorman had done it all, taken advantage of Basil's talking too much—an affliction which his real friends had always allowed for—in order to ruin him. The world was suddenly compact of villainy. He decided to go home.

In the coat room he was accosted by Bill Kampf: "Hello, Basil, how did you hurt your lip?"

"Cut it shaving."

"Say, are you going to this party they're getting up next week?"

"No."

"Well, look, I've got a cousin from Chicago coming to stay with us and mother said I could have a boy out for the weekend. Her name is Minnie Bibble."

"Minnie Bibble?" repeated Basil, vaguely revolted.

"I thought maybe you were going to that party, too, but Riply Buckner said to ask you and I thought——"

"I've got to stay home," said Basil quickly.

"Oh, come on, Basil," he pursued. "It's only for two days, and she's a nice girl. You'd like her."

"I don't know," Basil considered. "I'll tell you what I'll do, Bill. I've got to get the street car home. I'll come out for the week-end if you'll take me over to Wildwood now in your car."

"Sure I will."

Basil walked out on the veranda and approached Connie Davies.

"Good-by," he said. Try as he might, his voice was stiff and proud. "I had an awfully good time."

"I'm sorry you're leaving so early, Basil." But she said to herself: "He's too stuck up to have a good time. He thinks he's wonderful."

From the veranda he could hear Imogene's laughter down at the end of the pier. Silently he went down the steps and along the walk to meet Bill Kampf, giving strollers a wide berth as though he felt the sight of him would diminish their pleasure.

It had been an awful night.

Ten minutes later Bill dropped him beside the waiting trolley. A few last picnickers sauntered aboard and the car bobbed and clanged through the night toward St. Paul.

Presently two young girls sitting opposite Basil began looking over at him and nudging each other, but he took no notice — he was thinking how sorry they would all be — Imogene and Margaret, Joe and Hubert and Riply.

"Look at him now!" they would say to themselves sorrowfully. "President of the United States at twenty-five! Oh, if we only hadn't been so bad to him that night!"

He thought he was wonderful!

IV
. . . . .

Ermine Gilberte Labouisse Bibble was in exile. Her parents had brought her from New Orleans to Southampton in May, hoping that the active outdoor life proper to a girl of fifteen would take her thoughts from love. But North or South, a storm of sapling arrows flew about her. She was "engaged" before the first of June.

Let it not be gathered from the foregoing that the somewhat hard outlines of Miss Bibble at twenty had already begun to appear. She was of a radiant freshness; her head had reminded otherwise not illiterate young men of damp blue violets, pierced with blue windows that looked into a bright soul, with today's new roses showing through.

She was in exile. She was going to Glacier National Park to forget. It was written that in passage she would come to Basil as a sort of initiation, turning his eyes out from himself and giving him a first dazzling glimpse into the world of love.

She saw him first as a quiet handsome boy with an air of consideration in his face, which was the mark of his recent rediscovery that others had wills as strong as his, and more power. It appeared to Minnie—as a few months back it had appeared to Margaret Torrence, like a charming sadness. At dinner he was polite to Mrs. Kampf in a courteous way that he had from his father, and he listened to Mr. Bibble's discussion of the word "Creole" with such evident interest and appreciation that Mr. Bibble thought, "Now here's a young boy with something *to* him."

After dinner, Minnie, Basil, and Bill rode into Black Bear village to the movies, and the slow diffusion of Minnie's charm and personality presently became the charm and personality of the affair itself.

It was thus that all Minnie's affairs for many years had a family likeness. She looked at Basil, a childish open look; then opened her eyes wider as if she had some sort of comic misgivings, and smiled—she smiled—

For all the candor of this smile, its effect, because of the special contours of Minnie's face and independent of her mood, was of sparkling invitation. Whenever it appeared Basil seemed to be suddenly inflated and borne upward, a little farther each time, only to be set down when the smile had reached a point where it must become a grin, and chose instead to melt away. It was like a drug. In a little while he wanted nothing except to watch it with a vast buoyant delight.

Then he wanted to see how close he could get to it.

There is a certain state of an affair between young people when the presence of a third party is a stimulant. Before the second day

had well begun, before Minnie and Basil had progressed beyond
the point of great gross compliments about each other's surpass-
ing beauty and charm, both of them had begun to think about the
time when they could get rid of their host, Bill Kampf.

In the late afternoon, when the first cool of the evening had
come down and they were fresh and thin-feeling from swimming,
they sat in a cushioned swing, piled high with pillows and
shaded by the thick veranda vines; Basil put his arm around her
and leaned toward her cheek and Minnie managed it that he
touched her fresh lips instead. And he had always learned things
quickly.

They sat there for an hour, while Bill's voice reached them, now
from the pier, now from the hall above, now from the pagoda at
the end of the garden, and three saddled horses chafed their bits in
the stable and all around them the bees worked faithfully among
the flowers. Then Minnie reached up to reality, and they allowed
themselves to be found —

"Why, we were looking for you too."

And Basil, by simply waving his arms and wishing, floated
miraculously upstairs to brush his hair for dinner.

"She certainly is a wonderful girl. Oh, gosh, she certainly is
a wonderful girl!"

He mustn't lose his head. At dinner and afterward he listened
with unwavering deferential attention while Mr. Bibble talked of
the boll weevil.

"But I'm boring you. You children want to go off by yourselves."

"Not at all, Mr. Bibble. I was very interested — honestly."

"Well, you all go on and amuse yourselves. I didn't realize time
was getting on. Nowadays it's so seldom you meet a young man
with good manners and good common sense in his head, that an
old man like me is likely to go along forever."

Bill walked down with Basil and Minnie to the end of the pier.
"Hope we'll have a good sailing tomorrow. Say, I've got to drive

over to the village and get somebody for my crew. Do you want to come along?"

"I reckon I'll sit here for a while and then go to bed," said Minnie.

"All right. You want to come, Basil?"

"Why — why, sure, if you want me, Bill."

"You'll have to sit on a sail I'm taking over to be mended."

"I don't want to crowd you."

"You won't crowd me. I'll go get the car."

When he had gone they looked at each other in despair. But he did not come back for an hour — something happened about the sail or the car that took a long time. There was only the threat, making everything more poignant and breathless, that at any minute he *would* be coming.

By and by they got into the motorboat and sat close together murmuring: "This fall — " "When you come to New Orleans — " "When I go to Yale year after next — " "When I come North to school — " "When I get back from Glacier Park — " "Kiss me once more." . . . "You're terrible. Do you know you're terrible? . . . You're absolutely terrible——"

The water lapped against the posts; sometimes the boat bumped gently on the pier; Basil undid one rope and pushed, so that they swung off and way from the pier, and became a little island in the night . . .

. . . next morning, while he packed his bag, she opened the door of his room and stood beside him. Her face shone with excitement; her dress was starched and white.

"Basil, listen! I have to tell you: Father was talking after breakfast and he told Uncle George that he'd never met such a nice, quiet, level-headed boy as you, and Cousin Bill's got to tutor this month, so father asked Uncle George if he thought your family would let you go to Glacier Park with us for two weeks so I'd have some company." They took hands and danced excitedly around the room. "Don't say anything about it, because I reckon he'll have to write your mother and everything. Basil, isn't it wonderful?"

So when Basil left at eleven, there was no misery in their parting. Mr. Bibble, going into the village for a paper, was going to escort Basil to his train, and till the motor-car moved away the eyes of the two young people shone and there was a secret in their waving hands.

Basil sank back in the seat, replete with happiness. He relaxed — to have made a success of the visit was so nice. He loved her — he loved even her father sitting beside him, her father who was privileged to be so close to her, to fuddle himself at that smile.

Mr. Bibble lit a cigar. "Nice weather," he said. "Nice climate up to the end of October."

"Wonderful," agreed Basil. "I miss October now that I go East to school."

"Getting ready for college?"

"Yes, sir; getting ready for Yale." A new pleasurable thought occurred to him. He hesitated, but he knew that Mr. Bibble, who liked him, would share his joy. "I took my preliminaries this spring and I just heard from them — I passed six out of seven."

"Good for you!"

Again Basil hesitated, then he continued: "I got A in ancient history and B in English history and English A. And I got C in algebra A and Latin A and B. I failed French A."

"Good!" said Mr. Bibble.

"I should have passed them all," went on Basil, "but I didn't study hard at first. I was the youngest boy in my class and I had a sort of swelled head about it."

It was well that Mr. Bibble should know he was taking no dullard to Glacier National Park. Mr. Bibble took a long puff of his cigar.

On second thought, Basil decided that his last remark didn't have the right ring and he amended it a little.

"It wasn't exactly a swelled head, but I never had to study very

much, because in English I'd usually read most of the books before, and in history I'd read a lot too." He broke off and tried
again: "I mean, when you say swelled head you think of a boy just
going around with his head swelled, sort of, saying, 'Oh, look how
much I know!' Well, I wasn't like that. I mean, I didn't think I
knew everything, but I was sort of——"

As he searched for the elusive word, Mr. Bibble said, "H'm!"
and pointed with his cigar at a spot in the lake.

"There's a boat," he said.

"Yes," agreed Basil. "I don't know much about sailing. I never
cared for it. Of course I've been out a lot, just tending boards and
all that, but most of the time you have to sit with nothing to do.
I like football."

"H'm!" said Mr. Bibble. "When I was your age I was out in the
Gulf in a catboat every day."

"I guess it's fun if you like it," conceded Basil.

"Happiest days of my life."

The station was in sight. It occurred to Basil that he should
make one final friendly gesture.

"Your daughter certainly is an attractive girl, Mr. Bibble," he
said. "I usually get along with girls all right, but I don't usually
like them very much. But I think your daughter is the most attractive girl I ever met." Then, as the car stopped, a faint misgiving overtook him and he was impelled to add with a disparaging
little laugh. "Good-by. I hope I didn't talk too much."

"Not at all," said Mr. Bibble. "Good luck to you. Good-by."

A few minutes later, when Basil's train had pulled out, Mr.
Bibble stood at the newsstand buying a paper and already drying
his forehead against the hot July day.

"Yes, sir! That was a lesson not to do anything in a hurry," he
was saying to himself vehemently. "Imagine listening to that fresh
kid gabbling about himself all through Glacier Park! Thank the
good Lord for that little ride!"

* * *

On his arrival home, Basil literally sat down and waited. Under no pretext would he leave the house save for short trips to the drug store for refreshments, whence he returned on a full run. The sound of the telephone or the door-bell galvanized him into the rigidity of the electric chair.

That afternoon he composed a wondrous geographical poem, which he mailed to Minnie:

> *Of all the fair flowers of Paris*
> *Of all the red roses of Rome,*
> *Of all the deep tears of Vienna*
> *The sadness wherever you roam,*
> *I think of that night by the lakeside,*
> *The beam of the moon and stars,*
> *And the smell of an aching like perfume,*
> *The tune of the Spanish guitars.*

But Monday passed and most of Tuesday and no word came. Then, late in the afternoon of the second day, as he moved vaguely from room to room looking out of different windows into a barren lifeless street, Minnie called him on the phone.

"Yes?" His heart was beating wildly.

"Basil, we're going this afternoon."

"Going!" he repeated blankly.

"Oh, Basil, I'm so sorry. Father changed his mind about taking anybody West with us."

"Oh!"

"I'm so sorry, Basil."

"I probably couldn't have gone."

There was a moment's silence. Feeling her presence over the wire, he could scarcely breathe, much less speak.

"Basil, can you hear me?"

"Yes."

"We may come back this way. Anyhow, remember we're going to meet this winter in New York."

"Yes," he said, and he added suddenly: "Perhaps we won't ever meet again."

"Of course we will. They're calling me, Basil. I've got to go. Good-by."

He sat down beside the telephone, wild with grief. The maid found him half an hour later bowed over the kitchen table. He knew what had happened as well as if Minnie had told him. He had made the same old error, undone the behavior of three days in half an hour. It would have been no consolation if it had occurred to him that it was just as well. Somewhere on the trip he would have let go and things might have been worse—though perhaps not so sad. His only thought now was that she was gone.

He lay on his bed, baffled, mistaken, miserable but not beaten. Time after time, the same vitality that had led his spirit to a scourging made him able to shake off the blood like water, not to forget, but to carry his wounds with him to new disasters and new atonements—toward his unknown destiny.

Two days later his mother told him that on condition of his keeping the batteries on charge, and washing it once a week, his grandfather had consented to let him use the electric whenever it was idle in the afternoon. Two hours later he was out in it, gliding along Crest Avenue at the maximum speed permitted by the gears and trying to lean back as if it were a Stutz Bearcat. Imogene Bissel waved at him from in front of her house and he came to an uncertain stop.

"You've got a car!"

"It's grandfather's," he said modestly. "I thought you were up on that party at the St. Croix."

She shook her head. "Mother wouldn't let me go—only a few girls went. There was a big accident over in Minneapolis and mother won't even let me ride in a car unless there's someone over eighteen driving."

"Listen, Imogene, do you suppose your mother meant electrics?"

"Why, I never thought—I don't know. I could go and see."

"Tell your mother it won't go over twelve miles an hour," he called after her.

A minute later she ran joyfully down the walk. "I can go, Basil," she cried. "Mother never heard of any wrecks in an electric. What'll we do?"

"Anything," he said in a reckless voice. "I didn't mean that about this bus making only twelve miles an hour—it'll make fifteen. Listen, let's go down to Smith's and have a claret lemonade."

"Why, Basil Lee!"

THE CAPTURED SHADOW

Fitzgerald continued to write the lucrative Basil stories in Paris in September 1928, just before he returned to Delaware. In This Side of Paradise, *Amory Blaine and his friend Froggy Parker claim that "the greatest line in literature occurred in Act III of 'Arsene Lupin': 'If one can't be a great artist or a great soldier, the next best thing is to be a great criminal.'" Although it is not clear from his notebooks if he ever saw the Maurice Leblanc dramatic adaptation of the Arsene Lupin stories, Leblanc was one of Fitzgerald's favorite authors and his tales of a gentleman burglar worked their way into Fitzgerald's imagination. In January 1912, while attending Newman Academy, Fitzgerald began a play that he finished on the train home to St. Paul that summer. It became the young playwright's second offering for Elizabeth Magoffin's dramatic club in St. Paul. With the 15-year-old Fitzgerald as The Shadow,* The Captured Shadow *was performed August 23, 1912, at Mrs. Backus' School for Girls, located a short walk from the Fitzgerald home on Holly Avenue, the very street on which Fitzgerald had Basil live. Sixteen years later he would fictionalize the events of the play's production for this story. As a professional writer, Fitzgerald continued to use the stock gentlemen crook character in "Dalyrimple Goes Wrong," a story inspired by another St. Paul friend, Tubby Washington, and published in* The Smart Set *in 1920.*

The Saturday Evening Post, December 29, 1928
Collected in *Taps at Reveille* (1935)

I
. . . . .

BASIL DUKE LEE shut the front door behind him and turned on the dining-room light. His mother's voice drifted sleepily downstairs:

"Basil, is that you?"

"No, mother, it's a burglar."

"It seems to me twelve o'clock is pretty late for a fifteen-year-old boy."

"We went to Smith's and had a soda."

Whenever a new responsibility devolved upon Basil he was "a boy almost sixteen," but when a privilege was in question, he was "a fifteen-year-old boy."

There were footsteps above, and Mrs. Lee, in kimono, descended to the first landing.

"Did you and Riply enjoy the play?"

"Yes, very much."

"What was it about?"

"Oh, it was just about this man. Just an ordinary play."

"Didn't it have a name?"

"*Are You a Mason?*"

"Oh." She hesitated, covetously watching his alert and eager face, holding him there. "Aren't you coming to bed?"

"I'm going to get something to eat."

"Something more?"

For a moment he didn't answer. He stood in front of a glassed-in bookcase in the living room, examining its contents with an equally glazed eye.

"We're going to get up a play," he said suddenly. "I'm going to write it."

"Well — that'll be very nice. Please come to bed soon. You were up late last night, too, and you've got dark circles under your eyes."

From the bookcase Basil presently extracted *Van Bibber and*

Others, from which he read while he ate a large plate of straw softened with half a pint of cream. Back in the living room he sat for a few minutes at the piano, digesting, and meanwhile staring at the colored cover of a song from *The Midnight Sons.* It showed three men in evening clothes and opera hats sauntering jovially along Broadway against the blazing background of Times Square.

Basil would have denied incredulously the suggestion that that was currently his favorite work of art. But it was.

He went upstairs. From a drawer of his desk he took out a composition book and opened it.

BASIL DUKE LEE

ST. REGIS SCHOOL

EASTCHESTER, CONN.

FIFTH FORM FRENCH

and on the next page, under Irregular Verbs:

PRESENT

je connais   *nous con*

tu conais

il connaît

He turned over another page.

MR. WASHINGTON SQUARE

A Musical Comedy by

BASIL DUKE LEE

Music by Victor Herbert

ACT I

[*The porch of the Millionaires' Club, near New York. Opening Chorus,* LEILIA *and* DEBUTANTES:

We sing not soft, we sing not loud
   For no one ever heard an opening chorus.

We are a very merry crowd
　　But no one ever heard an opening chorus.
We're just a crowd of debutantes
　　As merry as can be
And nothing that there is could ever bore us
　　We're the wittiest ones, the prettiest ones
In all society
　　But no one ever herd an opening chorus.

LEILIA (*stepping forward*): Well, girls, has Mr. Washington Square been around here today?

Basil turned over a page. There was no answer to Leilia's question. Instead in capitals was a brand-new heading:

HIC! HIC! HIC!

A Hilarious Farce in one Act

by

BASIL DUKE LEE

SCENE

[*A fashionable apartment near Broadway, New York City. It is almost midnight. As the curtain goes up there is a knocking at the door and a few minutes later it opens to admit a handsome man in a full evening dress and a companion. He has evidently been imbibing, for his words are thick, his nose is red, and he can hardly stand up. He turns up the light and comes down center.*

STUYVESANT: Hic! Hic! Hic!
O'HARA (*his companion*): Begorra, you been sayin' nothing else all this evening.

Basil turned over a page and then another, reading hurriedly, but not without interest.

PROFESSOR PUMPKIN: Now, if you are an educated man, as you claim, perhaps you can tell me the Latin word for "this."

STUYVESANT: Hic! Hic! Hic!

PROFESSOR PUMPKIN: Correct. Very good indeed. I——

At this point *Hic! Hic! Hic!* came to an end in midsentence. On the following page, in just as determined a hand as if the last two works had not faltered by the way, was the heavily underlined beginning of another:

THE CAPTURED SHADOW
A Melodramatic Farce in Three Acts
by
BASIL DUKE LEE
SCENE

[*All three acts take place in the library of the* VAN BAKERS' *house in New York. It is well furnished with a red lamp on one side and some crossed spears and helmets and so on and a divan and a general air of an oriental den.*

When the curtain rises MISS SAUNDERS, LEILIA VAN BAKER *and* ESTELLA CARRAGE *are sitting at a table.* MISS SAUNDERS *is an old maid about forty very kittenish.* LEILIA *is pretty with dark hair.* ESTELLA *has light hair. They are a striking combination.*

The Captured Shadow filled the rest of the book and ran over into several loose sheets at the end. When it broke off Basil sat for a while in thought. This had been a season of "crook comedies" in New York, and the feel, the swing, the exact and vivid image of the two he had seen, were in the foreground of his mind. At the time they had been enormously suggestive, opening out into a world much larger and more brilliant than themselves that existed outside their windows and beyond their doors, and it was this suggested world rather than any conscious desire to imitate *Officer*

666, that had inspired the effort before him. Presently he printed ACT II at the head of a new tablet and began to write.

An hour passed. Several times he had recourse to a collection of joke books and to an old *Treasury of Wit and Humor* which embalmed the faded Victorian cracks of Bishop Wilberforce and Sydney Smith. At the moment when, in his story, a door moved slowly open, he heard a heavy creak upon the stairs. He jumped to his feet, aghast and trembling, but nothing stirred; only a white moth bounced against the screen, a clock struck the half-hour far across the city, a bird whacked its wings in a trée outside.

Voyaging to the bathroom at half-past four, he saw with a shock that morning was already blue at the window. He had stayed up all night. He remembered that people who stayed up all night went crazy, and transfixed in the hall, he tried agonizingly to listen to himself, to feel whether or not he was going crazy. The things round him seemed preternaturally unreal, and rushing frantically back into his bedroom, he began tearing off his clothes, racing after the vanishing night. Undressed, he threw a final regretful glance at his pile of manuscript — he had the whole next scene in his head. As a compromise with incipient madness he got into bed and wrote for an hour more.

Late next morning he was startled awake by one of the ruthless Scandinavian sisters who, in theory, were the Lees' servants. "Eleven o'clock!" she shouted. "Five after!"

"Let me alone," Basil mumbled. "What do you come and wake me up for?"

"Somebody downstairs." He opened his eyes. "You ate all the cream last night," Hilda continued. "Your mother didn't have any for her coffee."

"All the cream!" he cried. "Why, I saw some more."

"It was sour."

"That's terrible," he exclaimed, sitting up. "Terrible!"

For a moment she enjoyed his dismay. Then she said, "Riply Buckner's downstairs," and went out, closing the door.

"Send him up!" he called after her. "Hilda, why don't you ever listen for a minute? Did I get any mail?"

There was no answer. A moment later Riply came in.

"My gosh, are you still in bed?"

"I wrote on the play all night. I almost finished Act Two." He pointed to his desk.

"That's what I want to talk to you about," said Riply. "Mother thinks we ought to get Miss Halliburton."

"What for?"

"Just to sort of be there."

Though Miss Halliburton was a pleasant person who combined the occupations of French teacher and bridge teacher, unofficial chaperon and children's friend, Basil felt that her superintendence would give the project an unprofessional ring.

"She wouldn't interfere," went on Riply, obviously quoting his mother. "I'll be the business manager and you'll direct the play, just like we said, but it would be good to have her there for prompter and to keep order at rehearsals. The girls' mothers'll like it."

"All right," Basil agreed reluctantly. "Now look, let's see who we'll have in the cast. First, there's the leading man — this gentleman burglar that's called The Shadow. Only it turns out at the end that he's really a young man about town doing it on a bet, and not really a burglar at all."

"That's you."

"No, that's you."

"Come on! You're the best actor," protested Riply.

"No, I'm going to take a smaller part, so I can coach."

"Well, haven't I got to be business manager?"

Selecting the actresses, presumably all eager, proved to be a difficult matter. They settled finally on Imogene Bissel for leading lady; Margaret Torrence for her friend, and Connie Davies for "Miss Saunders, an old maid very kittenish."

On Riply's suggestion that several other girls wouldn't be pleased at being left out, Basil introduced a maid and a cook, "who could just sort of look in from the kitchen." He rejected firmly Riply's further proposal that there should be two or three maids, "a sort of sewing woman," and a trained nurse. In a house so clogged with femininity even the most umbrageous of gentleman burglars would have difficulty in moving about.

"I'll tell you two people we won't have," Basil said meditatively — "that's Joe Gorman and Hubert Blair."

"I wouldn't be in it if we had Hubert Blair," asserted Riply.

"Neither would I."

Hubert Blair's almost miraculous successes with girls had caused Basil and Riply much jealous pain.

They began calling up the prospective cast and immediately the enterprise received its first blow. Imogene Bissel was going to Rochester, Minnesota, to have her appendix removed, and wouldn't be back for three weeks.

They considered.

"How about Margaret Torrence?"

Basil shook his head. He had vision of Leilia Van Baker as someone rarer and more spirited than Margaret Torrence. Not that Leilia had much being, even to Basil — less than the Harrison Fisher girls pinned around his wall at school. But she was not Margaret Torrence. She was no one you could inevitably see by calling up half an hour before on the phone.

He discarded candidate after candidate. Finally a face began to flash before his eyes, as if in another connection, but so insistently that at length he spoke the name.

"Evelyn Beebe."

"Who?"

Though Evelyn Beebe was only sixteen, her precocious charms had elevated her to an older crowd and to Basil she seemed of the very generation of his heroine, Leilia Van Baker. It was a little like asking Sarah Bernhardt for her services, but once her name had occurred to him, other possibilities seemed pale.

At noon they rang the Beebes' door-bell, stricken by a paralysis of embarrassment when Evelyn opened the door herself and, with politeness that concealed a certain surprise, asked them in.

Suddenly, through the portière of the living room, Basil saw and recognized a young man in golf knickerbockers.

"I guess we better not come in," he said quickly.

"We'll come some other time," Riply added.

Together they started precipitately for the door, but she barred their way.

"Don't be silly," she insisted. "It's just Andy Lockheart."

Just Andy Lockheart — winner of the Western Golf Championship at eighteen, captain of his freshman baseball team, handsome, successful at everything he tried, a living symbol of the splendid, glamorous world of Yale. For a year Basil had walked like him and tried unsuccessfully to play the piano by ear as Andy Lockheart was able to do.

Through sheer ineptitude at escaping, they were edged into the room. Their plan suddenly seemed presumptuous and absurd.

Perceiving their condition Evelyn tried to soothe them with pleasant banter.

"Well it's about time you came to see me," she told Basil. "Here I've been sitting at home every night waiting for you — ever since the Davies dance. Why haven't you been here before?"

He stared at her blankly, unable even to smile, and muttered: "Yes, you have."

"I have though. Sit down and tell me why you've been neglecting me! I suppose you've both been rushing the beautiful Imogene Bissel."

"Why, I understand —" said Basil. "Why, I heard from somewhere that she's gone up to have some kind of an appendicitis — that is —" He ran down to a pitch of inaudibility as Andy Lockheart at the piano began playing a succession of thoughtful chords, which resolved itself into the maxixe, an eccentric stepchild of the tango. Kicking back a rug and lifting her skirts a little, Evelyn fluently tapped out a circle with her heels around the floor.

They sat inanimate as cushions on the sofa watching her. She was almost beautiful, with rather large features and bright fresh color behind which her heart seemed to be trembling a little with laughter. Her voice and her lithe body were always mimicking, ceaselessly caricaturing every sound and movement near by, until even those who disliked her admitted that "Evelyn could always make you laugh." She finished her dance now with a false stumble and an awed expression as she clutched at the piano, and Basil and Riply chuckled. Seeing their embarrassment lighten, she came and sat down beside them, and they laughed again when she said: "Excuse my lack of self-control."

"Do you want to be the leading lady in a play we're going to give?" demanded Basil with sudden desperation. "We're going to have it at the Martindale School, for the benefit of the Baby Welfare."

"Basil, this is so sudden."

Andy Lockheart turned around from the piano

"What're you going to give—a minstrel show?"

"No, it's a crook play named *The Captured Shadow*. Miss Halliburton is going to coach it." He suddenly realized the convenience of that name to shelter himself behind.

"Why don't you give something like *The Private Secretary*?" interrupted Andy. "There's a good play for you. We gave it my last year at school."

"Oh, no, it's all settled," said Basil quickly. "We're going to put on this play that I wrote."

"You wrote it yourself?" exclaimed Evelyn.

"Yes."

"My-y gosh!" said Andy. He began to play again.

"Look, Evelyn," said Basil. "It's only for three weeks, and you'd be the leading lady."

She laughed. "Oh, no. I couldn't. Why don't you get Imogene?"

"She's sick, I tell you. Listen——"

"Or Margaret Torrence?"

"I don't want anybody but you."

The directness of this appeal touched her and momentarily she hesitated. But the hero of the Western Golf Championship turned around from the piano with a teasing smile and she shook her head.

"I can't do it, Basil. I may have to go East with the family."

Reluctantly Basil and Riply got up.

"Gosh, I wish you'd be in it, Evelyn."

"I wish I could."

Basil lingered, thinking fast, wanting her more than ever; indeed, without her, it scarcely seemed worth while to go on with the play. Suddenly a desperate expedient took shape on his lips:

"You're certainly would be wonderful. You see, the leading man is going to be Hubert Blair."

Breathlessly he watched her, saw her hesitate.

"Good-by," he said.

She came with them to the door and then out on the veranda, frowning a little.

"How long did you say the rehearsals would take?" she asked thoughtfully.

II
. . . . .

On an August evening three days later Basil read the play to the cast on Miss Halliburton's porch. He was nervous and at first there were interruptions of "Louder" and "Not so fast." Just as his audience was beginning to be amused by the repartee of the two comic crooks — repartee that had seen service with Weber and Fields — he was interrupted by the late arrival of Hubert Blair.

Hubert was fifteen, a somewhat shallow boy save for two or three felicities which he possessed to an extraordinary degree. But one excellence suggests the presence of others, and young ladies never failed to respond to his most casual fancy, enduring his fickleness of heart and never convinced that his fundamental indifference might not be overcome. They were dazzled by his flashing self-confidence, by his cherubic ingenuousness, which concealed a shrewd talent for getting around people, and by his extraordinary physical grace. Long-legged, beautifully proportioned, he had that tumbler's balance usually characteristic only of men "built near the ground." He was in constant motion that was a delight to watch, and Evelyn Beebe was not the only older girl who had found in him a mysterious promise and watched him for a long time with something more than curiosity.

He stood in the doorway now with an expression of bogus reverence on his round pert face.

"Excuse me," he said. "Is this the First Methodist Episcopal Church?" Everybody laughed — even Basil. "I didn't know. I thought maybe I was in the right church, but in the wrong pew."

They laughed again, somewhat discouraged. Basil waited until Hubert had seated himself beside Evelyn Beebe. Then he began to read once more, while the others, fascinated, watched Hubert's efforts to balance a chair on its hind legs. This squeaky experiment continued as an undertone to the reading. Not until Basil's desperate "Now, here's where you come in, Hube," did attention swing back to the play.

Basil read for more than an hour. When, at the end, he closed the composition book and looked up shyly, there was a burst of spontaneous applause. He had followed his models closely, and for all its grotesqueries, the result was actually interesting — it was a play. Afterward he lingered, talking to Miss Halliburton, and he walked home glowing with excitement and rehearsing a little by himself into the August night.

The first week of rehearsal was a matter of Basil climbing back and forth from auditorium to stage, crying, "No! Look here, Connie; you come in more like this." Then things began to happen. Mrs. Van Schellinger came to rehearsal one day, and lingering afterward, announced that she couldn't let Gladys be in "a play about criminals." Her theory was that this element could be removed; for instance, the two comic crooks could be changed to "two funny farmers."

Basil listened with horror. When she had gone he assured Miss Halliburton that he would change nothing. Luckily Gladys played the cook, an interpolated part that could be summarily struck out, but her absence was felt in another way. She was tranquil and tractable, "the most carefully brought-up girl in town," and at her withdrawal rowdiness appeared during rehearsals. Those who had only such lines as "I'll ask Mrs. Van Baker, sir," in Act I and "No, ma'am," in Act III showed a certain tendency to grow restless in between. So now it was:

"Please keep that dog quiet or else send him home!" or:

"Where's that maid? Wake up, Margaret, for heaven's sake!" or:

"What is there to laugh at that's so darn funny?"

More and more the chief problem was the tactful management of Hubert Blair. Apart from his unwillingness to learn his lines, he was a satisfactory hero, but off the stage he became a nuisance. He gave an endless private performance for Evelyn Beebe, which took such forms as chasing her amorously around the hall or of flipping peanuts over his shoulder to land mysteriously on the stage. Called to order, he would mutter, "Aw, shut up yourself," just loud enough for Basil to guess, but not to hear.

But Evelyn Beebe was all that Basil had expected. Once on the stage, she compelled a breathless attention, and Basil recognized this by adding to her part. He envied the half-sentimental fun that she and Hubert derived from their scenes together and he felt a vague, impersonal jealousy that almost every night after rehearsal they drove around together in Hubert's car.

One afternoon when matters had progressed a fortnight, Hubert came in an hour late, loafed through the first act, and then informed Miss Halliburton that he was going home.

"What for?" Basil demanded.

"I've got some things I got to do."

"Are they important?"

"What business is that of yours?"

"Of course it's my business," said Basil heatedly, whereupon Miss Halliburton interfered.

"There's no use of anybody getting angry. What Basil means, Hubert, is that if it's just some small thing—why, we're all giving up our pleasures to make this play a success."

Hubert listened with obvious boredom.

"I've got to drive downtown and get father."

He looked coolly at Basil, as if challenging him to deny the adequacy of this explanation.

"Then why did you come an hour late?" demanded Basil.

"Because I had to do something for mother."

A group had gathered and he glanced around triumphantly. It was one of those sacred excuses, and only Basil saw that it was disingenuous.

"Oh, tripe!" he said.

"Maybe you think so—Bossy."

Basil took a step toward him, his eyes blazing.

"What'd you say?"

"I said 'Bossy.' Isn't that what they call you at school?"

It was true. It had followed him home. Even as he went white with rage a vast impotence surged over him at the realization that the past was always lurking near. The faces of school were around him, sneering and watching. Hubert laughed.

"Get out!" said Basil in a strained voice. "Go on! Get right out!"

Hubert laughed again, but as Basil took a step toward him he retreated.

"I don't want to be in your play anyhow. I never did."

"Then go on out of this hall."

"Now, Basil!" Miss Halliburton hovered breathlessly beside them. Hubert laughed again and looked about for his cap.

"I wouldn't be in your crazy old show," he said. He turned slowly and jauntily, and sauntered out the door.

Riply Buckner read Hubert's part that afternoon, but there was a cloud upon the rehearsal. Miss Beebe's performance lacked its customary verve and the others clustered and whispered, falling silent when Basil came near. After the rehearsal, Miss Halliburton, Riply, and Basil held a conference. Upon Basil flatly refusing to take the leading part, it was decided to enlist a certain Mayall De Bec, known slightly to Riply, who had made a name for himself in theatricals at the Central High School.

But next day a blow fell that was irreparable. Evelyn, flushed and uncomfortable, told Basil and Miss Halliburton that her family's plans had changed — they were going East next week and she couldn't be in the play after all. Basil understood. Only Hubert had held her this long.

"Good-by," he said gloomily.

His manifest despair shamed her and she tried to justify herself.

"Really, I can't help it. Oh, Basil, I'm so sorry!"

"Couldn't you stay over a week with me after your family goes?" Miss Halliburton asked innocently.

"Not possibly. Father wants us all to go together. That's the only reason. If it wasn't for that I'd stay."

"All right," Basil said. "Good-by."

"Basil, you're not mad, are you?" A gust of repentance swept over her. "I'll do anything to help. I'll come to rehearsals this week until you get someone else, and then I'll try to help her all I can. But father says we've got to go."

In vain Riply tried to raise Basil's morale after the rehearsal that afternoon, making suggestions which he waved contemptuously away. Margaret Torrence? Connie Davies? They could hardly play the parts they had. It seemed to Basil as if the undertaking was falling to pieces before his eyes.

It was still early when he got home. He sat dispiritedly by his bedroom window, watching the little Barnfield boy playing a lonesome game by himself in the yard next door.

His mother came in at five, and immediately sensed his depression.

"Teddy Barnfield has the mumps," she said in an effort to distract him. "That's why he's playing there all alone."

"Has he?" he responded listlessly.

"It isn't at all dangerous, but it's very contagious. You had it when you were seven."

"H'm."

She hesitated.

"Are you worrying about your play? Has anything gone wrong?"

"No, mother. I just want to be alone."

After a while he got up and started after a malted milk at the soda fountain around the corner. It was half in his mind to see Mr. Beebe and ask him if he couldn't postpone his trip East. If he could only be sure that that was Evelyn's real reason.

The sight of Evelyn's nine-year-old brother coming along the street broke in on his thoughts.

"Hello, Ham. I hear you're going away."

Ham nodded.

"Going next week. To the seashore."

Basil looked at him speculatively, as if, through his proximity to Evelyn, he held the key to the power of moving her.

"Where are you going now?" he asked.

"I'm going to play with Teddy Barnfield."

"What!" Basil exclaimed. "Why, didn't you know —" He stopped. A wild, criminal idea broke over him; his mother's words floated through his mind: "It isn't at all dangerous, but it's very contagious." If little Ham Beebe got the mumps, and Evelyn *couldn't* go away —

He came to a decision quickly and coolly.

"Teddy's playing in his back yard," he said. "If you want to see him without going through his house, why don't you go down this street and turn up the alley?"

"All right. Thanks," said Ham trustingly.

Basil stood for a minute looking after him until he turned the corner into the alley, fully aware that it was the worst thing he had ever done in his life.

III
· · · · ·

A week later Mrs. Lee had an early supper—all Basil's favorite things: chipped beef, french-fried potatoes, sliced peaches and cream, and devil's food.

Every few minutes Basil said, "Gosh! I wonder what time it is," and went out in the hall to look at the clock. "Does that clock work right?" he demanded with sudden suspicion. It was the first time the matter had ever interested him.

"Perfectly all right. If you eat so fast you'll have indigestion and then you won't be able to act well."

"What do you think of the program?" he asked for the third time. "Riply Buckner, Jr., presents Basil Duke Lee's comedy, *The Captured Shadow*."

"I think it's very nice."

"He doesn't really present it.'

"It sounds very well though."

"I wonder what time it is?" he inquired.

"You just said it was ten minutes after six."

"Well, I guess I better be starting."

"Eat your peaches, Basil. If you don't eat you won't be able to act."

"I don't have to act," he said patiently. "All I am is a small part, and it wouldn't matter—" It was too much trouble to explain.

"Please don't smile at me when I come on, mother," he requested. "Just act as if I was anybody else."

"Can't I even say how-do-you-do?"

"What?" Humor was lost on him. He said good-by. Trying very hard to digest not his food but his heart, which had somehow slipped down into his stomach, he started off for the Martindale School.

As its yellow windows loomed out of the night his excitement became insupportable; it bore no resemblance to the building he had been entering so casually for three weeks. His footsteps echoed symbolically and portentously in its deserted hall; upstairs there was only the janitor setting out the chairs in rows, and Basil wandered about the vacant stage until someone came in.

It was Mayall De Bec, the tall, clever, not very likeable youth they had imported from Lower Crest Avenue to be the leading man. Mayall, far from being nervous, tried to engage Basil in casual conversation. He wanted to know if Basil thought Evelyn Beebe would mind if he went to see her sometime when the show was over. Basil supposed not. Mayall said he had a friend whose father owned a brewery who owned a twelve-cylinder car.

Basil said, "Gee!"

At quarter to seven the participants arrived in groups — Riply Buckner with the six boys he had gathered to serve as ticket takers and ushers; Miss Halliburton, trying to seem very calm and reliable; Evelyn Beebe, who came in as if she were yielding herself up to something and whose glance at Basil seemed to say: "Well, it looks as if I'm really going through with it after all."

Mayall De Bec was to make up the boys and Miss Halliburton the girls. Basil soon came to the conclusion that Miss Halliburton knew nothing about make-up, but he judged it diplomatic, in that lady's overwrought condition, to say nothing, but to take each girl to Mayall for corrections when Miss Halliburton had done.

An exclamation from Bill Kampf, standing at a crack in the curtain, brought Basil to his side. A tall bald-headed man in spectacles had come in and was shown to a seat in the middle of the house, where he examined the program. He was the public. Behind those waiting eyes, suddenly so mysterious and incalculable, was the secret of the play's failure or success. He finished the program, took off his glasses, and looked around. Two old ladies and two little boys came in, followed immediately by a dozen more.

"Hey, Riply," Basil called softly. "Tell them to put the children down in front."

Riply, struggling into his policeman's uniform, looked up, and the long black mustache on his upper lip quivered indignantly.

"I thought of that long go."

The hall, filling rapidly, was now alive with the buzz of conversation. The children in front were jumping up and down in their seats, and everyone was talking and calling back and forth save the several dozen cooks and housemaids who sat in stiff and quiet pairs about the room.

Then, suddenly, everything was ready. It was incredible. "Stop! Stop!" Basil wanted to say. "It can't be ready. There must be something—there always has been something," but the darkened auditorium and the piano and violin from Geyer's Orchestra playing "Meet Me in the Shadows" belied his words. Miss Sunders, Leilia Van Baker, and Leilia's friend, Estella Carrage, were already seated on the stage, and Miss Halliburton stood in the wings with the prompt book. Suddenly the music ended and the chatter in front died away.

"Oh, gosh!" Basil thought. "Oh, my gosh!"

The curtain rose. A clear voice floated up from somewhere. Could it be from that unfamiliar group on the stage?

> I will, Miss Saunders. I tell you I will!
>
> But, Miss Leilia, I don't consider the newspapers proper for young ladies nowadays.
>
> I don't care. I want to read about this wonderful gentleman burglar they call The Shadow.

It was actually going on. Almost before he realized it, a ripple of laughter passed over the audience as Evelyn gave her imitation of Miss Saunders behind her back.

"Get ready, Basil," breathed Miss Halliburton.

Basil and Bill Kampf, the crooks, each took an elbow of Victor Van Baker, the dissolute son of the house, and made ready to aid him through the front door.

It was strangely natural to be out on the stage with all those eyes looking up encouragingly. His mother's face floated past him, other faces that he recognized and remembered.

Bill Kampf stumbled on a line and Basil picked him up quickly and went on.

MISS SAUNDERS: So you are alderman from the Sixth Ward?
RABBIT SIMONS: Yes, ma'am.
MISS SAUNDERS (*shaking her head kittenishly*): Just what is an alderman?
CHINAMAN RUDD: An alderman is halfway between a politician and a pirate.

This was one of Basil's lines that he was particularly proud of—but there was not a sound from the audience, not a smile. A moment later Bill Kampf absent-mindedly wiped his forehead with his handkerchief and then stared at it, startled by the red stains of make-up on it—and the audience roared. The theatre was like that.

MISS SAUNDERS: Then you believe in spirits, Mr. Rudd.
CHINAMAN RUDD: Yes, ma'am, I certainly do believe in spirits. Have you got any?

The first big scene came. On the darkened stage a window rose slowly and Mayall De Bec, "in a full evening dress," climbed over the sill. He was tiptoeing cautiously from one side of the stage to the other, when Leilia Van Baker came in. For a moment she was frightened, but he assured her that he was a friend of her brother Victor. They talked. She told him naïvely yet feelingly of her admiration for The Shadow, of whose exploits she had read. She hoped, though, that The Shadow would not come here tonight, as the family jewels were all in that safe at the right.

The stranger was hungry. He had been late for his dinner and so had not been able to get any that night. Would he have some crackers and milk? That would be fine. Scarcely had she left the room when he was on his knees by the safe, fumbling at the catch, undeterred by the unpromising word "Cake" stencilled on the safe's front. It swung open, but he heard footsteps outside and closed it just as Leilia came back with the crackers and milk.

They lingered, obviously attracted to each other. Miss Saunders came in, very kittenish, and was introduced. Again Evelyn mimicked her behind her back and the audience roared. Other members of the household appeared and were introduced to the stranger.

What's this? A banging at the door, and Mulligan, a policeman, rushes in.

We have just received word from the Central Office that the notorious Shadow has been seen climbing in the window! No one can leave this house tonight!

The curtain fell. The first rows of the audience — the younger brothers and sisters of the cast — were extravagant in their enthusiasm. The actors took a bow.

A moment later Basil found himself alone with Evelyn Beebe on the stage. A weary doll in her make-up, she was leaning against a table.

"Heigh-ho, Basil," she said.

She had not quite forgiven him for holding her to her promise after her little brother's mumps had postponed their trip East, and Basil had tactfully avoided her, but now they met in the genial glow of excitement and success.

"You were wonderful," he said — "Wonderful!"

He lingered a moment. He could never please her, for she wanted someone like herself, someone who could reach her through her senses, like Hubert Blair. Her intuition told her that Basil was of a certain vague consequence; beyond that his inces-

sant attempts to make people think and feel, bothered and wea-
ried her. But suddenly, in the glow of the evening, they leaned forward and kissed peacefully, and from that moment, because they
had no common ground even to quarrel on, they were friends for
life.

When the curtain rose upon the second act Basil slipped down
a flight of stairs and up to another to the back of the hall, where he
stood watching in the darkness. He laughed silently when the audience laughed, enjoying it as if it were a play he had never seen
before.

There was a second and a third act scene that were very similar.
In each of them The Shadow, alone on the stage, was interrupted
by Miss Saunders. Mayall De Bec, having had but ten days of rehearsal, was inclined to confuse the two, but Basil was totally unprepared for what happened. Upon Connie's entrance Mayall
spoke his third-act line and involuntarily Connie answered in
kind.

Others coming on the stage were swept up in the nervousness
and confusion, and suddenly they were playing the third act in the
middle of the second. It happened so quickly that for a moment
Basil had only a vague sense that something was wrong. Then he
dashed down one stairs and up another into the wings, crying:

"Let down the curtain! Let down the curtain!"

The boys who stood there aghast sprang to the rope. In a minute Basil, breathless, was facing the audience.

"Ladies and gentlemen," he said, "there's been changes in the
cast and what just happened was a mistake. If you'll excuse us
we'd like to do that scene over."

He stepped back in the wings to a flutter of laughter and applause.

"All right, Mayall!" he called excitedly. "On the stage alone.
Your line is: 'I just want to see that the jewels are all right,' and
Connie's is: 'Go ahead, don't mind me.' All right! Curtain up!"

In a moment things righted themselves. Someone brought water for Miss Halliburton, who was in a state of collapse, and as the act ended they all took a curtain call once more. Twenty minutes later it was over. The hero clasped Leilia Van Baker to his breast, confessing that he was The Shadow, "and a captured Shadow at that"; the curtain went up and down, up and down; Miss Halliburton was dragged unwillingly on the stage and the ushers came up the aisles laden with flowers. Then everything became informal and the actors mingled happily with the audience, laughing and important, congratulated from all sides. An old man whom Basil didn't know came up to him and shook his hand, saying, "You're a young man that's going to be heard from some day," and a reporter for the paper asked him if he was really only fifteen. It might all have been very bad and demoralizing for Basil, but it was already behind him. Even as the crowd melted away and the last few people spoke to him and went out, he felt a great vacancy come into his heart. It was over, it was done and gone—all that work, and interest and absorption. It was a hollowness like fear.

"Good night, Miss Halliburton. Good night, Evelyn."

"Good night, Basil. Congratulations, Basil. Good night."

"Where's my coat? Good night, Basil."

"Leave your costumes on the stage, please. They've got to go back tomorrow."

He was almost the last to leave, mounting to the stage for a moment and looking around the deserted hall. His mother was waiting and they trolled home together through the first cool night of the year.

"Well, I thought it went very well indeed. Were you satisfied?" He didn't answer for a moment. "Weren't you satisfied with the way it went?"

"Yes." He turned his head away.

"What's the matter?"

"Nothing," and then, "Nobody really cares, do they?"

"About what?"

"About anything."

"Everybody cares about different things. I care about you, for instance."

Instinctively he ducked away from a hand extended caressingly toward him: "Oh, don't. I don't mean like that."

"You're just overwrought, dear."

"I am not overwrought. I just feel sort of sad."

"You shouldn't feel sad. Why, people told me after the play ____"

"Oh, that's all over. Don't talk about that—don't ever talk to me about that any more."

"Then what are you sad about?"

"Oh, about a little boy."

"What little boy?"

"Oh, little Ham—you wouldn't understand."

"When we get home I want you to take a real hot bath and quiet your nerves."

"All right."

But when he got home he fell immediately into deep sleep on the sofa. She hesitated. Then covering him with a blanket and a comforter, she pushed a pillow under his protesting head and went upstairs.

She knelt for a long time beside her bed.

"God help him! help him," she prayed, "because he needs help that I can't give him any more."

FORGING AHEAD

On July 21, 1928, Fitzgerald wrote Maxwell Perkins, "I plan to publish a book of those Basil Lee Stories after the novel." In January 1929, with no novel in sight, Fitzgerald finished his seventh Basil story, "Forging Ahead." When Tender Is the Night *was still unfinished in May 1930, Fitzgerald mentioned to Perkins that Harold Ober felt he should publish the Basil Lee stories if his novel was not going to be ready for fall publication, "but I know too well by whom reputations are made + broken," Fitzgerald insisted, "to ruin myself completely by such a move." When he had still not completed his novel by September 1933, Fitzgerald asked Perkins if Scribner's could bring out a collection of the Basil stories and a similar set he wrote about Josephine, a girl who lived in Chicago and was modeled on Ginevra King. After the publication of* Tender Is the Night *in April 1934, Fitzgerald again wrote Perkins, suggesting the collection for that fall and proposing an extra story that brought Basil and Josephine together. In 1935 Scribner's released* Taps at Reveille, *which contained eight Basil and Josephine stories. All fourteen of the stories finally appeared in a 1973 collection. Fitzgerald based "Forging Ahead" on his brief stint as a summer workman for James J. Hill's Great Northern Railway. As in the story, he had a real-life* deus ex machina. *The death of his McQuillan grandmother in 1913 guaranteed he would be able to attend Princeton. "Grandmother dies," he wrote in his ledger. "Her last gift."*

The Saturday Evening Post, March 30, 1929
Collected in *The Basil and Josephine Stories* (1973)

I
`. . . . .`

BASIL DUKE LEE AND RIPLY BUCKNER, JR., sat on the Lees' front steps in the regretful gold of a late summer afternoon. Inside the house the telephone sang out with mysterious promise.

"I thought you were going home," Basil said.

"I thought you were."

"I am."

"So am I."

"Well, why don't you go, then?"

"Why don't you, then?"

"I am."

They laughed, ending with yawning gurgles that were not laughed out but sucked in. As the telephone rang again, Basil got to his feet.

"I've got to study trig before dinner."

"Are you honestly going to Yale this fall?" demanded Riply skeptically.

"Yes."

"Everybody says you're foolish to go at sixteen."

"I'll be seventeen in September. So long. I'll call you up tonight."

Basil heard his mother at the upstairs telephone and he was immediately aware of distress in her voice.

"Yes. . . . Isn't that awful, Everett! . . . Yes. . . . Oh-h my!" After a minute he gathered that it was only the usual worry about business and and went on into the kitchen for refreshments. Returning, he met his mother hurrying downstairs. She was blinking rapidly and her hat was on backward—characteristic testimony to her excitement.

"I've got to go over to your grandfather's."

"What's the matter, mother?"

"Uncle Everett thinks we've lost a lot of money."

"How much?" he asked, startled.

"Twenty-two thousand dollars apiece. But we're not sure."

She went out.

"Twenty-two thousand dollars!" he repeated in an awed whisper.

His ideas of money were vague and somewhat debonair, but he had noticed that at family dinners the immemorial discussion as to whether the Third Street block would be sold to the railroads had given place to anxious talk of Western Public Utilities. At half-past six his mother telephoned for him to have his dinner, and with growing uneasiness he sat alone at the table, undistracted by *The Mississippi Bubble,* open beside his plate. She came in at seven, distraught and miserable, and dropping down at the table, gave him his first exact information about finance — she and her father and her brother Everett had lost something more than eighty thousand dollars. She was in a panic and she looked wildly around the dining room as if money were slipping away even here, and she wanted to retrench at once.

"I've got to stop selling securities or we won't have anything," she declared. "This leaves us only three thousand a year — do you realize that, Basil? I don't see how I can possibly afford to send you to Yale."

His heart tumbled into his stomach; the future, always glowing like a comfortable beacon ahead of him, flared up in glory and went out. His mother shivered, and then emphatically shook her head.

"You'll just have to make up your mind to go to the state university."

"Gosh!" Basil said.

Sorry for his shocked, rigid face, she yet spoke somewhat sharply, as people will with a bitter refusal to convey.

"I feel terribly about it — your father wanted you to go to Yale. But everyone says that, with clothes and railroad fare, I can count on it costing two thousand a year. Your grandfather helped me to send you to St. Regis School, but he always thought you ought to finish at the state university."

After she went distractedly upstairs with a cup of tea, Basil sat thinking in the dark parlor. For the present the loss meant only one thing to him—he wasn't going to Yale after all. The sentence itself, divorced from its meaning, overwhelmed him, so many times had he announced casually "I'm going to Yale," but gradually he realized how many friendly and familiar dreams had been swept away. Yale was the far-away East, that he had loved with a vast nostalgia since he had first read books about great cities. Beyond the dreary railroad stations of Chicago and the night fires of Pittsburgh, back in the old states, something went on that made his heart beat fast with excitement. He was attuned to the vast, breathless bustle of New York, to the metropolitan days and nights that were tense as singing wires. Nothing needed to be imagined there, for it was the very stuff of romance—life was as vivid and satisfactory as in books and dreams.

But first, as a sort of gateway to that deeper, richer life, there was Yale. The name evoked the memory of a heroic team backed up against its own impassable goal in the crisp November twilight, and later, of half a dozen immaculate noblemen with opera hats and canes standing at the Manhattan Hotel bar. And tangled up with its triumphs and rewards, its struggles and glories, the vision of the inevitable, incomparable girl.

Well, then, why not work his way through Yale? In a moment the idea had become a reality. He began walking rapidly up and down the room, declaring half aloud, "Of course, that's the thing to do." Rushing upstairs, he knocked at his mother's door and announced in the inspired voice of a prophet: "Mother, I know what I'm going to do! I'm going to work my way though Yale."

He sat down on her bed and she considered uncertainly. The men in her family had not been resourceful for several generations, and the idea startled her.

"It doesn't seem to me you're a boy who likes to work," she

said. "Besides, boys who work their way through college have scholarships and prizes, and you've never been much of a student."

He was annoyed. He was ready for Yale a year ahead of his age and her reproach seemed unfair.

"What would you work at?" she said.

"Take care of furnaces," said Basil promptly. "And shovel snow off sidewalks. I think they mostly do that—and tutor people. You could let me have as much money as it would take to go to the state university?"

"We'll have to think it over."

"Well, don't you worry about anything," he said emphatically, "because my earning my way through Yale will really make up for the money you've lost, almost."

"Why don't you start by finding something to do this summer?"

"I'll get a job tomorrow. Maybe I can pile up enough so you won't have to help me. Good night, mother."

Up in his room he paused only to thunder grimly to the mirror that he was going to work his way through Yale, and going to his bookcase, took down half a dozen dusty volumes of Horatio Alger, unopened for years. Then, much as a postwar young man might consult the George Washington Condensed Business Course, he sat at his desk and slowly began to turn the pages of *Bound to Rise.*

II
. . . . .

Two days later, after being insulted by the doorkeepers, office boys and telephone girls of the *Press*, the *Evening News*, the *Socialist Gazette* and a green scandal sheet called the *Courier*, and assured that no one wanted a reporter practically seventeen, after enduring every ignominy prepared for a young man in a free country trying to work his way through Yale, Basil Duke Lee, too "stuck-up" to apply to the parents of his friends, got a position with the railroad, through Eddie Parmelee, who lived across the way.

At 6:30 the following morning, carrying his lunch, and a new suit of overalls that had cost four dollars, he strode self-consciously into the Great Northern car shops. It was like entering a new school, except that no one showed any interest in him or asked if he was going out for the team. He punched a time clock, which affected him strangely, and without even an admonition from the foreman to "go in and win," was put to carrying boards for the top of a car.

Twelve o'clock arrived; nothing had happened. The sun was blazing hot and his hands and back were sore, but no real events had ruffled the dull surface of the morning. The president's little daughter had not come by, dragged by a runaway horse; not even a superintendent had walked through the yard and singled him out with an approving eye. Undismayed, he toiled on—you couldn't expect much the first morning.

He and Eddie Parmelee ate their lunches together. For several years Eddie had worked here in vacations; he was sending himself to the state university this fall. He shook his head doubtfully over the idea of Basil's earning his way through Yale.

"Here's what you ought to do," he said: "You borrow two thousand dollars from your mother and buy twenty shares in Ware Plow and Tractor. Then go to a bank and borrow two thousand more with those shares for collateral, and with that two thousand buy twenty more shares. Then you sit on your back for a year, and after that you won't have to think about earning your way through Yale."

"I don't think mother would give me two thousand dollars."

"Well, anyhow, that's what I'd do."

If the morning had been uneventful, the afternoon was distinguished by an incident of some unpleasantness. Basil had risen a little, having been requested to mount to the top of a freight car and help nail the boards he had carried in the morning. He found that nailing nails into a board was more highly technical than nailing tacks into a wall, but he considered that he was progressing satisfactorily when an angry voice hailed him from below:

"Hey, you! Get up!"

He looked down. A foreman stood there, unpleasantly red in the face.

"Yes, you in the new suit. Get up!"

Basil looked about to see if someone was lying down, but the two sullen hunyaks seemed to be hard at work, and it grew on him that he was indeed being addressed.

"I beg your pardon, sir," he said.

"Get up on your knees or get out! What the h— do you think this is?"

He had been sitting down as he nailed, and apparently the foreman thought that he was loafing. After another look at the foreman, he suppressed the explanation that he felt steadier sitting down and decided to just let it go. There were probably no rail-road shops at Yale; yet, he remembered with a pang the ominous name, New York, New Haven and Hartford.

The third morning, just as he had become aware that his over-alls were not where he had hung them in the shop, it was an-nounced that all men of less than six months' service were to be laid off. Basil received four dollars and lost his overalls. Learning that nails are driven from a kneeling position had cost him only carfare.

III
. . . . .

In a large old-fashioned house in the old section of the city lived Basil's great-uncle, Benjamin Reilly, and there Basil presented himself that evening. It was a last resort—Benjamin Reilly and Basil's grandfather were brothers and they had not spoken for twenty years.

He was received in the living room by the small, dumpy old man whose inscrutable face was hidden behind a white poodle beard. Behind him stood a woman of forty, his wife of six months, and her daughter, a girl of fifteen. Basil's branch of the family had not been invited to the wedding, and he had never seen these two additions before.

"I thought I'd come down and see you, Uncle Ben," he said with some embarrassment.

There was a certain amount of silence.

"Your mother well?" asked the old man.

"Oh, yes, thank you."

Mr. Reilly waited. Mrs. Reilly spoke to her daughter, who threw a curious glance at Basil and reluctantly left the room. Her mother made the old man sit down.

Out of sheer embarrassment Basil came to the point. He wanted a summer job in the Reilly Wholesale Drug Company.

His uncle fidgeted for a minute and then replied that there were no positions open.

"Oh."

"It might be different if you wanted a permanent place, but you say you want to go to Yale." He said this with some irony of his own, and glanced at his wife.

"Why, yes," said Basil. "That's really why I want the job."

"Your mother can't afford to send you, eh?" The note of pleasure in his voice was unmistakable. "Spent all her money?"

"Oh, no," answered Basil quickly. "She's going to help me."

To his surprise, aid came from an unpromising quarter. Mrs. Reilly suddenly bent and whispered in her husband's ear, whereupon the old man nodded and said aloud:

"I'll think about it, Basil. You go in there."

And his wife repeated: "We'll think about it. You go in the library with Rhoda while Mr. Reilly looks up and sees."

The door of the library closed behind him and he was alone with Rhoda, a square-chinned, decided girl with fleshy white arms and a white dress that reminded Basil domestically of the lacy pants that blew among the laundry in the yard. Puzzled by his uncle's change of front, he eyed her abstractedly for a moment.

"I guess you're my cousin," said Rhoda, closing her book, which he saw was *The Little Colonel, Maid of Honor.*

"Yes," he admitted.

"I heard about you from somebody." The implication was that her information was not flattering.

"From who?"

"A girl named Elaine Washmer."

"Elaine Washmer!" His tone dismissed the name scornfully. "That girl!"

"She's my best friend." He made no reply. "She said you thought you were wonderful."

Young people do not perceive at once that the giver of wounds is the enemy and the quoted tattle merely the arrow. His heart smoldered with wrath at Elaine Washmer.

"I don't know many kids here," said the girl, in a less aggressive key. "We've only been here six months. I never saw such a stuck-up bunch."

"Oh, I don't think so," he protested. "Where did you live before?"

"Sioux City. All the kids have much more fun in Sioux City."

Mrs. Reilly opened the door and called Basil back into the living room. The old man was again on his feet.

"Come down tomorrow morning and I'll find you something," he said.

"And why don't you have dinner with us tomorrow night?" added Mrs. Reilly, with a cordiality wherein an adult might have detected disingenuous purpose.

"Why, thank you very much."

His heart, buoyant with gratitude, had scarcely carried him out the door before Mrs. Reilly laughed shortly and called in her daughter.

"Now we'll see if you don't get around a little more," she announced. "When was it you said they had those dances?"

"Thursdays at the College Club and Saturdays at the Lake Club," said Rhoda promptly.

"Well, if this young man wants to hold the position your father has given him, you'll go to them all the rest of the summer."

IV
. . . . .

Arbitrary groups formed by the hazards of money or geography may be sufficiently quarrelsome and dull, but for sheer unpleasantness the condition of young people who have been thrust together by a common unpopularity can be compared only with that of prisoners herded in a cell. In Basil's eyes the guests at the little dinner the following night were a collection of cripples. Lewis and Hector Crum, dullard cousins who were tolerable only to each other; Sidney Rosen, rich but awful; ugly Mary Haupt, Elaine Washmer, and Betty Geer, who reminded Basil of a cruel parody they had once sung to the tune of "Jungle Town":

> *Down below the hill*
> *There lives a pill*
> *That makes me ill,*
> *And her name is Betty Geer.*
> *We had better stop right here. . . .*
> *She's so fat,*
> *She looks just like a cat,*
> *And she's the queen of pills.*

Moreover, they resented Basil, who was presumed to be "stuck-up," and walking home afterward, he felt dreary and vaguely exploited. Of course, he was grateful to Mrs. Reilly for her kindness, yet he couldn't help wondering if a cleverer boy couldn't have got out of taking Rhoda to the Lake Club next Saturday night. The proposal had caught him unaware; but when he was similarly trapped the following week, and the week after that, he began to realize the situation. It was a part of his job, and he accepted it grimly, unable, nevertheless, to understand how such a bad dancer and so unsociable a person should want to go where she was obviously a burden. "Why doesn't she just sit at home and read a book," he thought disgustedly, "or go away somewhere — or sew?"

It was one Saturday afternoon while he watched a tennis tournament and felt the unwelcome duty of the evening creep up on him, that he found himself suddenly fascinated by a girl's face a few yards away. His heart leaped into his throat and the blood in his pulse beat with excitement; and then, when the crowd rose to go, he saw to his astonishment that he had been staring at a child ten years old. He looked away, oddly disappointed; after a moment he looked back again. The lovely, self-conscious face suggested a train of thought and sensation that he could not identify. As he passed on, forgoing a vague intention of discovering the child's identity, there was beauty suddenly all around him in the afternoon; he could hear its unmistakable whisper, its never-inadequate, ever-failing promise of happiness. "Tomorrow — one day soon now — this fall — maybe tonight." Irresistibly compelled to express himself, he sat down and tried to write to a girl in New York. His words were stilted and the girl seemed cold and far away. The real image on his mind, the force that had propelled him into this state of yearning, was the face of the little girl seen that afternoon.

When he arrived with Rhoda Sinclair at the Lake Club that night, he immediately cast a quick look around to see what boys were present who were indebted to Rhoda or else within his own sphere of influence. This was just before cutting-in arrived, and ordinarily he was able to dispose of half a dozen dances in advance, but tonight an older crowd was in evidence and the situation was unpromising. However, as Rhoda emerged from the dressing room he saw Bill Kampf and thankfully bore down upon him.

"Hello, old boy," he said, exuding personal good will. "How about dancing once with Rhoda tonight?"

"Can't," Bill answered briskly. "We've got people visiting us. Didn't you know?"

"Well, why couldn't we swap a dance anyhow?"

Bill looked at him in surprise.

"I thought you knew," he exclaimed. "Erminie's here. She's been talking about you all afternoon."

"Erminie Bibble!"

"Yes. And her father and mother and her kid sister. Got here this morning."

Now, indeed, the emotion of two hours before bubbled up in Basil's blood, but this time he knew why. It was the little sister of Erminie Gilberte Labouisse Bibble whose strangely familiar face had so attracted him. As his mind swung sharply back to a long afternoon on the Kampfs' veranda at the lake, ages ago, a year ago, a real voice rang in his ear, "Basil!" and a sparkling little beauty of fifteen came up to him with a fine burst of hurry, taking his hand as though she was stepping into the circle of his arm.

"Basil! I'm so glad!" Her voice was husky with pleasure, though she was at the age when pleasure usually hides behind grins and mumbles. It was Basil who was awkward and embarrassed, despite the intention of his heart. He was a little relieved when Bill Kampf, more conscious of his lovely cousin than he had been a year ago, led her out on the floor.

"Who was that?" Rhoda demanded, as he returned in a daze. "I never saw her around."

"Just a girl." He scarcely knew what he was saying.

"Well, I know that. What's her name?"

"Minnie Bibble, from New Orleans."

"She certainly looks conceited. I never saw anybody so affected in my life."

"Hush!" Basil protested involuntarily. "Let's dance."

It was a long hour before Basil was relieved by Hector Crum, and then several dances passed before he could get possession of Minnie, who was now the centre of a moving whirl. But she made it up to him by pressing his hand and drawing him out to a veranda which overhung the dark lake.

"It's about time," she whispered. With a sort of instinct she found the darkest corner. "I might have known you'd have another crush."

"I haven't," he insisted in horror. "That's a sort of a cousin of mine."

"I always knew you were fickle. But I didn't think you'd forget me so soon."

She had wriggled up until she was touching him. Her eyes, floating into his, said, "What does it matter? We're alone."

In a curious panic he jumped to his feet. He couldn't possibly kiss her like this — right at once. It was all so different and older than a year ago. He was too excited to do more than walk up and down and say, "Gosh, I certainly am glad to see you," supplementing this unoriginal statement with an artificial laugh.

Already mature in poise, she tried to soothe him: "Basil, come and sit down!"

"I'll be all right," he gasped, as if he had just fainted. "I'm a little fussed, that's all."

Again he contributed what, even to his pounding ears, sounded like a silly laugh.

"I'll be here three weeks. Won't it be fun?" And she added, with warm emphasis: "Do you remember on Bill's veranda that afternoon?"

All he could find to answer was: "I work now in the afternoon."

"You can come out in the evenings, Basil. It's only half an hour in a car."

"I haven't got a car."

"I mean you can get your family's car."

"It's an electric."

She waited patiently. He was still romantic to her — handsome, incalculable, a little sad.

"I saw your sister," he blurted out. Beginning with that, he might bridge this perverse and intolerable reverence she inspired. "She certainly looks like you."

"Does she?"

"It was wonderful," he said. "Wonderful! Let me tell you——"

"Yes, do." She folded her hands expectantly in her lap.

"Well, this afternoon——"

The music had stopped and started several times. Now, in an intermission, there was the sound of determined footsteps on the veranda, and Basil looked up to find Rhoda and Hector Crum.

"I got to go home, Basil," squeaked Hector in his changing voice. "Here's Rhoda."

"Take Rhoda out to the dock and push her in the lake." But only Basil's mind said this; his body stood up politely.

"I didn't know where you were, Basil," said Rhoda in an aggrieved tone. "Why didn't you come back?"

"I was just coming." His voice trembled a little as he turned to Minnie. "Shall I find your partner for you?"

"Oh, don't bother," said Minnie. She was not angry, but she was somewhat astonished. She could not be expected to guess that the young man walking away from her so submissively was at the moment employed in working his way through Yale.

V
. . . . .

From the first, Basil's grandfather, who had once been a regent at the state university, wanted him to give up the idea of Yale, and now his mother, picturing him hungry and ragged in a garret, adjoined her persuasions. The sum on which he could count from her was far below the necessary minimum, and although he stubbornly refused to consider defeat, he consented, "just in case anything happened," to register at the university for the coming year.

In the administration building he ran into Eddie Parmelee, who introduced his companion, a small, enthusiastic Japanese.

"Well, well," said Eddie. "So you've given up Yale!"

"I given up Yale," put in Mr. Utsonomia, surprisingly. "Oh,

yes, long time I given up Yale." He broke into enthusiastic laughter. "Oh, sure. Oh, yes."

"Mr. Utsonomia's a Japanese," explained Eddie, winking. "He's a sub-freshman too."

"Yes, I given up Harvard Princeton too," continued Mr. Utsonomia. "They give me choice back in my country. I choose here."

"You did?" said Basil, almost indignantly.

"Sure, more strong here. More peasants come, with strength and odor of ground."

Basil stared at him. "You like that?" he asked incredulously.

Utsonomia nodded. "Here I get to know real American peoples. Girls too. Yale got only boys."

"But they haven't got college spirit here," explained Basil patiently.

Utsonomia looked blankly at Eddie.

"Rah-rah!" elucidated Eddie, waving his arms. "Rah-rah-rah! You know."

"Besides, the girls here——" began Basil, and stopped.

"You know girls here?" grinned Utsonomia.

"No, I don't know them," said Basil firmly. "But I know they're not like the girls that you'd meet down at the Yale proms. I don't think they even have proms here. I don't mean the girls aren't all right, but they're just not like the ones at Yale. They're just coeds."

"I hear you got a crush on Rhoda Sinclair," said Eddie.

"Yes, I have!" said Basil ironically.

"They used to invite me to dinner sometimes last spring, but since you take her around to all the club dances——"

"Good-by," said Basil hastily. He exchanged a jerky bow for Mr. Utsonomia's more formal dip, and departed.

From the moment of Minnie's arrival the question of Rhoda had begun to assume enormous proportions. At first he had been merely indifferent to her person and a little ashamed of her lacy, oddly reminiscent clothes, but now, as he saw how relentlessly his services were commandeered, he began to hate her. When she complained of a headache, his imagination would eagerly convert it into a long, lingering illness from which she would recover only after college opened in the fall. But the eight dollars a week which he received from his great-uncle would pay his fare to New Haven, and he knew that if he failed to hold this position his mother would refuse to let him go.

Not suspecting the truth, Minnie Bibble found the fact that he only danced with her once or twice at each hop, and was then strangely moody and silent, somehow intriguing. Temporarily, at least, she was fascinated by his indifference, and even a little unhappy. But her precociously emotional temperament would not long stand neglect, and it was agony for Basil to watch several rivals beginning to emerge. There were moments when it seemed too big a price to pay even for Yale.

All his hopes centered upon one event. That was a farewell party in her honor for which the Kampfs had engaged the College Club and to which Rhoda was not invited. Given the mood and the moment, he might speed her departure knowing that he had stamped himself indelibly on her heart.

Three days before the party he came home from work at six to find the Kampfs' car before his door and Minnie sitting alone on the front porch.

"Basil, I had to see you," she said. "You've been so funny and distant to me."

Intoxicated by her presence on his familiar porch, he found no words to answer.

"I'm meeting the family in town for dinner and I've got an hour. Can't we go somewhere? I've been frightened to death your mother would come home and think it was fresh for me to call on you." She spoke in a whisper, though there was no one close enough to hear. "I wish we didn't have the old chauffeur. He listens."

"Listens to what?" Basil asked, with a flash of jealousy.

"He just listens."

"I'll tell you," he proposed: "We'll have him drop us by grampa's house and I'll borrow the electric."

The hot wind blew the brown curls around her forehead as they glided along Crest Avenue.

That he contributed the car made him feel more triumphantly astride the moment. There was a place he had saved for such a time as this — a little pigtail of a road left from the excavations of Prospect Park, where Crest Avenue ran obliviously above them and the late sun glinted on the Mississippi flats a mile away.

The end of summer was in the afternoon; it had turned a corner, and what was left must be used while there was yet time.

Suddenly she was whispering in his arms, "You're first, Basil — nobody but you."

"You just admitted you were a flirt."

"I know, but that was years ago. I used to like to be called fast when I was thirteen or fourteen, because I didn't care what people said; but about a year ago I began to see there was something better in life — honestly, Basil — and I've tried to act properly. But I'm afraid I'll never be an angel."

The river flowed in a thin scarlet gleam between the public baths and the massed tracks upon the other side. Booming, whistling, far-away railroad sounds reached them from down there; the voices of children playing tennis in Prospect Park sailed frailly overhead.

"I really haven't got such a line as everybody thinks, Basil, for I mean a lot of what I say way down deep, and nobody believes me. You know how much alike we are, and in a boy it doesn't matter, but a girl has to control her feelings, and that's hard for me, because I'm emotional."

"Haven't you kissed anybody since you've been in St. Paul?"

"No."

He saw she was lying, but it was a brave lie. They talked from their hearts — with the half truths and evasions peculiar to that organ, which has never been famed as an instrument of precision. They pieced together all the shreds of romance they knew and made garments for each other no less warm than their childish passion, no less wonderful than their sense of wonder.

He held her away suddenly, looked at her, made a strained sound of delight. There it was, in her face touched by sun — that promise — in the curve of her mouth, the tilted shadow of her nose on her cheek, the point of dull fire in her eyes — the promise that she could lead him into a world in which he would always be happy.

"Say I love you," he whispered.

"I'm in love with you."

"Oh, no; that's not the same."

She hesitated. "I've never said the other to anybody."

"Please say it."

She blushed the color of the sunset.

"At my party," she whispered. "It'd be easier at night."

When she dropped him in front of his house she spoke from the window of the car:

"This is my excuse for coming to see you. My uncle couldn't get the club Thursday, so we're having the party at the regular dance Saturday night."

Basil walked thoughtfully into the house; Rhoda Sinclair was also giving a dinner at the College Club dance Saturday night.

VI
. . . . .

It was put to him frankly. Mrs. Reilly listened to his tentative excuses in silence and then said:

"Rhoda invited you first for Saturday night, and she already has one girl too many. Of course, if you choose to simply turn your back on your engagement and go to another party, I don't know how Rhoda will feel, but I know how I should feel."

And the next day his great-uncle, passing through the stock room, stopped and said: "What's all this trouble about parties?"

Basil started to explain, but Mr. Reilly cut him short. "I don't see the use of hurting a young girl's feelings. You better think it over."

Basil had thought it over; on Saturday afternoon he was still expected at both dinners and he had hit upon no solution at all.

Yale was only a month away now, but in four days Erminie Bibble would be gone, uncommitted, unsecured, grievously offended, lost forever. Not yet delivered from adolescence, Basil's moments of foresight alternated with those when the future was measured by a day. The glory that was Yale faded beside the promise of that incomparable hour.

On the other side loomed up the gaunt specter of the university, with phantoms flitting in and out its portals that presently disclosed themselves as peasants and girls. At five o'clock, in a burst of contempt for his weakness, he went to the phone and left word with a maid at the Kampfs' house that he was sick and couldn't come tonight. Nor would he sit with the dull left-overs of his generation — too sick for one party, he was too sick for the other. The Reillys could have no complaint as to that.

Rhoda answered the phone and Basil tried to reduce his voice to a weak murmur:

"Rhoda, I've been taken sick. I'm in bed now," he murmured feebly, and then added: "The phone's right next to the bed, you see; so I thought I'd call you up myself."

"You mean to say you can't come?" Dismay and anger were in her voice.

"I'm sick in bed," he repeated doggedly. "I've got chills and a pain and a cold."

"Well, can't you come anyhow?" she asked, with what to the invalid seemed a remarkable lack of consideration. "You've just go to. Otherwise there'll be two extra girls."

"I'll send someone to take my place," he said desperately. His glance, roving wildly out the window, fell on a house over the way. "I'll send Eddie Parmelee."

Rhoda considered. Then she asked with quick suspicion: "You're not going to that other party?"

"Oh, no; I told them I was sick too."

Again Rhoda considered. Eddie Parmelee was mad at her.

"I'll fix it up," Basil promised. "I know he'll come. He hasn't got anything to do tonight."

A few minutes later he dashed across the street. Eddie himself, tying a bow on his collar, came to the door. With certain reservations, Basil hastily outlined the situation. Would Eddie go in his place?

"Can't do it, old boy, even if I wanted to. Got a date with my real girl tonight."

"Eddie, I'd make it worth your while," he said recklessly. "I'd pay you for your time — say, five dollars."

Eddie considered, there was hesitation in his eyes, but he shook his head.

"It isn't worth it, Basil. You ought to see what I'm going out with tonight."

"You could see her afterward. They only want you — I mean me — because they've got more girls than men for dinner — and listen, Eddie, I'll make it ten dollars."

Eddie clapped him on the shoulder.

"All right, old boy, I'll do it for an old friend. Where's the pay?"

More than a weeks' salary melted into Eddie's palm, but another sort of emptiness accompanied Basil back across the street — the emptiness of the coming night. In an hour or so the Kampfs' limousine would draw up at the College Club and — time and time again his imagination halted miserably before that single picture, unable to endure any more.

In despair he wandered about the dark house. His mother had let the maid go out and was at his grandfather's for dinner, and momentarily Basil considered finding some rake like Elwood Leaming and going down to Carling's Restaurant to drink whiskey, wines, and beer. Perhaps on her way back to the lake after the dance, Minnie, passing by, would see his face among the wildest of the revelers and understand.

"I'm going to Maxim's," he hummed to himself desperately; then he added impatiently: "Oh, to heck with Maxim's!"

He sat in the parlor and watched a pale moon come up over the Lindsays' fence at McKubben Street. Some young people came by, heading for the trolley that went to Como Park. He pitied their horrible dreariness—they were not going to dance with Minnie at the College Club tonight.

Eight-thirty—she was there now. Nine—they were dancing between courses to "Peg of My Heart" or doing the Castle Walk that Andy Lockheart brought home from Yale.

At ten o'clock he heard his mother come in, and almost immediately the phone rang. For a moment he listened without interest to her voice; then abruptly he sat up in his chair.

"Why, yes; how do you do, Mrs. Reilly. . . . Oh, I see. . . . Oh. . . . Are you sure it isn't Basil you want to speak to? . . . Well, frankly, Mrs. Reilly, I don't see that it's my affair."

Basil got up and took a step toward the door; his mother's voice was growing thin and annoyed: "I wasn't here at the time and I don't know who he promised to send."

Eddie Parmelee hadn't gone after all—well, that was the end.

". . . Of course not. It must be a mistake. I don't think Basil would possibly do that; I don't think he even knows any Japanese."

Basil's brain reeled. For a moment he was about to dash across the street after Eddie Parmelee. Then he heard a definitely angry note come into his mother's voice:

"Very well, Mrs. Reilly. I'll tell my son. But his going to Yale is scarcely a matter I care to discuss with you. In any case, he no longer needs anyone's assistance."

He had lost his position and his mother was trying to put a proud face on it. But her voice continued, soaring a little:

"Uncle Ben might be interested to know that this afternoon we sold the Third Street block to the Union Depot Company for four hundred thousand dollars."

VII

· · · · ·

Mr. Utsonomia was enjoying himself. In the whole six months in America he had never felt so caught up in its inner life before. At first it had been a little hard to make plain to the lady just whose place it was he was taking, but Eddie Parmelee had assured him that such substitutions were an American custom, and he was spending the evening collecting as much data upon American customs as possible.

He did not dance, so he sat with the elderly lady until both the ladies went home, early and apparently a little agitated, shortly after dinner. But Mr. Utsonomia stayed on. He watched and he wandered. He was not lonesome; he had grown accustomed to being alone.

About eleven he sat on the veranda pretending to be blowing the smoke of a cigarette — which he hated — out over the city, but really listening to a conversation which was taking place just behind. It had been going on for half an hour, and it puzzled him, for apparently it was a proposal, and it was not refused. Yet, if his eyes did not deceive him, the contracting parties were of an age that Americans did not associate with such serious affairs. Another thing puzzled him even more: obviously, if one substituted for an absent guest, the absent guest should not be among those present, and he was almost sure that the young man who had just engaged himself for marriage was Mr. Basil Lee. It would be bad manners to intrude now, but he would urbanely ask him about a solution of this puzzle when the state university opened in the fall.

AT YOUR AGE

"At Your Age," written in Paris in June 1929, brought Fitzgerald's story fee to $4,000, his lifetime high. Harold Ober thought it "the finest short story" Fitzgerald had ever written, and he was able to convince the Post *as well. The* Post *editor Lorimer gave "At Your Age" pride of place as the first piece of fiction in the August 17, 1929, issue. Although "At Your Age" claims to be set in Minneapolis, most of the locales are from St. Paul: the College Club (University Club), Downtown Club (Minnesota Club) and Crest Avenue (Summit Avenue). Always aware of social status, Fitzgerald also refers to "Nushka" in the story. Created in the mid-1880s to champion St. Paul's Winter Carnival, Nushka was "the most fashionable" of the sixty or so clubs that promoted tobogganing, snowshoeing and skating.*

The Saturday Evening Post, August 17, 1929
Collected in The Price Was High: The Last Uncollected Stories of F. Scott Fitzgerald (1979)

I

· · · · ·

Tom Squires came into the drug store to buy a toothbrush, a can of talcum, a gargle, Castile soap, Epsom salts, and a box of cigars. Having lived alone for many years, he was methodical, and while waiting to be served he held the list in his hand. It was Christmas week and Minneapolis was under two feet of exhilarating, constantly refreshed snow; with his cane Tom knocked two clean crusts of it from his overshoes. Then, looking up, he saw the blonde girl.

She was a rare blonde, even in that Promised Land of Scandinavians, where pretty blondes are not rare. There was warm color in her cheeks, lips, and pink little hands that folded powders into papers; her hair, in long braids twisted about her head, was shining and alive. She seemed to Tom suddenly the cleanest person he knew of, and he caught his breath as he stepped forward and looked into her gray eyes.

"A can of talcum."

"What kind?"

"Any kind. . . . That's fine."

She looked back at him apparently without self-consciousness, and, as the list melted away, his heart raced with it wildly.

"I am not old," he wanted to say. "At fifty I'm younger than most men of forty. Don't I interest you at all?"

But she only said, "What kind of gargle?"

And he answered, "What can you recommend? . . . That's fine."

Almost painfully he took his eyes from her, went out, and got into his coupé.

"If that young idiot only knew what an old imbecile like me could do for her," he thought humorously — "what worlds I could open out to her!"

As he drove away into the winter twilight he followed this train of thought to a totally unprecedented conclusion. Perhaps the time of day was the responsible stimulant, for the shop windows glowing into the cold, the tinkling bells of a delivery sleigh, the white gloss left by shovels on the sidewalks, the enormous distance of the stars, brought back the feel of other nights thirty years ago. For an instant the girls he had known then slipped like phantoms out of their dull matronly selves of today and fluttered past him with frosty, seductive laughter, until a pleasant shiver crawled up his spine.

"Youth! Youth! Youth!" he apostrophized with conscious lack of originality, and, a somewhat ruthless and domineering man of no morals whatsoever, he considered going back to the drug store to seek the blonde girl's address. It was not his sort of thing, so the half-formed intention passed; the idea remained.

"Youth, by heaven—youth!" he repeated under his breath. "I want it near me, all around me, just once more before I'm too old to care."

He was tall, lean, and handsome, with the ruddy, bronzed face of a sportsman and a just faintly graying mustache. Once he had been among the city's best beaus, organizer of cotillions and charity balls, popular with men and women, and with several generations of them. After the war he had suddenly felt poor, gone into business, and in ten years accumulated nearly a million dollars. Tom Squires was not introspective, but he perceived now that the wheel of his life had revolved again, bringing up forgotten, yet familiar, dreams and yearnings. Entering his house, he turned suddenly to a pile of disregarded invitations to see whether or not he had been bidden to a dance tonight.

Throughout his dinner, which he ate alone at the Downtown Club, his eyes were half closed and on his face was a faint smile. He was practicing so that he would be able to laugh at himself painlessly, if necessary.

"I don't even know what they talk about," he admitted. "They pet—prominent broker goes to petting party with débutante. What is a petting party? Do they serve refreshments? Will I have to learn to a play saxophone?"

These matters, lately as remote as China in a news reel, came alive to him. They were serious questions. At ten o'clock he walked up the steps of the College Club to a private dance with the same sense of entering a new world as when he had gone into a training camp back in '17. He spoke to a hostess of his generation and to her daughter, overwhelmingly of another, and sat down in a corner to acclimate himself.

He was not alone long. A silly young man named Leland Jaques, who lived across the street from Tom, remarked him kindly and came over to brighten his life. He was such an exceedingly fatuous young man that, for a moment, Tom was annoyed, but he perceived craftily that he might be of service.

"Hello, Mr. Squires. How are you, sir?"

"Fine, thanks, Leland. Quite a dance."

As one man of the world with another, Mr. Jaques sat, or lay, down on the couch and lit — or so it seemed to Tom — three or four cigarettes at once.

"You should of been here last night, Mr. Squires. Oh, boy, that was a party and a half! The Caulkins. Hap-past five!"

"Who's that girl who changes partners every minute?" Tom asked. . . . "No, the one in white passing the door."

"That's Annie Lorry."

"Arthur Lorry's daughter?"

"Yes."

"She seems popular."

"About the most popular girl in town — anyway, at a dance."

"Not popular except at dances?"

"Oh, sure, but she hangs around with Randy Cambell all the time."

"What Cambell?"

"D. B."

There were new names in town in the last decade.

"It's a boy-and-girl affair." Pleased with this phrase, Jaques tried to repeat it: "One of those boy-and-girls affair — boys-and-girl affairs——" He gave it up and lit several more cigarettes, crushing out the first series on Tom's lap.

"Does she drink?"

"Not especially. At least I never saw her passed out. . . . That's Randy Cambell just cut in on her now."

They were a nice couple. Her beauty sparkled bright against his strong, tall form, and they floated hoveringly, delicately, like two people in a nice, amusing dream. They came near and Tom admired the faint dust of powder over her freshness, the guarded sweetness of her smile, the fragility of her body calculated by Nature to a millimeter to suggest a bud, yet guarantee a flower. Her innocent, passionate eyes were brown, perhaps; but almost violet in the silver light.

"Is she out this year?"

"Who?"

"Miss Lorry."

"Yes."

Although the girl's loveliness interested Tom, he was unable to picture himself as one of the attentive, grateful queue that pursued her around the room. Better meet her when the holidays were over and most of these young men were back in college "where they belonged." Tom Squires was old enough to wait.

He waited a fortnight while the city sank into the endless northern midwinter, where gray skies were friendlier than metallic blue skies, and dusk, whose lights were a reassuring glimpse into the continuity of human cheer, was warmer than the afternoons of bloodless sunshine. The coat of snow lost its press and became soiled and shabby, and ruts froze in the street; some of the big houses on Crest Avenue began to close as their occupants went South. In those cold days Tom asked Annie and her parents to go as his guests to the last Bachelors' Ball.

The Lorrys were an old family in Minneapolis, grown a little harassed and poor since the war. Mrs. Lorry, a contemporary of Tom's, was not surprised that he should send mother and daughter orchids and dine them luxuriously in his apartment on fresh caviar, quail, and champagne. Annie saw him only dimly — he lacked vividness, as the old do for the young — but she perceived his interest in her and performed for him the traditional ritual of young beauty — smiles, polite, wide-eyed attention, a profile held obligingly in this light or in that. At the ball he danced with her twice, and, though she was teased about it, she was flattered that such a man of the world — he had become that instead of a mere old man — had singled her out. She accepted his invitation to the symphony the following week, with the idea that it would be uncouth to refuse.

There were several "nice invitations" like that. Sitting beside him, she dozed in the warm shadow of Brahms and thought of Randy Cambell and other romantic nebulosities who might appear tomorrow. Feeling casually mellow one afternoon, she deliberately provoked Tom to kiss her on the way home, but she wanted to laugh when he took her hands and told her fervently he was falling in love.

"But how could you?" she protested. "Really, you mustn't say such crazy things. I won't go out with you any more, and then you'll be sorry."

A few days later her mother spoke to her as Tom waited outside in his car:

"Who's that, Annie?"

"Mr. Squires."

"Shut the door a minute. You're seeing him quite a bit."

"Why not?"

"Well, dear, he's fifty years old."

"But, mother, there's hardly anybody else in town."

"But you mustn't get any silly ideas about him."

"Don't worry. Actually, he bores me to extinction most of the time." She came to a sudden decision: "I'm not going to see him any more. I just couldn't get out of going with him this afternoon."

And that night, as she stood by her door in the circle of Randy Cambell's arms, Tom and his single kiss had no existence for her.

"Oh, I do love you so," Randy whispered. "Kiss me once more."

Their cool cheeks and warm lips met in the crisp darkness, and, watching the icy moon over his shoulder, Annie knew that she was his surely and, pulling his face down, kissed him again, trembling with emotion.

"When'll you marry me then?" he whispered.

"When can you—we afford it?"

"Couldn't you announce our engagement? If you knew the misery of having you out with somebody else and then making love to you."

"Oh, Randy, you ask so much."

"It's so awful to say good night. Can't I come in for a minute?"

"Yes."

Sitting close together in a trance before the flickering, lessening fire, they were oblivious that their common fate was being coolly weighed by a man of fifty who lay in a hot bath some blocks away.

II

· · · · ·

Tom Squires had guessed from Annie's extremely kind and detached manner of the afternoon that he had failed to interest her. He had promised himself that in such an eventuality he would drop the matter, but now he found himself in no such humor. He did not want to marry her; he simply wanted to see her and be with her a little; and up to the moment of her sweetly casual, half passionate, yet wholly unemotional kiss, giving her up would have been easy, for he was past the romantic age; but since that kiss the thought of her made his heart move up a few inches in his chest and beat there steady and fast.

"But this is the time to get out," he said to himself. "My age; no possible right to force myself into her life."

He rubbed himself dry, brushed his hair before the mirror, and, as he laid down the comb, said decisively: "That is that." And after reading for an hour he turned out the lamp with a snap and repeated aloud: "That is that."

In other words, that was not that at all, and the click of material things did not finish off Annie Lorry as a business decision might be settled by the tap of a pencil on the table.

"I'm going to carry this matter a little further," he said to himself about half-past four; on that acknowledgment he turned over and found sleep.

In the morning she had receded somewhat, but by four o'clock in the afternoon she was all around him — the phone was for calling her, a woman's footfalls passing his office were her footfalls, the snow outside the window was blowing, perhaps, against her rosy face.

"There is always the little plan I thought of last night," he said to himself. "In ten years I'll be sixty, and then no youth, no beauty for me ever any more."

In a sort of panic he took a sheet of note paper and composed a carefully phrased letter to Annie's mother, asking permission to pay court to her daughter. He took it himself into the hall, but before the letter slide he tore it up and dropped the pieces in a cuspidor.

"I couldn't do such an underhand trick," he told himself, "at my age." But this self-congratulation was premature, for he rewrote the letter and mailed it before he left his office that night.

Next day the reply he had counted on arrived — he could have guessed its very words in advance. It was a curt and indignant refusal.

It ended:

> I think it best that you and my daughter meet no more.
> Very Sincerely Yours,
> MABEL TOLLMAN LORRY.

"And now," Tom thought coolly, "we'll see what the girl says to that."

He wrote a note to Annie. Her mother's letter had surprised him, it said, but perhaps it was best that they should meet no more, in view of her mother's attitude.

By return post came Annie's defiant answer to her mother's fiat: "This isn't the Dark Ages. I'll see you whenever I like." She named a rendezvous for the following afternoon. Her mother's short-sightedness brought about what he had failed to achieve directly; for where Annie had been on the point of dropping him, she was now determined to do nothing of the sort. And the secrecy engendered by disapproval at home simply contributed the missing excitement. As February hardened into deep, solemn, interminable winter, she met him frequently and on a new basis. Sometimes they drove over to St. Paul to see a picture or to have dinner; sometimes they parked far out on a boulevard in his coupé, while the bitter sleet glazed the windshield to opacity and furred his lamps with ermine. Often he brought along something special to drink—enough to make her gay, but, carefully, never more; for mingled with his other emotions about her was something paternally concerned.

Laying his cards on the table, he told her that it was her mother who had unwittingly pushed her toward him, but Annie only laughed at his duplicity.

She was having a better time with him than with anyone else she had ever known. In place of the selfish exigency of a younger man, he showed her a never-failing consideration. What if his eyes were tired, his cheeks a little leathery and veined, if his will was masculine and strong. Moreover, his experience was a window looking out upon a wider, richer world; and with Randy Cambell next day she would feel less taken care of, less valued, less rare.

It was Tom now who was vaguely discontented. He had what he wanted—her youth at his side—and he felt that anything further would be a mistake. His liberty was precious to him and he could offer her only a dozen years before he would be old, but she had become something precious to him and he perceived that drifting wasn't fair. Then one day late in February the matter was decided out of hand.

They had ridden home from St. Paul and dropped into the College Club for tea, breaking together through the drifts that masked the walk and rimmed the door. It was a revolving door; a young man came around in it, and stepping into his space, they smelt onions and whisky. The door revolved again after them, and he was back within, facing them. It was Randy Cambell; his face was flushed, his eyes dull and hard.

"Hello, beautiful," he said, approaching Annie.

"Don't come so close," she protested lightly. "You smell of onions."

"You're particular all of a sudden."

"Always. I'm always particular." Annie made a slight movement back toward Tom.

"Not always," said Randy unpleasantly. Then, with increased emphasis and a fractional glance at Tom: "Not always." With his remark he seemed to join the hostile world outside. "And I'll just give you a tip," he continued: "Your mother's inside."

The jealous ill-temper of another generation reached Tom only faintly, like the protest of a child, but at this impertinent warning he bristled with annoyance.

"Come on, Annie," he said brusquely. "We'll go in."

With her glance uneasily averted from Randy, Annie followed Tom into the big room.

It was sparsely populated; three middle-aged women sat near the fire. Momentarily Annie drew back, then she walked toward them.

"Hello, mother . . . Mrs. Trumble . . . Aunt Caroline."

The two latter responded; Mrs. Trumble even nodded faintly at Tom. But Annie's mother got to her feet without a word, her eyes frozen, her mouth drawn. For a moment she stood staring at her daughter; then she turned abruptly and left the room.

Tom and Annie found a table across the room.

"Wasn't she terrible?" said Annie, breathing aloud. He didn't answer.

"For three days she hasn't spoken to me." Suddenly she broke out: "Oh, people can be so small! I was going to sing the leading part in the Junior League show, and yesterday Cousin Mary Betts, the president, came to me and said I couldn't."

"Why not?"

"Because a representative Junior League girl mustn't defy her mother. As if I were a naughty child!"

Tom stared on at a row of cups on the mantelpiece—two or three of them bore his name. "Perhaps she was right," he said suddenly. "When I begin to do harm to you it's time to stop."

"What do you mean?"

At her shocked voice his heart poured a warm liquid forth into his body, but he answered quietly: "You remember I told you I was going South? Well, I'm going tomorrow."

There was an argument, but he had made up his mind. At the station next evening she wept and clung to him.

"Thank you for the happiest month I've had in years," he said.

"But you'll come back, Tom."

"I'll be two months in Mexico; then I'm going East for a few weeks."

He tried to sound fortunate, but the frozen city he was leaving seemed to be in blossom. Her frozen breath was a flower on the air, and his heart sank as he realized that some young man was waiting outside to take her home in a car hung with blooms.

"Good-by, Annie. Good-by, sweet!"

Two days later he spent the morning in Houston with Hal Meigs, a classmate at Yale.

"You're in luck for such an old fella," said Meigs at luncheon, "because I'm going to introduce you to the cutest little traveling companion you ever saw, who's going all the way to Mexico City."

The lady in question was frankly pleased to learn at the station that she was not returning alone. She and Tom dined together on the train and later played rummy for an hour; but when, at ten o'clock, standing in the door of the stateroom, she turned back to him suddenly with a certain look, frank and unmistakable, and stood there holding that look for a long moment, Tom Squires was suddenly in the grip of an emotion that was not the one in question. He wanted desperately to see Annie, call her for a second on the phone, and then fall asleep, knowing she was young and pure as a star, and safe in bed.

"Good night," he said, trying to keep any repulsion out of his voice.

"Oh! Good night."

Arriving in El Paso next day, he drove over the border to Juarez. It was bright and hot, and after leaving his bags at the station he went into a bar for an iced drink; as he sipped it a girl's voice addressed him thickly from the table behind:

"You'n American?"

He had noticed her slumped forward on her elbows as he came in; now, turning, he faced a young girl of about seventeen, obviously drunk, yet with gentility in her unsteady, sprawling voice. The American bartender leaned confidentially forward.

"I don't know what to do about her," he said. "She come in about three o'clock with two young fellows—one of them her sweetie. They had a fight and the men went off, and this one's been here ever since."

A spasm of distaste passed over Tom—the rules of his generation were outraged and defied. That an American girl should be drunk and deserted in a tough foreign town—that such things happened, might happen to Annie. He looked at his watch, hesitated.

"Has she got a bill?" he asked.

"She owes for five gins. But suppose her boy friends come back?"

"Tell them she's at the Roosevelt Hotel in El Paso."

Approaching, he put his hand on her shoulder. She looked up.

"You look like Santa Claus," she said vaguely. "You couldn't possibly be Santa Claus, could you?"

"I'm going to take you to El Paso."

"Well," she considered, "you look perfectly safe to me."

She was so young — a drenched little rose. He could have wept for her wretched unconsciousness of the old facts, the old penalties of life. Jousting at nothing in an empty tilt yard with a shaking spear. The taxi moved too slowly through the suddenly poisonous night.

Having explained things to a reluctant night clerk, he went out and found a telegraph office.

"Have given up Mexican trip," he wired. "Leaving here tonight. Please meet train in the St. Paul station at three o'clock and ride with me to Minneapolis, as I can't spare you for another minute. All my love."

He could at least keep an eye on her, advise her, see what she did with her life. That silly mother of hers!

On the train, as the baked tropical lands and green fields fell away and the North swept near again with patches of snow, then fields of it, fierce winds in the vestibule, and bleak, hibernating farms, he paced the corridors with intolerable restlessness. When they drew into the St. Paul station he swung himself off like a young man and searched the platform eagerly, but his eyes failed to find her. He had counted on those few minutes between the cities; they had become a symbol of her fidelity to their friendship, and as the train started again he searched it desperately from smoker to observation car. But he could not find her, and now he knew that he was mad for her; at the thought that she had taken his advice and plunged into affairs with other men, he grew weak with fear.

Drawing into Minneapolis, his hands fumbled so that he must call the porter to fasten his baggage. Then there was an interminable wait in the corridor while the baggage was taken off and he was pressed up against a girl in a squirrel-trimmed coat.

"Tom!"

"Well, I'll be——"

Her arms went up around his neck. "But, Tom," she cried, "I've been right here in this car since St. Paul!"

His cane fell in the corridor, he drew her very tenderly close and their lips met like starved hearts.

III
· · · · ·

The new intimacy of their definite engagement brought Tom a feeling of young happiness. He awoke on winter mornings with the sense of undeserved joy hovering in the room; meeting young men, he found himself matching the vigor of his mind and body against theirs. Suddenly his life had a purpose and a background; he felt rounded and complete. On gray March afternoons when she wandered familiarly in his apartment the warm sureties of his youth flooded back—ecstasy and poignancy, the mortal and the eternal posed in their immemorially tragic juxtaposition, and, a little astounded, he found himself relishing the very terminology of young romance. But he was more thoughtful than a younger lover; and to Annie he seemed to "know everything," to stand holding open the gates for her passage into the truly golden world.

"We'll go to Europe first," he said.

"Oh, we'll go there a lot, won't we? Let's spend our winters in Italy and the spring in Paris."

"But, little Annie, there's business."

"Well, we'll stay away as much as we can anyhow. I hate Minneapolis."

"Oh, no." He was a little shocked. "Minneapolis is all right."

"When you're here it's all right."

Mrs. Lorry yielded at length to the inevitable. With ill grace she acknowledged the engagement, asking only that the marriage should not take place until fall.

"Such a long time," Annie sighed.

"After all, I'm your mother. It's so little to ask."

It was a long winter, even in a land of long winters. March was full of billowy drift, and when it seemed at last as though the cold must be defeated, there was a series of blizzards, desperate as last stands. The people waited; their first energy to resist was spent, and man, like weather, simply hung on. There was less to do now and the general restlessness was expressed by surliness in daily contacts. Then, early in April, with a long sigh the ice cracked, the snow ran into the ground, and the green, eager spring broke up through.

One day, riding along a slushy road in a fresh, damp breeze with a little starved, smothered grass in it, Annie began to cry. Sometimes she cried for nothing, but this time Tom suddenly stopped the car and put his arm around her.

"Why do you cry like that? Are you unhappy?"

"Oh, no, no!" she protested.

"But you cried yesterday the same way. And you wouldn't tell me why. You must always tell me."

"Nothing, except the spring. It smells so good, and it always has so many sad thoughts and memories in it."

"It's our spring, my sweetheart," he said. "Annie, don't let's wait. Let's be married in June."

"I promised mother, but if you like we can announce our engagement in June."

The spring came fast now. The sidewalks were damp, then dry, and the children roller-skated on them and boys played baseball in the soft, vacant lots. Tom got up elaborate picnics of Annie's contemporaries and encouraged her to play golf and tennis with them. Abruptly, with a final, triumphant lurch of Nature, it was full summer.

On a lovely May evening Tom came up the Lorrys' walk and sat down beside Annie's mother on the porch.

"It's so pleasant," he said, "I thought Annie and I would walk instead of driving this evening. I want to show her the funny old house I was born in."

"On Chambers Street, wasn't it? Annie'll be home in a few minutes. She went riding with some young people after dinner."

"Yes, on Chambers Street."

He looked at his watch presently, hoping Annie would come while it was still light enough to see. Quarter of nine. He frowned. She had kept him waiting the night before, kept him waiting an hour yesterday afternoon.

"If I was twenty-one," he said to himself, "I'd make scenes and we'd both be miserable."

He and Mrs. Lorry talked; the warmth of the night precipitated the vague evening lassitude of the fifties and softened them both, and for the first time since his attentions to Annie began, there was no unfriendliness between them. By and by long silences fell, broken only by the scratch of a match or the creak of her swinging settee. When Mr. Lorry came home Tom threw away his second cigar in surprise and looked at his watch; it was after ten.

"Annie's late," Mrs. Lorry said.

"I hope there's nothing wrong," said Tom anxiously. "Who is she with?"

"There were four when they started out. Randy Cambell and another couple—I didn't notice who. They were only going for a soda."

"I hope there hasn't been any trouble. Perhaps—Do you think I ought to go and see?"

"Ten isn't late nowadays. You'll find—" Remembering that Tom Squires was marrying Annie, not adopting her, she kept herself from adding: "You'll get used to it."

Her husband excused himself and went up to bed, and the conversation became more forced and desultory. When the church clock over the way struck eleven they both broke off and listened to the beats. Twenty minutes later just as Tom impatiently crushed

out his last cigar, an automobile drifted down the street and came
to rest in front of the door.

For a minute no one moved on the porch or in the auto. Then
Annie, with a hat in her hand, got out and came quickly up the
walk. Defying the tranquil night, the car snorted away.

"Oh, hello!" she cried. "I'm so sorry! What time is it? Am I terribly late?"

Tom didn't answer. The street lamp threw wine color upon her
face and expressed with a shadow the heightened flush of her
cheek. Her dress was crushed, her hair was in brief, expressive dis-
array. But it was the strange little break in her voice that made
him afraid to speak, made him turn his eyes aside.

"What happened?" Mrs. Lorry asked casually.

"Oh, a blow-out and something wrong with the engine — and
we lost our way. Is it terribly late?"

And then, as she stood before them, her hat still in her hand,
her breast rising and falling a little, her eyes wide and bright, Tom
realized with a shock that he and her mother were people of the
same age looking at a person of another. Try as he might, he could
not separate himself from Mrs. Lorry. When she excused herself he
suppressed a frantic tendency to say, "But why should you go
now? After sitting here all evening?"

They were alone. Annie came up to him and pressed his hand.
He had never been so conscious of her beauty; her damp hands
were touched with dew.

"You were out with young Cambell," he said.

"Yes. Oh, don't be mad. I feel — I feel so upset tonight."

"Upset?"

She sat down, whimpering a little.

"I couldn't help it. Please don't be mad. He wanted so for me
to take a ride with him and it was such a wonderful night, so I
went just for an hour. And we began talking and I didn't realize
the time. I felt so sorry for him."

"How do you think I felt?" He scorned himself, but it was said now.

"Don't, Tom. I told you I was terribly upset. I want to go to bed."

"I understand. Good night, Annie."

"Oh, please don't act that way, Tom. Can't you understand?"

But he could, and that was just the trouble. With the courteous bow of another generation, he walked down the steps and off into the obliterating moonlight. In a moment he was just a shadow passing the street lamps and then a faint footfall up the street.

IV
. . . . .

All through that summer he often walked abroad in the evenings. He liked to stand for a minute in front of the house where he was born, and then in front of another house where he had been a little boy. On his customary routes there were other sharp landmarks of the 90's, converted habitats of gayeties that no longer existed — the shell of Jansen's Livery Stables and the old Nushka Rink, where every winter his father had curled on the well-kept ice.

"And it's a darn pity," he would mutter. "A darn pity."

He had a tendency, too, to walk past the lights of a certain drug store, because it seemed to him that it had contained the seed of another and nearer branch of the past. Once he went in, and inquiring casually about the blonde clerk, found that she had married and departed several months before. He obtained her name and on an impulse sent her a wedding present "from a dumb admirer," for he felt he owed something to her for his happiness and pain. He had lost the battle against youth and spring, and with his grief paid the penalty for age's unforgivable sin — refusing to die. But he could not have walked down wasted into the darkness without being used up a little; what he had wanted, after all, was only to break his strong old heart. Conflict itself has a value beyond victory and defeat, and those three months — he had them forever.

A FREEZE-OUT

"A Freeze-Out" was the last story Fitzgerald wrote in Europe before returning to America for good in September 1931, and it earned him his top-dollar fee, $4,000. His rate dropped in 1932 to $3,500, partly due to the Depression but also because magazine editors—and even his loyal agent—were complaining about the quality of his stories. For the most part, he had lost interest in creating stories about young love, his bread-and-butter formula. One last successful flicker of this story type came with "A Freeze-Out," which was both the last story he would set in St. Paul and the final reference to his hometown in his fiction. (A small Minnesota history note: the James-Younger gang robbed a bank in Northfield, not Stillwater, in September 1876. Fitzgerald may have been remembering that the Youngers were held in Stillwater Prison, where the doctor who delivered Fitzgerald, Benjamin H. Ogden, had cared for the bank robbers after their capture.) After this story was published, St. Paul appears only in his letters, sometimes mentioned disparagingly, but often invoked in a bittersweet note. Zelda, who had spent only a year in Minnesota, also retained a tender memory of their St. Paul summers. They both kept meaning to bring their daughter back, they said.

The Saturday Evening Post, December 19, 1931
Collected in The Price Was High: The Last Uncollected Stories of F. Scott Fitzgerald (1979)

I
. . . . .

HERE AND THERE IN A SUNLESS CORNER skulked a little
snow under a veil of coal specks, but the men taking down storm
windows were laboring in shirt sleeves and the turf was becoming
firm underfoot.

In the streets, dresses dyed after fruit, leaf, and flower emerged
from beneath the shed somber skins of animals; now only a few
old men wore mousy caps pulled down over their ears. That was
the day Forrest Winslow forgot the long fret of the past winter as
one forgets inevitable afflictions, sickness, and war, and turned
with blind confidence toward the summer, thinking he already
recognized in it all the summers of the past — the golfing, sailing,
swimming summers.

For eight years Forrest had gone East to school and then to college; now he worked for his father in a large Minnesota city. He
was handsome, popular, and rather spoiled in a conservative way,
and so the past year had been a comedown. The discrimination
that had picked Scroll and Key at New Haven was applied to sort-
ing furs; the hand that had signed the Junior Prom expense checks
had since rocked in a sling for two months with mild *dermatitis
venenata.* After work, Forrest found no surcease in the girls with
whom he had grown up. On the contrary, the news of a stranger
within the tribe stimulated him and during the transit of a popular visitor he displayed a convulsive activity. So far, nothing had
happened; but here was summer.

On the day spring broke through and summer broke through —
it is much the same thing in Minnesota — Forrest stopped his
coupé in front of a music store and took his pleasant vanity inside.
As he said to the clerk, "I want some records," a little bomb of excitement exploded in his larynx, causing an unfamiliar and almost
painful vacuum in his upper diaphragm. The unexpected detona-

tion was caused by the sight of a corn-colored girl who was being waited on across the counter.

She was a stalk of ripe corn, but bound not as cereals are but as a rare first edition, with all the binder's art. She was lovely and expensive, and about nineteen, and he had never seen her before. She looked at him for just an unnecessary moment too long, with so much self-confidence that he felt his own rush out and away to join hers — ". . . from him that hath not shall be taken away even that which he hath." Then her head swayed forward and she resumed her inspection of a catalogue.

Forrest looked at the list a friend had sent him from New York. Unfortunately, the first title was: "When Voo-do-o-do Meets Boop-boop-a-doop, There'll Soon be a Hot-Cha-Cha." Forrest read it with horror. He could scarcely believe a title could be so repulsive.

Meanwhile the girl was asking: "Isn't there a record of Prokofiev's 'Fils Prodigue'?"

"I'll see, madam." The saleswoman turned to Forrest.

"'When Voo —'" Forrest began, and then repeated, "'When Voo———'"

There was no use; he couldn't say it in front of that nymph of the harvest across the table.

"Never mind that one," he said quickly. "Give me 'Huggable———'" Again he broke off.

"'Huggable, Kissable You'?" suggested the clerk helpfully, and her assurance that it was very nice suggested a humiliating community of taste.

"I want Stravinsky's 'Fire Bird,'" said the other customer, "and this album of Chopin waltzes."

Forrest ran his eye hastily down the rest of his list: "Digga Diggity," "Ever So Goosy," "Bunkey Doodle I Do."

"Anybody would take me for a moron," he thought. He crumpled up the list and fought for air — his own kind of air, the air of casual superiority.

"I'd like," he said coldly, "Beethoven's 'Moonlight Sonata.'"

There was a record of it at home, but it didn't matter. It gave him the right to glance at the girl again and again. Life became interesting; she was the loveliest concoction; it would be easy to trace her. With the "Moonlight Sonata" wrapped face to face with "Huggable, Kissable You," Forrest quitted the shop.

There was a new book store down the street, and here also he entered, as if books and records could fill the vacuum that spring was making in his heart. As he looked among the lifeless words of many titles together, he was wondering how soon he could find her, and what then.

"I'd like a hard-boiled detective story," he said.

A weary young man shook his head with patient reproof; simultaneously, a spring draft from the door blew in with it the familiar glow of cereal hair.

"We don't carry detective stories or stuff like that," said the young man in an unnecessarily loud voice. "I imagine you'll find it at a department store."

"I thought you carried books," said Forrest feebly.

"Books, yes, but not that kind." The young man turned to wait on his other customer.

As Forrest stalked out, passing within the radius of the girl's perfume, he heard her ask:

"Have you got anything of Louis Arragon's, either in French or in translation?"

"She's just showing off," he thought angrily. "They skip right from Peter Rabbit to Marcel Proust these days."

Outside, parked just behind his own adequate coupé, he found an enormous silver-colored roadster of English make and custom design. Disturbed, even upset, he drove homeward through the moist, golden afternoon.

The Winslows lived in an old, wide-verandaed house on Crest Avenue — Forrest's father and mother, his great-grandmother, and his sister Eleanor. They were solid people as that phrase goes since the war. Old Mrs. Forrest was entirely solid; with convictions based on a way of life that had worked for eighty-four years. She was a character in the city; she remembered the Sioux war, and she had been in Stillwater the day the James brothers shot up the main street.

Her own children were dead and she looked on these remoter descendants from a distance, oblivious of the forces that had formed them. She understood that the Civil War and the opening up of the West were forces, while the free-silver movement and the World War had reached her only as news. But she knew that her father, killed at Cold Harbor, and her husband, the merchant, were larger in scale than her son or her grandson. People who tried to explain contemporary phenomena to her seemed, to her, to be talking against the evidence of their own senses. Yet she was not atrophied; last summer she had traveled over half of Europe with only a maid.

Forrest's father and mother were something else again. They had been in the susceptible middle thirties when the cocktail party and its concomitants arrived in 1921. They were divided people, leaning forward and backward. Issues that presented no difficulty to Mrs. Forrest caused them painful heat and agitation. Such an issue arose before they had been five minutes at table that night.

"Do you know the Rikkers are coming back?" said Mrs. Winslow. "They've taken the Warner house." She was a woman with many uncertainties, which she concealed from herself by expressing her opinions very slowly and thoughtfully, to convince her own ears. "It's a wonder Dan Warner would rent them his house. I suppose Cathy thinks everybody will fall all over themselves."

"What Cathy?" asked old Mrs. Forrest.

"She was Cathy Chase. Her father was Reynold Chase. She and her husband are coming back here."

"Oh, yes."

"I scarcely knew her," continued Mrs. Winslow, "but I know

that when they were in Washington they were pointedly rude to everyone from Minnesota — went out of their way. Mary Cowan was spending a winter there, and she invited Cathy to lunch or tea at least half a dozen times. Cathy never appeared."

"I could beat that record," said Pierce Winslow. "Mary Cowan could invite me a hundred times and I wouldn't go."

"Anyhow," pursued his wife slowly, "in view of all the scandal, it's just asking for the cold shoulder to come out here."

"They're asking for it, all right," said Winslow. He was a Southerner, well liked in the city, where he had lived for thirty years. "Walter Hannan came in my office this morning and wanted me to second Rikker for the Kennemore Club. I said: 'Walter, I'd rather second Al Capone.' What's more, Rikker'll get into the Kennemore Club over my dead body."

"Walter had his nerve. What's Chauncey Rikker to you? It'll be hard to get anyone to second him."

"Who are they?" Eleanor asked. "Somebody awful?"

She was eighteen and a débutante. Her current appearances at home were so rare and brief that she viewed such table topics with as much detachment as her great-grandmother.

"Cathy was a girl here; she was younger than I was, but I remember that she was always considered fast. Her husband, Chauncey Rikker, came from some little town upstate."

"What did they do that was so awful?"

"Rikker went bankrupt and left town," said her father. "There were a lot of ugly stories. Then he went to Washington and got mixed up in the alien-property scandal; and then he got in trouble in New York — he was in the bucket-shop business — but he skipped out to Europe. After a few years the chief Government witness died and he came back to America. They got him for a few months for contempt of court." He expanded into eloquent irony: "And now, with true patriotism, he comes back to his beautiful Minnesota, a product of its lovely woods, its rolling wheat fields——"

Forrest called him impatiently: "Where do you get that, father? When did two Kentuckians ever win Nobel prizes in the same year? And how about an upstate boy named Lind——"

"Have the Rikkers any children?" Eleanor asked.

"I think Cathy has a daughter about your age, and a boy about sixteen."

Forrest uttered a small, unnoticed exclamation. Was it possible? French books and Russian music — that girl this afternoon had lived abroad. And with the probability his resentment deepened — the daughter of a crook putting on all that dog! He sympathized passionately with his father's refusal to second Rikker for the Kennemore Club.

"Are they rich?" old Mrs. Forrest suddenly demanded.

"They must be well off if they took Dan Warner's house."

"Then they'll get in all right."

"They won't get into the Kennemore Club," said Pierce Winslow. "I happen to come from a state with certain traditions."

"I've seen the bottom rail get to be the top rail many times in this town," said the old lady blandly.

"But this man's a criminal, grandma," explained Forrest. "Can't you see the difference? It isn't a social question. We used to argue at New Haven whether we'd shake hands with Al Capone if we met him——"

"Who is Al Capone?" asked Mrs. Forrest.

"He's another criminal, in Chicago."

"Does he want to join the Kennemore Club too?"

They laughed, but Forrest had decided that if Rikker came up for the Kennemore Club, his father's would not be the only black ball in the box.

Abruptly it became full summer. After the last April storm someone came along the street one night, blew up the trees like balloons, scattered bulbs and shrubs like confetti, opened a cage full of robins, and, after a quick look around, signaled up the curtain upon a new backdrop of summer sky.

Tossing back a strayed baseball to some kids in a vacant lot, Forrest's fingers, on the stitched seams of the stained leather cover, sent a wave of ecstatic memories to his brain. One must hurry and get there—"there" was now the fairway of the golf course, but his feeling was the same. Only when he teed off at the eighteenth that afternoon did he realize that it wasn't the same, that it would never be enough any more. The evening stretched large and empty before him, save for the set pieces of a dinner party and bed.

While he waited with his partner for a match to play off, Forrest glanced at the tenth tee, exactly opposite and two hundred yards away.

One of the two figures on the ladies' tee was addressing her ball; as he watched, she swung up confidently and cracked a long drive down the fairway.

"Must be Mrs. Horrick," said his friend. "No other woman can drive like that."

At that moment the sun glittered on the girl's hair and Forrest knew who it was; simultaneously, he remembered what he must do this afternoon. That night Chauncey Rikker's name was to come up before the membership committee on which his father sat, and before going home, Forrest was going to pass the clubhouse and leave a certain black slip in a little box. He had carefully considered all that; he loved the city where his people had lived honorable lives for five generations. His grandfather had been a founder of this club in the 90's when it went in for sailboat racing instead of golf, and when it took a fast horse three hours to trot out here from town. He agreed with his father that certain people were without the pale. Tightening his face, he drove his ball two hundred yards down the fairway, where it curved gently into the rough.

The eighteenth and tenth holes were parallel and faced in opposite directions. Between tees they were separated by a belt of trees forty feet wide. Though Forrest did not know it, Miss Rikker's hostess, Helen Hannan, had dubbed into this same obscurity, and as he went in search of his ball he heard female voices twenty feet away.

"You'll be a member after tonight," he heard Helen Hannan say, "and then you can get some real competition from Stella Horrick."

"Maybe I won't be a member," said a quick, clear voice. "Then you'll have to come and play with me on the public links."

"Alida, don't be absurd."

"Why? I played on the public links in Buffalo all last spring. For the moment there wasn't anywhere else. It's like playing on some courses in Scotland."

"But I'd feel so silly. . . . Oh, gosh, let's let the ball go."

"There's nobody behind us. As to feeling silly—if I cared about public opinion any more, I'd spend my time in my bedroom." She laughed scornfully. "A tabloid published a picture of me going to see father in prison. And I've seen people change their tables away from us on steamers, and once I was cut by all the American girls in a French school. . . . Here's your ball."

"Thanks. . . . Oh, Alida, it seems terrible."

"All the terrible part is over. I just said that so you wouldn't be too sorry for us if people didn't want us in this club. I wouldn't care; I've got a life of my own and my own standard of what trouble is. It wouldn't touch me at all."

They passed out of the clearing and their voices disappeared into the open sky on the other side. Forrest abandoned the search for his lost ball and walked toward the caddie house.

"What a hell of a note," he thought. "To take it out on a girl that had nothing to do with it"—which was what he was doing this minute as he went up toward the club. "No," he said to himself abruptly, "I can't do it. Whatever her father may have done, she happens to be a lady. Father can do what he feels he has to do, but I'm out."

After lunch the next day, his father said rather diffidently: "I see you didn't do anything about the Rikkers and the Kennemore Club."

"No."

"It's just as well," said his father. "As a matter of fact, they got by. The club has got rather mixed anyhow in the last five years — a good many queer people in it. And, after all, in a club you don't have to know anybody you don't want to. The other people on the committee felt the same way."

"I see," said Forrest dryly. "Then you didn't argue against the Rikkers?"

"Well, no. The thing is I do a lot of business with Walter Hannan, and it happened yesterday I was obliged to ask him rather a difficult favor."

"So you traded with him." To both father and son, the word "traded" sounded like traitor.

"Not exactly. The matter wasn't mentioned."

"I understand," Forrest said. But he did not understand, and some old childhood faith in his father died at that moment.

II

. . . . .

To snub anyone effectively one must have him within range. The admission of Chauncey Rikker to the Kennemore Club and, later, to the Downtown Club was followed by angry talk and threats of resignation that simulated the sound of conflict, but there was no indication of a will underneath. On the other hand, unpleasantness in crowds is easy, and Chauncey Rikker was a facile object for personal dislike; moreover, a recurrent echo of the bucket-shop scandal sounded from New York, and the matter was reviewed in the local newspapers, in case anyone had missed it. Only the liberal Hannan family stood by the Rikkers, and their attitude aroused considerable resentment, and their attempt to launch them with a series of small parties proved a failure. Had the Rikkers attempted to "bring Alida out," it would have been for the inspection of a motley crowd indeed, but they didn't.

When, occasionally during the summer, Forrest encountered

Alida Rikker, they crossed eyes in the curious way of children who don't know each other. For a while he was haunted by her curly yellow head, by the golden-brown defiance of her eyes; then he became interested in another girl. He wasn't in love with Jane Drake, though he thought he might marry her. She was "the girl across the street"; he knew her qualities, good and bad, so that they didn't matter. She had an essential reality underneath, like a relative. It would please their families. Once, after several highballs and some casual necking, he almost answered seriously when she provoked him with "But you don't really care about me"; but he sat tight and next morning was relieved that he had. Perhaps in the dull days after Christmas——Meanwhile, at the Christmas dances among the Christmas girls he might find the ecstasy and misery, the infatuation that he wanted. By autumn he felt that his predestined girl was already packing her trunk in some Eastern or Southern city.

It was in his more restless mood that one November Sunday he went to a small tea. Even as he spoke to his hostess he felt Alida Rikker across the firelit room; her glowing beauty and her unexplored novelty pressed up against him, and there was a relief in being presented to her at last. He bowed and passed on, but there had been some sort of communication. Her look said that she knew the stand that his family had taken, that she didn't mind, and was even sorry to see him in such a silly position, for she knew that he admired her. His look said: "Naturally, I'm sensitive to your beauty, but you see how it is; we've had to draw the line at the fact that your father is a dirty dog, and I can't withdraw from my present position."

Suddenly in a silence, she was talking, and his ears swayed away from his own conversation.

". . . Helen had this odd pain for over a year and, of course, they suspected cancer. She went to have an X ray; she undressed behind a screen, and the doctor looked at her through the machine, and then he said, 'But I told you to take off all your clothes,' and Helen said, 'I have.' The doctor looked again, and said, 'Listen, my dear, I brought you into the world, so there's no use being modest with me. Take off everything.' So Helen said, 'I've got every stitch off; I swear.' But the doctor said, 'You have not. The X ray shows me a safety pin in your brassiere.' Well, they finally found out that she'd been suspected of swallowing a safety pin when she was two years old."

The story, floating in her clear, crisp voice upon the intimate air, disarmed Forrest. It had nothing to do with what had taken place in Washington or New York ten years before. Suddenly he wanted to go and sit near her, because she was the tongue of flame that made the firelight vivid. Leaving, he walked for an hour through feathery snow, wondering again why he couldn't know her, why it was his business to represent a standard.

"Well, maybe I'll have a lot of fun some day doing what I ought to do," he thought ironically — "when I'm fifty."

The first Christmas dance was the charity ball at the armory. It was a large, public affair; the rich sat in boxes. Everyone came who felt he belonged, and many out of curiosity, so the atmosphere was tense with a strange haughtiness and aloofness.

The Rikkers had a box. Forrest, coming in with Jane Drake, glanced at the man of evil reputation and at the beaten woman frozen with jewels who sat beside him. They were the city's villains, gaped at by the people of reserved and timid lives. Oblivious of the staring eyes, Alida and Helen Hannan held court for several young men from out of town. Without question, Alida was incomparably the most beautiful girl in the room.

Several people told Forrest the news — the Rikkers were giving a big dance after New Year's. There were written invitations, but these were being supplemented by oral ones. Rumor had it that one had merely to be presented to any Rikker in order to be bidden to the dance.

As Forrest passed through the hall, two friends stopped him and with a certain hilarity introduced him to a youth of seventeen, Mr. Teddy Rikker.

"We're giving a dance," said the young man immediately. "January third. Be very happy if you could come."

Forrest was afraid he had an engagement.

"Well, come if you change your mind."

"Horrible kid, but shrewd," said one of his friends later. "We were feeding him people, and when we brought up a couple of saps, he looked at them and didn't say a word. Some refuse and a few accept and most of them stall, but he goes right on; he's got his father's crust."

Into the highways and byways. Why didn't the girl stop it? He was sorry for her when he found Jane in a group of young women reveling in the story.

"I hear they asked Bodman, the undertaker, by mistake, and then took it back."

"Mrs. Carleton pretended she was deaf."

"There's going to be a carload of champagne from Canada."

"Of course, I won't go, but I'd love to, just to see what happens. There'll be a hundred men to every girl—and that'll be meat for her."

The accumulated malice repelled him, and he was angry at Jane for being part of it. Turning away, his eyes fell on Alida's proud form swaying along a wall, watched the devotion of her partners with an unpleasant resentment. He did not know that he had been a little in love with her for many months. Just as two children can fall in love during a physical struggle over a ball, so their awareness of each other had grown to surprising proportions.

"She's pretty," said Jane. "She's not exactly overdressed, but considering everything, she dresses too elaborately."

"I suppose she ought to wear sackcloth and ashes or half mourning."

"I was honored with a written invitation, but, of course, I'm not going."

"Why not?"

Jane looked at him in surprise. "You're not going."

"That's different. I would if I were you. You see, you don't care what her father did."

"Of course, I care."

"No, you don't. And all this small meanness just debases the whole thing. Why don't they let her alone? She's young and pretty and she's done nothing wrong."

Later in the week he saw Alida at the Hannans' dance and noticed that many men danced with her. He saw her lips moving, heard her laughter, caught a word or so of what she said; irresistibly he found himself guiding partners around in her wake. He envied visitors to the city who didn't know who she was.

The night of the Rikkers' dance he went to a small dinner; before they sat down at table he realized that the others were all going on to the Rikkers'. They talked of it as a sort of comic adventure; insisted that he come too.

"Even if you weren't invited, it's all right," they assured him. "We were told we could bring anyone. It's just a free-for-all; it doesn't put you under any obligations. Norma Nash is going and she didn't invite Alida Rikker to her party. Besides, she's really very nice. My brother's quite crazy about her. Mother is worried sick, because he says he wants to marry her."

Clasping his hand about a new highball, Forrest knew that if he drank it he would probably go. All his reasons for not going seemed old and tired, and, fatally, he had begun to seem absurd to himself. In vain he tried to remember the purpose he was serving, and found none. His father had weakened on the matter of the Kennemore Club. And now suddenly he found reasons for going — men could go where their women could not.

"All right," he said.

The Rikkers' dance was in the ballroom of the Minnekada Hotel. The Rikkers' gold, ill-gotten, tainted, had taken the form of a forest of palms, vines, and flowers. The two orchestras moaned in pergolas lit with fireflies, and many-colored spotlights swept the floor, touching a buffet where dark bottles gleamed. The receiving line was still in action when Forrest's party came in, and Forrest grinned ironically at the prospect of taking Chauncey Rikker by the hand. But at the sight of Alida, her look that at last fell frankly on him, he forgot everything else.

"Your brother was kind enough to invite me," he said.

"Oh, yes," she was polite, but vague; not at all overwhelmed by his presence. As he waited to speak to her parents, he started, seeing his sister in a group of dancers. Then, one after another, he identified people he knew: it might have been any one of the Christmas dances; all the younger crowd were there. He discovered abruptly that he and Alida were alone; the receiving line had broken up. Alida glanced at him questioningly and with a certain amusement.

So he danced out on the floor with her, his head high, but slightly spinning. Of all things in the world, he had least expected to lead off the Chauncey Rikkers' ball.

III

· · · · ·

Next morning his first realization was that he had kissed her; his second was a feeling of profound shame for his conduct of the evening. Lord help him, he had been the life of the party; he had helped to run the cotillion. From the moment when he danced out on the floor, coolly meeting the surprised and interested glances of his friends, a mood of desperation had come over him. He rushed Alida Rikker, until a friend asked him what Jane was going to say. "What business is it of Jane's?" he demanded impatiently. "We're not engaged." But he was impelled to approach his sister and ask her if he looked all right.

"Apparently," Eleanor answered, "but when in doubt, don't take any more."

So he hadn't. Exteriorly he remained correct, but his libido was in a state of wild extroversion. He sat with Alida Rikker and told her he had loved her for months.

"Every night I thought of you just before you went to sleep," his voice trembled with insincerity, "I was afraid to meet you or speak to you. Sometimes I'd see you in the distance moving along like a golden chariot, and the world would be good to live in."

After twenty minutes of this eloquence, Alida began to feel exceedingly attractive. She was tired and rather happy, and eventually she said:

"All right, you can kiss me if you want to, but it won't mean anything. I'm just not in that mood."

But Forrest had moods enough for both; he kissed her as if they stood together at the altar. A little later he had thanked Mrs. Rikker with deep emotion for the best time he had ever had in his life.

It was noon, and as he groped his way upright in bed, Eleanor came in in her dressing gown.

"How are you?" she asked.

"Awful."

"How about what you told me coming back in the car? Do you actually want to marry Alida Rikker?"

"Not this morning."

"That's all right then. Now, look: the family are furious."

"Why?" he asked with some redundancy.

"Both you and I being there. Father heard that you led the cotillion. My explanation was that my dinner party went, and so I had to go; but then you went too!"

Forrest dressed and went down to Sunday dinner. Over the table hovered an atmosphere of patient, puzzled, unworldly disappointment. Finally Forrest launched into it:

"Well, we went to Al Capone's party and had a fine time."

"So I've heard," said Pierce Winslow dryly. Mrs. Winslow said nothing.

"Everybody was there — the Kayes, the Schwanes, the Martins, and the Blacks. From now on, the Rikkers are pillars of society. Every house is open to them."

"Not this house," said his mother. "They won't come into this house." And after a moment: "Aren't you going to eat anything, Forrest?"

"No, thanks. I mean, yes, I am eating." He looked cautiously at his plate. "The girl is very nice. There isn't a girl in town with better manners or more stuff. If things were like they were before the war, I'd say——"

He couldn't think exactly what it was he would have said; all he knew was that he was now on an entirely different road from his parents'.

"This city was scarcely more than a village before the war," said old Mrs. Forrest.

"Forrest means the World War, granny," said Eleanor.

"Some things don't change," said Pierce Winslow. Both he and Forrest thought of the Kennemore Club matter and, feeling guilty, the older man lost his temper:

"When people start going to parties given by a convicted criminal, there's something serious the matter with them."

"We won't discuss it any more at table," said Mrs. Winslow hastily.

About four, Forrest called a number on the telephone in his room. He had known for some time that he was going to call a number.

"Is Miss Rikker at home? . . . Oh, hello. This is Forrest Winslow."

"How are you?"

"Terrible. It was a good party."

"Wasn't it?"

"Too good. What are you doing?"

"Entertaining two awful hangovers."

"Will you entertain me too?"

"I certainly will. Come on over."

The two young men could only groan and play sentimental music on the phonograph, but presently they departed; the fire leaped up, day went out behind the windows, and Forrest had rum in his tea.

"So we met at last," he said.

"The delay was all yours."

"Damn prejudice," he said. "This is a conservative city, and your father being in this trouble——"

"I can't discuss my father with you."

"Excuse me. I only wanted to say that I've felt like a fool lately for not knowing you. For cheating myself out of the pleasure of knowing you for a silly prejudice," he blundered on. "So I decided to follow my own instincts."

She stood up suddenly. "Goody-by, Mr. Winslow."

"What? Why?"

"Because it's absurd for you to come here as if you were doing me a favor. And after accepting our hospitality, to remind me of my father's troubles is simply bad manners."

He was on his feet, terribly upset. "That isn't what I meant. I said I had felt that way, and I despised myself for it. Please don't be sore."

"Then don't be condescending." She sat back in her chair. Her mother came in, stayed only a moment, and threw Forrest a glance of resentment and suspicion as she left. But her passage through had brought them together, and they talked frankly for a long time.

"I ought to be upstairs dressing."

"I ought to have gone an hour ago, and I can't."

"Neither can I."

With the admission they had traveled far. At the door he kissed her unreluctant lips and walked home, throwing futile buckets of reason on the wild fire.

Less than two weeks later it happened. In a car parked in a blizzard he poured out his worship, and she lay on his chest, sighing, "Oh, me too — me too."

Already Forrest's family knew where he went in the evenings;

there was a frightened coolness, and one morning his mother said:

"Son, you don't want to throw yourself away on some girl that isn't up to you. I thought you were interested in Jane Drake."

"Don't bring that up. I'm not going to talk about it."

But it was only a postponement. Meanwhile the days of this February were white and magical, the nights were starry and crystalline. The town lay under a cold glory; the smell of her furs was incense, her bright cheeks were flames upon a northern altar. An ecstatic pantheism for his land and its weather welled up in him. She had brought him finally back to it; he would live here always.

"I want you so much that nothing can stand in the way of that," he said to Alida. "But I owe my parents a debt that I can't explain to you. They did more than spend money on me; they tried to give me something more intangible—something that their parents had given them and that they thought was worth handing on. Evidently it didn't take with me, but I've got to make this as easy as possible for them." He saw by her face that he had hurt her. "Darling——"

"Oh, it frightens me when you talk like that," she said. "Are you going to reproach me later? It would be awful. You'll have to get it out of your head that you're doing anything wrong. My standards are as high as yours, and I can't start out with my father's sins on my shoulders." She thought for a moment. "You'll never be able to reconcile it all like a children's story. You've got to choose. Probably you'll have to hurt either your family or hurt me."

A fortnight later the storm broke at the Winslow house. Pierce Winslow came home in a quiet rage and had a session behind closed doors with his wife. Afterward she knocked at Forrest's door.

"Your father had a very embarrassing experience today. Chauncey Rikker came up to him in the Downtown Club and began talking about you as if you were on terms of some understanding with his daughter. Your father walked away, but we've got to know. Are you serious about Miss Rikker?"

"I want to marry her," he said.

"Oh, Forrest!"

She talked for a long time, recapitulating, as if it were a matter of centuries, the eighty years that his family had been identified with the city; when she passed from this to the story of his father's health, Forrest interrupted:

"That's all so irrelevant, mother. If there was anything against Alida personally, what you say would have some weight, but there isn't."

"She's overdressed; she runs around with everybody——"

"She isn't a bit different from Eleanor. She's absolutely a lady in every sense. I feel like a fool even discussing her like this. You're just afraid it'll connect you in some way with the Rikkers."

"I'm not afraid of that," said his mother, annoyed. "Nothing would ever do that. But I'm afraid that it'll separate you from everything worth while, everybody that loves you. It isn't fair for you to upset our lives, let us in for disgraceful gossip——"

"I'm to give up the girl I love because you're afraid of a little gossip."

The controversy was resumed next day, with Pierce Winslow debating. His argument was that he was born in old Kentucky, that he had always felt uneasy at having begotten a son upon a pioneer Minnesota family, and that this was what he might have expected. Forrest felt that his parents' attitude was trivial and disingenuous. Only when he was out of the house, acting against their wishes, did he feel any compunction. But always he felt that something precious was being frayed away—his youthful companionship with his father and his love and trust for his mother. Hour by hour he saw the past being irreparably spoiled, and save when he was with Alida, he was deeply unhappy.

One spring day when the situation had become unendurable, with half the family meals taken in silence, Forrest's great-grandmother stopped him on the stair landing and put her hand on his arm.

"Has this girl really a good character?" she asked, her fine, clear, old eyes resting on his.

"Of course she has, gramma."

"Then marry her."

"Why do you say that?" Forrest asked curiously.

"It would stop all this nonsense and we could have some peace. And I've been thinking I'd like to be a great-great-grandmother before I die."

Her frank selfishness appealed to him more than the righteousness of the others. That night he and Alida decided to be married the first of June, and telephoned the announcement to the papers.

Now the storm broke in earnest. Crest Avenue rang with gossip—how Mrs. Rikker had called on Mrs. Winslow, who was not at home. How Forrest had gone to live in the University Club. How Chauncey Rikker and Pierce Winslow had had words in the Downtown Club.

It was true that Forrest had gone to the University Club. On a May night, with summer sounds already gathered on the window screens, he packed his trunk and his suitcases in the room where he had lived as a boy. His throat contracted, and he smeared his face with his dusty hand as he took a row of golf cups off the mantelpiece, and he choked to himself: "If they won't take Alida, then they're not my family any more."

As he finished packing, his mother came in.

"You're not really leaving." Her voice was stricken.

"I'm moving to the University Club."

"That's so unnecessary. No one bothers you here. You do what you want."

"I can't bring Alida here."

"Father——"

"Hell with father!" he said wildly.

She sat down on the bed beside him. "Stay here, Forrest. I promise not to argue with you any more. But stay here."

315

"I can't."

"I can't have you go!" she wailed. "It seems as if we're driving you out, and we're not!"

"You mean it looks as though you were driving me out."

"I don't mean that."

"Yes, you do. And I want to say that I don't think you and father really care a hang about Chauncey Rikker's moral character."

"That's not true, Forrest. I hate people that behave badly and break the laws. My own father would never have let Chauncey Rikker——"

"I'm not talking about your father. But neither you nor my father care a bit what Chauncey Rikker did. I bet you don't even know what it was."

"Of course I know. He stole some money and went abroad, and when he came back they put him in prison."

"They put him in prison for contempt of court."

"Now you're defending him, Forrest."

"I'm not! I hate his guts; undoubtedly he's a crook. But I tell you it was a shock to me to find that father didn't have any principles. He and his friends sit around the Downtown Club and pan Chauncey Rikker, but when it comes to keeping him out of a club, they develop weak spines."

"That was a small thing."

"No, it wasn't. None of the men of father's age have any principles. I don't know why. I'm willing to make an allowance for an honest conviction, but I'm not going to be booed by somebody that hasn't got any principles and simply pretends to have."

His mother sat helplessly, knowing that what he said was true. She and her husband and all their friends had no principles. They were good or bad according to their natures; often they struck attitudes remembered from the past, but they were never sure as her father or her grandfather had been sure. Confusedly she supposed it was something about religion. But how could you get principles just by wishing for them?

The maid announced the arrival of a taxi.

"Send up Olsen for my baggage," said Forrest; then to his mother, "I'm not taking the coupé; I left the keys. I'm just taking my clothes. I suppose father will let me keep my job down town."

"Forrest, don't talk that way. Do you think your father would take your living away from you, no matter what you did?"

"Such things have happened."

"You're hard and difficult," she wept. "Pease stay here a little longer, and perhaps things will be better and father will get a little more reconciled. Oh, stay, stay! I'll talk to father again. I'll do my best to fix things."

"Will you let me bring Alida here?"

"Not now. Don't ask me that. I couldn't bear——"

"All right," he said grimly.

Olsen came in for the bags. Crying and holding on to his coat sleeve, his mother went with him to the front door.

"Won't you say good-by to father?"

"Why? I'll see him tomorrow in the office."

"Forrest, I was thinking, why don't you go to a hotel instead of the University Club?"

"Why, I thought I'd be more comfortable——" Suddenly he realized that his presence would be less conspicuous at a hotel. Shutting up his bitterness inside him, he kissed his mother roughly and went to the cab.

Unexpectedly, it stopped by the corner lamp-post at a hail from the sidewalk, and the May twilight yielded up Alida, miserable and pale.

"What is it?" he demanded.

"I had to come," she said. "Stop the car. I've been thinking of you leaving your house on account of me, and how you loved your family—the way I'd like to love mine—and I thought how terrible it was to spoil all that. Listen, Forrest! Wait! I want you to go back. Yes, I do. We can wait. We haven't any right to cause all this pain. We're young. I'll go away for a while, and then we'll see."

He pulled her toward him by her shoulders.

"You've got more principles than the whole bunch of them," he said. "Oh, my girl, you love me and, gosh, it's good that you do!"

IV
· · · · ·

It was to be a house wedding, Forrest and Alida having vetoed the Rikkers' idea that it was to be a sort of public revenge. Only a few intimate friends were invited.

During the week before the wedding, Forrest deduced from a series of irresolute and ambiguous telephone calls that his mother wanted to attend the ceremony, if possible. Sometimes he hoped passionately she would; at others it seemed unimportant.

The wedding was to be at seven. At five o'clock Pierce Winslow was walking up and down the two interconnecting sitting rooms of his house.

"This evening," he murmured, "my only son is being married to the daughter of a swindler."

He spoke aloud so that he could listen to the words, but they had been evoked so often in the past few months that their strength was gone and they died thinly upon the air.

He went to the foot of the stairs and called: "Charlotte!" No answer. He called again, and then went into the dining room, where the maid was setting the table.

"Is Mrs. Winslow out?"

"I haven't seen her come in, Mr. Winslow."

Back in the sitting room he resumed his walking; unconsciously he was walking like his father, the judge, dead thirty years ago; he was parading his dead father up and down the room.

"You can't bring that woman into this house to meet your mother. Bad blood is bad blood."

The house seemed unusually quiet. He went upstairs and looked into his wife's room, but she was not there; old Mrs. Forrest was slightly indisposed; Eleanor, he knew, was at the wedding.

He felt genuinely sorry for himself as he went downstairs again. He knew his role—the usual evening routine carried out in complete obliviousness of the wedding—but he needed support, people begging him to relent, or else deferring to his wounded sensibilities. This isolation was different; it was almost the first isolation he had ever felt, and like all men who are fundamentally of the group, of the herd, he was incapable of taking a strong stand with the inevitable loneliness that it implied. He could only gravitate toward those who did.

"What have I done to deserve this?" he demanded of the standing ash tray. "What have I failed to do for my son that lay within my power?"

The maid came in. "Mrs. Winslow told Hilda she wouldn't be here for dinner, and Hilda didn't tell me."

The shameful business was complete. His wife had weakened, leaving him absolutely alone. For a moment he expected to be furiously angry with her, but he wasn't; he had used up his anger exhibiting it to others. Nor did it make him feel more obstinate, more determined; it merely made him feel silly.

"That's it. I'll be the goat. Forrest will always hold it against me, and Chauncey Rikker will be laughing up his sleeve."

He walked up and down furiously.

"So I'm left holding the bag. They'll say I'm an old grouch and drop me out of the picture entirely. They've licked me. I suppose I might as well be graceful about it." He looked down in horror at the hat he held in his hand. "I can't—I can't bring myself to do it, but I must. After all, he's my only son. I couldn't bear that he should hate me. He's determined to marry her, so I might as well put a good face on the matter."

In sudden alarm he looked at his watch, but there was still time. After all, it was a large gesture he was making, sacrificing his principles in this manner. People would never know what it cost him.

An hour later, old Mrs. Forrest woke up from her doze and rang for her maid.

"Where's Mrs. Winslow?"

"She's not in for dinner. Everybody's out."

The old lady remembered.

"Oh, yes, they've gone over to get married. Give me my glasses and the telephone book. . . . Now, I wonder how you spell Capone."

"Rikker, Mrs. Forrest."

In a few minutes she had the number. "This is Mrs. Hugh Forrest," she said firmly. "I want to speak to young Mrs. Forrest Winslow. . . . No, not to Miss Rikker; to Mrs. Forrest Winslow." As there was as yet no such person, this was impossible. "Then I will call after the ceremony," said the old lady.

When she called again, in an hour, the bride came to the phone.

"This is Forrest's great-grandmother. I called up to wish you every happiness and to ask you to come and see me when you get back from your trip if I'm still alive."

"You're very sweet to call, Mrs. Forrest."

"Take good care of Forrest, and don't let him get to be a ninny like his father and mother. God bless you."

"Thank you."

"All right. Good-by, Miss Capo—Good-by, my dear."

Having done her whole duty, Mrs. Forrest hung up the receiver.

A LETTER FROM ZELDA FITZGERALD

F. Scott Fitzgerald died, of a heart attack, on December 21, 1940. He was forty-four years old. He had been living in and around Hollywood since the summer of 1937, drawn there by the chance of screenwriting work. But in his final year he devoted himself to a major novel, The Last Tycoon, *which he left unfinished. Shortly after his death, Zelda Fitzgerald evidently received a condolence letter from their old St. Paul friends Xandra and Oscar Kalman. She wrote back to Oscar Kalman from Alabama, where she was living with her mother in between stays at a mental hospital. Her response to the Kalman letter, written in January 1941, evokes once again the bittersweet memories of St. Paul and White Bear that both Fitzgeralds seemed to sustain to the end.*

322 Sayre St.
Montgomery, Ala.
{January 1941}

Dearest Kollie:

Scottie and I are grateful to you for remembering us so kindly. So many years have passed since summers lost themselves in the green valleys of White Bear and Time floated immutable and eternal above the blue sleek surface of the lake. We had so many happy hours together. I know that Scott is, elsewhere, recognizant of your goodwill, and thankful, as I am, for the warmth of friendly remembrance.

He loved his friends deeply, deriving his deepest inspiration and his greatest solace from the poignancy of human aspirations and from the significance of long and faithful efforts. Always, we hoped to someday be able to offer testimonial to the courtesies that were extended us, from so many kind hearts, in so many lonesome places.

Now that he won't be coming East again with his pockets full of promises and his notebooks full of schemes, and new refurbished hopes, life doesn't offer as happy a vista. My only consolation is that he died mercifully, without suffering. Whereas he might have spent years confined to his room by the tiredness of a heart that had always felt so deeply. I know that Scott would have wanted to finish the novel about Hollywood on which he was working, and that he would have liked to see his friends again.

We wanted to bring Scottie to St. Paul some summer: it is so good to have a sense of the roots from which one is sprung, and there were lots of things still undone. However, life has a way of closing its books as soon as one's category is fulfilled, and I suppose the time had come.

Even the deepest of grief and bereavement, were one able to change the destiny by which one is pursued, such might be a very regrettable instance.

God is Just and Merciful.

If you are going to stop in Montgomery anyway, please call, and have lunch — or something. I live with my mother at 332 Sayre St. Her telephone Walnut 2643. Her name is Mrs. A.D. Sayre. She is 80, and charming, and will always be happy to see you and Sandy whenever you are around. If when things have resolved themselves more tangibly, I want to know how to find my way about in the bread-line, I will write you —

Don't forget me: maybe some mutual purpose will someday arise anew —

Anyway, we all loved you —

Zelda

Acknowledgements

F. Scott Fitzgerald invoked St. Paul again and again in his fiction. But what qualifies as a Fitzgerald "St. Paul story" must finally be acknowledged as a matter of editorial judgment and taste. We have gathered a selection, not compiled a compendium. We could not include, for example, the wonderful (and wonderfully apt) story "The Popular Girl," because it is almost novella length. The light we train on Fitzgerald is meant to illuminate an aspect of his imagination that remained forever attached to his home place in some of his most vivid short stories.

Many people helped to bring this collection of Fitzgerald's stories together. In the bibliography we have tried to acknowledge our debt as editors to the biographers, literary critics, and historians whose work informed or aided our own.

But our gratitude extends beyond professional scholars. In particular we wish to thank Eleanor Lanahan, Robert Clark, Phebe Hanson, Eleanor Heginbotham, Mary Jane LeVigne, Jack Koblas, Sybil Kretzmer, Eileen McCormack, Judy Morgan, Stephen P. Williams, and Terrence Williams.

We have been especially fortunate in the editorial and production team at Borealis Books. The idea for a collection of Fitzgerald's St. Paul stories met with immediate enthusiasm and sustained commitment there. Special thanks to publisher Gregory M. Britton and to production manager Will Powers. Our editor, Ann Regan, was the book's most steadfast friend.

Selected Bibliography

WORKS BY F. SCOTT FITZGERALD

All the Sad Young Men. New York: Charles Scribner's Sons, 1926.

The Basil and Josephine Stories of F. Scott Fitzgerald, ed. Jackson R. Bryer and John Kuehl. New York: Scribner, 1973, 1997.

Before Gatsby: The First Twenty-Six Stories, ed. Matthew J. Bruccoli with the assistance of Judith S. Baughman. Columbia: University of South Carolina Press, 2001.

Correspondence of F. Scott Fitzgerald, ed. Bruccoli with the assistance of Margaret M. Duggan. New York: Random House, 1980.

The Crack-Up, ed. Edmund Wilson. New York: New Directions, 1945.

F. Scott Fitzgerald: A Life in Letters, ed. Bruccoli with the assistance of Baughman. New York: Scribner's, 1994.

F. Scott Fitzgerald's Ledger: A Facsimile. ed. Bruccoli with the assistance of Baughman. Washington, D.C.: A Bruccoli Clark Book, 1972.

Flappers and Philosophers. New York: Charles Scribner's Sons, 1920; New York: Penguin USA, 1999.

The Great Gatsby. New York: Charles Scribner's Sons, 1925, 1995.

"Minnesota's Capital in the Role of Main Street," *Literary Digest International Book Review,* 1 (March 1923): 35–36. Review of Grace Flandrau's *Being Respectable.*

The Price Was High: The Last Uncollected Stories of F. Scott Fitzgerald, ed. Bruccoli. New York: Harcourt Brace Jovanovich, 1979.

The Short Stories of F. Scott Fitzgerald: A New Collection. ed. Bruccoli. New York: Charles Scribner's Sons, 1989.

Tales of the Jazz Age. New York: Charles Scribner's Sons, 1922; Philadelphia: University of Pennsylvania Press, 2003.

Taps at Reveille. New York: Charles Scribner's Sons, 1935, 1976.

Tender Is the Night. New York: Charles Scribner's Sons, 1934, 1995.

WORKS ABOUT FITZGERALD & ST. PAUL

Bruccoli, Matthew J. *Some Sort of Epic Grandeur: The Life of F. Scott Fitzgerald.* Rev. ed. Columbia, S.C.: University of South Carolina Press, 2002.

Bryer, Jackson R., ed. *New Essays on F. Scott Fitzgerald's Neglected Stories.* Columbia, Mo.: University of Missouri Press, 1996.

Donaldson, Scott. *Hemingway vs. Fitzgerald: The Rise and Fall of a Literary Friendship.* New York: Penguin, 2001.

Hill, Louis W. Letter to Maudie Hill, April 23, 1920. Louis W. Hill Papers, James J. Hill Reference Library, St. Paul.

Hook, Andrew. *F. Scott Fitzgerald: A Literary Life.* New York: Palgrave Macmillan, 2002.

Maccabee, Paul. *John Dillinger Slept Here: A Crooks' Tour of Crime and Corruption in St. Paul, 1920–1936.* St. Paul: Minnesota Historical Society Press, 1995.

Mellow, James R. *Invented Lives.* New York: Houghton Mifflin Co, 1984.

Page, Dave, and John Koblas. *F. Scott Fitzgerald in Minnesota: Toward the Summit.* St. Cloud, Minn.: North Star Press, 1996.

Potts, Stephen W. *The Price of Paradise: The Magazine Career of F. Scott Fitzgerald.* San Bernardino, Calif: The Borgo Press, 1993.

Rahm, Virginia L. "The Nushka Club," *Minnesota History* 43 (Winter 1973): 303–307.

Wingerd, Mary Lethert. *Claiming the City: Politics, Faith, and the Power of Place in St. Paul.* Ithaca, N.Y.: Cornell University Press, 2001.

PATRICIA HAMPL is Regents' Professor of English at the University of Minnesota and author of several books, including *A Romantic Education* and *I Could Tell You Stories: Sojourns in the Land of Memory*, which was a finalist for a National Book Critics Circle Award. She has won NEA, Bush, Guggenheim, Bellagio, McKnight, Fulbright, and MacArthur fellowships.

DAVE PAGE is co-author of *F. Scott Fitzgerald in Minnesota: Toward the Summit* and was the co-chair of the 2002 International Fitzgerald Conference. He teaches writing at Inver Hills Community College in Minnesota.

The Saint Paul Stories of F. Scott Fitzgerald was designed and set in type by Will Powers at Borealis Books, and was printed by Maple Press, York, Pennsylvania. The type is American Garamond, designed in 1919 by Thomas Maitland Cleland and Morris Fuller Benton for the American Typefounders Company.